TRUST NOT THE HEART

TRUST NOT THE HEART

Published by Rainy Valley Press, Salem, Oregon.

Library of Congress Control Number: 2020922539

ISBN e-book: 978-0-9974387-6-5

ISBN trade paperback: 978-0-9974387-7-2

Cover design by Kim Killion of Killion Publishing.
https://thekilliongroupinc.com/

TRUST NOT THE HEART

An Eden Beach Main Street Novel

LIZ HARTLEY

Rainy Valley Press: Salem, Oregon

Elizabeth McCracken
Barbara Nelson
Kathy Gredzens

Your loving hearts and brilliant smiles are sorely missed.

"A coward is incapable of exhibiting love; it is the prerogative of the brave."

Mahatma Ghandi

CHAPTER 1

CASSIE FRANKLIN LIFTED HER FOOT from the speed control and let her Foredom motor tool hang from its hook. She blew debris from the wax ring model she was carving and took a look at it. It would be the perfect home for the rhodolite garnet she'd purchased at the Tucson gem show in February.

So why wasn't she excited about it?

She shrugged mentally. *I'm just at that stage of the work*, she thought.

Cassie frowned. She'd been at "that stage of the work" for months now, on all her work. What was bothering her?

Setting the model on her bench, she stood up to stretch and roll her shoulders and wrists. She hung her magnifying head piece on a hook above her bench, untied her apron, and tossed it on her chair.

As she pulled the wooden pin out of her hair, the long, dark brown mass fell loose behind her shoulders. Running her hands up underneath her heavy mane, she massaged her scalp. It made the streak of gray hair at her right temple more visible.

Cassie stepped down from the platform that held her benches.

Her shop was built over rising bedrock, so while the showroom was at ground level, her benches were two steps up. The workshop, where she did her casting and finishing, was three steps higher. The benefit was that, from either of her benches or from the workshop, she could see all the cases in the tiny display area. A glass barrier in front of the benches reduced the noise and dust in the show room, and kept idle fingers from roaming her work space.

Cassie no longer noticed her store's unique layout, but customers were always intrigued.

She pulled a bottle of iced tea from the small fridge under the counter and decided to take a break. What good was working at the beach if you didn't enjoy it once in a while?

September was the best month in Eden Beach. The Festival of the Masters was over, Labor Day was behind them, and schools were back in session. There were still plenty of visitors, but the overwhelming crush was gone. Residents once again owned the town.

On top of that, the weather was perfect. The fog hadn't returned in the mornings yet, and although the temperature was in the nineties, the onshore breeze tempered the heat. This time of year had always been *her* summer.

She grinned, thinking of the Septembers that she and her best friend, Anna Rodriguez, had cut classes and driven up and down the coast in an old VW bug—when Anna could borrow it from her brother, Fernando—singing "Harden My Heart" at the tops of their voices along with Quarterflash. They'd body-surfed every beach for fifty miles in either direction and flirted with boys much older than they were.

They'd been very careful not to go beyond that. They both had plans that didn't include early pregnancies. Cassie's mom had been seventeen when Cassie was born. Beth

Franklin had never given her daughter anything but love, but Cassie had always known her mom's life would have been different if she hadn't been an unwed teen mother.

Anna's five brothers and father had also been a potent form of chastity control.

Anna was married now, though, and Consuelo Rodriguez was beginning to mention grandchildren frequently.

Cassie smiled. That would make her an auntie. She would teach her nieces and nephews to skateboard the Third Avenue hill.

Every kid should have a broken arm in their past, she thought.

Idly, she rubbed her left arm, remembering. She was twenty-nine now, and a serious business owner, but she'd never forget the feel of the street racketing under her wheels as she reached light speed, the sound of Anna whooping behind her.

She closed her eyes and leaned against the front of the building. She sighed contentedly as the luscious heat of the bricks penetrated the white tank top and her shoulders began to relax. Within moments the sun began prickling her long, bare legs from the edge of her thigh-length denim skirt to her toes in flat-soled sandals. The cold bottle of iced tea in her hand began to drip condensation over her fingers. Heaven.

With her eyes shut, the sounds of the town intensified. The vast expanse of air and ocean muffled the thump and hiss of the surf just a stone's throw away across the highway. The shrieks of small children racing away from the waves and the catcalls from the volleyball net were like sounds from another world. It was a happier, freer world than the one occupied by the drivers on the Pacific Coast Highway, right in front of her, who gunned their engines angrily when the lights changed.

Two seagulls streaked overhead, laughing raucously. Sometimes Eden Beach drove her crazy with its tourist hordes and petty, small-town politics. But she loved it, too, for just those things. She wouldn't live anywhere else.

She took a drink of her tea and tipped her face up to the sun.

Nora cringed every time Cassie pulled another bottle out of the endless cache of the over-sweetened tea, but Cassie lived on it. Caffeine and sugar and maybe a little sunshine. What more did a jewelry designer-slash-bench jeweler need?

Her smile faded and she opened her eyes. *Customers would be nice*, she thought, her dark brown eyes serious. She watched people walking by. They glanced in store windows and sometimes slowed, but they didn't go into many shops. The bumpy economy had everyone—even the wealthy folks in the estates up and down the coast—clutching their money extra tightly. They'd all thought the milk-and-honey days of the 1980s would last.

They'd been wrong.

The talk now was all about recession. President Clinton kept saying things were getting better, but here in Eden Beach, the merchants didn't see it.

Delia Owen stepped out of her dress shop next door to water the plants. The pots bright ceramic pots in front of her windows were now chained to iron eyes in the concrete after Delia had lost a number of them.

"Hey, Cassie! You playing hooky?"

Cassie lifted her tea in salute. "You're reading my mind," she called back.

Delia set the watering can down and walked over. Fashion-model thin and almost as tall as Cassie's 5'9", Delia's figure was perfect to show off the stylish clothes she sold in her store.

"Killer outfit." Cassie nodded at the swirly, olive-green skirt printed with large red and pink flowers and topped with gray-green camisole under a fuchsia jacket.

"Thanks." Delia pushed her perfectly styled gray hair off her face. "Great day," she added looking across the highway at the park. "It's good to have things a bit quieter again."

"Maybe a bit *too* quiet," said Cassie.

Delia nodded. "I don't know about you, but this summer's been so slow I could have closed my doors for the last three months and made almost as much money." She shook her head. "I'm about ready to stock T-shirts. It seems like the only thing selling around here."

"I hope you don't," said Cassie. "You've got the best clothes in town. But you're right. I've never seen it this slow."

"And you've been here longer than I have," said Delia.

"Yep. Pretty much all my life. Jim took me on as his apprentice when I was fifteen." Cassie puckered her forehead in thought. "1980-ish?" She waggled her hand in a give-or-take gesture. "But he opened the shop in the mid-seventies, and I was under his feet from the start."

"So weird what happened to him," said Delia.

"Umm." Cassie didn't like talking about Jim's disappearance. It had left a huge hole in her heart and in her life.

Two kids on skateboards roared past them, weaving around the pedestrians, distracting Delia.

"They're going to kill someone someday," said Delia.

Cassie took another swallow of tea to avoid answering and to hide her smile.

"So have you checked out the new restaurant up on Ocean yet?" asked Delia.

"It's open?" asked Cassie, surprised.

"End of the month, is what I hear," said Delia. "Contractors are putting in long hours to get it done. Must be a fortune in overtime. Margot says she saw the new owner having lunch with Carla Towne at the Pelican."

Cassie snorted. "Wonder how high Carla's father jacked the rent up after they drove Ron Baxter out." She shook her head. The merchants in the area had been horrified at what Alden Towne had done to Ron. Many of them rented space from Towne, via the Eden Beach Land Management Company.

Delia rolled her eyes. "Alden Towne. Our own slumlord."

Cassie nodded. "The new owner better watch his back if he's getting cozy with the Townes, is all I can say."

"Yes, well, from what Margot said, it looked like it was getting *very* cozy," said Delia. "She said Carla looked even more like a shark than normal. Like she was circling a tasty morsel."

Cassie raised an eyebrow. "You suppose that's why the Townes pushed Ron out? This guy is Carla's new love interest?"

Delia shrugged. "Could be. Margot said he was a hunky hot number." Delia shook her hands like she was trying to cool them. "That seems to bring out the predator in Carla."

"So I've heard," said Cassie. "Anna's pretty tied into the gossip grapevine at Captain Jack's bar."

"I wonder if the new guy paid Carla a bonus to get Ron out so he could have the space," said Delia. "Love interest or not. Carla's all about the money."

Carla—either on her own or working with her father—was insinuating herself into a lot of the rental property in town. She would offer a landlord two or three times the rent the current tenant was paying. When she got her hands on the space, she'd turn around and sublet it for even more, usually to a vanilla-flavored national chain.

Cassie pulled at her tea. "She and Alden are really something." She shook her head. "You know, if they keep driving out all the cute, quirky little shops that give Eden Beach its personality, tourists will have no reason to come down here. I sometimes wonder if that's part of the reason all our sales are off this year."

"Well, the economy is sagging pretty badly right now," said Delia.

"I can't argue with that, but if you think about it, why should anyone come to an art colony to shop if all they can find are the same stores they have in South Coast Plaza?

"I mean, personally, I'm not sorry to see macramé hangings going out of style," she continued, and Delia laughed. "But some of the galleries are replacing original painting and sculpture with prints and reproductions." She gestured toward Delia's clothes. "And places like yours, with original clothes, are filling up with T-shirts."

Delia nodded. "The manager at the Clay Corner," she said, mentioning an Eden Beach landmark that featured the work of craft potters, "told me they're really beginning to feel the impact of all the imported ceramics."

"That's what I mean," said Cassie. "It won't be long and the artists in Eden Beach will become an endangered species."

They were quiet for a moment, gloomily thinking about the changes in town.

"So," said Delia casually, her eyes on the people passing by, "speaking of love lives, anything going on with you?"

Cassie sighed inwardly. Delia was a great business neighbor and a lot of fun, but she was the same age as Cassie's mom would have been. She seemed to think it was her job to match make.

Especially after she'd witnessed that ugly scene between Cassie and Phil's wife.

Cassie shoved the memory away.

More than a year later, she was still mortified by the encounter. The thought of making such a stupid mistake again made her whole body tense up. She wasn't sure she was willing to trust anyone ever again.

Besides. She had Nora to think about.

"Nope. Enjoying the single life." Cassie didn't look at Delia.

There was an awkward silence. Delia shook her hair out of her face and cleared her throat.

"Speaking of the shark," she said, like she'd never digressed, "did I tell you she gave my shop the once over the other day?"

"What? Delia, no!" Cassie snapped upright, stepping away from the wall.

"Yep. Walked in bold as brass. Went right on through into the back while I was with a customer."

"She didn't say anything?"

"Hah! Speak to the likes of me? Just because it's my shop?" Delia's voice dripped flames. "She didn't say a thing. Not good morning. Nothing. Just walked in.

"By time I excused myself and got back there, she was heading toward the front. When I asked what she thought she was doing, she said, 'sizing up the property.' Then she just walked out."

Delia snorted in disgust. "Queen Carla."

Cassie stared at Delia in disbelief. "Jeez!" she said finally. "That's outrageous, even for Carla!" She shook her head. "What gives her the right?"

Delia rubbed her thumb and middle finger together. "Money. And the Towne name."

"The Towne name," said Cassie darkly. "The two of them keep buying up everything at this rate and they'll change our name from Eden Beach to Towne Center South." She sighed and shook her head. "You know, we call her a shark, but there's something clean and honest about a shark. The Townes are more like piranha. Working in a pack to tear the living flesh off a body."

Delia guffawed.

It wasn't good news to know the Townes had their sights

set on this building. But it was hardly surprising. It was a prime piece of property, with its five shops and landmark movie theater sitting right on Coast Highway directly across from Main Beach in the heart of town. Cassie didn't think their landlord, Rachel Meyers, would sell, but how long would she hold out against the Townes. Especially now that Jim was gone?

A chill ran up her back. Maybe Carla was acting like she owned them because she and Rachel were already talking?

No, thought Cassie. *Rachel would not do that to us.*

It was a disturbing idea nonetheless.

She shook the thought off as she heard Delia continue. "Yep. The times they are a-changin', as the song says."

Cassie laughed out loud. Delia looked at her puzzled.

"I was just standing here feeling old, thinking of Anna having kids and me becoming an auntie," she said when she finally stopped laughing. "But that is a seriously old song! Bob Dylan, isn't it? I think my mom used to play that album."

Delia put her hands on her hips and gave Cassie a mock glare. "Cassie Franklin are you saying I'm old?"

"No, no." Cassie waved away the suggestion and smiled. "You're just an admirer of the classics."

"Absolutely." Delia grinned in return.

A couple of women turned into Delia's shop. Delia rolled her eyes and held up crossed fingers.

"Go get 'em," said Cassie with a laugh as Delia turned away.

Cassie went back to sipping tea and watching traffic— human and automobile. By the sheer numbers of both, it would not appear that times were tight. The highway and sidewalks were about as busy as they ever were this time of year, but sales everywhere were down.

Even the summer art and craft fairs had been slow this year. Less traffic, fewer sales.

Cassie shared a booth at the Pepper Tree Art and Craft Show with her housemate, Nora Cassidy, a weaver. She featured earrings at the show—they didn't need sizing, prices were in the impulse purchase range, and women usually bought more than one pair. It wasn't unusual for Cassie to make enough to cover all her annual expenses just from the show, and Nora usually had enough commissions to keep her busy all winter. This summer, though, Cassie'd made just enough to cover the shop rent for the year and pay her share of the property taxes on the house. Nora had done even worse. Cassie's shop earnings would have to pay for silver, the little gold she used, gemstones, supplies, food, utilities, insurance. While she had some savings, with things this slow, it was going to be a squeeze.

Now Carla was swimming around. *How many other businesses will the Townes tear apart and swallow up?* Cassie thought. Far in the back of her mind echoed another unwanted thought, *Will I be next?* Other custom design jewelers, like her, were struggling. A number of them had shifted to selling ready-made pieces to the tourists in order to survive.

Jim always made it work, she thought firmly. Cassie was determined to make things work for her, too. She hoped that Jim would be proud of her, even though she had resigned herself to him never coming back. The problem was that costs were so much higher now for Cassie. As the affluent bought up and demolished the tiny individual bungalows in the canyons, and filled the properties with multi-level, multi-million dollar villas, taxes all over town skyrocketed. Cassie and Nora were holding onto their house—thanks to her mom's life insurance—but others had been forced to sell.

As the daughter of a hippie, Cassie had always considered herself a "free spirit," whatever that meant. During those crazy, carefree days with Anna, she'd never thought she'd become a settled business person worrying about sales and property taxes. *Things are different when you're staring at thirty*, she thought.

Or when you have kids.

Cassie smiled sadly. Growing up she'd never thought of her mom in the same breath as life insurance. But it turned out Beth had bought the policy not long after Cassie was born.

Beth hadn't been much more than a kid herself.

A wave of sadness swept over Cassie. She sighed deeply.

So much lost. First Beth. Then Jim.

She stood in the sunshine for a few more minutes watching a parade of sunburned shoulders and white knees. The smell of waffle cones from the ice cream shop at the end of the building and the burned coffee smell from the coffee shop in the other direction mingled with the salt air and merged in front of her. Her stomach growled. She'd forgotten lunch again. She'd have to call Susie's Thai House and ask Freddie to run an order of *phad thai* to her.

She shoved off from the wall, finished her tea, and paused to look at her front window. Cassie changed the jewelry display every day or two to keep things looking fresh, but lately, it didn't pull in customers like it used to.

Worrying won't help, she thought, and went back inside and back to her bench. She pulled on her apron, twisted her hair up, and staked it with the long wooden hair pin that had been her mom's.

She picked up the wax, put it gently on her scale, and did the math in her head to estimate how much it would weigh in silver. A little heavy. She'd have to lighten it up a bit to make it comfortable to wear.

She plucked it off the scale and looked it over again. The shapes were good, the balance was good, the asymmetry was enough to make it interesting but not so much it would scare off buyers. The gold bezel and gold accents she planned to add would really make the rhodolite garnet pop. She wished she could afford to use white gold instead of sterling and pavé-set some diamonds along that outside curve.

But the cost of the little gold she was already using would push the price of this ring up. Diamonds would make it unaffordable in this economy. In addition, while her standard setting skills were excellent—Jim had seen to that—she'd never learned things like pavé and channel setting. She'd have to hire someone to do it for her, raising the price even higher.

The door pinged, and a woman in a print sundress came in. She was probably ten years older than Cassie. Her hair was shingled in a geometric cut that Cassie admired but could never have worn. It framed the woman's face perfectly.

"Hi! Welcome back," she said.

The woman looked startled. "You remember me?"

Cassie laughed. "I remember the great haircut and how well it suited you," she admitted. "It's been a while, though, since you've been in."

The woman smiled broadly and relaxed.

She reached into her handbag, pulled out a box, and handed it to Cassie.

"Maybe you can make this suit me, too."

Cassie opened it to find a wedding set with a moderately sized diamond and graduated smaller stones.

"I just got rid of my worthless husband and I want something completely different," the woman said.

Cassie gestured to the chair at the design counter. "Why don't you sit down and tell me what you're thinking," she said.

An hour or so later, the counter was littered with sketches, and the customer—Peggy—had settled on a new ring and a pendant and given Cassie a deposit. Cassie didn't punch the air when Peggy left, but her mood picked up.

She was putting the job envelope into her work box when another customer came in to pick up a ring she'd bought and had re-sized. Between that, the custom deposit, and the repairs earlier in the day, it was enough for groceries and utilities for a month or so. *Worth keeping the doors open*, thought Cassie. When the door pinged again, Cassie looked up from her carving. One more customer would make the best day she'd had for a while.

It was Carla Towne.

Cassie's shoulders tightened, and an adrenaline surge spiked her heart rate.

After her conversation with Delia, Cassie knew what this visit meant.

It was going to ruin her afternoon.

"Hi, Carla," Cassie managed to say nonchalantly. As she turned back to her wax, she had the satisfaction of seeing the momentary hitch in Carla's walk and the brief irritated frown. *She thinks I'm presuming to know her*, thought Cassie. *I'm too far down the food chain for her to remember meeting me.*

Carla's smile flashed on quickly. "Mind if I look around?" she asked.

"Help yourself," said Cassie. She fiddled with the wax carving but kept glancing back at the realtor.

Tall and slim, the realtor's tawny hair (*That cost a lot*, thought Cassie) was perfectly cut and styled. Her cream-colored blouse was silk as was the straight, dark beige skirt just skimming her knees. The perfect three-inch pumps matched the skirt. Her hoop earrings were gold as was the watch on her left wrist. Her tan was perfect—not too much, not too pale. A golden girl. Cassie was quite sure that was the effect Carla wanted to give. The look screamed "money."

But then it should. Alden Towne was the owner, builder and conceptual genius behind the Towne Center, a high-end fashion mall on the top of the bluff in Newport. His fortune from that was what had allowed him to expand into other commercial properties, including buying up property in Eden Beach and the surrounding area.

Cassie mentally contrasted her own appearance to Carla's. Hair in a messy knot, three earrings in one ear, two in the other, one of which was linked to an ear cuff above it. White tank, short denim skirt, strappy sandals she'd bought at the Pepper Tree show. She could imagine what the realtor thought. She didn't care.

Carla was obviously more interested in the shop space than she was in the jewelry in the cases, as Cassie had known she would be. The realtor studied the view out the window, the exposed brick wall between Cassie's shop and Delia's next door, the high ceilings. She thought she was being subtle, but Cassie saw her pace off the square footage.

Carla's professional smile flashed again as she started walking toward the security gate. "Mind if I look in the back?" she asked, obviously expecting agreement.

Cassie kept her eyes on her wax, turning it from side to side, blowing invisible debris from the wax surface. From the corner of her eye, she saw the break in Carla's stride as her hand reached for the gate and she realized it was locked. Cassie was pleased to see the realtor's flash of annoyance.

"Actually, I do mind," said Cassie.

Carla's smile was back. She reached in her purse and pulled out a card.

"I'm sorry. I should have introduced myself," she said. "I'm Carla Towne. I'm a realtor here in Eden Beach." She leaned toward Cassie's bench holding out the card. Cassie glanced up.

"Yes," Cassie said pleasantly. "I know." She did not reach for Carla's card. "We met opening night at the Festival of the Masters last year. Lou Pallis introduced us." *Again.*

Carla gave a light, false laugh and drew the card back. "Then you know you can trust me in the back with all your jewels!" Her condescension told Cassie she didn't think there was anything in the shop worth stealing.

"Sorry, no tours today." Cassie flashed a fake smile back at Carla and deliberately turned back to the wax. She noticed her hands were shaking.

"Not even if I ask nicely?" Carla's flirty voice had an edge to it. "You know realtors! We're always interested in novel spaces, just in case they come on the market." Another false laugh.

"This one's not coming on the market," said Cassie flatly. *Not unless I'm dead.*

Carla tried again. "Still, I'm told this shop is really unusual. I just wanted to take a little peek." Carla held up a hand with thumb and forefinger half an inch apart. Cassie wondered that the smile didn't crack her face.

Carla was right, though. The shop was certainly novel. Built up against rocks that the contractor had not bothered to blast away, you actually had to climb steps cut into the rock face to get to the bathroom. Needless to say, the plumbing was interesting.

"Even if *I* asked nicely," said Cassie, "I don't suppose you'd appreciate it if I walked into your home, without invitation, and started rummaging in the closets and bathrooms. I'm sure it's a novel space, too." *I'll bet every wall is mirrored.*

Carla's smile slipped, and Cassie saw anger flash in her eyes. "Well, of course not," Carla replied with a hint of impatience. "A home is not a public space."

"My shop is not a public space." Cassie set the wax onto her bench. Her hands were clenching. She'd spent too many hours carving that wax to risk breaking it. "An artist's workshop is like her home. It's not open to idle curiosity."

"An *artist*!" snorted Carla, not smiling now. "Is *that* what you think you are?"

Cassie's mouth moved before her brain engaged. "A *realtor*? Is that what you think *you* are?"

Stunned fury blotched Carla's face erasing any attractiveness. "Excuse me? I studied long and hard and had to pass a state board exam to get my license. What did you do? Learn to bend spoons from that ignorant hippie before you? And you call yourself an *artist*?" She waved her hand dismissively at the cases around her. "Making cheap souvenirs for tourists doesn't make you an artist. Nobody with any taste would buy this...this..." Words apparently failed her.

Cassie took a moment before she allowed herself to speak. "The door is behind you," she said quietly, her voice shaking only slightly. "Don't come back."

"Oh, I'll be back," sneered Carla. "I'll be back with your eviction notice. I'm sure your landlord will be happy to take twice the amount of rent you're paying now."

I'd like to hear that *conversation*, thought Cassie. *I hope you mention the ignorant hippie.*

"If she is, I'm sure she'll tell me," said Cassie. She pointed at the door with the carving tool in her hand. Then she picked up her wax and ignored Carla.

Without another word, the realtor turned and stalked out. Cassie saw her march past the front window, her steps short, her mouth tight, and her face pinched and pointed.

When Carla was out of sight, Cassie laid her work down gently. She got up carefully, went up the three steps to the back room, picked up a tapered steel ring mandrel, took a good grip, and slammed it into the scarred wood bench that held her buffing machine. The loose buffs jumped, and a stick of polishing compound rolled to the floor.

"You slimy, bottom-feeding, scum-sucking..." she remembered the tawny realtor's pointed face, "ferret!" she shouted to the walls. Cassie and Anna rarely swore. Consuelo Rodriguez had literally scrubbed both their mouths with soap when they were twelve and trying out the words they'd heard at school. They'd both become creative in making insults after that.

It made her feel a little better. She set the mandrel down, took a few deep breaths, went back to the front of the store, and pulled out an iced tea. Cassie spent the next hour calming down and wondering which of the other merchants would help her get rid of Carla's body.

CHAPTER 2

TATE GARNER STEPPED BACK TO THE CURB and looked at the front of his restaurant. His! In a few weeks, the remodeling would be done, and the doors would be open. He imagined a balmy night like this, the big glass windows on either side of the double doors folded back to let in the light and air. Happy voices would spill out, a counterpoint to the live music. Irresistible aromas would drift out from the kitchen. His menu would change every week, with every season, except for a few regular offerings. He could see people sitting on the side patio near the bar in the back. A low wall would separate the patio from the street, and planters with trellises would screen the diners but let passersby have a peek in. Eventually Tate would commission a mural for the wall on the building facing the patio.

He grinned. The vision almost made him hungry.

Tate's sous-chef, Domingo Rivera, came out of the door and stopped.

"Man, that look on your face," he said.

"What look?" asked Tate.

"Like you're getting all excited looking at this building. That's really kinky, man."

Tate grinned and spread his arms out as if he would embrace the building. "*Mi amor!*" he said.

"You're sick, man."

Tate laughed and locked the front door. He *was* in love. His dream was coming true.

Tate had worked in kitchens since he was fifteen. He'd worked with fine chefs all over Europe and the US—some in top restaurants and others in little holes-in-the-wall. He'd learned not only cooking and the creation of menus, but business and administration. By watching, he'd figured out some of the pitfalls of restaurant ownership. He'd talked about the psychology of food, eating, and people with friends, chefs, bartenders, wait staff, and customers. It had been a long time coming, but he was finally confident he could bring it all together in a winning combination.

He stretched his arms over his head and took a deep breath of the warm evening air. The Santa Ana winds were blowing from the desert to the sea and the air was crystal clear.

"Man, it feels great to be out of the kitchen," he said to Domingo. They'd been standing all day working on new recipes while the construction crew worked on the dining room.

They were all up against a hard deadline. The restaurant was scheduled to open at the end of September. In early May, though, Tate had decided to dramatically change the restaurant's focus. It had meant lots of interior design reworking for the architects, and overtime for the construction crew. Tate had scrapped the original menu plan, so he and Domingo were working long hours coming up with a new one.

"That's the truth. I can't believe there really *is* sun in sunny California. I thought that's what you all called the moon." Domingo lifted his shoulders and rolled his head back and forth. He lifted his T-shirt, sniffed, and winced. "I think I'm turning into a head of garlic," he said. "I'm ready for a shower."

Tate grinned. "Yeah, but all that garlic died in a good cause." He slapped Domingo on the shoulder as they turned to walk toward the beach.

"Not all of it," said Domingo.

A couple of the recipes they'd worked out had been winners, at least according to the workmen Tate had tried them out on. There'd also been one spectacular failure, according to Domingo. Tate grinned at Domingo's blunt assessment of that entrée, now resting at the bottom of the dumpster out back.

Tate turned and walked backward for a few steps, facing Domingo. "Hey, even Picasso had an off day." He shrugged, holding his hands wide.

Domingo snorted. "A Picasso is about what that one plate looked like."

Tate laughed and turned around again.

On the whole, the opening menu was taking shape, which is why they were taking a rare evening off. While Tate still wanted to come up with some complementary bar food ideas, those could come last after the main menu was fleshed out.

As the sun headed toward the ocean, the hills behind them turned golden except for one broad swath where fire had burned them black the year before. Lavender shadows were pooling in the canyons, but the hilltops were sharply defined against a sky that was deep, clear, and blue.

At least the hills behind Eden Beach hadn't changed in his fourteen years of self-exile.

Tate took another deep breath of the clean, warm air, and let it out in a sigh.

"So. You glad you came back?" asked Domingo.

"Yeah, I am." *At least I hope so,* he thought to himself.

"Sounds like there's a 'but' in there somewhere," said Domingo.

Tate cut his eyes to his friend. He sometimes thought Domingo read minds on his days off.

Domingo noticed the look and grinned, but said nothing.

After a few more steps, Tate finally answered. "I have to admit, it's not entirely what I remember. Last time I was here, there were Volkswagen bugs and buses everywhere. Now it's all Mercedes."

"Good for business," said Domingo. "No?"

"Yeah. Probably." Tate was reluctant to agree. "But look at the stores. Some of my best memories are of days I spent here with my mom and Tia prowling around the funky shops or visiting artist studios in the hills. Now look at it."

They'd reached the corner of Ocean and Pacific Coast Highway. Tate gestured to the stores south of the intersection. "What do you see here that you can't see in New York or even Paris? Chain stores. National brands. Imports." He shook his head. "Used to be, the shops sold handmade stuff, like candles and tie-dye."

"Man, give up the restaurant and go work for the Chamber of Commerce. You missed your calling," said Domingo.

Tate glared at him, but Domingo just shrugged.

"You can't go home again, man. Isn't that what they say? My mom, she found that out when she took us back to Puerto Rico when we were kids, after my dad left. Everything was poorer and smaller than she remembered." He laughed. "It really pissed her off."

Tate sighed. "Yeah. Maybe you're right. But I just think…" He paused, then went on. "I think, if Eden Beach loses its artists, its soul will die." What he was really afraid of was that his memories would die with it.

The light changed and the two crossed to the park.

"Kinda late to think about that now," said Domingo. The traffic roared to a start behind them as the light went green.

It was. Tate had bought a house and signed a lease on the restaurant. He was committed.

"Yeah, you're right," Tate nodded.

They crossed to the boardwalk and headed along the bay, Tate bouncing on one foot and then the other as he pulled off his sandals. The sand-gritty, sun-warmed boards that curved around the pretty bay brought back great memories.

It felt good to stretch his long legs, and this path was familiar. Since he'd arrived in early spring, he'd spent his mornings running along the beach and the boardwalk. Occasionally while running, he'd caught a glimpse of a tall, dark-haired woman walking in the park or up the canyon road. Lately, he'd caught himself looking for her. He smiled to himself. Maybe someday he'd meet her.

"Besides, it must have been destiny, us getting such a great location," he said. The restaurant was right on Ocean, one of the main arteries of downtown Eden Beach, and only a block from the beach. There was parking just steps away, the patio he'd dreamed of, and a lot of the plumbing and electrical he needed was already in place.

Domingo made a non-committal noise.

"I know, I had my doubts, too, at the beginning," he said, as if Domingo had spoken. "But you got to admit, Carla came through."

Tate would never have chosen Carla Towne as his realtor. She was a little too polished. A little too...entitled. When he'd met her, she had insisted they'd gone to Costa del Sol High together, but Tate had no recollection of her at all. He'd certainly known a lot of girls *like* her. Moneyed. Well-dressed in designer jeans and handmade boots, with expensive haircuts and superior attitudes. If Carla had noticed him—the loner, the wild boy on the motorcycle—he was pretty sure she would have had nothing good to say about him.

But Sam Tyler, who had helped Tate buy his house on the bluff, had had a small heart attack,and gone in for bypass surgery before he could help Tate find a restaurant location. Sam had recommended Carla saying she knew the town well.

Domingo grimaced, shrugged and looked out to sea.

"What?" Tate stopped and turned toward his friend. "Look. She found us a great space. I saved beaucoup bucks because it was already set up for a kitchen. And at least she's been supportive. Sam thought I was nuts opening another restaurant here. Said the town's almost choking on them. But Carla's been enthusiastic from the start."

"Yeah? She didn't seem so happy when you asked for all those contract changes. Seems you had to push pretty hard to get her to take your counter offer to the agent."

Domingo was right. Tate's attorney had strongly recommended some changes in the rental agreement. At first Carla had resisted taking them to the landlord, Eden Beach Land Management, and when she had finally agreed, the agent had pushed back.

"Yeah, but in the end, she got a good contract, five years with no increase."

"That cost you, though." Tate had ended up paying a premium for making the contract changes and locking in the rate. "Just hope it doesn't end up costing you more. She might think you owe her for the favor. If you know what I mean."

It was an ongoing argument. "I keep telling you. I'm not interested in Carla." Though Tate had to say the whole location search had been much more pleasant because Carla was so easy to look at.

Domingo lifted a shoulder.

"Maybe not. But she looks at you like she's just waiting for 'Amen' to start eating."

Tate grinned as he turned to continue down the board-walk. "Can't help it if I'm male perfection, guy."

Domingo snorted. "If she was looking for male perfection, man, she'd be following *me* around." Domingo, who wasn't taller than 5'6", wiggled his eyebrows at Tate. "Like they say, great things in small packages." He made his eyes droopy and his lips pouty in his parody of a sexy face.

Tate guffawed. Domingo grinned at him.

They walked in silence a while before Domingo finally asked, "So, what did you decide about the advertising?"

Tate sighed. "Not much to decide. The changes and over-time pretty much ate the budget for it." He shrugged. "I'm going to have to depend on word-of-mouth."

"Yeah, well that only works if you get people to come in in the first place. Otherwise, they got nothing to talk about," said Domingo.

Tate hesitated. "Actually, about that. Carla had a pretty good idea the other night."

He felt Domingo turn and stare at him. "The other night," he said flatly.

"We had dinner." Tate shrugged. Carla had been trying to arrange it for a couple weeks, and Tate had finally agreed. He didn't tell Domingo that Carla had tried to get Tate to cook for her at home. He could imagine what she'd have said about his fixer-upper.

"She suggested we have an open house. Invitation only. She said she'd talk to some of her clients and people around town she knows. We have them in for samples, drinks, maybe get some buzz going. I already talked to some merchants. Invited them, too."

Domingo walked on silently for a while. "Might drum up some catering biz for the holidays," he said.

Tate nodded. "That would sure help get us back in the black."

"Hate to say it, but it's a good idea. Maybe invite a couple reviewers, too."

"Double-edged sword, there, if they don't like it," said Tate.

Domingo shrugged. "They say any advertising is good advertising."

"Let's just hope it works," said Tate, holding up crossed fingers.

They paused as a mom herded three pink, damp, shivering kids across the boardwalk in front of them. She had a large bulging bag across her body and carried a couple beach chairs and a cooler. The kids were wrapped in sandy beach towels.

Tate grinned as they started walking again.

"I remember those days," he said.

"You were a mom once?" asked Domingo. "Dude! You never told me."

Tate shook his head.

"My mom used to bring us down here. We loved the Pepper Tree show. You'll have to go next summer." This past summer, the two of them had never gotten out of the kitchen.

"What? I get a day off?"

"Shut up," said Tate. "I unlocked your chain tonight, didn't I?"

It was Domingo's turn to grin. "Yeah, yeah. So. What's a Pepper Tree show?"

"It's one of the art fairs they hold here every summer. There are tons of funky booths along these little twisting lanes all covered with sawdust. Smells like a mill. Or a forest. At night, with the lights and incense, it's like magic.

"Last time we were here, Tia was just seven," Tate pointed his finger at the ground and twirled it around, "like a tiny tornado spinning up and down the aisles. My mom bought her this crown-like thing," Tate gestured to his head, "woven out of dried flowers and ribbons." Tate laughed. "She got one for herself, too. And bracelets. *And* sandals. She looked like she belonged behind a booth, not buying things from one." His mom had looked like a girl herself, her blond hair in a braid down her back, ribbons fluttering behind the garland on her head, laughing with Tia.

"We ate lunch here in the park. Tia fell asleep." Tate could see his little sister in his mind, shadows playing on her face, his mother stroking her hair as he ran to the water and body-surfed in his cut-offs.

He didn't realize his smile had turned sad.

A year later, his mother was gone, lost to a heart attack at thirty-eight.

While a shocked and grieving fifteen-year-old Tate comforted his young sister, Martin remarried. When his father had tried to throw out Lydia's "arty junk," Tate had locked himself in Lydia's studio and, sobbing, called Lydia's best friend, Sheila, who immediately came and got it all. Just recently, Tate, Tia, and Sheila had gone through the boxes. Tia couldn't remember their mother's face, but she had burst into tears at the sight of the dried flower hair wreaths with their faded ribbons.

They came to a stop at the volleyball nets. Half a dozen young women were having an intense game.

Tate grinned.

Domingo was a New Yorker to the bone and Tate had had a hard time convincing him to move west.

"I don't know, man," Domingo had said, when he'd arrived at the coast early in the spring on a particularly clear and superbly beautiful day. "All this clean air." He'd waved a hand at the ocean. "Can't be good for you."

Then he'd seen the bikinis on the beach.

"This goes on all the time?" he'd asked Tate, jerking his

chin toward a couple of girls, their browned figures shown off to perfection at the volleyball net.

"Yep," Tate had told him. "No snow in California."

"You didn't tell me about the fringe benefits, man."

"Only the best for my sous-chef." Tate had grinned at him.

"So." Domingo had hitched up his pants and rolled his shoulders. "Maybe I can get used to all the air."

They watched the game going on now for a few minutes. "I'm going to have to learn to play this," Domingo said. Tate just laughed at him.

"I've got a beer calling my name. Want to join me?" Domingo asked.

Tate shook his head. "Thanks. I think I'll walk a bit more, then maybe…"

"Go back and work out a few more recipes?"

Tate gave him a lopsided smile. "Yeah. Maybe."

"You want help?"

"No, man. You go get your beer. Take the night off. I've just got a couple bar snacks I thought I'd try to develop. Not even sure I'll go back, but…"

Domingo grinned. "Glad I'm not the *jefe*. I got a life."

"Not for long," said Tate. "After we open, don't count on seeing the light of day."

"Then I'd better enjoy my fringe benefits while I can."

Tate laughed. Domingo saluted, then headed across the sand, angling around the volleyball game.

CHAPTER 3

TATE WATCHED HIS FRIEND GO BEFORE heading down the boardwalk.

Domingo was probably the best friend Tate had ever had and an excellent chef in his own right. He'd unwittingly saved Tate from making a huge mistake, too. Tate owed a lot to Domingo and that one simple recipe.

I don't dare tell him that, thought Tate, *or there would be no working with him.*

Tate smiled to himself. He already knew that, once the restaurant was on a solid footing, he was going to ask Domingo to be his partner.

At the end of the boardwalk, Tate turned and looked back along the curve of the bay, gazing out across the ocean to where Catalina Island lay, a purple shadow at the horizon's edge. Delighted screams floated on the evening air from the amusement pier on Halo Point a mile across the water.

He took a deep breath and the muscles in his back relaxed. Any lingering doubts about his decision vanished.

This was the right move, he thought, *coming back here. This is home.*

Eden Beach was the place that spoke to his heart. Not Newport, where he'd been raised, but this strip of beach with the golden hills behind it. No matter where he'd traveled in the world, this little town had always loomed large in his mind.

He sat down on a nearby bench, the sun warm on his face, and watched the water change.

As he sat there, hands locked behind his head, legs stretched in front of him and, from the corner of his eye he saw the glances cast his way. Tate knew he was good looking. He could hardly avoid knowing. At 6'3", with long, strong legs, and sun-bleached hair reaching to the neck of his T-shirt, he'd always drawn women. All the hiking and skiing in Europe, all the wrestling of the big motorcycles he loved, showed in the well-muscled arms and broad chest.

In his teens and twenties, he would have looked back at the women passing by and let it lead wherever. But he'd gotten bored with the chase, the expectations, the scenes when things broke up.

Face it, Garner, he thought, *you're getting old.*

In reality, it was the ugly split with Avril in Paris that had made him bitter. And cynical.

Tate didn't need Domingo to tell him Carla Towne was flirting with him. And, yeah, maybe he *was* flirting back a bit. But flirting was one thing. Getting involved with Carla was another. He didn't want another Avril.

He shook his head, anger rising as it always did. He didn't want to think about Avril. A stupid mistake. One that had almost cost him the dream of having the restaurant. It had certainly delayed it. Now that it was in his hands, he wouldn't do anything to put it at risk again. That meant no girlfriends. He wanted to focus on only one thing: making this a success.

Tate smiled wryly to himself, and the anger faded. There would be little chance of him making the same mistake again.

Not with Domingo here. His friend was one of the few people who knew about the fiasco with Avril. Domingo was as down-to-earth as they came. Since he'd learned the story—the night they'd killed a couple six packs of Heineken—he'd kept a sharp eye on Tate's heart when he thought Tate was getting careless with it.

Like now.

Tate watched the sun sink for a bit longer, idly running recipe ideas through his head.

The hell with it, he thought. *No more work tonight. I'll just head home. There's plenty to do there.*

As he crossed the highway, he noticed the theater was playing a new movie, "A Clear and Present Danger," with Harrison Ford. He'd have to take Tia to see it. Ford was one of her favorites. Action for him, eye-candy for her.

Even though it was almost six, the lights were still on at the little shop with the bay window next to the theater's small plaza. Tate ambled over to look. The Green Lotus. *Strange name for a jewelry store, even in Eden Beach*, he thought. The work, however, was nice. It looked very Eden Beach, reminding him of the pieces his mother had loved. He didn't know anything about jewelry, but he recognized the crafts-manship. He appreciated that in any artist—chef, kite maker, or jeweler. *I'd like to meet this guy*, he thought.

He glanced through the window and was surprised. Or not really. Like many Eden Beach jewelers, this one had a young woman working for him, only this one was working at the bench. He watched her for a while, her dark head bent over her work. He found himself smiling. He could hear Domingo's warning echo in his brain. *Just because I've sworn off relationships*, he thought, *it doesn't mean I can't admire the view.*

The low sun was making a mirror of the window, and Tate realized that maybe he wasn't in the best shape to meet anyone. He looked more like a beach bum than a soon-to-be-successful restauranteur. His old T-shirt was emblazoned with cartoon characters on various kinds of wheeled vehicles from tricycles to unicycles. The legend read "Tour de Farce." He was more than an hour past a five o'clock shadow. His hair was a bit wild. He had a bad habit of running his hands through it when he thought, and he'd been thinking a lot today. Like Domingo, he smelled a bit garlicky.

The heck with it, he thought, reminding himself that he didn't care whether women looked at him or not. He ignored the little voice in his head—which sounded a lot like Domingo—jeering, *yeah, sure*. He also tried to ignore his hands which tried to tame his hair a bit before they twitched to straighten the worn T-shirt.

The woman at the bench glanced up when the door pinged softly and smiled. "Hi," she said. "It's a great evening, isn't it?"

Tate almost stumbled. It was the woman he'd seen walking in the mornings. He hadn't been able to tell from a distance, or even from the front window, how beautiful she was. Widely spaced brown eyes, so dark the pupils almost seemed to disappear, surrounded by long lashes. Skin perfectly tan with a hint of pink underneath. A small straight nose and soft, sensuous lips. Her dark hair was deep, rich brown, like strong coffee. It was pinned up at the back of her head in a way that said she'd often taken it down during the day. Tate thought he might enjoy seeing it loose. He was pretty sure he'd enjoy getting closer to those lips.

All thoughts of Avril and Carla vanished along with his certainty that he was through with women for a while. Avril and Carla would look their age in another ten years. This woman would be stunning at eighty.

Oh. She'd said something. He scrambled his brain to respond.

"It is," he agreed, a bit belatedly. "Mind if I look?" Though it wasn't the jewelry he wanted to see more of.

"Help yourself," said Cassie. "I'm just finishing up here." She bent back to her work, and her hand tool began to whir.

Tate tore his eyes away and looked around. The shop was tiny and spare. One wall held a triple case of earrings. The three small, glass-topped wood cases—custom-made by the look of them—held pendants, a few bracelets and some rings. There was a pin his mom would have bought in a minute. Most of the jewelry in the cases was silver, but that was to be expected this close to the beach. The lower price would probably appeal to beach traffic, and the style should be popular with the tourists.

The bare brick walls held some of the most amazing paintings he'd ever seen—one next to the door, another one, smaller on the wall next to the benches where the woman was working, two small ones between the earring case and the bay window in the front. They were abstracts, but they really gave him a sense of the bleached hills, the beach, the fog, and the sea. He wondered idly who'd painted them. He wanted local art for the restaurant.

There was a low counter next to the door, with a window looking onto the theater plaza. There was more jewelry under the glass top, but there was also a binder lying open, with photos and drawings of jewelry. To the right of that was a small security gate and a few steps up to the work benches. Even higher, behind the design counter and the benches was a glass wall in front of the workshop. Tate was fascinated to see all the equipment. It looked like some kind of foundry.

As he roamed, Tate kept stealing looks at the woman. She was oblivious to him, totally focused on her work. His estimation of her as a craftsperson went up. *This one's not just ornamental*, he thought. But he kept thinking of that thick waterfall of hair. It looked fine and soft. He found himself smiling.

Stop that, he told himself.

She finally finished, stood up, and took her apron off. She was very tall, he was surprised to see, and slender without being thin, her waist invitingly narrow in a well-defined figure that said she didn't always sit at a bench. Tate quickly turned away so she wouldn't see the look of longing that washed through him. *Get a grip, Garner!* he thought.

She released the security gate and came onto the show-room floor. Tate grabbed a quick look at her long bare legs as she turned to pull the gate closed. "Let me know if you have questions about any of the pieces," she said. "Everything here is handmade."

Close up he could see she was about his age—late twenties, early thirties. He was intrigued that she didn't color the gray streak that ran from her right temple into that gorgeous hair. *She's young to be going gray*, he thought, but he could also see the fine lines around her eyes that said she'd seen her share of worry, grief, and unhappiness.

She had two earrings, plus an ear cuff, in one ear, three earrings in the other. They all looked like they came from the shop. No rings or bracelets, but then, like Tate, she worked with her hands. He would bet that when she wasn't working, she wore a lot more.

Over her white tank and denim skirt, she wore a patch-work blue and white jacket that looked like it had been made from old summer kimonos like those he'd seen in Japan. She was close to 5'9" in her lightweight sandals. Many tall women slouched, he'd noticed, but not her. She carried herself with confidence and looked the world in the eye.

Tate liked her immediately.

He liked that she had come out to greet him and treated him as a serious customer even though he didn't look like one. A number of owners and salespeople at the shops he'd gone into had just given him the once over and pretty much ignored him until he'd introduced himself. Even then they hadn't been warm and welcoming. He had been just another merchant, not a potential customer.

Tate found himself smiling again, and stepped toward her, his hand out. "Well, you're a welcome surprise," he said. "I was beginning to think it was a city ordinance that everyone who worked on this street had to be ugly as dirt. Nice to know that's not the case. If I'd known that, I'd have been down here sooner."

What on earth was that? he thought. *What just fell out of my mouth?*

She drew back slightly, and the tightening around her eyes told him he had stepped wrong, but hell. She was so gorgeous she had to have heard worse. He hadn't meant to sound like he was coming on to her, although he wanted to come on to her. Jeez. She had him so nervous he was acting like a kid in junior high with his first crush. What was with that?

She took his hand without hesitation, though, her grip strong, no doubt from using the hand tools she'd been working with when he'd come in.

"I'm Tate Garner," he said, trying to salvage his dignity. "My place is up on Ocean, up past the alley. I'm opening a restaurant in a couple weeks."

"I heard," she said. "Cassie Franklin. I wish you luck with it."

Tate could tell she meant it. He warmed to her even more.

"Thanks. Not everyone feels that way. Si Corwin made a point of telling me most restaurants went out of business in six months," said Tate. "I had the distinct feeling he was hoping I'd be one of them."

He was gratified when she laughed. "Well, I'm afraid Si doesn't like anyone opening a new place that might take a customer or two away from The Eden Beach Table," she said. "I'm not sure why he worries. Although maybe he should. He often has seating open when the other restaurants are packed."

"Oh?" said Tate. "Food's not good?"

"I guess the food is good," said Cassie. "He gets decent reviews."

"Only good," asked Tate, "not great?"

"I couldn't say," said Cassie. "I've never eaten there."

"Why not?"

She hesitated, seeming a little surprised at the questions. She looked away, out the front window briefly. Tate figured she had something to say but didn't know him well enough to risk saying something negative that might get back to Corwin. He waited.

"No particular reason," she finally said. "Well, yes, a particular reason. His prices are very high—way out of my budget, I'm afraid." She smiled apologetically. "Si caters to a very..." she chose her words carefully, "elite...clientele. I hear a lot of celebrities eat there, a lot of the very wealthy from down the coast." She paused, appeared to want to say one thing, then shrugged and said something else. "I guess there's a niche market for everyone," Cassie finally said with an apologetic disclaimer. "And Si's isn't mine, so I probably don't have a right to say anything."

Tate waited a moment. "There's something else you're not saying," he finally said. When she still hesitated, he added, "I'm not trying to get you to put down another merchant. I just wonder if he's doing something I should be aware of." Now he *did* sound like he was muckraking. He hurried on. "So I don't do the same thing," he explained. "Something that could hurt my business here in Eden Beach."

She seemed to understand. "No, there's nothing like that. Not that I know of. It's more a personal thing." She paused, thought, and finally decided to say it. "Si has a lot of staff turnover. I've had friends who have worked there. He doesn't treat his people very well." As if sorry she'd said anything, she quickly added, "But I'm sure he's under a lot of pressure with the kind of customers he draws. Maybe he just doesn't deal with it well and takes it out on those who work for him."

Tate had only met Si once, but he'd bet the restauranteur took out his ill temper on anyone except, probably, the wealthy and famous who came into his place.

"Ah, well," said Tate. "One thing I do understand is that a good staff is beyond price. I've worked in way too many lousy kitchens, with too many *prima donna* chefs. I certainly don't want to be one of them. I hope to find really good people. And when I do, I intend to pay them well and treat them well so they'll stay."

"Good to hear," said Cassie.

"So," Tate went on, "if Si's place is expensive, and he has just 'good' food, maybe he should be worried. I'll have *great* food."

Cassie laughed again. "You're right. Then maybe he should worry."

She laughed easily, Tate thought, not because she was nervous or silly, but because, despite the evidence of the streak of gray in her hair, she seemed to find life joyful. She certainly made him feel lighthearted.

"If you don't go to The Eden Beach Table," he asked curiously, "where do you go? When you want a special meal."

"Don't know if it's up to your standards or not," she said smiling, "but I love Clancy's up at Smuggler's Cove on the Island." She tipped her head to the north. "Looks right onto the marina, and we can watch the boats coming in or the sun going down, though usually we go for brunch."

"We?" Tate tried to ask it casually.

Cassie smiled again. "My housemate, Nora and I, usually.

She has a thing for their Seafood Florentine. Though I go there with other friends occasionally."

"So," said Tate, "Do you go out much?"

Cassie's face immediately shut down again. Tate winced. What was he saying?

"I'm sorry," he said, reaching for his wallet. "That sounded like a pick up line." Her raised eyebrow said, *You're telling me.*

"I didn't mean it like it sounded." In the back of his mind, though, Tate suspected he had meant it exactly like it sounded. He was going to have to have a talk with his subconscious.

He rushed on before his face could betray him. "I've just been working in the kitchen for twelve and fourteen hours a day for the last week or so. I'm not sure my brain hasn't turned to soup."

She smiled slightly. "Long hours," she said. "And you're not even open."

Tate shook his head. "My own fault," he said. "I came here with one idea for the restaurant, then, just a few months ago, I changed my idea radically. The architect is about ready to kill me. He had to completely redesign the interior. And the exterior. The contractor is loving it because his people are making a ton of overtime. And Domingo—he's my sous-chef —Domingo and I, we're working round the clock trying to develop the new menu." Tate grinned. "So far he's only sworn at me in Spanish. He hasn't chased me out with a cleaver."

Cassie laughed. At the sound, Tate felt something release deep in his chest, something he hadn't known was tight.

"So what made you change your mind?" Cassie asked him.

Tate hesitated, about to wave off the question, but the way she was looking at him, the way she'd asked the question —she really was interested. Tate found himself reaching for the words to tell her the truth.

"Well," he started slowly, "I've worked in restaurants all

my life. I always wanted to be a chef. Anyway Martin, my dad, thought it was a waste of time." *To say the least*, thought Tate. The storm of ugly words had driven Tate around the world. "I left home and never looked back."

His voice had gotten tight, the anger of a lifetime still there, still rankling. Tate tried to lighten it up.

"Like any young guy who leaves home with a chip on his shoulder, I had grandiose dreams of coming back, opening a five-star restaurant in Eden Beach. Kind of an 'I'll show him' thing," Tate said, and stopped, stunned. He'd never told anyone that. He'd never realized it himself, until just now. He looked at Cassie, suddenly afraid, now that he'd put so much of himself out there, that she'd make some kind of joke.

But Cassie was listening intently, her head slightly cocked to one side, her eyes on his. His fear slid away. For a moment, he forgot what he was saying. When she frowned slightly, he realized he hadn't finished.

"Anyway," he said, scrambling to catch the thread of his thoughts, "one night Domingo and I were working late. We were tired. Nothing had gone right. We were starving, believe it or not, in a kitchen full of failed recipes. Then Domingo pulled together this rice and bean and tomato thing that was a variation on something his grandmother used to make. It wasn't the same because we hadn't intended to make it. It was the same idea, but not the same because we had to use what we had left over from other recipes." He looked at Cassie quizzically. "Do you know what I mean?" he asked. "I'm not making myself clear."

Cassie nodded. "You're clear," she said.

"Well, I suddenly realized that everything was wrong," he said, looking into her serious brown eyes. "My concept, my effort to prove Martin wrong. Digging into that non-Puerto Rican Puerto Rican dish made me remember that it's always been the small, ethnic restaurants I love. Didn't matter if I was in Chicago, or New York, or some village in Greece or Italy or Japan. I love the regional specialties, the family restaurants, the tiny spots you take your friends." He paused. "Anyway. I realized I couldn't go on with my original idea. I'd had it for all the wrong reasons. Martin wouldn't give a damn no matter what I did. Eventually, I would have come to hate the restaurant. And myself."

Tate stopped. He couldn't believe he'd told her all this. He hadn't told anyone. Certainly not the part about wanting to prove himself to Martin.

"You love your work," said Cassie. "When you're passionate about something, you have to trust your heart." She nodded, as if to herself. "I'm sure you'll make a success of it."

Tate laughed, embarrassed. "Yes, well, I hope you're right. Because all the changes and the costs have wiped out my budget for promotion. All the ads I was going to run are so much smoke, now."

He looked at the wallet in his hand as if surprised he was holding it. "And that's what brings me in," he said. "I've been going door-to-door... Well, not exactly. I'm trying to meet some of the folks in the businesses around me." He opened his wallet and pulled out a couple invitations and handed them to her. She seemed to take them reluctantly.

"I'm having an open house," he said. "Invitation only. I want people in the area to get to know me and my food. Then I hope they'll recommend me to their friends and their customers. And come back themselves."

"Good idea," said Cassie cautiously. Then she grinned wickedly. "Are you inviting Si?"

"I should, shouldn't I?" Now it was Tate's turn to laugh.

"Any ideas of who else I should include, though?" he asked her.

Cassie thought for a minute, then recommended a couple

of candy shops, an antique shop, the owners of a few B&Bs, and a couple jewelers. "Talk to Art Jackson," she said, "and Lou Pallis. They're two of the best jewelers in Eden Beach and they have a lot of wealthy customers who eat out a lot. Lou will be invaluable," she laughed. "He loves to gossip. And don't be put off by Art's grumpy demeanor. He plays the temperamental artist card—and, boy, he plays it well!" She grinned at him, and Tate couldn't help but smile back. "But he's very visible, very vocal here in Eden Beach. Having him in your corner could do you a world of good."

"Thanks," said Tate. "I've visited a couple jewelry stores, but not those two."

She thought again. Seemed to hesitate. Then said, "I'm guessing you want people who can spread the word about the restaurant to others in the community—customers, friends..."

Tate nodded.

"But it might not hurt to include some of the community service people—like firefighters or police. Or the executive director at the South Coast Heritage Park." She grinned at him. "Though that will mean you'll be asked to donate eventually."

He grinned back. "An excellent idea," he said, and he really thought it was. "Thanks.

"Oh. And Margot Somerset. She owns the gallery at the top of the hill on the highway."

Tate nodded.

"Look, I hope you'll come," he said. "Bring your boss. Bring dates if you'd like. The invitations are for two," he said, though he was hoping she'd come without a date. Certainly without a husband. "I think you'll like the food, and I plan to have..."

He suddenly caught her look. Though he'd annoyed her with his accidental pick-up lines, she'd quickly gotten over them. But now, he'd definitely pissed her off.

"Did I say something wrong?" he asked, at a loss.

"My boss," she said quietly.

"Yes?" said Tate. The moment he spoke, he knew what he'd done.

"*I'm* the owner here," said Cassie quietly, although there was an edge to her voice. "And the designer. And the maker. You're talking to the *boss*."

Shit, he thought, closing his eyes briefly. *Stupid, stupid, stupid*. It had been quite clear she was not an employee if he'd only paid attention. But she'd thrown him so off balance.

"I'm sorry," he said into the frigid silence. "I really put my foot in it. That was a stupid assumption on my part. But you really can't blame me. Seems like most of the jewelers I've talked to have beautiful young women selling their work for them." *Oh, crap! That was really the wrong thing to say*, his subconscious told him.

He smiled to show he was joking, but she didn't respond. Instead, she set the invitations aside on the counter. Tate felt his heart sink with disappointment.

"Tate, I don't mean to rush you, but I have to get some more work done before my day is finished..." she said.

Okay, that's it, he thought. *Time to make a graceful exit, Garner. Try again another time.*

He held up his hands as his smile faded. "Sure," he said. "I don't mean to keep you. And look, I'm really sorry. I should have realized you were the jeweler here." His tongue wasn't going to quit. "It's just there aren't many women jewelers I've met."

"No, there aren't many," was all she said. Still no smile.

"Sorry. I guess I'd better leave you to your work," he said reluctantly.

"Yes, please," said Cassie.

Ouch. That was cold. He winced mentally and hoped it didn't show on his face.

Tate reached out and tapped the invitations. "Look, I hope you'll forgive me and put these to use. We'll have great food and an open bar. Maybe we can have a drink and start over. I'm usually not this stupid. Or this chauvinistic."

"Thanks, but I don't drink," said Cassie. "I'm pretty busy right now. I put in a lot of late nights. I wouldn't count on me making it to your party."

She was not making this easy.

He made one last attempt. "Well, if your work opens up, I hope you'll have the chance to come by, either then or another time," he said.

He took a step toward the door. As he did, he nodded toward the display cases. "You have nice pieces here. A very nice Eden Beach look. I expect that during the summer you do a great business with all the visitors, especially with this location."

Again there was silence.

Now what? he thought.

"An Eden Beach look?" she asked quietly

"Yeah, you know," said Tate, fumbling. He knew he'd said something wrong again, but for the life of him he couldn't think what it might be. "Sort of freeform. Big stones. All off center," he said. "My mom used to love the Pepper Tree show. She'd come down here whenever she wanted something different. Drove Martin nuts. Not what he thought the wife of a Newport Beach financier should wear, I guess. Too artsy. He was all about classic lines and elegance and diamonds." He laughed self-consciously.

There was an embarrassed silence as Tate stuttered to a stop.

It was clear he hadn't made things better.

"Tate, I'm sure you think you've given me a compliment," she said briskly. "But artists don't generally like to be called 'artsy.' As for tourists, The Green Lotus is a bit more than a cheap souvenir stand."

Definitely pissed, thought Tate. But now he was annoyed, too.

"Look," he said. "I didn't mean to insult you. I'm trying to apologize." He threw his hands up. "Why does every merchant in town pretend they don't court the tourists? Eden Beach is all *about* tourists. It always has been. Without tourists the place would be an empty beach. Look at the art festivals. They're *meant* to draw in tourists!"

"I can't speak for other merchants," said Cassie stiffly, "but I have a very broad-based clientele."

Hell, thought Tate, *she sounds like Corwin.*

"I doubt that," said Tate, knowing as he said it that he was burning a bridge here. "Everyone knows the real money in town is spent up in Newport. Certainly for jewelry."

"Then I'm surprised you didn't set your restaurant up in Newport," said Cassie.

"Because everyone also knows that folks with money like to rub elbows with the artsy types here in Eden Beach," he said, deliberately using the word that had gotten under her skin the first time.

He saw her take a deep breath.

"I don't think this is going anywhere," said Cassie. "I have work to do, if you'll excuse me."

"You're right, it's not," he said. He started to turn away, then he stepped back toward her. She stood her ground.

"You know, when I first saw you, I thought I'd met a real person," he said sadly. "In fact, you reminded me of my mom, a little. That's a compliment, before you get huffy again. But now I'm not so sure that you're any different than Si Corwin and all the other Corwins running businesses here. You want to pretend you're something you're not.

"Now don't let me keep you from your work." He looked

pointedly at the job box on her bench. It held only three work envelopes. "I know you're busy."

He turned and left the store. Just before the door closed completely behind him, he was sure he heard her say, "Don't let the door hit you in the ass as you go!"

44

CHAPTER 4

THE SEVENTEEN-MINUTE WALK HOME to the tiny bungalow she shared with Nora usually gave Cassie time to decompress, analyze designs that didn't work, plan new designs, or simply enjoy the evening light. Tonight, the sunset, the balmy air, the view of the ocean—all of it was wasted on her.

What a jerk! She thought, her anger pounding in time with her footsteps. "Seems like most jewelers have beautiful young women working for them," she muttered aloud, mimicking Tate. Like that was supposed to make her feel better about him assuming neither she nor any woman could be making jewelry and running her own shop.

What really irked her was that she'd liked him. Despite what Delia had said about him being friendly with Carla, Cassie had liked him. He hadn't been all brawn and no brain. Tate's passion for his work practically vibrated from him. He was clearly excited by the turn it had taken.

It hadn't hurt that he was so good looking, either.

He had a nice face. Maybe not conventionally handsome, but strong, open. Straight nose. Bushy eyebrows that suited the tousled hair, bleached by the sun. Laugh lines showed through his tan around his fascinating eyes. Cassie had had a hard time concentrating on what he was saying because she kept trying to figure out what color they were. Blue? Gray? Maybe greenish?

All in all, it was an honest face. A face she would not mind seeing more of.

A body she would not mind seeing more of.

She squashed that thought, but not fast enough.

She thought most chefs were overweight from eating their own cooking, but not Tate. From the snug, faded, silly T-shirt, to the tattered jeans that hugged his long legs, Cassie had not seen—and she had looked, though she wasn't acknowledging that, either—an ounce of fat on him. Obviously he kept in shape, but he didn't have the look of a weight lifter. A swimmer maybe, or a runner.

Suddenly Cassie flashed on the memory of a long-legged blond runner pounding down the boardwalk when she'd been out walking a couple mornings ago.

The runner she'd liked the look of and wondered how to meet. Well, now she'd met him.

And he was a chauvinistic jerk.

Deep in her heart, Cassie knew she was partly angry because she was disappointed. Tate had looked comfortable in his own skin. Not caring about the old T-shirt or the tattered jeans. Confident in his skills, his dream, but not arrogant. He listened. He made her laugh. She'd found herself wanting to sit down over coffee and talk. He was, she had thought, someone who might understand her dreams, her desires, her doubts.

Instead, he was just like every other guy she seemed to meet. Sure he was so much better than she was. *After all,* she thought bitterly, *hadn't he pointed out he was the son of a Newport financier?*

Cassie was still fuming when she walked into the house and dropped her backpack on the floor next to the hall table.

Nora was sitting at the table in the tiny alcove that had once been Cassie's bedroom and that they now called a dining room. She was putting the finishing touches on a couple Chinese chicken salads. She glanced up, smiling, "Hungry..." she started to ask, then saw the tightness on Cassie's face. "Or seriously pissed off?" she finished.

Cassie looked back. "I don't suppose you know anyone who'd help me dig a double grave?" she asked.

"Day that good?"

Cassie blew out a breath and shoved her hands in her hair, loose now that she was away from the bench. "I don't even know where to begin," she said, leaning back against the counter next to the sink.

"Did you eat at all today?"

"Nora! I had the day from hell and all you can say is did I eat?" Cassie really shouldn't have been surprised. Nora had always been the one to see that they all ate.

"In other words, no," said Nora calmly.

"I had a granola bar."

"In other words, no," repeated Nora. "And let me get you a glass," she added as Cassie yanked open the fridge, pulled out a bottle of tea, and set it on the table. Nora reached for her canes to get up.

"I'll get it," said Cassie, going to the cupboard. "I'm up."

"I'll get the rolls then," said Nora, levering herself to her feet. "I forgot them."

Cassie knew better than to offer to get those, too.

Nora Cassidy had been Beth Franklin's best friend. Like Cassie and Anna, they'd spent more time out of school than in it. In the 1960s, they'd been drawn inexorably to Eden Beach and the hippie life blooming there, working in the shops and restaurants, doing their art work at night and on weekends, living in the studios of friends. By the time she was not quite seventeen, thought, Beth had found herself pregnant by a boyfriend who had already left. Her parents had insisted she give the baby up for adoption. Instead, she and Nora had found this small, run-down, two-bedroom house to rent and alternated care of Cassie.

The accident that had killed Beth had crippled Nora. Doctors had been dubious about her regaining the ability to walk, but they had reckoned without Nora's determination not to be a burden on Cassie. Nora had also had the help of one of their former roommates—a very skilled physical therapist. Though she was dependent on crutches and could not drive or walk far, Nora could take care of herself and insisted on doing as much as she could—both for herself and for Cassie.

Cassie put the glass on the table, sat, and poured her tea. She watched her friend maneuver herself around the kitchen. Nora's gray-brown hair was tucked behind her ears. Bangs fell across her face and skimmed the tops of red eyeglasses that slightly magnified her hazel eyes. The cotton twill jumper, dark green with patch pockets, was faded with the years, as was her long-sleeved red T-shirt. Cassie felt a rush of love for this woman who'd been a second mother as well as close friend.

Nora set the basket of rolls on the table, then reseated herself.

"Now," said Nora, "tell me about the day from hell."

In between bites of salad—Cassie really was pretty hungry as she'd never gotten her *phad thai*—she told Nora about Carla Towne's nasty comments about Cassie's—and Jim's—work, and about Carla threatening to have the landlord throw her out of the shop.

"*That* should be an interesting conversation," laughed Nora. "You didn't tell her Rachel was Jim's sister, did you?"

"Oh, no," said Cassie. "I thought I'd let Rachel tell her. But her crack about my work really made me want to strangle her. Then that new restaurant owner came in. What a jerk."

"Oh? What new restaurant owner?"

"The one that took over Ron Baxter's old place on Ocean."

Nora shook her head. Like many Eden Beach's residents, Nora was still angry at the way Ron had been shoved out. She tore off a piece of roll. "So, what was his story?" she asked before popping it into her mouth.

Cassie explained Tate's visit and how he'd assumed she was an employee, then said her work had a great "Eden Beach look."

"I swear, Nora. He acted like I should have applauded him for using the word. Artsy. Sheesh."

"Ah," said Nora. "First Carla saying you weren't an artist, then this guy—what's his name?"

"Tate, of all things," said Cassie. "Tate Garner."

"Then Tate calls you artsy. I can see this would make a bad day." Nora's tone was light.

Cassie stabbed her fork into her salad. "I would have thought you of all people would understand."

"Understand what? That there are mean, vindictive people in the world? Or that some are clumsy with their compliments?"

"What are you talking about?" Cassie's brows came together. "These people come into my store—*my* store—and proceed to talk down to me, insult me and my work like they have the right, and you act like it's no big deal!"

Nora looked at Cassie for a long time, and Cassie saw the depth of pain and love in her eyes. She felt anger draining away, leaving her feeling sheepish and childish. She was still annoyed, however.

"Cassiopeia," said Nora. "If you try to live your life, or

make your work to please others, you'll always be disappointed. No. Carla insulting you and your work is not a big deal. That's who she is. You know that, just like you've known for a while that she would try to take your shop. Who cares what she says? She's a bitch."

Cassie barked a laugh and shook her finger at Nora. "I'm so going to tell Consuelo on you!"

Nora smiled. "I expect Consuelo would make an exception and agree with me on this. As for...Tate?" Cassie nodded. "It sounds like he was trying to compliment your work, he just didn't know how to do it in an 'acceptable'," Nora's hands made air quotes, "manner."

Seeing Cassie's face, Nora went on. "Don't get pouty."

"I'm not pouty."

Nora raised an eyebrow and looked at her for a moment, then went on.

"I think, my dearest Cassie," she said, "they both ticked you off because they hit a sore spot."

"They ticked me off because they were obnoxious and rude." Cassie pushed aside her almost empty salad bowl and crossed her arms on the table, ready to fight.

Nora smiled and continued as if Cassie hadn't spoken.

"In different ways, they both spoke the truth that no artist in Eden Beach wants to hear: that we're all making work for tourists," said Nora.

"I'm not!" said Cassie hotly.

"Aren't you?"

Cassie looked at her friend defiantly but an awful feeling stirred in her gut.

"It hurts, but it's true." Nora shrugged. "We do live off the tourists. I've just had more time to come to terms with it than you have. We've learned what tourists like and expect and we give it to them. If we don't, we starve, or we end up waiting tables, working in a T-shirt shop, or tending bar, like Anna."

"But I want to be known for more than that," said Cassie, wincing at the whine she heard in her voice.

"Then do more than that," said Nora.

"What?" said Cassie, sitting up stunned.

"For a long time," said Nora gently, "I think you've been unhappy with your work." She put up a hand as Cassie started to protest. "Yes, you have. Or, let's say, not as enthusiastic as you've been in the past. I think something's been missing, some spark, and you've been trying to ignore it."

Cassie sat back in her chair, twisted her hair up on top of her head and held it there. She gazed past Nora to their backyard and the tiny shed where her mom had once made pots, where Jim had first cut stones and made jewelry. Nora sat quietly, watching her.

It was as if Nora had shone a bright light into the dark corners of Cassie's heart harshly illuminating all her self-doubt. Cassie knew she was right. The proof was in the beautiful wax sitting on her bench right now. It was a workmanlike job, done with skill and dedication. But Cassie didn't feel that gut-deep excitement about it, the way she once would have. Carla's remark, about Cassie not being an artist, had hit hard because it was exactly the question Cassie's subconscious had been asking for longer than she wanted to admit.

Then there was Tate's comment about being "artsy." Was he right, too? Was she depending on an "Eden Beach look" to sell her work to tourists? Was she the artist she thought she was, the artist she wanted to be? Or was she taking the easy way out, becoming what she despised?

"You're right," she finally said. "I'm stuck, creatively. I haven't wanted to admit it. I was hoping it was just a phase." Cassie brought her focus back to Nora's steady hazel eyes. "What am I going to do?"

"Try something new," said Nora.

"Like what?" Cassie, irritated, dropped her arms back to the table. Her hair tumbled down her back. "I've been making jewelry since I was a kid. And I'm damn good at it. I don't want a new career."

Nora shook her head. "Cassie, open your mind and listen for a minute. I'm not talking about a new career. What I'm saying is that you have become comfortable with what you've been doing. It's sold well, and would probably continue to sell well except for the economy right now." Nora brushed her hair out of her face and took a deep breath. Cassie could tell she was getting annoyed.

"You're right about your skills," she went on. "Jim taught you well. Probably too well. Jim didn't care about his work the way you do. He was good at his craft but he was more than happy to give tourists what they wanted. Good heavens, if there is an 'Eden Beach look,' Jim probably helped create it.

"But you're more like Anna," Nora went on. "I suspect you've been wanting to say something with your work for a long time, make people look at things differently. The only person I know who's doing that here is Art Jackson. He's the only jeweler in town whose work stands out starkly from everyone else's."

Cassie snorted. "Mr. Ego."

"Yes, well. Give the devil his due. He has a right to have a big ego," said Nora. "His work speaks for itself. He doesn't have to be modest or personable. He gives people the artistic personality, and they buy his work because it's so far above everyone else's. That's why you—and everyone else—have always admired him. Or been jealous of him. Maybe you should stop admiring his work and *look* at it. Then figure out how to make him admire you."

"I doubt he even looks at anyone else's work," said Cassie.

"Oh, I guarantee you he looks," said Nora. "That's how he

stays out in front. You watch him at the Masters. He takes a lot of breaks while someone works his booth. He's always walking around, looking at work, talking to people. He doesn't just look at the jewelers, either. He's looking at the sculptors and the painters. I've even seen him fingering woven work. I've watched him cruise the Pepper Tree, too. He disparages the artists there, but don't let him fool you. Art is stealing ideas all the time. He just changes them up so much, no one realizes it."

Cassie reached for a roll and silently took it apart for a while, thinking about Art Jackson's jewelry. The workmanship was incomparable. Art was a magician in gold. He spoke its secret language. But what was more important was his imagination. His work was always innovative and breathtaking.

Art was one jeweler who couldn't care less about tourists' expectations. Yet they were drawn to his store like pilgrims on a holy search.

Into her silence, Nora said, "Maybe it's time for you to aim at the Masters."

Cassie looked at her in disbelief. "Now? We're sitting here talking about my work being...stale," though *boring* was the word that came to her mind, "and you suggest I enter the primo art show in Eden Beach?"

The Eden Beach Festival of the Masters had been the heart of an Eden Beach summer since forever. Between the Fourth of July and Labor Day, the show drew millions of visitors. Successful artists could often make their living—and their reputation—on just the one show.

"Why not?" said Nora. "Maybe that's what you need. A major challenge to shove you out of complacency."

"That's a challenge, all right," said Cassie. "Make a fool of myself in front of the entire town."

"Oh, really? No one in Eden Beach has anything better to do than to wait for you to fail?"

Cassie glared. "You know what I mean."

"No, Cassie," said Nora, irritated. "Actually I don't."

"Look around," said Cassie, sweeping her arm out in an arc meant to encompass the whole town. "Who do you see? Is it people like you and me and Mom and Jim? No. It's all investment bankers and lawyers and, heaven help us, land moguls." She shook her head. "I told you what Carla said today. She'd love to see the 'hippies' run out of town." Cassie collapsed back in her chair. "She'd like nothing better than for me to try to get into the Masters and fail. I can't let Jim down by embarrassing myself like that."

Nora shot forward in her chair, eyes burning. "No, ma'am. No," she said, jabbing her finger into the table for emphasis. "You will not make this about Jim. This is about *you*. *Your* work. Don't you hide behind Jim."

Cassie felt like she'd been slapped. Nora sometimes got angry, but never like this. And never at Cassie.

"Don't you act like you're protecting his legacy. He would be the first to tell you to grow up. Get on with your own life. Do your own work. Jim never worried about what people said about him *or* his work. He stayed out there, learning, trying, doing new things. Bolo ties don't sell any more? Let's try spoons. Spoon jewelry fading away? Let's do something else."

Nora leaned back, her eyes boring into Cassie's. Cassie was afraid to say a word.

Nora took a deep breath and blew it out through her nose.

"If you're so interested in protecting his legacy, maybe that's the one you should protect," she said, her voice calmer but still angry. "If you want to embarrass him, keep acting like a child with a big chip on your shoulder, making excuses about why you can't do something."

Cassie stared at Nora feeling absolutely naked. *Is she right?* Cassie wondered with growing horror. *Am I hiding behind Jim?*

The silence in the kitchen stretched out.

"Okay," Cassie finally said, her voice small. "Suppose I do try. And let's say, by some miracle, I get in. Look at the costs. I would have to work more in gold—and diamonds. Where will I find that money?"

"Cassiopeia Andromeda Franklin!" said Nora sternly but without heat, making Cassie smile. Hearing her full name always did that to her. What had her mother been thinking? "Where's my can-do girl?" continued Nora, trying hard not to smile herself.

"Yes. Well, your can-do girl took a few body blows today," said Cassie ruefully. "Suppose the jurors think my work is just as kitschy as everyone else does?" Unlike the Pepper Tree show, work entered into the Festival of the Masters was juried by a panel of seven artists that changed every year.

"By everyone, do you mean Carla Towne and a guy you've only met once?"

Cassie nodded. "Carla's representative of a lot of the folks with money in Eden Beach—and in Newport. And yeah, I may only have met the guy once..." *and too bad he was such a toad*, she thought, *he had fascinating eyes and a very nice rear*. The flashing thought surprised her so much she almost forgot what she was saying. "...but...maybe he just said what other people haven't said. The ones who haven't bought my jewelry all summer."

Nora didn't miss Cassie faltering at the thought of Tate. She raised an eyebrow, but simply said, "Cassie. No one has sold well this summer. Or last. Why are you taking this so personally?"

Cassie sat quietly for a minute, turning her fork in her empty bowl. "Nora," she said finally, then stopped. Nora waited patiently. "Nora," Cassie started again, eyes on the fork in her hand. "What if they're right?" She looked up, pain in her eyes. "What if I'm *not* good enough? What if all this...

ego…on my part has been just that?" *What if putting down the Masters and the artists who get in is simply sour grapes on my part?* Cassie felt tears sting her eyes. "I can't imagine doing anything else."

Nora leaned forward and gently put her hand on Cassie's arm. "That's your answer," she said. "You can't think of doing anything else. You won't fail. You'll find your way through this…midnight of the soul. I think Bradbury was talking about something else, but it's true here, too. Any artist hits this point sometime. Maybe several sometimes. It always feels like the end. It usually isn't." She patted Cassie's arm. "You'll find the way," she said again.

"And I don't want to hear any more garbage about letting anyone down. Or ego." Nora sat back in her chair. "There is a difference between ego and self-confidence. You are not egotistical. Right now, your self-confidence has taken a beating. So I'd start there, building that back up."

Cassie snorted. "I'll put it on my to-do list."

Nora shook her finger at Cassie. "Don't you get snippy with me, miss."

Cassie laughed and saluted. She started to stack up the dishes to clear the table, then stopped.

"Nora," she said tentatively, "do you think…*really* think I could get into the Masters?"

Nora didn't hesitate. "Of course you can. I have no doubt of it." She waited for a moment. "But first you have to fall in love with your work again," she quietly added.

"I still like it," said Cassie, then sighed. "But you're right. I don't *love* it anymore."

"Then you'll have to find a way to get unstuck," said Nora. "When that happens, I'm willing to bet that you'll have so much love for it, you won't be able to stop working."

"Unstuck," said Cassie. "I really have no idea how to do that."

"When I get stuck," said Nora, "I try a new fiber, a new technique. In the past, I've even tried to learn new skills. I attempted watercolor once."

Cassie frowned. "I don't think watercolor will help me."

"Cassie, sometimes you can be extremely literal," said Nora, with exasperation. "I'm not talking about watercolors per se. I'm talking about a serious investigation into other materials, other approaches to your work. When I tried watercolors, I was looking at new ways of working with color, not thinking about using paper in my weaving, though I have done that, too."

"The only other materials I can make jewelry from are gold and more expensive stones," said Cassie, looking past Nora to the studio in the yard. "I'm not in a position to invest in them, then have them fail to sell." She frowned. Something in her words echoed in her head.

"Well," said Nora dryly, and the ghost of the thought flitted away from Cassie, "at least you have a positive attitude."

She fitted her arms into her crutches and stood up. "Until you stop feeling sorry for yourself, and decide to think outside the box—like an artist—then I have only one more thing to say."

Cassie looked up at Nora, this tiny woman of indomitable strength. "What's that?" she asked without an edge.

"Find what you love. Material, texture, color—whatever it is, be passionate about it. Otherwise you'll find yourself in another box. Don't worry about what anyone thinks. If you love it, it'll be right."

Cassie sighed and gave Nora a soft smile. "Okay. I'll do that as soon as I'm done being pissed off."

"That's all I can ask," said Nora, and smiled. "The dishes, I believe, are yours." She walked carefully down the hall and into her bedroom. In a few minutes, Cassie heard the thump of the loom.

Cassie sat for a long time, staring at the shabby shed in the backyard. She thought about Jim. Nora was right. He had started by making bolo ties out of the stones he'd cut, then moved on, changing his style, changing the work, improving his skills. Jim had enjoyed making jewelry. He had a knack for it. But he wasn't passionate about it.

He was passionate about bikes, thought Cassie, *and the road. Now he's gone. But maybe that's what passion is all about. Taking it to the limit.*

She thought some more about her own work. Nora was right. Cassie *did* want her work to be more. She just didn't know what.

A couple hours later, after Cassie had cleaned up the kitchen, and spent some time sitting in the dusty studio out back, spinning the potter's wheel and thinking about her mom, she came in, dished up a couple bowls of ice cream, and took them to Nora's room.

"Need a break?" she asked.

The loom that filled half the room stopped, and Nora looked up. "Is it Rocky Road?"

Cassie gave her a look. "Since when is there any other kind in our freezer?"

"Then the answer is yes." Nora extended her hand.

Cassie settled herself on the edge of the bed, and they savored the ice cream quietly together for a few minutes.

Finally Nora asked, "So. Besides the fact that he got your goat, what's this new restaurant owner like?"

Cassie almost choked. "You mean besides the fact he's a chauvinistic jerk?"

"Besides that, yes." Nora smiled wryly.

Cassie shrugged. She really didn't want to talk about Tate. Now that Nora had almost talked her out of being annoyed with him, Cassie could see her friend was right. Tate had just been clumsy about complimenting her work. After all, he'd told her he was tired and not thinking straight. If she gave him that, though, then she also had to admit his assumption that she was simply a male jeweler's assistant was understandable, given the number of male jewelers in town and the number of female assistants they had. If she gave in on *that* point, however, she would also have to think a little bit about how he had looked at her with those interesting eyes—gray? green?—and about how she might have felt. How she *had* felt.

If he hadn't been a clumsy chauvinist.

"I'm sure Anna would tell you he's good looking," Cassie tried to say off-handedly. "Very tall. Longish hair. Sandy blond. Typical surfer look." She spooned up more ice cream.

"Ah," said Nora.

"What 'ah'?" said Cassie.

"Phil-ish, then." Phil Trainer had been Cassie's previous boyfriend. Gone for a year and a half, but the wounds, anger, and embarrassment he'd left behind were still very much present.

"Low blow, Nora."

"Just because Phil was a jerk..." continued Nora.

"...liar, cheat..." Cassie filled in.

"...it doesn't mean all men—even blond surfer types—are jerks."

"No, they're not. Jim was a jewel," said Cassie.

"Jim was a hippie not a surfer," said Nora primly, and Cassie laughed out loud. Nora smiled.

"But I'd had a run of jerks, too," said Nora. "If I'd closed my heart, Jim and I would never have happened. I'd have missed some of the happiest years of my life," she finished quietly.

"Yeah. Me, too," said Cassie.

After a moment, Cassie went on. "I guess one of the

drawbacks to living in Eden Beach," she said, "is that most guys come down here looking to score."

"Not true," said Nora.

Cassie set her bowl on her lap and held out both hands with forefingers pointing toward herself. "Case in point. I'm here because some guy was wanting to score."

Nora smiled. "Cassie, it was the '6os. Everyone—women included—was looking to score, as you so quaintly put it."

Cassie knew Nora was right. As she'd grown up, she'd asked her mom about her dad. Beth had always said he wasn't important. By listening at doors, though, when Beth and Nora talked at night, she'd discovered that Beth hadn't been sure who Cassie's father was. She'd had a couple boyfriends about the time she got pregnant. It could have been either of them.

"This...Tate?...well, he can't be just looking to score," said Nora. "He's invested a lot to open a restaurant in a town almost overpopulated by restaurants. He must have something on the ball."

"He can't be that smart if he rented from the Townes," said Cassie.

"I rest my case," said Nora. "You're judging him without knowing him. Not everyone knows the Townes like we do. He may be regretting it already."

"The point I'm making, Nora," said Cassie, trying to get away from talking about Tate, "is that it never occurs to the guys I meet that a woman living and working in Eden Beach has a brain or a dream or something she wants to accomplish in her life. They think of her as a quick one night stand and, baby, they're gone. This guy was no different." *And too bad*, a little voice in her head said. She ignored it.

"I could see it in the way he was looking at me. It was in all his double entendres. He thought he was so smooth. I'm just so tired of it." She took the last bite of her ice cream.

"Ah, well, then," said Nora. "Maybe not. But I'm just saying, Cassiopeia, don't close your heart. You might end up locking out the one person you should let in."

"Guarantee it wasn't this guy," said Cassie.

She sighed, got up and reached for Nora's empty bowl. "I think I'm going to bed. My indignation is in tatters, and I don't think I can take any more," she said.

Nora laughed and handed her bowl over. "You'll survive," she said.

CHAPTER 5

HWACK!

Tate slammed the cleaver through the onion with unnecessary force. They were working on brunch recipes and nothing was coming out the way Tate wanted. He couldn't seem to focus on the work.

Not that it had anything to do with the beautiful woman he'd managed to tick off and insult yesterday. The woman who made him think thoughts he'd sworn he wouldn't think.

He saw Domingo glance up at him from across the work table.

"What?" asked Tate irritably, pausing with the cleaver in the air.

"Whoa!" said Domingo, stepping back and dramatically raising his hands. "I don't know who pissed you off, but I'm pretty sure it wasn't me, and it wasn't that onion."

Tate smiled ruefully. "Bad evening." *That's putting it mildly,* he thought. *I sounded like a slimy lounge lizard in front of the only woman who's truly gotten my attention in years.*

"Yeah, I can see that," said Domingo. "But still, man, you shouldn't take it out on the vegetables. It's not their fault.

More Zen and less anger in the kitchen," he added, smiling slightly. "Isn't that what you always say?"

"Guilty," said Tate, putting the cleaver down.

"So what happened? When I left you last night, you were all happy. Man, how can you get into trouble in a few hours?" He gave Tate a look. "Just tell me it's not the blond."

"No," said Tate, absently, his mind still on Cassie. "No! It's not the blond." *Definitely not the blond*, he thought.

"So?"

"It's nothing."

"Nothing," Domingo repeated. "That means it's a girl. You find a fringe benefit you liked?" He grinned.

"What? No, don't be an idiot. It's not a girl," said Tate. Especially after the way his conversation with Cassie had deteriorated, definitely not *that* girl.

Which was too bad. He had finally gotten up at 2 a.m. to roam the streets of Eden Beach for an hour, trying to walk Cassie out of his mind. No luck. Sure, she was beautiful, with a figure he could almost feel in his hands. But it was more than that. Her warm, easy laugh, her lack of self-consciousness, made him just want to stop and spend time with her. He admired the tremendous self-confidence and talent she had to do the work she did. How could he have been so stupid as to expect a guy to be running the show? The signs had all been there. There were female chefs he'd worked with who would have taken a cleaver to him and turned him into a soprano.

"Uh-hunh," said Domingo.

"You've got a one track mind, Mingo. Anyone ever tell you that?"

Domingo grinned. "You. All the time."

"No. No fringe benefit. It's the town. It's...different."

"Yeah, so you said."

"No, it's not just the shops. It's the people. The people are different."

"Like how?" asked Domingo, coming around the work table. "Move over and let me do that, man. You're dangerous when you're like this."

Tate moved aside at a jab of Domingo's elbow. "Like what?"

"All introspective and shit," said Domingo, starting to chop.

Tate snorted. "Introspection's got nothing to do with it," he said, stepping back and leaning on a counter. "It's just different. It's... When I was here last, when I used to come down with my mom and Tia, people were relaxed, casual. It was a beach town. The residents were all...themselves. They didn't care about politics or clothes or business as business."

"Man, you were here in the seventies. They were all high!" laughed Domingo. "Of *course*, they didn't care about all that shit."

Tate glared at him. "Do you want this answer or not?"

Domingo grinned back. "Yeah, sure. If it'll help you work out your issues so you don't beat up on the vegetables."

Tate made as if he were going to slug Domingo, but his sous-chef held up the cleaver like a shield. "No roughhousing in the kitchen with knives in hand. House rules." he said.

Tate grinned at him. "I'll get you later," he said.

"Yeah, whatever." Domingo turned back to chop another onion. "So now everybody's gotten all business-like, yeah?"

"Yeah." Tate sighed. "They're all, like, worried about their 'broad-based clientele.'" He immediately felt guilty mimicking Cassie even though she wasn't there to hear him. He knew he'd goaded her into making that comment. "I don't care where my clientele comes from," he said in his own voice. "I just want to serve people great food and have them appreciate it."

Maybe that's what Cassie wants, too, he thought.

He was quiet for a minute while Domingo, done with the onions, went to get a bowl.

"And I want to have fun doing it," he added.

"Man, you're making me cry, here," said Domingo, eyes watering from the onions.

Tate reached out and slapped him on the shoulder. Domingo grinned and scooped the onions into the bowl.

"That's what made it different before," said Tate. "Everyone was just doing their thing. Good, bad, indifferent. They were having fun, loving what they were doing and making a living at it. Now... Now I'm not sure people are still loving what they're doing. They're more interested in their piece of the action."

He still couldn't believe that Cassie was like that. *Can't or don't want to?* asked his useless subconscious. It had been asking him that all night.

"Too bad," said Domingo.

"Yeah, it is too bad," said Tate. "People should love what they do." He heard the front door open and began to move toward the front of the restaurant as he heard footsteps on the tile.

"No, man, not that," said Domingo, putting aside the onions, and beginning to mince cilantro. "I can't help you fix that. I meant, too bad it's not a girl. All you have to do is go down to the beach to fix that."

Tate glared at him. "Put that cleaver down."

Domingo shook his head and kept chopping. "No way," he laughed. "You get out of the kitchen and cool off. I got this covered."

"So what's this about a girl?"

Tate turned to see a small, pretty, pony-tailed blond, with a dainty elfin face, poking her head in the kitchen door. She was wearing cutoffs and a UCI T-shirt. Small diamonds glinted in her ears.

Tate grinned. "Tia!" he said, folding her into a tight hug and kissing the top of her head. When she stepped back and looked up at him, it was like looking into the face of his mother. He was sure this was what Lydia had looked like when she'd gone to school in Paris.

"You're not in town six months and already you've got a girl?" she said. "*Another* girl?"

"Yeah, and no sooner has he got the girl, then he has girl trouble," said Domingo.

Tate turned to glare, and Tia saw Domingo.

"Who's this?" asked Tia. "I thought *you* were the chef, big brother."

"I *am* the chef," said Tate. "This is my pain-in-the-ass sous-chef. Tia, meet Domingo Rivera. Mingo, my sister, Tia."

Domingo stopped chopping and looked up. "I'd shake hands but...oh, *wow*, man!" He made his eyes big. "More fringe benefits."

"Don't even think about it," said Tate, glaring at him, "or I'll cancel your contract." Tia looked confused.

Domingo grinned. "Nice to meet you, Tia. Hard to believe this crabby dude has such a cute sister. You must be adopted, right?"

"Yep," she said. "Left on the doorstep by elves."

Domingo winked at her. She blushed.

"So," she said, turning to her brother, "I see onions chopped. Does that mean I get an omelet before you put me to work?"

Domingo deftly dumped some chopped onions on the work top, used his cleaver to divide out a small pile, and pushed them toward Tate. Then he scooped up the rest and dumped them back in the bowl.

Tate rolled his eyes. "I guess that's a yes," he said. He went to the refrigerator to get the other ingredients. "Domingo, I expect you want one, too?"

Domingo looked hurt. "Man, didn't you say food came with the job?"

"Yeah, right. More fringe benefits?"

"Right there in the contract."

Tate grabbed a bowl and started breaking eggs. He appropriated Domingo's pile of cilantro. Domingo sighed and went to get another bunch of cilantro to mince.

In moments, it seemed, Tate had butter melting, mushrooms, garlic, roasted peppers, onions, and sun-dried tomatoes chopped, and two types of cheese grated.

"What's the crabby dude got you doing?" said Domingo to Tia, setting the cilantro aside in a bowl. In the next breath, he said to Tate, "If you're going to be ready for those tomatoes after we finish eating, I'll get them blanched while you're doing that." The question was really moot. Domingo already had the water boiling.

Tate simply nodded. Domingo moved to the refrigerator, and got the tomatoes, saying "So?" to Tia over his shoulder.

"I think I'm helping unpack, set up, wash, and put away," she said, looking at Tate with a raised eyebrow. Tate nodded.

"Usual slave wages?" asked Domingo.

"Yeah," said Tia. "He drove off the freeway and saw my sign: Starving student will work for food."

"Figures," said Domingo.

"You two are in the wrong business," said Tate. "You should audition for the Comedy Store."

He glanced up from the omelet pan in time to see Tia and Domingo exchange a smile. He was startled to see how the smile transformed the small man's face. He'd seen Domingo grin, but it had always been wry. This was like a bright light had turned on inside him. Then Tate noticed Tia's eyes were lit, too. *Well, well*, he thought and smiled to himself.

"Those tomatoes are going to rot and root, at this rate," he glared at Domingo. Domingo held his hands up in surrender and winked at Tia before reaching for the first tomatoes and dropping them into the water.

Tia turned to her brother. "So what's the secret here?" she asked him as he started adding ingredients to the pan. "I'm fainting from hunger and that fantastic smell is about to kill me."

"He never taught you how to do this?" Domingo asked over his shoulder.

"No," said Tia. "He tried once, but my dad about flipped out."

"About an omelet?" Domingo was incredulous.

"The omelet was just the tip of the iceberg," said Tate, stirring the sauté. "It was bad enough that Martin thought cooking was for servants. But omelets were all my mom could afford to make when she was studying painting in Paris. He hated to be reminded of her bohemian past. To him, omelets meant living in tiny walk-up rooms and buying clothes at the open air market. Omelets were entirely too artsy, like my mom."

His words were like a blow to his chest. *My God,* he thought, *Of course Cassie was pissed off when I called her work artsy.* His dad had always meant the term with contempt.

Tate was mortified. *How could I say that to a fine craftsperson?*

He realized that he had paused, hand stilled above the pan.

"Anyway," he went on, rounding up his thoughts and focusing on the omelet, "that was part of why he threw me out when I was seventeen. Thought I was a bad influence on Tia. Teaching her to make an omelet."

Domingo glanced at Tia, about to ask a question. She was fiddling with the salt shaker on the work top and not meeting Tate's eye. Domingo shut his mouth and turned back to his work.

Tate looked at Tia spinning the salt shaker. "He might

have thrown you out, but you didn't have to leave me," Tia said quietly.

Tate flushed with her gentle admonition. Sheila had warned him that Tia had things to say to him, but this was the first time since he'd been home that it had come up.

"No. I didn't. You're right," he said. "It was a bad decision, Ti. I think I knew it even then. I was just so angry—and full of myself. I never stopped to think that it wasn't all about me."

Tia set the shaker back into place and looked up at him. "No, it wasn't," she said. "I wasn't quite ten and you were all I had." Tia paused. "I've been angry, too."

Tate forced himself to hold his tongue and wait.

"Sometimes, I'm still angry," she went on. "But I've had a lot of years living with him, now, and I think I understand why you had to go so far away." She made a face. "Believe me, I understand. He really can't stand it when he can't bend you to his will."

"Yeah," said Tate.

"Anyway," she said, taking a deep breath. "I'm sure I'll be angry off and on in the future, but right now, I'm just so glad you're home."

She gave him their mother's smile. "So. Is that thing done or am I going to fall down and starve right here?"

"It's done," said Tate, sliding the last omelet onto a plate. "Mingo! Fringe benefit's ready."

"About time." Domingo pulled the last of the tomatoes out of the boiling water and slipped their skins. "I was going to come over and start making them myself."

"Remind me again why I hired you?"

"All my mama's recipes you want me to give you," said Domingo, as the three of them, inhaling the fragrance of onions and garlic, sat down at a small kitchen table.

Tia closed her eyes in ecstasy at the first bite. "This is *so* good," she said, as she swallowed. "Now that I'm not living at home any more, you'll have to teach me to make this."

"Deal," said Tate.

"So. Domingo," said Tia, as she lifted another bite of omelet, "what's your story? What got you into the restaurant business?"

"Simple," he said, reaching for a piece of toast. "Free food." She laughed. For the next few minutes, while they ate, Domingo entertained her with the story of his life in the kitchen. When he started on stories about Tate, Tate called a halt.

"Okay," he said. "I think it's time we all get to work."

Domingo winked at Tia. "I'll tell you more later," he said, stacking their plates.

"Not if I can help it," said Tate. Domingo just grinned and headed for the dishwasher. He began singing softly in Spanish.

"Why didn't she ever divorce him?" Tia asked Tate quietly. Tate knew she wasn't talking about Domingo.

"I couldn't tell you," said Tate. He'd wondered that himself so many, many times. "Maybe she meant to. Maybe not. I don't know. Maybe he wouldn't agree to a divorce. Maybe it was all about control. After he got that restraining order against me, so I couldn't see you, I wondered if he'd threatened that he'd take us away from her." He lifted his shoulders. "But I really don't know."

"Tate," said Tia firmly. "You have to tell me everything about her, everything you remember. He won't tell me anything. Just says, 'There's nothing to tell.'"

Tate smiled at her and squeezed her hand. "That I *will* promise you," he said.

Her brilliant smile made his heart ache.

CHAPTER 6

"Now that I'm fueled up," said Tia, putting her hands on the table and pushing her chair back, "where do we start?"

"Dining room," said Tate. "Domingo, I'll be back in five and we can get started on 'your mama's recipes.'" Domingo waved a hand in acknowledgement.

The dining room was a chaotic sea of furniture and boxes. More than forty tables were jumbled in one half of the room. Pristine wooden chairs with woven seats and backs were carefully wrapped in plastic and taped to keep them clean. Plastic-wrapped seat cushions leaned against one wall. The linen service had delivered table cloths and napkins the previous day. Plain white, plain blue, and white-and-blue-checked, they sat on the bar and a couple of nearby tables. Boxes of cutlery sat next to them. Heavy crates of glasses and dishware sat on the floor everywhere.

Tate ran both hands through his hair—Carla kept hinting it was too long—and thought about priorities.

"Start with the dishes, glasses, and cutlery," he said. "It all has to be run through the dishwasher and then put away. It'll mean walking back and forth, I'm afraid. Domingo and I are going to be using up all the space in the back."

"No problem," said Tia. "Just show me what buttons to push, give me a box cutter, and I'll take it from there."

Tate gave her a rundown on the dishwasher, showed her where everything would be stored, and gave her a box cutter. "Once that's all loaded and running," he told her, "maybe you can start placing tables and chairs in some kind of order. But leave the cushions and chairs wrapped for now. There's still some finishing work to do and I want them to stay clean. When all the construction is done—which should be next week—we'll dust everything down, clean it thoroughly, then put out the linens, and fill the service islands."

"How do you want me to arrange everything?" asked Tia.

Tate gave a small shrug and the ghost of a crooked smile. "Doesn't really matter," he said. "I'm sure I'll rearrange everything four or five times before we open. Just for now, though, keep the bar and the patio door area clear. The carpenters are still working there."

"Where are they today?" Tia asked.

"Another job. We made so many changes, they have to fit us in around other commitments."

Tia nodded. "Okay," she said. "Now go invent food." As she headed toward the first box, Tate returned to Domingo. "So. Where are we?" he asked.

For the next several hours, Tia shuttled between the dining room and kitchen, unpacking, running loads of dishes and glasses, putting them away, setting up tables, occasionally joining the banter between her brother and Domingo, and acting as a guinea pig, tasting recipes. Between the dishwasher and the cooking, the kitchen began to heat up and her hair began to curl around her face. She didn't notice the looks Domingo cast her way as she went back and forth, but Tate did. He kept his observations to himself.

As she passed through the kitchen for maybe the tenth time, her arms full of bubble wrap and flattened cardboard boxes destined for the dumpsters out back, Tate paused.

"Domingo, time for a break," he said as he came out of the fridge with a pitcher of iced tea.

"When I finish this," Domingo said.

Tate poured a couple glasses of iced tea and went out to the dining room. His heart skipped a beat. Tia had started setting tables on a loose diagonal. The look was casual, not rigid. It would be easy for wait staff to move through them quickly from the kitchen, and easy to shift them into larger configurations for big parties. A lot of the bar was now clear, and the boxes were definitely fewer.

A few minutes later, Tia joined him. He silently handed her the tea. She drank half of it off immediately. "You were reading my mind," she said.

"Tia," he said, "This looks great. I... It... It's great. Up until now, it's just been in my head. Now, it's real." He put his arm around her, pulled her close and kissed the top of her head. "Maybe you should give up landscape architecture and think about the restaurant business. I could use a good manager. That's a position I haven't filled yet."

Tia looked up at him. "Actually, I've already been thinking about the first part of that."

Tate looked confused. "Come again?"

"I'm going to try out these chairs," she said, pulling away. Despite his instructions, she'd unwrapped a set of four chairs and cushions, and put them at one table. "I think I've earned a few minutes to sit down."

"All of us have," said Tate. "Domingo!" he called into the kitchen. "Come on! Bring the tea with you."

Then he seemed to register what his sister had said. "Sorry," he said, sheepishly. "Maybe you don't want to talk in front of Domingo?"

"It's not really a secret," said Tia as Domingo came out of the kitchen with a tray holding a refilled pitcher of tea, sugar and lemon, another glass rattling with ice, and three pieces of lemon cheesecake.

"What's not a secret?" asked Domingo, setting the tray on the table.

"I'm thinking of changing my career," said Tia. "Well, maybe not changing, but expanding. Or, maybe not expanding as much as moving in another direction."

Tate laughed. "Sounds like changing to me."

"Stay out of the restaurant business," said Domingo. "Long hours, lousy pay."

"Excuse me?" said Tate.

"Usually lousy pay," amended Domingo. "Hours are still long. Hey," he added, looking at Tate's glare. "That part you know is true."

Tia grinned. "No, not the restaurant business." She looked nervously at Tate. "I'm leaving the architecture office."

"You're an architect?" asked Domingo.

"Landscape architect. Very junior."

"Isn't that just a fancy name for gardener?" asked Domingo, refilling Tia's glass.

Tia smiled at him. "Yeah, well, I guess in some ways it is," she said. "A landscape architect does what a really good gardener can do—lay out the grade of a site, suit the plants to the site and to each other, actually paint with plants."

"I'll bet being a landscape architect pays better than being a gardener, too," said Domingo.

Tia laughed. "I suspect it does," she said. She took a deep breath. "I guess I'm about to find out."

"Wait. What?" said Tate, concern on his face. "You want to become a gardener?"

"Yes. Well, no... Well..."

Tate raised an eyebrow. "Maybe you just don't like *this* job?"

Tia made a face. "I like my job. Well, I like the people, and love designing gardens. But I'm just making preliminary drawings. I'm not involved in *building* them." She picked up her fork. "That's one thing I enjoyed about the biology— being hands on."

"Biology?" asked Domingo. "Like cutting up frogs?" He shrugged. "Not so different from being a chef in France," he said. "Maybe you *are* cut out for the restaurant business."

Tia laughed. "I don't think so. I didn't like that part so much. I was thinking about going into marine biology."

"So why'd you give it up?"

She grinned. "I realized that maybe I didn't want to be in biology as much as I wanted to be stranded on a boat with Phillipe Cousteau."

Tate threw back his head and laughed so hard tears came to his eyes. "You and about a million other girls," he finally gasped, wiping his eyes with the heels of his hands.

Domingo looked hurt. "What is it about the French? Why don't girls think Puerto Ricans are sexy? I mean, hasn't anyone seen 'West Side Story'?"

Tia glanced at Domingo, then smiled shyly at her plate. She cut into the cheese cake and took a bite. Her eyes got enormous. "This!" she said, pointing to her plate with her fork. "This is even better than the omelet! Which of you geniuses made this?"

Before Tate could answer, Domingo said, "Your brother got it up at some place up in Costa Mesa called the Pie Picker, or something."

"You know, Domingo," said Tate. "If you didn't bake this well, I'd really send you back to New York. There has to be someone who will give me less grief than you."

"Where would be the fun in that?" Domingo grinned.

"Mingo," said Tia, "I can see I'm going to gain weight in no time if I keep coming here."

Domingo shrugged modestly.

"So getting back to your new career," said Tate. "What brought on this change of heart?"

Tia took another bite of cheesecake and closed her eyes in ecstasy for a moment. "We had a client who wanted a garden of drought-tolerant or native plants. She insisted the foliage had to be interesting, too. I'd never really thought about foliage, so I started reading about it and going to nurseries, and I realized I was missing the fun stuff. The colors, the shapes, the textures. The fragrances. I used to love working in Sheila's garden. Making something out of nothing." She shrugged. "I kind of like getting my hands dirty, too."

She glanced at Tate. "I guess I'm something like you and Mom. I need to do something more creative than just sit in an office all day. I still want to use my training, designing gardens. But I want to find a nursery, or even a gardening company," a quick grin at Domingo, "that helps people design their own yards. Something that would let me actually pick out the plants, set them out, see the final result."

"You've already given notice at the company up in LA?"

Tia nodded. "I've already started putting in applications at nurseries here, in Eden Beach, and up in Mission Viejo, Irvine, Costa Mesa. There's one in Irvine that's really promising."

"You're not looking in LA?"

Tia gave a tiny shake of her head. "If I'm going to change jobs, I might as well be down here, closer to you. We have a lot of years to make up."

Tate looked into her eyes and nodded once. "We do. But like Domingo said, it won't pay much."

"No, it won't," she agreed. "But I talked to an old friend

from UC Irvine. She lost one of her roommates. I can move in with her and the other two at the beginning of the month."

Tate was quiet for a minute. Tia looked down at her plate and nervously mashed a few cheesecake crumbs.

"Maybe I can help give you a start," Tate said finally. "I need plants for the dining room, patio, and restrooms."

"Really?" asked Tia, brightening up. "You'd let me do that?"

"Sure. Why don't you think about it, shop around, and give me a budget. They'll have to be tough to kill, though," he added. "I'm not that great with remembering to water plants."

Tia's eyes lit, and she tipped her head. "Maybe you need to give me a contract to care for them, too," she said.

Tate laughed. "Maybe I do." He picked up his glass and drained his tea.

"Tate," said Tia shyly. "You don't mind me doing this, do you? I mean, after you helped me get my certificate and all." Tate waved the question away. "You must think I'm such a dilettante, going from one thing to another."

Thinking of what he'd said to Domingo that morning, Tate said, "It's more important that you do what you love. I don't want you ending up nasty and bitter like Martin." He put his hand on her arm. "And do *not* hesitate to ask if you need help."

"I will. Thanks." Tia changed the subject. "You're opening the end of the month, you said. So I have until then to find you plants?"

"Three weeks," said Tate. "Until the open house."

"Open house?"

He nodded. "Word-of-mouth advertising is the best for restaurants, but getting that buzz going, that's the hard part. Carla came up with the idea of inviting local people with connections, let them taste the food, see the place, and hope they'll come back, and tell their friends and clients."

"Carla?" asked Tia, puzzled. "Isn't she your realtor?"

Tate opened his mouth, but Domingo was quicker.

"You met her?" asked Domingo. When Tia shook her head, he went on. "A very slick babe. She's hot for your brother."

"Oh?" asked Tia. "This is the woman trouble you two were talking about when I got here?"

"She's definitely trouble," said Domingo, suddenly serious. "A wolf in stiletto heels, that one." He shook his head. "I don't care how nice her ass is. I keep telling your bro she'll bite his balls off, he lets her get too close."

"Domingo," said Tate warningly.

Domingo turned back to Tia. "Sorry," he said. "I shouldn't have used the word stiletto." Tia laughed.

"And as I keep telling Domingo," Tate glared as his friend, "she's my realtor, nothing more."

Domingo raised his fork, unfazed by Tate's look. "Yeah, well, from what I've seen," he said, "she sure wants more. And she hasn't been getting much discouragement from you."

Domingo saw just a little bit too much, thought Tate, irritably. But he'd completely given up the idea of flirting with Carla after he'd met Cassie.

Cassie.

He sighed mentally.

"Mingo, you're making a big thing about this."

Domingo leaned toward Tate urgently. "Maybe you're not making a big enough thing about it." Tate started to say something, but Domingo kept going, a hint of anger in his voice. "Look, man. I was there. I remember what you were like when you got back from Paris."

He paused. Tate, watching his eyes, saw him change his mind about something.

Domingo sat back, and put his hands up in surrender. "I guess you want to put yourself into the jaws of a shark again, that's up to you," he said, the heat gone from his words, his bantering tone back. "But me, I don't want to live with that. You're a pain in the ass to work with when it goes south."

"Because it's all about you," said Tate.

Domingo raised his eyebrows questioningly and put out his hands, palms up. "There's someone else?"

Tate put his hand on Domingo's shoulder and shoved. The smaller man pretended the chair was about to topple. Tate grinned, his irritation gone.

"Look, Domingo, we need all the friends we can get right now." Domingo gave Tate the "Oh, yeah?" look he knew too well. "Carla has got connections in the community. We need her to be on our side."

"That kind of help comes with strings, man. Or, in her case, enough rope to hang you."

"You're reading too much into this," said Tate again.

"Maybe," said Domingo. "I just think you don't watch it, she'll have you carved up on a plate."

The front door opened, and they all turned at the sound.

"Sorry, we're not..." Tate started, and stopped when he saw it was Carla Towne. He got up and walked over to meet her.

"And the devil pops up," said Domingo under his breath. Tia looked at him as he stood. "You finished?"

"I haven't licked the plate yet," she said, but her smile faded as she saw Domingo's face. She glanced at Carla, and then stood to help him pile dishes on the tray. "She's really that bad?" she asked quietly, her back to the newcomer.

Domingo shrugged. "You judge," he said, then gave her a small smile. "Maybe I'm just jealous it's not *me* she's hot for." He took the tray and headed into the kitchen.

"I ran into Ken Huff a while ago," Carla was saying to Tate

with a smile. "He said you were making a lot of changes, but with the barriers up out front, I haven't been able to see them. When I saw they were down, I couldn't resist coming in to get a little peek." She held her thumb and forefinger an inch apart and gave Tate a cute smile. Neither of them saw Tia roll her eyes.

"Not much to see, yet," said Tate.

The high wattage smile dimmed. Carla reached into her bag, pulled out a folder and handed it to him. "I also wanted to bring you that list."

Tate flipped it open. Inside were two typed pages of names, businesses, phone numbers.

"They know you'll be calling," said Carla.

"Thanks, Carla," he said, and meant it. "This will be a good start."

"Well, actually, Tate," Carla's laugh was condescending, "It's more than a start." She gestured to the list in his hand. "Those are some of the most influential people on the South Coast."

Domingo's remark about strings and rope flashed into Tate's head, but they really did need a fast start. And Domingo had also been right about picking up catering contracts for the holidays.

Like it or not, he needed Carla's contacts.

Carla was pointing out names on the list. "You remember Bev Hutchins from high school, of course." Tate didn't. "Though you probably won't recognize her. She had her nose redone a few years ago. Doesn't really suit her." Carla shook her head. "But she's married to the top litigator in Orange County. And Sue French," Carla leaned into Tate a bit, her breast brushing his forearm. "Her husband is a vice president at Wells Fargo." She looked up at him coyly. "A nice friend to have when you want to expand."

Tate tried to nod non-committedly.

"I knew some of our old high school friends would want to support you." She laid her hand on his arm. "Especially the girls."

Tate tried not to wince. *Girls?* he thought.

"I know they never said," Carla continued, "but they all thought you were just the sexiest thing. A dangerous bad boy."

She wants to show me off, Tate thought with utter clarity. *She wants to show them she's tamed the bad boy.*

A surge of anger and resentment flashed through him. It took all his self-control not to let it show.

"I didn't know this would be a class reunion." It came out sounding harsher than Tate intended. Carla's flirty look vanished. She straightened up and away from Tate. "But I really appreciate your help, Carla." Tate scrambled to salvage what he could. He closed the folder and gestured with the list. "This is really great."

Carla, barely mollified, gave him a small smile.

"Well," she said, dropping her handbag on a nearby table. "Let's see what Ken was raving about."

She put her hands on her hips and twisted sideways to survey the room, a move calculated to show off her figure. As his eyes slid over her curves, Tate felt like a bit of a hypocrite after what he'd said to Domingo about not being interested in Carla.

An image flashed into his mind: Cassie as she stepped onto her show room floor, smiling unselfconsciously as she reached for his hand.

Carla frowned and moved a bit farther into the room. "I thought from what Ken said you were almost finished," she said.

"We are," Tate told her. "There's some more finish work to be done around the bar. And they're going to lay the patio in a few days."

"But this looks more like a cafeteria." Carla turned back to him with a look of distaste.

Across the room, Tia was opening boxes and stacking glasses on a tray. Tate saw her jaw drop as she froze for a moment, box cutter mid-slice. She caught his eye, then quickly snatched up the partially filled tray of glasses and hurried into the kitchen.

Tate knew his sister's look was mirrored on his own face. He had a hard time holding onto his temper. "I'm not sure what you mean," he finally said.

"It's obvious," said Carla, sweeping her arm out. "This is not the high-end, exclusive restaurant you described when you first talked about renting this space. For starters, it's all a bit...Spartan. The furniture looks like it belongs in a street café. And tile on the floor? Awfully noisy. I thought this would be some place...intimate. Not quite so open." She nodded toward the folding glass doors that led onto the street and onto the terrace off the bar. The frown deepened. "Where people could have private conversations, do business." She turned back to him. "I imagined something more upscale. Something more like—but nicer than—The Eden Beach Table."

"Originally, yes," said Tate, hiding his anger. "It was going to be like that. But then a few months ago, late one night, we were tired, and Domingo pulled together a family recipe from Puerto Rico. And it was just...*right*."

"Puerto Rico?" said Carla, her voice brittle.

"Yeah," said Tate ignoring the disapproval that radiated from Carla like heat from a bread oven. "So we started kicking ideas back and forth. We came up with a menu that's ethnically based, but with a new take, using all fresh local ingredients, when we can get them."

"Hmm." She said, and turned again. He noticed her face became a bit pointed when she disapproved of something.

"As for the floor..." Tate shrugged. "I've never thought it was a good idea to combine carpet with food and drinks, especially at the beach when you throw sand into the mix. Now that it's sealed, the slate will be easy to clean. As for the noise, the table cloths, the pads on the tables, and the acoustical ceiling will absorb a lot. But a certain level of noise makes it friendlier, happier, more European, than a dark, executive cave with carpeting on the floor.

"And that's what I want," he went on. "Lydia's should be a place where people can feel comfortable sitting with friends for a while after a meal. Where they don't feel hurried. I wanted bright, light, friendly, inclusive, where food and friends are the focus."

The frown seemed stuck. "It's just that Eden Beach could use a really good upscale, exclusive restaurant," she said.

"Then someone else will have to open it," said Tate bluntly. He saw the surprise on Carla's face. He dropped the folder holding her guest list onto the table next to her handbag, pulled the cushions off the chairs where they'd taken a break, and took them back to the box where they'd stay clean. Tia came back in from the kitchen, tray empty, a questioning look on her face.

"Tia, come meet Carla, my realtor," he said, not seeing Carla's eyes narrow as he labeled her. "Carla Towne, Tia Garner. My sister."

Carla's smile went to full wattage again. "Well, hello!" she said, putting her hand out to Tia. "It's a pleasure."

"Same here," said Tia, taking Carla's hand and smiling politely.

"Tia's been helping me set things up," said Tate.

"Oh! You're an interior designer?" asked Carla.

"No, I'm just a younger sibling lured into hard labor by the promise of food," said Tia. She grinned at Tate.

"Oh, too bad." Tate saw Carla dismiss his sister. "There's lots of work for a good interior designer in this area."

Tia saw the interest fade, too. "If you'll excuse me, I still have some work to do on the bar."

Carla didn't even acknowledge Tia. She was smiling up at Tate.

"I'm sorry, Tate," she said. "I guess I'm just a bit frank. It's just that this is so different from what you said you were planning."

Carla looked back at Tia as the younger woman unwrapped checked table cloths and carried them to the kitchen. "Still, it could be a good stepping stone," she said almost to herself.

"Stepping stone?" Tate asked.

"Yes." She turned her high wattage smile back to Tate. "You're right. Eden Beach probably isn't the best location for the type of restaurant you first talked about. I know of some excellent venues coming up for lease in Corona del Mar. There's even one in the Towne Center," she said, nodding. "Yes. I'll check into those for you."

"What? Carla. I haven't even opened this one yet." Tate looked at her puzzled. "I certainly don't want another one."

"Well," she cocked her head and gave him a little flirty grin. "It never hurts to keep your options open."

Tate was at a loss as what to say. It didn't matter. Carla was charging on as she began to walk around the restaurant.

"I like the European angle," she said slowly. "You should emphasize that in your advertising. Who's doing your PR?" she asked. "I know a couple PR specialists in Newport who could get your ad into the local city magazine, or get you some spots on the radio." She came back toward Tate.

"No budget for advertising," said Tate. "The remodel ate most of it up. I'm hoping the open house will pay off. It's a great idea."

He gestured to the list on the table. "I really appreciate your recommendations of people to invite." A parade of conflicting emotions on Carla's face. For a moment, he thought she would take the list back.

"Well, they *are* some of the most influential people in the area," she said hesitantly. "But I have to tell you, Tate, they're not expecting something...ethnic." Though she used the same word Tate had, he could tell she didn't feel about it the way he did. "Maybe you should have some of the food you originally talked about."

"I think the food we're planning will impress them," he said.

"Well..." Carla drew the syllable out doubtfully.

"It was a good idea to ask some of our old classmates from high school." Tate hated himself for saying it, but Carla began to preen a bit.

Well, why not? he justified himself. It wouldn't hurt to play the local-boy-makes-good angle. He wasn't going to tell Carla that he'd be surprised if he remembered two people from high school.

"I've invited some of the merchants, too," said Tate, walking back to the set up table and tucking the chairs in.

"Merchants?" asked Carla, her voice going up a bit. "Why?"

"Visitors always ask shop owners and hotel staff for recommendations for places to eat."

"Tourists?" Her voice was definitely sharper. "I thought you were targeting residents of the South Coast."

"Carla," said Tate, leaning on the back of a chair, "I can't afford to be exclusive. I think I have something for everyone. Local folks from Eden Beach. Folks from Newport, San Diego, Costa Mesa. Heck, Minnesota or Tennessee." He shrugged. "Everyone."

"What merchants have you been talking to?" Tate could see her mentally doing damage control.

For a brief moment, Tate considered giving Carla her list back. He was beginning to regret accepting her offer of help. Instead, he shrugged again. He needed all the friends he could get right now. He couldn't afford to alienate her. "The fellow who runs the imported pottery shop," he finally said. "Alexis, who makes those great truffles. That woman jeweler around the corner."

Carla's brows crashed into a frown. "Well, the first two are fine. They sell some of the best products in Eden Beach," she said. "But the jeweler's a mistake."

Tate was taken aback at her vehemence.

"Why?" he asked against his will. "What's wrong with Cassie Franklin?"

Carla almost snorted. "What's *not* wrong?" she said. "First, she makes cheap silver jewelry. Then there's the drug-dealing hippie who gave her the shop, who's probably her father, though no one knows. Then there's the whole commune she comes from. You've seen how she dresses," Carla went on. "Like something out of an old movie. But what really annoys me is that she's holding down the best location in town. Someone who claims to be an 'artist' and dresses like a throwback to the '70s," she scoffed. "If her landlord was smart, she'd throw her out and put in a business that's more appropriate to that location."

There was silence for a minute. Tate could see Tia at the bar had stopped unwrapping glasses and was staring.

"Gee, Carla," said Tate. "Why don't you tell me how you really feel about her?"

Carla took a deep breath. "Sorry. It just angers me to see people holding Eden Beach back from what it could be."

From what it can be or from what you want *it to be*, thought Tate. *I wonder if I fall into that category now, too.*

"I liked her work," said Tate mildly.

Carla waved her hand airily. "Well, it hardly matters," she said. "I've already contacted her landlord. I told her I could get more money for the space."

"You what?" said Tate, shocked.

Carla did the hand wave again. "She's going out of business anyway. Hippies are dead. People want quality nowadays. They don't want stuff like that." She made a face. "I expect someone else will be in that spot next summer."

"Anyway," she segued suddenly, seeming to read Tate's face. "What are you going to call it? Your restaurant."

Tate stared at her for a minute. "Lydia's," he said finally. "I originally thought about Lydia's Eden Beach Bistro, but decided to shorten it."

Carla's frown returned. "Oh," she said. "Why Lydia's?"

"I liked the name," he lied. At this moment, he didn't want to tell Carla anything about himself or his life.

"Oh," said Carla. "Don't you think it sounds a little... I don't know. Amateurish. Like someone operating from their kitchen."

Tate just looked at her.

"I don't mean to criticize," said Carla, in a hurry. "I mean, it's a good start. But maybe I could help you brainstorm some names. Something that will have a more elegant sound."

Tate shook his head as he glanced at the clock and pulled his apron off. "Not interested in elegant. Besides, the sign's coming tomorrow." His quick glance told him that Carla was annoyed.

"Ah. A done deal, then," she said.

"Yep, a done deal," said Tate.

Carla's face clouded and she glanced at the folder on the table. *She's going to withdraw her support*, he thought. An amateurish bistro, with a noisy slate floor, and local merchants and their customers as diners. *Too déclassé for words.*

He picked up a pile of plastic wrap and jammed it into an empty box. Tia came over and took it from him.

"You really named it Lydia's?" his sister asked him quietly.

He smiled softly and nodded, noting the tears that came to her eyes.

"I like it," she said. "It's perfect." Without a look at Carla, Tia took the trash toward the kitchen.

Tate turned back to the realtor. Let her take her list if she wanted to. He couldn't grovel any more. Domingo was right. He was starting to strangle in Carla's strings.

"Carla, I don't have any more time. I have someone coming in for a bartending interview in a minute." Just then the door pushed open, and a small Latina in her late twenties walked in. Tate saw the dark spiked hair tipped with blond, the big silver earrings, and he smiled broadly.

He turned to Carla. "I'll look forward meeting some of your friends," he couldn't resist saying. "And maybe seeing some folks from high school."

"Sure," said Carla. She turned, caught sight of the young woman coming in the door, and paused. Then she snatched up her handbag and walked out without another word.

Tate turned to the newcomer. "You're Anna Rodriguez? Here about the bartending job?"

"That's me," she said.

"Come on in, Anna. I'm Tate."

CHAPTER 7

ANOTHER NO SALE.

Cassie unlocked the front window to return the neckpiece she'd shown to the woman now walking out the door. She stood for a moment, looking out at the park and the boardwalk. Big clouds streamed across the sky, hurried by the wind. A few tourists drifted by eating ice cream. They glanced in her window and drifted on. Cassie doubted they'd even registered the jewelry.

She sighed. She wondered what she would do if the fears about the economy didn't ease.

She was staring out the window at some place halfway between the beach and Catalina when Cassie realized someone was making a face at her through the window. Anna stuck her tongue out when she saw Cassie look at her. Cassie stuck out her tongue in return. Anna laughed and headed around the side of the building.

The only door into The Green Lotus opened onto the tiny plaza between the shop and the movie theater next door. Cassie turned to meet Anna as she came through the door dragging in the scent of fresh popcorn as the theater got ready for the matinee.

"I've got to learn to lock that door," she said to Anna. "Just anyone can walk in when I leave it open."

"Be nice," said Anna, waving a brown bag bearing a pirate logo. "I bring gifts."

At the aroma of burgers and fries, Cassie's stomach growled loudly.

"Gotcha!" Anna laughed.

Cassie groaned. "Busted! I'd walk to San Diego for a burger right now."

She unlocked the security gate and waved Anna through to the design desk. Cassie had a small table set up behind it just for their occasional lunches together.

The two women had been best friends since junior high, bonding over their love of art and their mutual outsider status. Anna's parents were immigrants from Mexico. Her father, Luis, trained horses for many of the wealthy families whose kids Anna saw in class. Cassie's family consisted of unrelated artists and friends. They'd often been mocked by classmates for those reasons and because of the difference in their heights—Anna didn't top five feet compared to Cassie's 5'9".

While Anna got the food out, Cassie pulled a tea out of the fridge for her and grabbed a Coke for Anna.

"So the bleach job is new," she said, gesturing to her friend's blond-tipped dark hair. "I thought you were going natural."

"Dale liked the blond," she said. "This is a compromise."

"Ah," said Cassie as, she opened the bottle and the can and set them on the table. "Well, keep that man happy. When I make a lot of money, I'll want him to build me more cases." Anna's husband was a firefighter who made beautiful wood furniture on his days off.

They had started on their burgers before Anna asked, "So what was that scary face all about?"

Cassie chewed and swallowed. "What scary face?"

"The one you were wearing when I looked in the window," said Anna. "That was enough to drive away customers, assuming there was anyone out there with any potential."

"Yes, well, that's the reason for the scary face," said Cassie, grabbing a fry. "No business. I took in one small repair this morning and had a couple lookers. That's it."

"That bad?" asked Anna, her face getting serious.

Cassie waggled her hand back and forth. "It's not good. I don't know if it's 'that bad' yet. But it sure could be better."

"We're packing them in at Jack's," said Anna.

"Yeah. Burgers and T-shirts. That's all anyone's buying." Cassie sighed. "T-shirts. Everyone thinks they need just one more. No one thinks they need jewelry."

"Of *course* they need jewelry!" said Anna, with mock outrage. "Isn't jewelry, like, one of the basic food groups?"

Cassie grinned at her tiny friend. "Maybe earrings," she said, looking pointedly at Anna's. No matter how big Cassie made her earrings, Anna's outsized personality always seemed to counterbalance them. She reached out and squeezed her friend's arm. "What would I do without you? You always make me laugh."

"You'd have to go into a convent or something, I'm sure. The kind where no one talks," said Anna.

"As long as they feed me," said Cassie as she dipped a fry in ketchup.

"So. The business," said Anna, leaning back in her chair and setting her burger down. "What about applying to the Masters?"

Surprised, Cassie paused with the fry half way to her mouth. Then she gave Anna a suspicious look. "Did Nora call you?" she asked.

"What? No," said Anna. Then she raised her eyebrows. "Oh! I get it. I'm not the only one to bring it up."

"No, you're not."

"So? You used to talk about it."

"I used to be eighteen, too."

"So at twenty-nine you can't dream anymore?"

"Yeah, yeah," said Cassie making talking motions with her hand, and popping the fry into her mouth.

"Unh-uh, no," said Anna. "You are not getting out of it." She bent down, reached into the oversized bag on the floor next to her and pulled out some forms. She slapped them on the design desk.

"One for you, one for me," she said defiantly.

Cassie stared at the application forms for a minute, then looked at Anna. "*You're* applying to the Masters?" she asked. "You've always said it was bogus elitism or some such bull-drizzle. What brought on this change of heart?"

Anna grinned sheepishly. "Yeah, well. You're not the only one getting pushed. Dale's shoving pretty hard, too." She picked her burger back up. "And maybe I'm older. Maybe I think we both need some recognition," she said, unusually serious.

"And maybe you're too chicken to do it on your own?"

Anna grinned and wiggled her eyebrows. "Yeah, maybe there's some of that. But wouldn't it just set some folks on their heads if we got in?"

Cassie spun the application around, shuffling it back and forth on the desk.

"I don't know, Anna. I'm..."

Anna waited. Finally she asked, "You're what?"

"I don't know," said Cassie. "I'm just feeling...stuck. Stagnant."

Anna raised a pierced eyebrow. "Scared?"

Cassie forced a small, rueful laugh. "Yeah, well, that too.

But mostly, I'm not sure I have the confidence I need to pull off an entry."

"Then you'll just have to trust me. I have confidence in you. I'm sure you'll get in," said Anna.

"It's not getting in that worries me. Well, it worries me that I might *not* get in. But then it worries me that I *will* get in."

Anna shook her head. "You always were confused."

"Thank you so much," said Cassie.

Anna laughed. "So, why would you worry about getting in? That's a good thing."

"Yes, it would be a good thing." *Correction*, thought Cassie. *It would be freaking great*! "But the costs, Anna," said Cassie. "There's building a booth, and money for the metal and stones to make the jewelry to put in it. Then there are advertising costs—postcards, photos, mailings. I'd have to hire someone to man the booth during the day, because I still have to be here in the shop to keep the work going out the door."

"Not insurmountable," said Anna. "Everyone else does it, too. And the booth, *pheh*," she made a disparaging noise. "Dale can do that or no sex for a month."

Cassie threw back her head and laughed. "What *does* that man see in you?" she was finally able to say.

Anna grinned. "I feed him, too." She bounced her eyebrows again and snatched the last fry.

Cassie began to pick up all the burger papers and containers. "Seriously, Anna. Suppose I do all that and I'm *not* successful? I'm out of business."

Anna's smile stopped. "Are things that close?"

Cassie made the hand waggle gesture again. "If I don't get into the Masters, and things stay the same, I can struggle along for a few more years, hoping things pick up," said Cassie. *Hoping I'll find my way out of this creative box*, she thought. "But if I *do* get into the Masters and don't do any better than I'm doing now, I won't last through next summer. The extra costs will sink me."

Cassie had talked to a few people who had counted on the Masters, and who had gone under or come close to it. She feared that fate. More, she feared that a failure would simply reinforce everyone's opinion of her, despite Nora's lecture the previous night.

"Then what you're saying is that your choices are kind of like ripping off a Band-Aid slowly and torturing yourself, or getting it over quickly," said Anna.

"In other words, go down in a ball of flame if I'm going?" asked Cassie.

"Absolutely."

Cassie looked at her friend for a moment. "Anna, if I lose this," she waved her hand at the store, "I don't have a fall back, like tending bar. What would I do?"

Anna made a sound of disgust. "Cassie Franklin. Don't make me come over there and slap you!"

Cassie started to answer but Anna interrupted. "You go to work for someone else. You learn to do something else. Yes, it would be a set-back, but not the end of the world. Lots of people start again. And do better the second time." She gave her friend a mock glare. "Now are you going to make me forge that Masters application for you?"

Cassie looked back at her sheepishly. "You'd do that for me?" she asked sadly.

Anna started to answer, then looked at Cassie again. "You're yanking my chain." She balled up an empty French fry bag and threw it at Cassie.

Cassie dodged and started to laugh so hard she started crying. When she could finally speak, she wiped the tears out of her eyes and said, "I love it when you get all self-righteous and mother-henny and come galloping to the rescue."

"You really are despicable," said Anna. "When was the last time you saw a mother hen on a horse?"

When they stopped laughing and were able to breathe again, Cassie said, "Thanks, anyway, Anna. I was feeling a little...cowardly."

"I'll remind you of that when you're a big success, and they're writing you up in *Town and Country*."

Cassie shook her head, smiling.

"And once you're famous," Anna went on, "All my earrings will be worth a bunch of money. I'll be able to retire."

"Oh, no!" said Cassie. "You have to keep working at Captain Jack's so if I go bust, I'll still be able to eat. The jerk may pay like crap but at least his food is good."

"Yeah, well, with any luck I may not be working there much longer."

"Anna? Why? What's happened?"

"Oh, nothing yet!" said Anna quickly. "Talk about getting mother-henny. But you're right, he does pay crap. So I just applied at that new place, up on Ocean. Ron's old place. You heard it's changed hands."

Cassie's face closed down. She started to say something but Anna plunged on. "And, wow, Cass, if I get this job, you *have* to come visit me while I'm working! The new owner is one very hot guy! His name is Tate and..."

"We've met," said Cassie.

"Then you..." Anna paused, narrowed her eyes. "Wait. I know that voice. You're doing your Margaret Hallstrom imitation."

Cassie started laughing again. She *had* sounded like Margaret Hallstrom, a snooty pain in the butt from their high school days who'd had contempt for everyone and everything.

Anna looked at her. "How could you not like him? He's a great guy. Very easy going. Easy to talk to."

"Must have been his evil twin in my shop last evening, then," said Cassie ruefully.

"Whoa!" said Anna. "You want to talk about it?"

Reluctantly Cassie told Anna about her run in with Carla and with Tate, and the conversation with Nora.

Anna listened without interruption. When Cassie was finished, she said, "Well. That explains the whole self-doubt thing you were giving me earlier."

Cassie sighed. "It just seems like a bad time to apply to the Masters."

Before she even finished the sentence Anna was shaking her head. "Nope. Still not getting out of it. I agree with Nora. Now's the time."

Cassie pushed the application around a bit. Then looked up at Anna. "You really *are* applying, too?" she asked.

"Yes, heaven help me. I'll never hear the end of it if I don't."

Cassie smiled wickedly. "Or no sex for a month?"

"Hey! Don't give him any ideas," said Anna.

She got up to leave. Cassie rose with her.

"Cass, seriously," said Anna. "Nora's right. Carla's a bitch. You can ignore her. Rachel will never sell you out. In fact, she's probably all hot air. Carla probably won't even contact Rachel."

"Oh, yes, she will," said Cassie. "She already did. Rachel called this morning."

"Get out!" said Anna. "What did she say?"

"She said Carla offered her a *lot* of money," said Cassie, "though she didn't say how much. And Carla wants not only my shop, but Delia's *and* Connie's."

"The greedy turd!"

"I agree. Rachel told Carla no, she was happy with her tenants and liked the eclectic mix. But the saddest part is that she said, 'Jim would be furious if I threw you out.'"

"Oh, Cassie. That *is* sad." She shook her head. "She just can't come to terms with it, can she?"

"No, she can't. Three years, and she's still convinced her brother will walk back in."

Anna tsked. Then she opened her arms and gave Cassie a hug.

"Well, if he does come back some day," said Anna, "he's got a smack coming from me for worrying everyone for so long."

"I agree," said Cassie. "And I wish he would. But he's not."

She straightened up and said briskly, "You'd better get to work. You don't have that other job yet."

"Well, he'd be a fool not to hire me," said Anna.

"I agree with that, too," said Cassie. She hesitated. "Anna. Before I threw him out, he did say he pays good wages and treats his people right. I hope that's not just hot air."

Anna nodded. "He is offering really good wages for the right experience, and that's something I certainly have."

That was true, thought Cassie. Anna had been working bars since before she was legal. She could mix anything and handle anyone, small stature notwithstanding. That spiky hair wasn't all for show.

"Well," said Cassie, "the food better be good or I'm going to force you to go back to Captain Jack's. I want to be able to eat well if I'm going to be selling beaded bracelets on the sidewalk next year."

"Never happen," said Anna. "Remember, you're going to be so famous, they're going to name the Masters after you." She paused and struck a thoughtful pose. "Or maybe me." Cassie laughed. "Just let me visit Alcatraz before I head out."

When Anna came back, Cassie walked her friend to the door. "Let me know what you hear about the job," she said.

"I will," said Anna.

"And Anna," said Cassie. "I do wish you luck with it. Tate

and I may not see eye to eye, but if he pays you well and treats you well, that will make up for a lot."

"Thanks, *amiga*." Anna gave her another hug. "Late night tonight?"

"Yeah," said Cassie. "Casting night. I want to get a couple more pieces made if you're dragging me into the Masters. Tomorrow I'll have to call Sean Cleaver, see if I can get on his schedule."

"Whoa! You're going to have Sean Cleaver shoot your work?" asked Anna. "You really are going to go broke."

Cassie laughed. "I've already talked to him about doing a portfolio for me. We're trading. I'm making wedding rings for him and his lady. But I don't have a date for shooting. I'll have to hurry if I'm going to apply with you. Sean's in high demand for Masters shots."

"See?" said Anna. "I knew you were a shrewd business woman. You were already planning this." Cassie raised an eyebrow at her, and Anna laughed. "I'll call you tomorrow." She headed out the door and waved one last time as she went past the front window.

Cassie's smile faded as Anna disappeared from view. "What have I gotten myself into?" she asked the empty shop.

CHAPTER 8

CASSIE HAD A HARD TIME SLEEPING that night. Now that Anna had cornered her into applying to the Masters, she kept waking up to panic, thinking about all the things that could go wrong. She was more and more certain, as the night wore on, that trying to enter with her current work would be doomed to failure. She had done what she had promised Anna—she'd called Sean Cleaver and gotten on his calendar. The shoot was just over four weeks away. In such a short time, how could she come up with an incredible new look that would leave Art Jackson envious? She would not only have to develop the concept and make three pieces good enough to photograph. She'd still have to keep up with the work in the shop, too. Perhaps it was a good thing that she didn't have many custom commissions right now.

Maybe I don't have much custom because the work isn't good enough, said the little voice that kept her awake. Art Jackson never seemed to have trouble finding custom work, even though he, too, was complaining about business being slow.

But then, she thought, Art complained about almost everything.

Nora was having an unusually restless night, too. Every time Cassie woke up to think and worry, she heard the quiet "knock, knock" of Nora at her loom. It had been a regular night-time sound for Cassie's entire life. But it seemed that Nora worked her loom late more often now, ever since the accident.

Nora was usually in some pain—sometimes worse than others—but she rarely spoke about it. Sitting or lying down and being still, she said, made it worse, so sleep came with difficulty. Often, she would get up and work at her loom until she was so tired she could sleep for a while. Nora had certainly done her share of drugs in the '60s, but now she was wary of all prescription medication, even most over-the-counter pain relievers. When she took her prescribed medication, Cassie knew she was really hurting. However, Nora said, usually the movement and sound of the loom eased the pain and lulled her to sleep. Cassie was sure that there were many nights that Nora essentially slept at the loom or was so deep into meditation that she might as well have slept. Tonight it seemed, was one of those nights.

Cassie finally gave up trying to go back to sleep at 5 a.m. She tugged on sweat pants and warm socks and, old wood floors creaking, she went down the hall and slipped into the kitchen to start coffee. It was the one time of day she made an exception to her iced tea regimen.

Cassie pulled her favorite chair closer to the tiny bay window in the front of the house and laid her sketchpad on the table at her elbow. She pulled one of Nora's woven shawls over her shoulders and put her feet up onto the window seat.

She slipped her hand into the slot on the side of the steaming mug. Her mother had shaped the hand warmer pocket in the shape of a dragon wing. Cassie sipped her coffee and looked out into the tiny garden at the front of the house. A light fog softened the light from the streetlamps and porch lights across the way, but she could still clearly see the benches and arbors her mother and Nora had built over the years. The other art in the garden had been contributed by the transient artists who had lived with them—it was often their only form of "rent." Odd as they had been, they'd been Cassie's family and she had loved them—most of them. Some had been too weird for words, but those usually didn't last long.

She looked down at the well-loved mug in her hand. Nestled in the dragon's coils on the side nearest her was a hummingbird. The winged reptile gazed benevolently at her from the opposite rim of the mug. Cassie stroked its head with her thumb, remembering why and when her mom had made it.

Not four days after starting middle school, Cassie had crashed through the front door, slammed her backpack onto the floor, stormed through the kitchen, and hurled herself out the back door, shouting "I'm not going back! The girls are mean, and the boys are ugly and stupid!" Then she was across the small yard to her "tree house."

In a tiny house usually filled with adults, there was little space for a young girl to be alone with her daydreams. Cassie, with help from Nora and Beth, had hung old blankets from the branches of the wispy Palo Verde tree in the corner of the yard and furnished the space inside them with tie-dyed pillows and Indian-print bedspreads culled from yard sales and swap meets.

That's where Beth found her that day.

She poked her head in between two blankets. "Can I come in?" she asked.

Cassie, face buried in a pillow, shrugged one shoulder.

Beth crawled in, arranged a few pillows, then settled back, arms around her legs, next to her daughter.

"So," she said finally. "No boyfriend potential there."

Cassie made retching sounds into her pillow. She didn't see her mother smile. "Ah, well. Guess you'll have to wait until high school. They'll definitely get better looking." She paused. "I can't guarantee they'll get smarter."

Cassie rewarded her by snorting and raising her tear-wet face from the pillow.

"Mean girls, unfortunately, will still be there in high school," Beth told her, "and even afterwards. They're the pits. So. What did this group say?"

"Stuff."

"What kind of stuff?"

A shoulder shrug.

Beth tried another tack. "Didn't you see any of your friends from fifth grade?"

Cassie began to rage.

It had been Paulette, a former friend from elementary school. Anxious to ingratiate herself with the older girls, she'd told them everything about Cassie, from her love of dragons, to her fatherless state, to the artists who lived with them, to the fact that she still shared a room with her mother, "like a baby."

"Ah. Paulette," Beth said simply. She'd been one of several girls Cassie had invited to a backyard sleepover the previous summer to celebrate their elementary school graduation. They'd put up blanket tents, and Beth thought they'd been having a good time. But not long after ten, Paulette had demanded to go home, and her mom had picked her up. Later, Paulette's mom had called Beth ranting. Why had the girls slept outside? Who were the strange men in the house? She'd never have let Paulette spend the night if she'd known that neither Beth nor Nora were married. And so on.

Beth had not thought it would create a backlash like this.

"I'm not going back," Cassie told her mom again.

"Hmm," her mother replied. "I certainly understand why you're angry. I'm afraid school's not optional, though."

"But you didn't finish school," Cassie protested. "Neither did Nora. And neither did Jim! Why should I have to go to school?"

"You're right. I didn't finish *high* school," Beth agreed, looking into Cassie's obstinate face. "That was a mistake I'm not going to let you make."

"But *Mom*..." Cassie started to whine.

Beth laid a gentle finger over her daughter's lips and took a deep breath.

"Cassiopeia. There will always be mean girls trying to make you feel small if you're different. Especially if you're a young woman with limited education."

"Nobody is ever mean to you and Nora," Cassie said.

Beth looked into Cassie's eyes, and Cassie still remembered the pain in her mother's face. It had been her first inkling that the grown-up world was not as perfect as she thought it would be.

"Yes, they are," Beth finally said. "It's not a nice feeling.

"No high school diploma means less money, too, when you go to work later," Beth added.

"I could go to work for Jim," Cassie said excitedly. "He won't care if I don't go to school. I already help him at the Pepper Tree."

"No, you can't," Beth told her firmly. "Because I won't let you. And Jim would very much care. He wouldn't let you work for him either."

"I'll run away."

"Yes, you could do that," Beth agreed calmly. "You're very smart and resourceful. I'm sure you could hide from the police and their dogs and helicopters. Because I would send them after you, you know." She tapped Cassie's nose. "I'm certain Jim and his motorcycle club would search for you, too." Beth wiped the tears off Cassie's face with a hand that always seemed to smell of earth and clay. "But you could never, ever hide from me," she said, kissing Cassie's forehead. "You can't hide from mother radar. It's infallible. I would find you." She smiled. "And I'd still make you go to school."

She pulled Cassie more tightly to her. "What we need, though," she said, looking up through the lacey Palo Verde branches, "is a mean girl counter offensive."

"Poison," Cassie suggested.

"A good potential back-up plan," Beth laughed. "But let's start with something less lethal."

The counter offensive had ended up, surprisingly, being led by Jim. He'd been furious about Cassie's treatment at school.

"It's not right," he said that evening. "I won't have her come home crying like that again."

He'd personally evicted their artist friends despite Beth's and Nora's concerns about paying the mortgage.

"I'll take care of it," he said.

And he had. He'd found a small shop where he could sell his jewelry year round rather than just at craft fairs and the Pepper Tree show. That weekend, he and a friend had shifted their tiny Formica-topped table into the just-as-tiny kitchen, and converted the 8' x 8' dining alcove between the kitchen and living room into a bedroom for Cassie. He had begun teaching his future apprentice to make jewelry as a bribe to keep her in school.

Beth had made Cassie the dragon hummingbird mug. "Remember," she told her daughter. "Mothers are like dragons. Fierce and gentle. I will always protect you. But even young dragons have to go to school."

Two weeks later, the mean girls were forgotten. Anna

Rodriguez, eighty pounds of fight, and a dragon lover to boot, had walked into her third period art class. Cassie had never needed another friend.

Cassie smiled sadly, missing Beth with an aching heart.

On the front porch and in the arbor, a gentle breeze rang the wind chimes Jim had made from silver-plated flatware in his spoon-jewelry period.

Cassie smiled again, drank some coffee and bent over her drawing pad.

As the morning light became stronger, she sketched and scratched out, sketched and scratched out. Finally, she tossed the pad onto the table in disgust. Realizing the loom had stopped, Cassie went out to the kitchen.

Nora glanced up when Cassie stalked in. "You got up on the wrong side of the bed," she said.

"There wasn't a right side this morning," said Cassie, dumping cold coffee down the sink and opening the fridge to get an iced tea.

"Eggs?"

"Yes, please," said Cassie, twisting open the lid of the tea. "Nora, I've been in there for hours and can't come up with anything that isn't a copy of something or a retread of something I've done before. How will I ever get into the Masters?"

"Would you chop some chives for me?" asked Nora, as she cracked the eggs into a bowl. "And cut some bread for toast, please?"

"Of course," said Cassie, putting the tea down. Nora so rarely asked her to help in the kitchen, Cassie quickly moved to do as requested.

"I've always found that when you run out of ideas, that's usually when you get the best ones," said Nora, beating feta into the eggs. "Keep pushing. Think so far out of the box it's not on anyone's radar. Even yours."

"Like what?" asked Cassie, dropping bread into the toaster. "Give me a hint."

Nora smiled. "I don't know. See if you can get anyone to sell you moon rocks, maybe."

"That would only be a gimmick," laughed Cassie, "even if I could find them." She felt something ghost across the back of her mind. She frowned. It was gone before she could grab it. She shrugged, clipped chives from the box on the window sill, pulled a knife out, and started chopping.

"Then you'll have to look inside yourself," said Nora. "Find out who you are as an artist. What moves you? What do you love?"

Cassie sighed. "I loved Mom," she said quietly. She set down the knife and picked up her mug, running her hands over the surface. "I love the memory of her hands working the clay." She smiled slightly. "I could never get the hang of that."

Nora nodded. Cassie set the mug back down to finish the chives. "And I loved Jim," she said. "I was just thinking about him."

"Hmm," Nora nodded. "I heard the chimes, too. He'll always be with us."

They worked silently beside each other for a while. Nora mixed the chives into the eggs and poured them into the hot skillet. Cassie finished the toast and got out the jam that Nora made every year. They would not have eaten nearly as well as they had when she was growing up if it hadn't been for Beth and Nora and their "earth mother" ways. Nora had once wanted chickens, too, for their own eggs. The Eden Beach town council had been dead set against it. Nora had lost that battle.

"You were up most of the night," said Cassie finally. "You were hurting?"

Nora made a face and waved her hand, brushing away the

question. "Your questions and concerns about your work got me thinking," she said. "Maybe you're not the only one who's fallen into a safe rut. Doing the same patterns, using the same colors, the same fibers. So I was thinking a lot." She smiled. "I always think best when the loom is moving. You know that."

"I do," said Cassie. "Oddly, I usually sleep best when your loom is moving." She patted Nora's hand. "I've been so lucky," she said.

Nora laid her hand over Cassie's. "Me, too," she said. "Now we'd better eat these before they get cold."

By the time they'd eaten, and Cassie had cleaned up the kitchen, it was not quite 8 a.m. She was too restless to sit and draw, and nothing was coming of it anyway. She glanced out the window. The fog had gotten thicker as the light had gotten stronger. The first sign that fall was coming.

She took a quick shower, dressed in leggings, tank and cropped T-shirt, added socks and her walking boots, threw her sandals into her backpack, and headed to the kitchen to toss a lunch together.

"You're off early," said Nora, as Cassie packed a peanut butter sandwich, chips, and a pickle into her pack.

"I need to think," said Cassie.

Nora nodded. "See you later, then," she said and bent again to the woven swatches she was examining in the light from the kitchen window.

Cassie stopped and planted a quick kiss on Nora's cheek. It was not something she did often. "Good luck with your thinking, too," she said.

"Thanks," said Nora.

Cassie grabbed her heavy sweatshirt from the hook next to the front door and pulled it on as she headed out. She had it zipped, the hood up, and the pack shouldered before she emerged from the arbor at the sidewalk. She turned and headed down to the beach.

There were few other walkers in the park. The water was so still, there weren't even any surfers out. As Cassie hit the boardwalk and turned north toward the bluff, a pod of dolphins broke the ocean's glassy surface a little way out in the bay. Gulls flickered in and out of the fog like apparitions, their cries the only indication they were real. Over the scent of the sea, Cassie smelled bacon, probably drifting down from the Hotel Eden Beach.

Her face was damp with fog, and the chilly breeze curled her hair around her face, as she set what she thought of as her thinking pace. The hollow sound of the boardwalk beat like a metronome under her feet. She let the sound gradually empty her mind of doubt.

Cassie climbed the stairs to Bayview Park at the top of the bluff, her boots crunching on the gritty surface. The ocean shattered itself at the base of the cliff, water glittered on black rocks, and white rivulets slipped back into the bottle-green sea to merge with lacy foam.

She walked through the park, past the art museum to where Cliff Street joined the highway. Crossing the highway, she went up into the quiet neighborhoods that overlooked the park, circled back past the galleries on the highway, turned up Canyon Boulevard and passed the site of the Pepper Tree show. The fog intensified the scent of the chaparral and she drew the fragrance deeply into her lungs. When the canyon started to narrow, she turned and walked back to the beach.

By the time she got downtown again, she was feeling determined, not worried. She crossed over to Main Beach Park and sat down on a bench.

The sun had begun to burn through the fog, and Cassie watched patches of blue appear and disappear. Rays of sun shot through the breaks to glint on the tattered fronds of the palms near the boardwalk. She took a deep breath of the damp, clean air and, as she watched, the fog lifted like a veil and the purplish hump of Catalina appeared to rise like magic from the sea.

Nora had asked her what she loved. Suddenly, she knew clearly what that was. It was this. Eden Beach. She loved the colors of the hillsides, the smell of dust and dried chaparral in the summer. The water on the sand and rocks. The sight and sound of the swirling gulls. She even, heaven help her, loved the tourists. Their excitement, the kids on the beach, the flashing kites, the burned bodies, and silly beach towels.

How can I put that into jewelry? she thought. If she were a painter, maybe, like Anna. Or even a sculptor. *But I'm a jeweler.*

The ghost of an idea floated across the back of her mind, again, as formless and elusive as a handful of the morning fog that had all but disappeared. The idea slipped away as Cassie reached for it.

But the hint of it wouldn't leave her.

Sculptor, she thought. *I am a sculptor. I carve wax.*

She got up, went quickly back across the highway and picked up a couple donuts at Connie's bakery before opening her shop.

Cassie got everything set up, cleaned the cases, and then, ignoring the rough castings she needed to finish, she sat down at her design desk, pulled a sketchbook out of the drawer, and started working.

CHAPTER 9

SATURDAY FOUND CASSIE UNLOCKING THE SHOP at 7 a.m. Her feverish day of drawing had produced a few exciting design ideas. She'd itched to start carving on Friday, but she'd been frustrated, in a good way. In stark contrast to recent months, the store had been busy, with repairs being dropped off and picked up, several earring sales, and a long conversation about a possible custom order. Though she'd managed to get a couple waxes roughed out, it wasn't until she'd locked up at 8 p.m. that she'd been able to really concentrate. She'd skipped dinner, and not gotten home until almost eleven that evening.

Cassie went straight to her wax bench, pulled her apron on, knotted her hair, and flicked on KEBR, the local radio station. Then she started preparing the three finished wax models for casting. She carefully attached thin wax rods and wires to the model, "sprues" that would create the passages that would let melted wax run out and molten silver to flow into the plaster mold. It was a vital and painstaking process. If not done correctly, the metal would not fill the hollow mold completely and the models she had worked so hard on would be lost.

When she was finished, the models looked like Dr. Seuss trees—the sprues, like strange trunks and limbs, made of one color of wax, and the weird top of the tree—her pendants—in another color. She carefully fixed the trunk of each tree into a separate rubber base, then snapped the bases, like Tupperware lids, onto three separate small casting flasks, sections of stainless steel tubing two inches across and three inches long.

She smiled. She always thought the flasks, at this point, looked like the frozen orange juice containers her mom opened every morning when Cassie was a kid. Instead of orange juice, these held weird wax trees.

On masking tape, she wrote the amount of silver she would need to cast the piece and put the tape around the top of the tube. Once the flasks were filled with plaster, she would not know which piece was in which tube.

Setting her timer, she carefully measured, mixed and poured the high-temperature investment slowly into each flask, watching as the white plaster flowed around the waxes, filling all the crevices and openings. Investing was a precise process. Any errors in measurement or mixing times, and the casting process could fail. Once she started, Cassie could not stop until she was finished. She always invested before the store was open so she would have no interruptions and could concentrate fully on the work.

She placed the flasks on the table of her vacuum machine, covered them with the bell, and began to vibrate and vacuum the flasks. The vacuum would pull out all the extra bubbles of air around the models. During burn out, bubbles turned to spaces that filled with molten metal when she cast, leaving extra blobs stuck onto the pieces. Bubbles could obliterate design elements and required lengthy grinding to remove.

Once she was finished, she set the flasks aside where they

could set up and harden undisturbed. In several hours, they would be fully cured and ready to burn out. She took a deep breath then blew out a gusty exhale. She stretched and rolled her shoulders. Investing, working against the clock, always tested her nerves.

It was nearly nine. She quickly set up her cases and the front window, cleaned the glass, and ran the vacuum. Then she grabbed an iced tea, sat at her metal-working bench, and began cleaning up the castings from the night before. By the time she opened at eleven, she had the sprues removed, small irregularities filed away, and was ready to start polishing.

When she unlocked the door, the custom design customer from Friday was waiting outside, and Cassie was delighted to take a down payment. By the time five o'clock rolled around, she had managed to finish polishing the castings, start on a complex repair, and sell three more pairs of earrings. *If this keeps up*, she thought, *I'm going to have the best month in a long time*. The coward in her heart briefly thought, *Maybe I won't have to enter the Masters at all*. She winced at what Anna and Nora would have to say about that.

When the last earring customer left, Cassie went up into her back room. The plaster in the flasks was hard and ready for the oven. She peeled the tape off and, using a knife, she scratched the weight of the silver she needed for each piece into the plaster of each flask. She pulled the rubber bottoms off the flasks, exposing the tips of the sprues. She scraped them flat, then loaded the flasks, sprues downward, into the kiln. She set the oven so that the temperature would ramp up in certain increments, to a peak, then come back down to 1000°, the temperature at which she would cast. It would take about five hours. She flipped on the ventilation fans and went back to the front of the shop.

Cassie tried to start her burnout as close to closing as she could. The smell of burning wax was strong in the small shop.

Cassie didn't mind it. Knowing what came out of the kiln, she always thought the smell exciting. But in the early days, a few customers had remarked on the odor. To avoid sending customers out the door, casting meant late nights in the summer, when, Fridays and Saturdays, Cassie kept the shop open until eight.

After about an hour, the bulk of the melting was done. Cassie pulled out the drip pan and replaced it with another. It wouldn't eliminate the wax smell, but it did reduce it. She was glad none of her late afternoon customers seemed to be bothered by it.

When Cassie was finally able to lock the door at eight, she called her friend, Susie Anavil who owned the Thai House up on Ocean, and placed a to-go order. She picked it up on the way home.

"We have *Mrs. Doubtfire* and *The Fugitive* tonight," said Nora, coming into the kitchen as Cassie was dishing food into bowls. Nora didn't believe in eating out of the to-go cartons. "Humor or suspense, do you think?" Take-out and a movie was their Saturday ritual.

"I hope you don't mind if we do the movie tomorrow night," said Cassie, taking the bowls to the table. "I have some casting I want to do."

"I thought you cast last night," said Nora, looking puzzled.

"I did." Cassie poured their Thai iced teas into glasses. "This is something else. I'm trying something new."

"Oh? Part of the reinvention of Cassie Franklin?"

"Yes." Cassie smiled.

"Well, then. I guess I can wait a night. What time do you have to get back?"

Cassie glanced at the kitchen clock. It was quarter to nine. "I've got until 10:15," she said.

"Good," said Nora. "Plenty of time to enjoy dinner. You did remember the fresh spring rolls, didn't you?"

The fog was starting to drift up from the sea when Cassie left the house and headed back down to the shop. Nora didn't like her walking at night and went through periods of trying to convince Cassie to drive to the shop when she worked late. But Cassie enjoyed walking at night, when everything had closed up. Eden Beach was mostly a sleepy beach town after dark. She'd had a couple of verbal encounters with a homeless guy or two, but nothing frightening. The night duty police patrol, too, knowing her habits, kept an eye out for her.

Cassie let herself into the shop, locked the door behind her, and flicked off the alarm. The night light in the back was enough to guide her.

Her back room, where she kept the dirty work of jewelry making, was divided into two, oddly shaped spaces. On the left, behind the design desk, was her centrifugal casting machine, the kiln, and all her tools for casting. On the right, behind her benches, was the polishing motor, the sink with the steamer, and her ultrasonic. Glass walls separated the workshop from the front so that Cassie could keep an eye on the showroom floor. The ventilation fans, sonic, and steamer were all too noisy for her to hear the door chime if someone came in while she was working in the back. She needed a clear line of sight.

Just as she was about to turn on the lights in the back, Cassie glanced through the glass partition, through the shop, and out the front window. Tate Garner was passing, heading toward his restaurant. *Guess I'm not the only one working late,* she thought. A spark of grudging admiration flared. He apparently had the same dedication to his business that she had to hers to be working this late when he wasn't even open. She quickly extinguished the spark. She wasn't sure she was ready to forgive his remarks, no matter what Nora said.

She also wondered what that urge to hold a grudge said about her.

Maybe Nora's right, she thought. *I need to grow up.*

With that uncomfortable thought, Cassie flipped the light switch and checked the kiln temperature. It was perfect. She opened the safe, got out her silver casting grain, and measured out the amounts she needed for each small flask. Her stomach was tense with excitement. If these design elements came out the way she hoped, they could form the basis of a new line. She would make molds of them so she wouldn't have to carve them fresh each time.

She laid out her tools—tongs, borax shaker, quartz stirring rod—and put on her leather apron. She'd balanced the casting machine wrong once, when she was learning, and tossed molten silver all over. She'd never done it again, but she always wore the leather apron Jim had insisted on since that day.

Cassie set the crucible in the casting machine, adjusted the balancing weight, rotated the casting arm to tighten the powerful spring, and pulled the pin out to hold the arm in place. Then she poured the shiny pellets of sterling silver into the open mouth of the crucible. She turned on the gas and oxygen tanks and flicked her sparker in front of the torch. The flame snapped on, big, hot and blue. Cassie reduced the oxygen so the metal would not blacken unnecessarily.

When the flame was bushy and yellow, she began heating the crucible, circling the clay vessel with the flame to get everything evenly hot. The silver inside would come up to temperature gradually, but it was important that the crucible be just as hot so the metal would not start to cool before it entered the flask. It was hard to believe that, at such intense temperatures, even a few hundred degrees could make a difference in whether a casting was successful or not.

She put the torch to the metal and watched with the same

fascination she always felt. Like investing, the process took all her attention. The metal had to get to just the right temperature. Too cool, and the silver wouldn't flow and fill the hollow in the flask properly. Too hot, and she might burn off the alloys, resulting in a pitted casting. There was no thermometer. The right temperature was determined by watching the metal changes closely.

Gradually, the sterling began to sweat, the grains softening at the edges. Keeping the torch on the metal, moving it constantly, she was just reaching for the kiln latch with her free hand when she heard someone knocking on the window next to the shop's front door.

Shit, she thought, *I'm closed*. Even if she weren't, she couldn't stop now. The metal would be ready to cast in a heartbeat.

She glanced at the window and her heart gave a lurch. It was Tate with a box in his hand. He waved and pointed at the door, indicating he wanted to come in. She frowned, shook her head, and nodded toward the torch.

Quickly she re-focused her attention on her work. She pulled open the kiln door. A wave of scorching heat rolled out. With her tongs, Cassie reached in and pulled out the steel flask, placed it gently into the cradle, and, still using the tongs, pushed the crucible against the flask. Keeping one eye on the silver in the crucible, with her free hand, she shut the kiln door.

The metal began to puddle, a bright, silver mirror. With the quartz rod, Cassie poked the molten silver, making sure there were no solid spots. Feeling like an alchemist, she picked up her container of borax and dashed a small amount into the silver. The surface swirled, dark and bright.

With her free hand, she pulled the weighted end of the casting arm back slightly, and the release pin dropped. Cassie let go of the arm and pulled the torch away from the crucible in one smooth movement. The balance weights in the caster whipped around, driven by the powerful spring, throwing the crucible and flask into a high-speed spin. The same force that holds water in a bucket when it's spun around, hurled the molten silver into the hollow left in the plaster when the wax melted out.

Cassie had done this same, simple process hundreds of times, just as centuries of jewelers before her had done. It always thrilled her.

She glanced back at the window. Tate was gone. Cassie shrugged. She'd stop by and apologize another time.

When the casting machine had slowed almost completely, she stopped it, pulled the flask out, and set it on a firebrick. She set the machine up again, added the silver for the next flask, and began the process over.

When she was done casting, Cassie turned off the torch. She put on a dust mask and flipped on the ventilation fans. With tongs, she picked up the first flask, still blisteringly hot, and plunged it into a galvanized bucket of water. Steam shot out of the bucket as the water boiled instantly from both ends of the stainless steel flask. The thermal shock and boiling action broke the investment plaster. The silver casting fell to the bottom of the bucket. Cassie reached in pulled it out, put it into a bowl of water in the sink, then quenched the remaining two flasks.

Cassie scrubbed the castings free of investment and dumped the plaster-laden water into the bucket. She'd let it settle, filter the water off the top, then bag the slurry and put it into the trash. She had enough plumbing problems without sending pounds of plaster down the sink or toilet.

Normally, she would go home now, but she had to see if her new idea would work. She put on her magnifier and looked the castings over. The quality was good. There was no pitting, and the details were all there. She reached automatically for her jeweler's saw and, although it was almost midnight, she began to clean them up.

It was two in the morning when Cassie finally quit working. The pieces were good, she thought, and she might be able to use them, or pieces of them in her work. But they weren't going to take her into the Masters. They were too trite.

Suddenly, she was exhausted.

She sat there for a long time, staring at Anna's painting on the long brick wall next to the front door. Although there was nothing "real" in the painting, Cassie could clearly see the cliffs rising out of the fog, the trees indistinct at the bluff top. She could almost hear the gulls. If she could only do in jewelry what Anna did with paint.

It was late. Or early. Cassie sighed and got up to go. She made sure all the gas was off, the pressure was released from the steamer, the safe was locked, and everything was ready to leave. Tomorrow was Sunday. She'd earned a day of rest.

She shut off all the lights, set the alarm, locked the door, and double checked it as she always did. The theater was dark, the last show having finished hours before. The streets were deserted except for one lone car heading south on Coast Highway, its lights hazy in the fog.

Cassie pulled her jacket up around her neck, glad she'd brought it with her. The wind off the ocean had the chill of fall in it.

She was just turning the corner into her street when she remembered Tate. She wondered what he had wanted.

CHAPTER 10

CASSIE WOKE TO THE SOUND OF NORA'S loom. Sunlight was shooting prisms onto her wall through the old chandelier crystal hanging at her window. She rolled over groggily to look at the clock. It was almost nine. She never slept this late.

She scrubbed her face with her hands and wondered if she had to get up at all. Maybe she should never get up again. Groaning, Cassie threw her arm over her eyes as if she could block out the memory of the previous night's disaster.

The loom stopped. Nora's crutches tapped down the hall.

"I heard the groaning so I knew you were alive," said Nora, poking her head in the door.

"Do me a favor," said Cassie without removing her arm from her eyes. "Shoot me."

"Don't tell me you're hung over," said Nora, and Cassie could tell she was smiling.

Cassie dropped her arm away from her eyes and looked at Nora. "I thought I had this great idea. How to capture how I feel about Eden Beach in elements I could mix and match in my jewelry. But it was so kitschy I can hardly bear to think about it." While she'd been only unsatisfied with the castings when she'd left the shop the night before, by the time she'd gotten home, she'd felt embarrassed by how average they'd really been.

She shoved her hands up into her hair. "How could I have let you and Anna talk me into this? How could I ever think I'd be good enough for the Masters?"

Nora was silent.

Cassie dropped her hands and shoved herself upright in bed, scooting back to lean against the wall. "If you've got any words of wisdom," she said bitterly, "now's the time."

Nora gave her a small smile. "No words of wisdom. Just some encouragement from someone who has been there."

Cassie waited. Finally, she said, "Well? I can certainly use encouragement. I'm thinking of having Anna teach me how to tend bar."

Nora moved into the room and sat on the edge of Cassie's bed. After Beth had died, Cassie had taken to sleeping in her mom's room to comfort herself. When it was clear the move was going to be permanent, Jim had removed the folding doors between the kitchen and the alcove Cassie had been using as a bedroom, and converted it back into a dining area.

A breeze through the open window moved the crystal sending a rainbow of colors across Cassie's face.

"Ah! A good omen." Nora smiled more broadly.

"What?" Cassie batted at the rainbow as if she could wave it away.

"Pot of gold at the end of the rainbow." Nora pointed at Cassie's face.

Cassie raised an eyebrow and made a face at her.

"I guess you can look at it as the first failure over with," said Nora. "You have to work out the bad, unoriginal ideas first. Get them out of the way so that the fresh ones have room to bubble up. So. If you look at it that way, your first failure was good. One down."

"First failure. Good," said Cassie. "You mean I have more to look forward to?"

Nora shrugged. "Highly likely. Sorry. Creativity is not painless. Or instant."

Cassie shut her eyes and dropped her head back against the wall with a thump. "Like I said. Shoot me."

"How about I feed you instead?" Nora struggled to her feet. "I'm starved. I woke up thinking we hadn't been to Clancy's up on the Island for months. I think now would be a good time."

Cassie lifted her head. "Right. I'm soon going to be out of work, we'll be starving and living on the beach, and you want to go out to brunch?"

Nora shook her head. "Such a drama queen. If you feel that way, don't eat. But get up and drive. I can't get there on my own. There's a Seafood Florentine calling my name." She headed out and down the hall. "I'll be ready in half an hour," she called back to Cassie.

Cassie groaned again, then threw back the covers, got up, and staggered into the bathroom.

An hour later, she had the top down on their ancient VW Rabbit, and they were heading up the Coast Highway. With the sun, the ocean air whipping the hair out of her braid, and Nora teasing her, Cassie felt her spirits lift.

"Now if Jim were here," she shouted over the buffeting wind, "we could be on the motorcycle."

"You'd have to strap me on like luggage," Nora shouted back.

"I could do that," said Cassie. "Or talk Jim into putting the sidecar on."

Nora laughed. "I'd rather be strapped over the fender like a dead moose!"

Cassie drove into the marina, dropped Nora at the front door to Clancy's, then found a place to park. A gentle swell had found its way into the sheltered marina and the forest of masts rocked hypnotically. The otherwise placid water reflected the hulls of the boats moored there, many with sails furled. As Cassie walked back to the restaurant, she watched a moderately sized catamaran work its way out toward the bay.

"We'll probably have to wait hours," said Cassie as she joined Nora on the bench outside the front door. There were probably another twenty people waiting.

"Only about forty-five minutes," said Nora. "But with this weather, who's complaining?"

The sun was pleasantly warm. A cool breeze carried the scent of broiling fish and fresh bread from the restaurant to them along with just a whiff of diesel from one of the boats. Occasionally the water slapped the boats with a hollow sound. Happy, hungry voices rose and fell around them. It seemed no time at all until they were seated inside, pulling apart and buttering warm bread.

After they'd ordered, Nora said, "So tell me about this grand idea that failed."

Cassie sighed. Then she told Nora how she'd thought about what she'd said, about finding what she loved. How she'd wanted to do something that would evoke the shapes and colors of Eden Beach, but how she could only come up with the same overdone ideas in all the tourist shops. "You know, things that looked like whales and dolphins and waves."

"Couldn't you push it further?" asked Nora.

Cassie shook her head. "It's too trite. I can't get out of that box. I don't know where to go next."

"Well, at least you found one wall of the box. There has to be a door there somewhere," said Nora.

"I hope so," said Cassie.

Their lunch came, and they left Cassie's dilemma alone while they ate, concentrating on the quality of the food. They even split a chocolate cheesecake.

"That really was a last meal," said Cassie as they left the marina. "I don't think I've eaten so much in weeks."

"Well, I expect you'll be working late nights for a long while, trying to find your way out of that box. Plenty of time to work it off."

They drove quietly for a while.

"Nora," asked Cassie finally. "Do you really think I can find the way out?"

"As long as you keep looking, I do," she said. "Cassie, you're feeling discouraged because you've had the courage to try to break out, do something different. You've scared your creative instincts all to death. You fell back on what seems trite, but you made the first attempt. That takes courage. If you keep trying, sooner, I hope, rather than later, you'll find the key. You'll break through that wall. And it will be amazing."

"Really," said Cassie.

"Really," said Nora.

"I'll take that as a Delphic prophesy." Nora simply smiled.

They drove the rest of the way into Eden Beach in companionable silence. When Cassie stopped at the light at Canyon and Coast Highway, she turned to Nora. "Are you up for going to the store?"

"After that paltry selection you brought home the last time you went on your own? Absolutely," said Nora. "Otherwise I'll starve. Or be reduced to drinking that horrible tea."

Cassie grinned and drove past their turn off and down to Ralph's. The lot was as crowded as usual on Sunday. Again, she dropped Nora by the door and parked. The day had turned summer-time warm, so Cassie peeled off her light jacket and tossed it into the back seat. The sun felt delicious on her bare arms.

By the time Cassie caught up with her, Nora had a cart, her crutches laid over the top, and was just inside the door. Cassie grabbed a basket. They worked as a team, Nora shopping the outside aisles for the healthy food, Cassie working the inside aisles for crackers, canned soups, toilet paper, her tea. Then she'd hit the dairy case and the lunch-meat counter. As her basket filled, she'd find Nora and transfer the heavier items into the cart, then she'd be off again. By the time she'd gotten everything, the cart would be a bit heavy for Nora to push. Cassie would take over, Nora would take back her canes, and they'd finish up, usually arguing over what ice cream to get: Rocky Road or Rocky Road.

They were on their final round, and Cassie was in charge of the cart, when Nora decided to add chips to their selection. "Chips?" asked Cassie. "Salt? Fat? Calories? Are you feeling all right?"

Nora gave her a look. "I'll meet you at the front," she said and tapped off.

Cassie smiled and turned down the wine aisle. The labels always amazed her. So many designs for, really, a handful of wines—cabernets, Rieslings, merlots, chardonnays, pinots—from different wineries. They all advertised essentially the same thing, but the label made the difference between someone picking up something new, or leaving it on the shelf. She wondered how many label designs had failed before the winery found the right one. And how many wineries had failed before they found the right label.

Is jewelry any different? she wondered. It's all pendants and earrings, rings and bracelets by different designers. You just have to find the label—the style—that works. Maybe Nora was right. Her trite efforts to find her way out of her creative box had to be seen as just one step in the right direction, the first bad label.

She started to turn toward the cart when a voice at her shoulder said, "That's pretty intense scrutiny for someone who doesn't drink."

Startled, Cassie turned to see Tate standing at her elbow, wearing a small smile.

"What?" she said.

"Didn't you tell me you didn't drink when I came in the other day?"

"I don't," she said, irritably. "I didn't realize that meant I couldn't look at the wine labels."

She saw his smile fade and realized he'd been joking.

"What did I say this time?" he asked.

What, indeed, she thought.

It wasn't his fault she was in this mess, taking on the biggest challenge of her career, but Cassie knew she was taking it out on him. His words, that afternoon in her shop, had pushed her shortcomings into her face. That irritated her. She was jealous, too. He'd hired Anna. No more lunches at her shop. Though she'd enjoyed their burgers from Jack's for years, she didn't want to be beholden for any lunch goodies Anna might bring from Tate's restaurant.

None of this made any sense, and she knew it. It was childish, foolish, and put her out of sorts.

"Nothing," she said finally. "Sorry. Just cranky this morning." *I wasn't cranky until just now*, she thought. "I have to go." She turned away.

"Wait. Cassie," he said, taking her arm and pulling her gently back toward him.

His touch was warm where his hand rested, just above her elbow, but that didn't explain the flush of heat that washed through her, traveling to places that hadn't felt warm for a while.

Places she didn't want to feel warm. Not from Tate's touch.

She did not want to go down this path. Letting desire take control never went well. *Look at Phil*, she thought. *Look where that got me. Talk about desire making me blind.* Right now she needed all her attention on her work. She had to focus on saving her shop. On being able to take care of Nora.

She had no time or desire for Tate.

No time anyway.

With his gentle touch sending waves of heat through her, she felt transparent. Surely he could read her mind. She felt herself blushing.

This was ridiculous. She didn't blush.

"Look," she heard him saying, as she tried to get a grip on her emotions. "I know I put my foot in it the other day, and I'm sorry. I want to set things straight between us." His face softened toward a smile. "We are, after all, almost neighbors."

Hey, Baby, let's be friendly. We're neighbors, Cassie thought, and tensed. Yet another pick up line.

Irritation overpowered...whatever it was she was feeling. Whatever she was determined *not* to feel.

Her annoyance must have shown on her face. She saw Tate's smile fade again.

"Cassie," he said. "I'm trying to apologize. I don't really think there's any reason to stay angry."

"I'm not angry," she said, though she was. Angry at him. Angry at herself. "Just busy. Bad couple days."

"Is that why you wouldn't open the door last night?"

"I was working."

"You couldn't stop for a minute?"

"Not when I'm casting. I do it late at night so I won't be interrupted." It came out more pointed than she'd intended.

She took a breath and reached for civility. "Sorry. Not your fault. It didn't go well."

His hand was so warm on her skin. She could smell the soap or shampoo he'd used that morning. Her body wanted to move closer to him. Her head just wanted him to leave before she did or said something stupid.

He smiled again, and nodded. The smile was a bit crooked. It went very well with his green…gray?…eyes. Her heart picked up a beat.

Stop it, stop it, stop it, she told herself sternly.

"I'm like that, too," he said. "When I'm working on a new recipe. Especially now with the restaurant opening so soon. When it doesn't go well, Domingo tells me I get crabby."

He hesitated. "Please don't take this the wrong way, but I was a little worried when I saw you walk by the restaurant. I came over to be sure nothing was wrong. When I saw you working, I went back to get some of the new dessert I'd made. One that did go right." He smiled. "I was bringing some as a peace offering."

"Thanks for the thought," she said, though she knew she sounded anything but grateful. She was desperately trying to find balance here, but as her next words came out, she realized she hadn't found it. "But I really couldn't stop. And I work late all the time. I'm fine." She gave up. She'd done the best she could do with her heart racketing in her chest. "Now, if you'll let me go, someone is waiting for me."

Tate looked down. He seemed surprised to find his hand on her arm and he immediately released her.

The loss of his touch somehow left her feeling abandoned.

"Maybe you'll reconsider my invitation to the open house," said Tate, "and you can try the dessert there."

"Thanks," she said, and tried to mean it. "But I'll have to see."

She turned before he could say anything else and pushed the cart down the aisle. Her hands were shaking. *Stop it, stop it, stop it*, she told herself again.

She saw Nora at the end of the aisle a few feet away, looking at her strangely. Cassie's face was still hot, and she knew Nora could see it.

"Are you ready?" she asked Nora brightly. "Did you find what you wanted?"

Nora nodded and set the bag of chips in the cart. "Are you okay?"

"I'm fine," lied Cassie.

With her chin, Nora pointed up the aisle toward where Tate had been—and might still be—standing. Cassie did not look around. "Who was that?"

"Nobody," said Cassie, but she wasn't sure she believed it herself.

CHAPTER 11

CASSIE WAS BUSY SETTING STONES when the door pinged open the following Tuesday, ushering in happy sounds from the beach. She glanced up as a small, pretty blond came in, wearing shorts and a tank top. An oversized shirt hung down to well-tanned thighs. Diamonds glittered in her ears. After seeing the earrings, Cassie was surprised to see heavily tarnished bronze bangles on the young woman's wrist.

"Hi," said Cassie. "Great day to be at the beach. Again."

"Yeah, it is," said Tia. "But then, it's always a great day at the beach."

Cassie smiled. "I have to agree."

"Do you mind if I look around a bit?"

"Please do," said Cassie. "Let me know if you have questions. I just want to finish this job for a customer. She's picking it up tomorrow."

Cassie continued setting while Tia moved slowly from case to case. She spent a lot of time in front of the earring case.

Cassie glanced up at one point to see Tia shaking her head. "You look puzzled," she said.

"Oh, it's the garnet pendant here," said Tia, tapping a finger on the glass of one of the free-standing cases. "Garnets are my birthstone."

"You sound like you don't like them much," said Cassie, stopping her work and flipping up the lens of her head magnifier.

"Not really," said Tia. "This one's pretty for a garnet, but generally, I think they're kind of boring. My mom had some kind of antique garnet necklace that she loved. They were her birthstone, too. I never saw why she liked it."

"Ah," said Cassie. She smiled as she got up from the bench, tossed her head magnifier onto her chair, and rubbed her forehead. "They're my birthstone, too," she continued. "And I love them!"

"Why?" Tia looked at her incredulously.

Cassie smiled again, holding up a finger like she was about to impart some great wisdom. "I see you do not really know about garnets."

Tia smiled back at her. "I guess maybe I don't. What do you mean?"

"One moment."

Cassie went into her back room, withdrew a small, narrow box from the safe, and came back to the showroom floor.

"First of all, a lot of the beauty of gemstones comes from the cutting," said Cassie, walking out to Tia. She loved talking stones. "In fact, a lot of gemstones are pretty ugly when they're first found. But Jim, the guy who started this shop, taught me that you have to look beneath the skin. Something ugly—or boring—on the outside, might yield something beautiful on the inside."

A memory flitted at the back of Cassie's mind, something important, but it slipped away as she reached for it.

She shook her head slightly and went on. "Do you know what geodes are?" she asked Tia.

Tia nodded. "The round stones with the crystals on the inside."

"Yes," said Cassie. "You'd never know the beauty was there unless you cut it open. The same is true of most gemstones in their rough state."

She set the small box on the glass, unlocked the case, and pulled out the garnet pendant. "This garnet is beautiful, first, because its color is so rich and red. But because it's been so superbly cut, light can bring out that beautiful color." She turned the pendant so that deep flashes of blood red shot out of it. "Some of the old antique garnets were not particularly well cut, which may be why you don't like them." She shrugged. "And a lot of garnets are just plain dark.

"I see," said Tia.

Cassie smiled. "But you're still not convinced garnets are worth it."

Tia made a rueful face. "Sorry."

"Don't be," said Cassie. "You may not like the color of this garnet," she gestured at the pendant, "but did you know that garnets come in almost every color of the rainbow?"

"Seriously?" asked Tia.

"Yep, seriously," said Cassie, tucking the pendant back in the case and relocking it. "Yellow, gold, orange, pink, purple, and green. Some even change color depending on the light."

"No way!"

"Way," said Cassie, grinning. "They come in every color but blue. I like to think it means that you can't be unhappy if you're wearing garnets." She picked up the small box on the case.

"Do you have some in different colors?" asked Tia.

"I thought you'd never ask," said Cassie, unlatching the small box and holding it toward Tia. Inside, on a depression in the white velvet, sat a row of twelve cushion-cut garnets ranging from pale yellow to deep violet.

"Holy wow!" breathed Tia. "They're all garnets?" She looked at Cassie in disbelief.

"There is a garnet for every mood and for every woman whose birthstone it is," said Cassie. She smiled at the look of surprise on Tia's face, pleased as a magician showing the inside of a trick.

"So which is your favorite?" she asked Tia.

Tia pointed immediately to a golden orange stone. "That one," she said.

"Hessonite garnet," said Cassie. "An excellent choice. One of those would go beautifully with your blond hair."

Tia smiled at Cassie. "Which is *your* favorite?" she asked.

"This one," said Cassie, pointing to a brilliant, slightly bluish green stone. "Tsavorites. From only one place in the world. The Tsavo valley in Kenya. Always makes me think of exotic places and beautiful wild animals."

"What a great job you have," sighed Tia. "I'd love to be able to work with beautiful stones and silver and gold all day."

Cassie laughed and closed the box gently.

"Well, the outcome is beautiful if you do it right, but it's a lot of hard work." She held out a hand, smudged with black. "And dirty."

"It would be worth it to make such beautiful jewelry. You make everything yourself?"

"I do," said Cassie.

"How did you learn?"

"A friend taught me," she said. "I took a couple classes. Read books. Burned up a lot of metal. Broke a lot of stones."

Tia laughed. "You still do that?"

"Only very occasionally and only when I'm careless," said Cassie.

Tia seemed to hesitate, glancing back into the cases.

"Do you only work with silver?" she finally asked.

"Usually," said Cassie. "I work in gold occasionally for a special piece or commissions."

"I meant something less precious," said Tia shyly.

Cassie looked at her curiously.

"It's just that…" Tia paused.

"Yes?"

"Well," Tia put her arm out and slid the tarnished bangles off her wrist. "These are not expensive," she said apologetically. "They're not gold or anything. But they were my mom's. They haven't been worn for maybe fifteen years. I want to wear them but they're tarnished pretty badly."

Cassie nodded at the bracelets. "They look like something that came from the Pepper Tree show."

"They did!" said Tia. "My mom loved that show. We used to come down every year I can remember."

"You lost your mom?" Cassie asked carefully.

Tia nodded. "Yeah. She died when I was eight."

"I'm sorry," said Cassie. "I can't imagine how hard that must have been. I lost my mom just a few years ago and it was…"

"Beyond awful," said Tia.

"Yes. Beyond awful," Cassie agreed.

Tia gestured at the bracelets. "Do you think you can clean them up at all or are they ruined?"

"Nope, not ruined," said Cassie smiling. "I can clean them up in a few minutes. Do you have time or would you like to come back?"

"You can do it now?" Tia brightened, handing the bracelets to Cassie.

"Sure," said Cassie. Then she did something she almost never did. "Would you like to watch me?"

"Can I?" asked Tia, surprised. "I'd love that!"

Cassie unlocked the gate and the two of them climbed the

few stairs to the back room. "If I get another customer," she said, "I'll have to stop. But it shouldn't take long."

When they got into the workshop, Cassie tucked the box of garnets back into her safe, then stepped to the polishing table. She saw Tia looking with disbelief at the bedrock in the corner.

"What on earth?" she said.

Cassie made a face. "Imaginative builder. Guess he thought he'd save money on dynamite."

Tia laughed.

"Where does the door go to?" she asked.

"The bathroom, if you can believe it," said Cassie.

Tia laughed again. "I guess I have to. There isn't anywhere else it could be."

"No, it's a pretty cozy space," said Cassie.

Cassie made sure her hair was secure and out of the way, then flipped on the buffing machine. She put the stick of polishing compound against the blur of the spinning buff to charge it, then picked up a bracelet and laid it into the wheel.

"Wow," said Tia, as the bangle in Cassie's hand began to quickly shine again. "I have to get one of those!"

Cassie laughed. "Bring them back any time," she said. "I'll be happy to touch them up for you."

Cassie quickly finished polishing the bracelets. She flipped off the machine, then scrubbed the bangles with a soft brush, soap and water. After that, she hung them on wires in the ultrasonic.

"What's that do?" asked Tia, as the equipment started to buzz.

"It uses sound to vibrate the cleaning solution and removes all the debris from polishing. It's especially good at getting gunk out of all tiny details, like the cracks between the braids and twists on your bracelets."

When the dirt stopped rising from the bracelets, Cassie

plucked them out, dried them with a towel, then used compressed air to blow them completely dry. She handed them back to Tia. "Like new," she said.

Tia slipped them on her wrist and held her arm out to admire them.

"Thanks," she said. "I really appreciate it. What do I owe you?"

"Not a thing," said Cassie. "My pleasure." She meant it. The smile on Tia's face was all the payment she needed.

"Thanks, then," said Tia. She turned and moved back down the steps. Cassie unlatched the security gate and let her into the showroom.

Tia stopped and turned back. "Would you mind if I came back some time and watched you work?"

"Not at all," said Cassie. "Any time."

"Thanks. I'm Tia," she said, holding out her hand.

"Cassie." She smiled warmly. "Glad to meet you."

CHAPTER 12

"GREAT, FRED. LOOK FORWARD to seeing you there." Tate waved at the manager of the gift shop as he left.

Where next? he wondered, as he scanned the directory in the little Tropicana Shopping Plaza. One notice caught his eye: Lou Pallis Jewelry Design. Second floor.

One of the jewelers Cassie had mentioned.

The one who liked to gossip.

Tate took the stairs two at a time. At the top, on the right, a small window display with extravagant—and expensive-looking—jewelry in gold, diamonds, and gemstones told Tate he'd found the place.

Inside was a small display space. A guy in his early to mid-40s was working at a bench. Like Cassie, he wore a magnifier on his head. When Tate walked in, he flipped it up to look Tate over.

"Howdy," he said. "Looking for anything special or just looking?"

"Actually, I'm here to introduce myself. Tate Garner. I'm just about to open a restaurant over on Ocean."

"Hey," said the jeweler, standing up and coming around the bench. "I thought it looked like it was just about done. Saw the sign go up the other day." He held out his hand and Tate took it. "Lou Pallis."

Pallis was shorter than Tate—about 5'10", he guessed—but broad across the shoulders. Although he carried a slight paunch in front, and his dark hair, just touched with gray, was thinning on top, he was a good-looking man. Dark eyes, olive skin. Italian or Greek background, thought Tate. His dark green shirt was rolled up to the elbows, his jeans were old and faded. His hand in Tate's was strong, hard, and callused.

"So when are you opening?" asked Lou as they shook.

"A couple weeks from Thursday, barring hurricanes, floods, tornadoes..." said Tate.

"Look forward to giving it a try," said Lou.

"Actually, I'm here to invite you to the open house the Wednesday before. I'm asking a number of merchants and others in the area. Food samples, drinks."

"You can count on me," grinned Lou. "I never turn down free food and booze. Against my religion."

"My kind of man," said Tate, grinning back. He pulled out a couple invitations and handed them to Lou.

"Actually, another jeweler here in town recommended I talk to you," said Tate.

"Who's that?" asked Lou

"Cassie Franklin? Owns The Green Lotus on Coast Highway?" Tate thought he asked the question casually.

"Sure, I know Cassie," said Lou. "I know most of the jewelers in town. She does really nice work. I was glad she took over the shop when Jim disappeared."

"Jim?" asked Tate.

"Jim Davies. It was his shop. Cassie was like a daughter to him. He taught her the business."

"You said he disappeared?"

"Yeah, weird thing. He and a buddy went off on a motorcycle trip. Think they were heading to Texas or some place in the southwest. They drove off the map. Just vanished. No one heard from him again."

"That is strange," said Tate. "Could it have been drug related?"

Lou gave him a strange look.

"Sorry," said Tate. "Someone mentioned the previous shop owner had been a drug dealer."

Lou snorted. "Bullshit. Jim smoked some dope, but who doesn't? He was a great guy. Smart, funny, hard-working, but very mellow and relaxed. Great laugh. Very skilled jeweler."

Tate held up a hand. "Sorry. I guess I really got the wrong information." *I wonder why Carla told me he dealt drugs?* thought Tate. "I guess you knew him well."

"Sure. Everyone knew Jim. He started in the '70s, like a bunch of us down here. A few guys never got past the Indian-style jewelry phase and faded away. But Jim was always looking at old pieces, reading what there was. Said he learned more from his screw-ups than he ever did from doing something right. He never made the same mistake twice, though. Anybody making jewelry here in town today, if they're honest, will lay their influence at Jim's door. I do. I went my own way, but Jim helped me out when I started."

Lou shook his head. "Drug dealer. I don't know who told you that, but they're full of crap, and they never knew Jim. He would never have put his family at risk like that. That's what made it so weird. He loved that family. Unless he was abducted by aliens or something, nothing would have stopped him coming back to them."

"When did he disappear?"

Lou took a deep breath, leaned against his bench, crossed his arms, and thought. "Three years ago? Something like that. Cassie kept waiting, wondering, worrying. Nora, I think she was just furious that Jim would go off and leave like that." Lou grimaced. "Frankly, I think anger was her way of dealing with the fear he was dead. They were together a long time."

Lou shrugged a bit. "Anyway. His bike finally turned up in the desert some place. Completely burned up. No sign of Jim. Cassie and Nora were pretty shattered by that. Cassie shut the store for a couple months. She wasn't up to facing people. I went down to help her finish up their custom work and repairs so her customers could pick things up. For a while, I wasn't sure she would open again." Lou grinned. "I shouldn't have worried. That girl's got polishing compound in her blood. Been making jewelry since she was old enough to stand, practically."

Tate nodded. "I should have guessed that. The rings and things in her cases looked well made."

"They are," agreed Lou.

"Well, I'd better let you get back to work," said Tate.

Lou held up the invitations. "Thanks for these. I guess I'll see you then."

"I look forward to it," said Tate, and turned to head out the door.

"By the way," said Lou, and Tate turned back. "I don't want to tell you how to put together your guest list, but you might want to talk to Melody Jansen, at the clothing boutique downstairs. She carries a high-end product and caters to a lot of the professional women in and around town. She might be a good person to have on your side."

"Thanks for the tip," said Tate. "I'll stop by."

"You'll meet Nora, too," said Lou. "She's a weaver. Sells her work at Melody's." Lou grinned at him. "Don't mention that drug-dealing bullshit to her. You won't live long enough to regret it."

Tate winced. "Thanks. I don't think I'll make that mistake again."

As Tate poked around the little plaza looking for Melody's, he thought about what Lou had said. Both Lou and Carla had implied Jim was not Cassie's dad, but Lou had said the three of them had been a family. *The woman on crutches I saw with her must be her mom*, he thought. He wondered how Nora had been disabled.

He spotted a shop window filled with clothing made of unusual fabrics. *Must be the place*, he thought. He hesitated before he went in. He wasn't sure of his welcome by Nora.

Only one way to find out, he thought.

Taking a deep breath, he pushed the door open. A gentle bell rang, the sound almost eclipsed by the chattering of women gathered in a small group in the back corner. There was laughter and one of the women pulled away and came toward him.

"How can I help you?" she asked.

"I'm looking for Melody Jansen?"

"You found her."

"Tate Garner," he said, holding out his hand. "I'm opening the restaurant over on Ocean next week." As he spoke, he saw one of the women in the group look up at him. It was, as he'd expected, the woman Cassie had been with at the grocery store.

"Great to meet you!" Melody was saying. "We've all been waiting for you to open. Come over and tell us all about it." She took Tate's arm and pulled him toward the group. She introduced them all, but the only name he paid attention to was Nora Cassidy's. He briefly wondered why she and Cassie didn't share the same name, then spent the next fifteen minutes explaining what his food would be like. He ended up inviting them all to the open house.

While Nora wrote up orders for jackets and runners for the holidays, Tate made small talk with Melody. Later he couldn't remember what they had talked about. He'd been conscious throughout of Nora's sharp hazel eyes watching him behind her red-framed glasses.

As the women filtered out, Nora pulled her crutches out from under her loom. "Melody, I think I'll go outside and get some air while there's a break. Tate, would you keep me company? I have some questions about this restaurant of yours."

They found a bench in the shade outside where it was quiet. Tate reached for her arm as she sat.

"Thanks, but I can manage," said Nora as she'd settled herself. Tate took the hint and sat down next to her.

"What can I tell you about the restaurant?" he asked.

"Nothing, actually," said Nora. "I really wanted to talk to you about Cassie."

"Oh?" he said, for lack of something more intelligent to say. *Now what?*

"I overheard some of your conversation at the store the other day. She was pretty short with you."

"No, it's my fault," said Tate. "I'm afraid I insulted her pretty badly the first day we met."

"Well, you did push a great many of her buttons," said Nora, with a small smile.

"Ah. She told you." Tate wondered if the whole village knew what had happened.

"She did. You should know that, normally, Cassie would have laughed it off. It's just she's pretty stressed right now."

"What's wrong?"

"Nothing's really wrong. She's just under pressure from a number of things," said Nora. She shifted and made herself more comfortable on the bench.

"As I'm sure I don't have to tell you, the economy the last couple years has been... Well, it's been a disaster. None of the businesses down here are doing what they should."

Tate winced. "Sounds like I picked a bad time to go into business."

Nora made a face. "I hope that's not true. Though, honestly," she raised her eyebrows, "the timing could have been better."

Another one for blunt talk, thought Tate. *I guess it runs in the family*.

"But for Cassie, it's more personal," Nora was continuing. "If you haven't heard by now, you will soon, that Jim, the former owner of the shop...well, he disappeared. He trained Cassie and left the shop to her. She feels a personal obligation to make sure it survives. To see it fail would be to fail Jim. If that's not bad enough, her new work isn't going well, and she's afraid she'll lose all she's worked for. All Jim worked for."

"But her work is beautiful," said Tate. "She's an excellent craftsman. Woman."

Nora nodded. "She is. And she probably won't lose the store, but you can't tell her that," Nora continued. She looked at Tate as if she were evaluating him. It was an uncomfortable feeling. "I expect you have the same worries about your new venture."

"I certainly do," said Tate fervently. "Lots of sleepless nights."

Nora nodded once, paused then went on. "If that's not enough, she feels obligated to me."

"That I understand," said Tate. "I was close to my mom, too."

Nora looked at him strangely. "I'm not Cassie's mom," she said.

Tate's head spun. "I'm sorry?"

"Her mom and I were in a car accident seven years ago," Nora told him. "It left me like this. Beth died."

Tate sat back and stared at Nora. For a moment, the grief of his own loss blindsided him. He never got used to it surprising him at odd moments. He felt a deep kinship with Cassie. He knew that sorrow. He'd never been able to outrun it.

Only seven years, and then to lose Jim, too.

"I'm so sorry for you both," he said.

Nora nodded. "Beth was my best friend. We'd been friends since childhood. Just like Cassie and Anna."

"Anna?" he asked.

"Your new bartender," she said.

"This town is shrinking around me," said Tate, making a face.

Nora laughed. "Yes, well, wait until you're here thirty years or more if you want that small town feel," she said. "Anyway, it's been a rough time for Cassie and she's lost her sense of equilibrium. And her sense of humor. I just thought you should know. Give her the benefit of the doubt, if you can."

"I will. More than you know," said Tate.

"Oh," said Nora, smiling, "I think I know." She pulled her canes over, leaned on them, and got to her feet.

"It's been nice talking to you, Tate. I hope you meant that invitation to the opening."

"I did," he said. "I've already given invitations to Cassie, but I think she may have burned them. Or driven a stake through them." Nora laughed. "I'd love it if you could change her mind, get her to come."

"I will," said Nora. "The 28th, you said?"

"Yes," said Tate. "Wednesday, the 28th."

"We'll be there." Nora turned carefully, and tapped her way slowly back to Melody's shop.

LIGHT FOG WAS SHREDDING OVER BAYVIEW Park as the sun rose, tatters of it drifting down Coast Highway. Palm fronds rustled while, hidden in them, half the sparrows in California argued about territory. Below the bluff, the ocean, like rumpled gray silk, slipped relentlessly into the beach, flashing in the sunlight where it broke onto the sand.

Cassie sat on a bench in the park, hugging her heavy sweatshirt around her against the dampness. Occasionally, on the path behind her, came the thudding footsteps and ragged breathing of early morning runners. Cassie hardly heard them. She was trying not to cry.

Seven years, she thought. *Everyone said it would get better with time. Why does it still hurt like this?*

But it wasn't just the anniversary of her mom's death that was hitting her so hard. Every day that passed made it look more and more like she would lose Jim's business.

Her business.

Her mom and Nora had made it on far less. Jim had made it. Why couldn't she? Was she lying to herself about her abilities? If she couldn't work as an artist, who was she? What was left? Despite Anna's brave words, Cassie wasn't sure she could do anything else, not without losing herself.

She bit her lip and took a deep shaky breath.

Every waking minute in the past week, she had shoved at the walls of her creative box with all the strength and ingenuity she could muster. No matter what she tried, though, the new work wasn't developing.

She'd tried being outrageous, but the pieces looked like something she'd made in high school. When she'd tried quirky, they just looked sad. She'd thought about enameling and stone inlay as ways to add more color to her work. But with the photo shoot only weeks away, she didn't have time to learn either technique, certainly not to the level she would need to enter the Masters. Cassie wasn't sure they would give her what she wanted, anyway. Both techniques felt too... controlled. Too polished.

Despite Nora urging her on, Cassie felt like a failure.

Anna was having self-doubts, too. She didn't want to talk about her work and, unusually for Anna, she was very irritable. Cassie smiled to herself. Anna muttered to herself in Spanish when she was stressed. Cassie knew enough Spanish to know Anna was in for it if Consuelo heard her.

Then there was Tate.

Thinking about him made her feel even lower.

Just the night before, Nora had sat on the end of Cassie's bed and talked to her about the way she had treated Tate at the grocery store.

"I talked to him, Cassie. I saw the way he talked to the women at Melody's. The way he joked with them, the way he honestly admired Melody's shop. Even those crazy women clients of mine—he treated them like ladies."

"You realize the cynical part of me says he was simply

promoting his business," said Cassie. "He needs customers, too, you know."

"I took that into consideration. But I think he truly is sorry for the mess he made of his start with you."

"Nora..." she tried to interrupt, but Nora just talked over her.

"And frankly, I'm glad he stopped by the shop the other night, when you went to cast. I worry about you, sometimes, down there late and walking home. If someone else is looking out for you, he's okay in my book."

Cassie thought she'd rather have her eyes poked out before she'd admit that she, too, didn't mind if someone checked on her occasionally, though she would have preferred it hadn't been Tate.

At least that was what she was telling herself.

"Nora, please..."

Nora held up her hand. "Before you say anything, yes, I do think he's interested in you. Who could blame him? But that shouldn't prevent you from being friendly, or at least civil, as business owners working in the same block."

We're almost neighbors, Tate had said.

"I don't have the energy to be nice or to worry about Tate. And I *really* don't have the energy to get involved with anyone. Or the desire."

"Well, you should find the energy," said Nora sternly. "You're right that Tate is trying to get business owners and hotel managers on his side. He needs referrals for his business to grow. It helps to have friends in the community."

Nora paused

"And it can hurt if you have enemies," she said.

"What does that mean?" asked Cassie, frowning at her.

"If Tate's business grows, even if *he* doesn't talk badly about you—and you know how people talk at a bar—if he talks up other jewelers in town instead, it could hurt your business."

"That sounds so...calculating." Cassie's eyes narrowed. "That's not like you."

"Your behavior is not like *you*, Cassiopeia," said Nora. "Tate's clumsy attempts at friendliness, or to pick you up, or whatever," Nora waved a hand to dismiss the protest Cassie was about to make, "would usually never faze you. I know you're worried about the business. And now the work isn't going well..."

"The work is crap," interjected Cassie.

"As I said, it isn't going well," repeated Nora, "and that's making you grouchy. But it's no reason to take it out on people who are trying to be pleasant. No matter how badly they're doing it."

"Nora, I can't pretend to be crazy about the guy when I'm not." *Liar, liar.* The little voice in her head was getting tedious. Cassie wished it would shut up.

Nora just looked at her.

"I'm not," insisted Cassie.

"Fine. You're not," said Nora. "But at least give him a chance. You might find he can be a friend, or at least someone you don't hate, if you just give it room to breathe. After all, his business is also facing an uphill struggle."

"You do know I'm going to be thirty in January, don't you?" asked Cassie.

"Really. And here you're acting like you're sixteen." Nora hefted herself onto her crutches. "I was here then, you know. I remember."

She leaned over awkwardly and kissed Cassie on the forehead. "And *you* do remember that I love you more than I can ever say?"

Tears stung Cassie's eyes. "I know," she said huskily. "I know."

So why did she feel so bereft? Like she was all alone on an island, a thousand miles from anyone?

She had been so close to her mom, even in the years they'd fought over school. As Cassie had gotten older, she, Beth, and Nora had sometimes felt like sisters. They were a trio, like the Cartier ring she'd sized once: three interlocked bands of white, yellow, and rose gold. Now one of those bands was gone. It could never be replaced.

In the back of her mind, she registered the changing timbre of footsteps as a runner went from the hard path to the grass. Suddenly, Tate was at the end of her bench bending over, winded.

"May I join you?" he asked breathlessly. "I won't be annoying. I just need a break."

"Sit," said Cassie, hearing Nora in her head, "before you fall over."

"Thanks," he said and collapsed onto the bench.

They sat quietly for a while as Tate tried to catch his breath. Cassie stole a look at him: baggy shorts, white T-shirt, wet with sweat, gray battered sweatshirt tied around his waist, running shoes that had seen some miles. Unaware of her sidelong look, Tate wiped at the sweat on his forehead with the inside of his elbow.

Though she was trying to figure out a Nora-approved way to get up and leave, in part of her mind, Cassie was casting about for a way to start a non-threatening conversation.

Direct, she thought. *It's the only way for me to be.*

"Tate," she said finally, to the air in front of her. "I've been really obnoxious to you, and I want to apologize. I really do have a lot on my mind—I know you do, too, with the restaurant opening in a little while—but I've let it get the better of me. I'm not usually so...bitchy."

She felt Tate looking at her. Then he said, very carefully,

as if he were testing her, "You're doing very well for someone who doesn't get much practice."

She shot him a glance and saw the small smile on his face. She couldn't help it. She laughed shortly. "Well, maybe I *have* had some practice in the past," she admitted.

Now Tate laughed.

"Fair enough," he said. "I'm not usually so stupid with words, either. Well, I'm better with food." He swiped at his face again, running his hand up into his hair, scratching the back of his head.

"At the risk of breaking this fragile truce, though, and in my own defense, I have to say you just flustered the heck out of me the day we met. I just…found the wrong words coming out." He put his hand over his heart. "I ask you to forgive me, and I'll try to do better."

She gave him a small smile. "So will I," she said.

"So," he said, into the awkward pause, "Do you run, too?"

Cassie shook her head. "Too much like work. If I want speed, give me a long hill and a skateboard." She was satisfied to see Tate's surprise. "I'm a walker," she went on. "I do my best thinking while walking. And while watching the ocean from here." She nodded to the gray-blue waves rolling in from Asia.

"What are you thinking about today?" he asked lightly.

Cassie hesitated, then surprised herself by saying, "My mother." She felt her throat close up.

"Ah," he said. "I'm very sorry. I heard she died a while back."

"Seven years today." Cassie paused and swallowed hard.

Tate let her get control over her voice.

"Mostly I think I'm past it," she finally went on. "Past the worst of it, anyway. I don't think I'll ever be truly over it." Cassie rubbed the thigh of her jeans with her thumb. Tate sat still as a stone watching her. "But sometimes…sometimes I just wish she were here to talk to. I'm very lucky to have Nora. But my mom…she was the best. And the most incredible potter Eden Beach will ever see."

Tate nodded. "I met Nora the other day. She's a terrific weaver. And a gifted storyteller!"

"She is that," Cassie agreed.

"You're right about never getting over it," said Tate, after another pause. Cassie looked up at him. "I lost my mom when I was fifteen. Heart attack. She was thirty-eight." He shook his head. "I still can't believe it sometimes. Especially now. My younger sister, Tia, looks just like her."

"Tia? asked Cassie, surprised. "Tiny. Pretty blond. Mid-twenties?"

Tate nodded. "You polished our mom's bracelets the other day. You made her day."

"She's very nice," said Cassie, then frowned. "She must have been very young when your mom died."

"She was just eight." Tate looked out to the ocean. He seemed to think about what he would say next. "She doesn't really remember much about our mom."

"That's hard. At least I have lots of years of memories. Tia was lucky to have you, though," said Cassie, "and, I assume, your dad?"

Tate snorted. "Yeah, well. That's a story."

He hesitated, but Cassie had the feeling he wanted to talk, so she prodded.

"Oh?"

Tate glanced at Cassie, then out to the ocean again. "Martin—my dad—and I…we didn't see eye to eye on most things." He made a sound that was supposed to be a laugh, Cassie thought. "Especially when the subject was me. But I was just fifteen. I'd lost my mom. I was full of anger at the world, grief I couldn't express any other way. Especially when Martin married not even a year later," he said bitterly. "So I got wild. Got a motorcycle as soon as I got my license. Well, almost had my license. Grew my hair long." He gestured to his head. "Old habit." A crooked grin.

Now it was Cassie's turn to sit quietly.

"I was an embarrassment," he said. "Big name financier," Tate waggled his hands in front of him in a "big deal" gesture, "long-haired, motorcycle-riding delinquent for a son." He sighed. "There was a lot of yelling about family name." He turned to Cassie. "My grandfather was a big land investor in the 1930s. Meaning he bought land from destitute farmers for a pittance." He shook his head and turned back to the ocean.

Lights went on for Cassie. "Wait. Garner," she said. "*Martin Garner* is your father?" Phil Trainer, her former boyfriend, was a financial consultant. He'd talked with near-religious ardor about Martin Garner as the money behind Alden Towne and Towne Center.

"That's him," said Tate. His eyes on the ocean, Tate didn't see the shock on Cassie's face.

"Anyway, Martin decided I was too difficult," Tate went on, staring into the past as much as he was staring at the sea. "Which meant he couldn't control me. Martin doesn't like anything or anyone he can't control. So he threw me out at seventeen." Tate took a deep breath, then turned toward Cassie. "I didn't much care. I'd been working in restaurants since my mom died—my way to cope, I guess." He shrugged. "My mom taught me to cook," he explained. "Being in kitchens, I felt close to her. She always wanted a restaurant."

He looked back at the horizon. Cassie wondered if he'd ever said any of this to anyone. He seemed to find it easier to talk without looking at her.

"Then I found out how vindictive Martin could be," said Tate, after a pause.

"What do you mean?" asked Cassie. She saw Tate clench and unclench a hand.

"I went back to the house to see Tia, not long after I'd moved out. Martin stopped me," said Tate, his voice shaking a bit with remembered fury and resentment. "Told me not to come back. He'd gotten a restraining order against me. Said I was a danger to Tia." The bitterness in his voice was enough to peel the paint off the bench. "I was so angry it's a wonder I didn't try to kill him."

He stopped speaking.

Cassie watched him stare at the ocean, looking older, remembering dark and lonely times. His throat was working as if he was trying to swallow tears. She didn't wonder. It was such a monstrous thing to do, she could think of nothing to say.

"So I got on the motorcycle and took off. I thought if I couldn't see Tia, I might as well leave California. Went to Chicago, New York, London, Paris, all over Italy, Greece and Spain. Just a backpack. Picking up languages and working in kitchens."

"You left Tia alone with Mr. Warmth?" Cassie heard the hardness in her voice. "Sorry," she said. "I shouldn't have said that."

Tate grimaced. "Believe me. I've said worse to myself. But I was seventeen, and it was all about me." He shook his head. "Stupid and selfish." He shrugged. "I got smart. Eventually. Or smarter, anyway. I wrote her, through a friend of our mom's. She wrote back."

"Still, not the same as having you here," said Cassie.

"No. No, not the same." He gave a hollow laugh. "For either of us."

"Well," said Cassie. "It sounds like a great adventure, but I'm surprised Tia speaks to you."

"Fortunately," said Tate, "Tia's the mature one of the family. I include Martin in that. She's made sure I knew how she felt over the years, though," he said, giving her a lopsided grin. "Too much like me. And Martin, I guess."

Cassie found herself liking Tia more. And Tate.

"How long were you gone?" she asked.

"Fifteen years," he said. "I didn't come back to the US until Tia was over twenty-one and my father didn't have control anymore. Didn't come back to California until last spring."

"Long time," said Cassie. Tate nodded

"So you came back to see Tia and start your mom's restaurant," said Cassie. "I'm guessing her name was Lydia?"

Tate looked at her.

"I can read," she said. "I saw the sign."

"Oh, yeah," said Tate, sheepishly. "Obvious, I guess, huh?"

He heaved a sigh, tugged the sweatshirt from around his waist and pulled it over his head.

"Yeah, I came back from New York where I ended up. That's where I met Domingo."

"Who's that?" asked Cassie.

"Well, officially he's my sous-chef, second in command. But I'm not so sure he doesn't really run the place. Along with your friend, Anna."

Cassie laughed out loud. "I don't know your friend Domingo, but I guarantee you Anna *will* run the place within six months! Consider yourself warned!"

"She's dynamite, isn't she?" said Tate, grinning.

"Well, look at you," said Cassie. "You finally said something right." Tate raised an eyebrow. "Anna is simply the best. If you say nice things about my friend, I can forgive a lot."

"You've known her a long time?"

"Forever. We met at the beginning of junior high. Both of us with lots of attitude. We used to cut classes even then. We spent more time either on the beach or grounded than we spent in school. Our mothers managed us as a unit."

"What do you mean?" asked Tate.

Cassie smiled. "We once tried that old game—only once! —I'll say I'm staying at your house, you say you're staying at mine. But my mom called Consuelo—Anna's mom—to be sure it was okay for me to spend the night. Consuelo told her, there must be some mistake. Anna was staying with *us*. After that, the phone line was on fire between them. I don't think I ever left the house without mom or Nora calling Consuelo."

Tate laughed. "I should have known you then," he said. "Sounds like the three of us would have been wild together."

"No, no," she said, waving a finger at him. "No boys."

"Oh, I can't believe that!" said Tate.

"Believe it," she said. "Anna has five brothers. Her parents knew all about boys." She shook her head negatively. "No one, and I mean *no one* messed with Anna—or me. Luis—her dad —and her brothers, were a very strong deterrent." She looked at Tate. "Very strong."

Tate laughed.

"You laugh now," said Cassie, with the hint of a smile, "but wait until you meet Luis and his sons. I love him like my own father, but he and the boys were very protective of Anna and I. They still are."

"I'll watch my step."

"Now, of course, there's Dale, too," said Cassie.

"Anna's husband?" asked Tate.

"Have you met him?"

"Not yet, though Anna hardly stops talking about him," said Tate, grinning.

"They're an unexpected couple, but very, very good together." Cassie smiled. "Glad you like Anna. You treat her well, or you'll answer to me—and all the Rodriguezes."

Tate laughed. "Believe me, I treasure Anna. She's smart, funny. Great ideas about the bar, the food." He shook his head. "Between Mingo and Anna, I have ninety-five percent of a great restaurant."

"It's going well then," said Cassie.

"Yeah, well, we'll know more when I open. But so far, yes, it is," said Tate. He hesitated a moment. "It would go better if you and Nora would come to the open house at the end of the month."

It was Cassie's turn to be quiet. "I was bitchy about that, too, wasn't I?" she asked.

Tate shrugged one shoulder. "You had a right," he said. "I'd just called you 'artsy.'"

He grinned. Cassie noticed his smile was crooked. How had she missed that before? And his front tooth turned a little to the side. Her heart did a little stutter beat.

"Yes. Well. We'll just call it 'one'," she said, feeling a flush rising slowly all the way up from her feet. "Just remember, I have plenty of heavy tools to throw at you should it happen again."

"Noted." He smiled.

A small silence grew between them. Cassie's thoughts went back to what he'd said earlier.

She took a breath and hoped she'd sound offhand.

"So. Your dad." Tate frowned a bit. "That's how you know Carla?"

The frown turned to puzzlement.

"Carla?"

"Towne," she said.

"My realtor?"

Cassie nodded.

Tate shook his head. "My first realtor recommended her." He looked at Cassie strangely. "Why do you think my dad knows her?"

"Oh. Well." Cassie was starting to get embarrassed. "It's

just... I understood Martin Garner provided the funding for the Towne Center. So I assumed..." She trailed off.

"Towne Center? The big shopping mall up in Newport?" Tate's puzzled frown deepened. "I'm not following."

"Carla's dad's developed it," said Cassie. "Since your dad provided funding..."

Understanding dawned on Tate's face. "Ah. No." He shook his head. "I haven't spoken to Martin since I was seventeen. I didn't have any interest in what he did then. I certainly don't now." He shrugged. "Sam just said that Carla knew the town and the properties that might be available."

"Oh." Cassie let it drop as if it wasn't important.

There was a long pause. Cassie suddenly realized that they were staring at each other, and both of them had gone quiet again.

"Well," she said into the awkward silence. "I'd better get to the shop. I have to get some decent work done." She stood and Tate stood with her. "Something artsy," she said, smiling up at him. With her height, she didn't look up for many people.

He had taken a step toward her and was standing very close. Cassie found herself staring into those eyes. Green. Today they were green. The fog and the running had left damp curls at his neck and temples. He hadn't shaved yet that morning, and she wanted to touch his face, feel the roughness under her hand. She felt a pull toward him, from the center of her chest, that was almost tidal in power. Irresistible as the ocean. She swayed gently and felt his arm go around her waist. He bent his head toward her.

Stop, stop, stop! said a small voice in her head. *I don't want this.*

Don't you? asked another voice.

Cassie put her hand firmly on his chest, feeling his steady heartbeat under the sweatshirt. "Whoa. Sorry," she said. "I guess I got a bit dizzy. Too much walking without breakfast." She stepped back deliberately and, after the slightest resistance, Tate let her go.

"Cassie," he said.

"I'd better go find some donuts. Though maybe I shouldn't say that to a European-trained chef. And I'm sure you need to get to the restaurant," she babbled, "otherwise, Anna will have taken over." She smiled awkwardly. Her mouth did not want to be speaking right now. It wanted to be kissing Tate.

Was her entire body turning against her?

"It was good talking to you, Tate," she said into his silence. "I'm glad we cleared the air."

He gave her a small smile. "I am, too." He reached out and gently touched her arm. Even through her heavy sweatshirt, she felt the heat, as if someone had opened a kiln door. It was the grocery store all over again. Except now, her defensive anger was gone.

"Cassie, maybe I just rushed things a bit," he said. "Maybe we could have lunch on a day you're closed? If you and Anna spent so much time on the beaches, surely you know a place for a picnic. We've still got a bit of summer left." The lines at the corners of his eyes tilted, as if his smiles started there. "I know a great chef."

She hesitated. *Say yes,* she heard Nora's voice urging her. *What's one date?*

Yes, well Nora didn't know Tate was Martin Garner's son. Despite Tate's obvious dislike of his father, Cassie wasn't sure she wanted to have even one date with anyone even remotely associated with Eden Beach's slumlord. Or his despicable daughter.

Excuses, whispered her subconscious. *You're afraid.*

She was going to strangle that little voice in her head if she ever got her hands on it.

"Tate, thank you, but really, my head is just too full right now to think about dating or doing anything but getting this work done."

Tate gave her his small crooked smile, and Cassie again felt that oceanic pull. "I understand," he said a little sadly. "At least I hope to see you at the open house. And maybe, once your work gets going a little better..." He trailed off.

"Maybe." Cassie stepped back and quickly turned away, waving a hand over her shoulder as she walked at a fast pace down the hill to her store.

CHAPTER 14

The following Tuesday, Cassie was trying to catch up on repairs. She'd spent a frustrating hour on a ring that had gone through a garbage disposal. The job was not going smoothly, and it was going to take more time than she'd estimated. She was going to lose money on it. She decided to stop and take care of a few simpler repairs before annoyance caused her to make a mistake.

She adjusted the flame on her torch and deftly soldered a broken chain link, then dropped the piece into the pickle pot where the weak acid would clean the heat-darkened metal. She pulled the next job out of the box, read her notes on the envelope, and was just slipping the piece out to examine it when Tia walked in.

"Hi," said Tia, smiling as the door closed behind her, shutting out the chilly mist that, as yet, showed no signs of burning off. "How's it going?"

"Not too well today," said Cassie, laying the repair on the bench, and flipping up her magnifier.

Tia's step faltered. "Oh. Sorry. Maybe I should have called to see if it was okay to come in."

Cassie's hesitated a fraction. "No. It's fine," she said, sighing inwardly. Her confused feelings about Tate were no reason to be rude to his sister. "It's one of my jobs. It's not cooperating. I just switched over to another one. So your timing is good, actually."

"If you're sure..."

"I am." Cassie smiled and got up to unlock the security gate. "Come on in. Coffee?"

"I'd love some." Tia hunched her sweatshirt around her. "It's sunny up in Irvine. I didn't expect it to be so cold here."

"Yes," grinned Cassie, as she poured coffee into a Eden Beach mug. "The beach betrayal."

"Yeah. You'd think we'd learn." Tia took the hot mug, cupping it in both hands. "Just because it's hot inland doesn't mean it will be a sunny beach day. At least I wore jeans and not shorts."

Cassie grabbed an iced tea. The weather never seemed to affect her choice of beverage. "So, what do you know about jewelry?"

"Besides it's beautiful? Nothing," said Tia.

"Then let me give you the basics."

Cassie spent a half hour or so, explaining her equipment —what tools she used for wax working, which she used to cut, shape, solder and clean metal—and how casting worked. She explained stone setting, and showed Tia jewelry in all states of process. The younger woman was all eyes, looking closely at everything, asking Cassie a constant stream of questions.

Cassie was surprised. She usually had a wax project going on behind her booth at the Pepper Tree show, but visitors only rarely asked questions. She'd learned to keep her answers short or people's eyes got a glazed look. So after she had demonstrated wax carving, she impulsively asked Tia if she wanted to try it.

"Me?" she asked nervously. "What happens if I make a mistake or it breaks? Seems fragile."

"It's wax," Cassie told her. "You just melt more, stick the broken pieces together with it and, when it's solid again, go back to work. Remember, wax is just the first step. It makes the hollow in the plaster that you cast the melted metal into."

"Yeah. Sure. Okay."

"Okay then," Cassie smiled, handing Tia an apron. "First rule," she told her, pointing at Tia's hair, which swung freely below her shoulders. "Always tie your hair back."

"Oh?"

Cassie nodded. "You won't be using anything motorized, but if a motorized tool—like the buffing machine back there," she gestured to the back room, "catches any stray hair, it will tear out a chunk of scalp faster than you can blink."

Tia looked startled. "Seriously?"

"Oh, yeah."

"Did that ever happen to you?"

Cassie shook her head. "No. But it happened to Jim in his early days. He said the headache lasted three days. And the hair never really grew back in the bald spot. He was a fanatic about me keeping my hair up and back. It's a good habit to get into from the beginning."

"Got it," said Tia and deftly wove her hair into a French braid.

Cassie watched admiringly. "Sissy used to do that for me," she said as she gave Tia an elastic band to secure the braid. "But I never got the hang of it." She immediately wished the words back. Seeing Tia's hands in her hair, the name had just popped out.

"Your sister?" Tia asked, as she stepped around the chair to sit down.

"Careful!" said Cassie, putting her hand on Tia's arm to stop her. "Sit down from the other side." She pointed at the torch in its rest on the metal-working bench. Tia had come very close to the blue flame.

"Yikes," said Tia quietly, moving away from the heat of the torch and sitting down.

"I keep it burning when I'm working on repairs or building a new piece. Saves time if I don't have to re-light it every time I reach for it."

Before Tia could ask more about Sissy, Cassie put a pre-cut, one-by-six-inch slab of blue wax in front of her. Then she took a wax model she'd been working on earlier—a fairly simple pendant—and set it where Tia could see it. "This will give you something to copy, just to start," she said. "Do you remember how I laid out a design on the wax earlier?"

Tia nodded. "I've used a compass and calipers before. In a sculpture class," she said.

"Then you should be right at home here. Lay out a circle about the same size as the pendant, then use the saw," Cassie pointed, "to cut off the excess wax. Cut just outside your scribed line. Use the wax file," she set it on the bench top, "to true up your edges."

Tia nodded.

Cassie reached to the tool board behind the benches and picked off another head magnifier. "You'll need this," she said, helping Tia put it on and adjust it.

With further instructions on how to keep the saw vertical and brace the work on the bench pin sticking out of the front of the bench, Cassie let her go and went back to her repair.

A short while later, she glanced up to see that Tia had finished sawing and had picked up a wax tool to begin carving. Cassie smiled to herself. The cutting lines were wavy, as was to be expected.

"Use the wax file and get your edges trued up," she reminded. "Then use the knife to get your rough shape before going to the wax tools."

Tia looked up, realized she couldn't see with the magnifier over her eyes, and flipped up the lens. Cassie laughed.

"Now you look like a jeweler," she said.

Tia reached for the knife.

"Be careful, because it's really sharp," said Cassie, then smiled. "But I have lots of Band-Aids."

"I'm not sure that's reassuring," said Tia. She pointed to the wax tool. "This looks like something my dentist would use."

"It's the same thing. Dentists make crowns the same way," Cassie told her. "Once you get the feel of the wax, if you want, I'll show you how to use the motorized handpiece. You use it the same way, it's just a whole lot faster for removing a lot of wax."

As Tia flipped the magnifier back into place, Cassie went back to her work, too.

A few minutes later she asked Tia, "So. When you're not auditioning to be a jeweler, what kind of work do you do?"

"Well, I majored in biology in college," Tia said absently, slicing off a few curls of wax. "Thought I'd be a marine biologist. But got sidetracked by a class in native plants. Switched to landscape architecture. Worked in an office in LA. But after Tate came home, I quit. Moved back down here. I've gotten a job working at a nursery in Mission Viejo."

"I'm surprised with all the new housing going up you weren't able to find something at an architect's office." Cassie's hand moved deftly, picking up tiny squares of solder with a pick and placing them on the piece she was repairing.

Tia sighed. "I did a few interviews, but..." She picked up the wax file and reshaped an area of her design.

"But..." prompted Cassie when Tia seemed to forget she'd been speaking.

"Oh. But I realized I liked working with the plants more

than working with the drawings." A small shrug. "Like the color. Smell of the dirt."

"Still, the pay hit must be substantial."

"Yeah, but I'm sharing a house with three other women in Irvine, so rent's pretty cheap."

Cassie found herself smiling as she moved the torch over a solder joint. "Roommates can be the best or the worst."

"I'm lucky. I have the best ones." Tia chuckled. "Or maybe I should say, at least we haven't gotten on each other's nerves yet."

"I expect you moved down here to be close to your family?" Cassie asked.

"I wanted to be close to Tate," Tia corrected. "He moved out when I was pretty young—he's seven years older than I am. Spent a lot of time in Europe."

"He mentioned that." Her repair sizzled as Cassie dipped it into her pickle pot. "That must have been amazing."

"Most of it was," said Tia. "But he had a pretty bad time in Paris."

There was a snap.

"Oh, no!" cried Tia, looking at the two pieces of wax in her hand.

"No problem," said Cassie. "It's wax. We'll mend it." She got up, moved around to Tia's right, and turned on the wax pen. When it was hot, she showed Tia how to use it to melt wax and heal the break.

"That is so cool!" said Tia.

"Everything about making jewelry is cool, I think," said Cassie.

The door pinged, and Cassie looked up under the edge of her magnifier. Her pulse started dancing when she saw it was Tate.

No, she told herself firmly. Her heart ignored her.

Tia looked up, blinded by her magnifier, then flipped it up. Tate saw her and laughed.

"That's a good look on you," he told his sister. He held up a stack of white boxes. "Domingo said you were down here. I brought us lunch."

"It's lunch?" said Tia, swiveling to look at the clock over the design desk. She turned back to Cassie. "I've been here two hours already?"

Cassie smiled. "It sucks you in," she said, as she stood and took off her magnifier. "About time. We should have taken a break a while ago." She rolled her shoulders as Tia stood up and groaned.

"Oh, wow," she said. "I didn't think you could get so stiff from sitting."

"Do you have a place in back to eat?" asked Tate.

Cassie shook her head. "Not enough room for all three of us. But I have an old blanket. We can eat in the park across the street."

Tate raised an eyebrow. "The store?"

Cassie reached under the design desk. "Sign in the window," she said, holding it up. "Tuesdays are usually slow anyway."

"Yeah, well if it works like the restaurant business," said Tate, "just as you send some of the staff home, you get a group of about thirty in for a late lunch."

"If you bringing lunch in here turns out to work like that," Cassie told him, "I'll have you bring lunch every day."

She regretted the remark immediately as a soft look of pleasure came to Tate's face. She didn't want to encourage him, though her heart quickened at the thought of seeing him so often.

Cassie shook herself mentally. *Fellow business owners. That's all*, she thought.

She hung the sign, locked the door, and the three of them

went across to sit on the grass in the sun that was boldly burning its way through the overcast. Cassie sat facing the shop to keep an eye out for customers.

Tate had brought a selection of sandwiches—meat, cheese, veggies—along with deep fried sweet potatoes and cheesecake. The three of them began reducing it all to crumbs.

"You really are much better with food," Cassie told Tate.

"Thank you." He gave her a half bow and turned to Tia, grinning. "Thinking about changing your career from garden designer to jewelry now?"

Cassie smiled and said, teasingly, "You're getting the hang of wax carving so quickly, maybe you should consider it."

Tia laughed. "It's fun, isn't it?"

"I'm curious," asked Cassie. "You mentioned sculpture. Why didn't you study art instead of biology at college?"

Tia snorted. "I wanted to, but when I mentioned it to my dad, he about had a fit."

Cassie laughed, but she saw Tate's face tighten.

"What is it about art that makes parents throw fits?" she asked the palm fronds above her. Looking back at Tia she said, "My mom's folks had a fit, too," she said.

"What did she do?"

Cassie hesitated.

"She ran away."

"She what?" Tia was shocked.

"She ran away. Came down here to live with friends and learned to pot. Had me." Cassie shrugged and feigned interest in some people who had stopped to look in the shop window.

"How old was she?"

"Fifteen."

"*Fifteen?*"

Cassie nodded. "Yeah," she said, looking at Tia's stricken face. "Freaks me out, too, every time I think about it."

"Didn't her parents come after her?"

Cassie's face clouded. She shook her head. "Tough love. They thought if they left her on her own, she'd learn the hard way and come back." She grinned. "They obviously didn't know how stubborn my mom was."

"Did mom run away, too?" Tia asked her brother.

He shook his head. "Scholarship," he told her. Cassie looked at him with a question in her eyes. "Our mom went to art school in Paris."

"Wow," said Cassie. "On scholarship. What school?"

Tate shook his head ruefully. "I don't know. I'm sure she probably told me, but I don't remember."

"Dad doesn't know either," said Tia.

"Oh, I'm sure he knows," said Tate. "He's just trying to erase that, like everything else about her." He leaned forward, resting his elbows on his knees and shook his head. "Worst thing that happened to her in Paris. She met Martin. And never finished school."

"Hey!" Tia slapped him on the arm. "Where would we be if that hadn't happened?"

He grinned. "You have a point."

The sunlight, growing in strength, pierced the palm fronds, turning the blond heads golden. As they smiled at each other, Cassie felt...something...turn in her chest. Regret for the siblings she never had? Envy of the bond between the two sitting in front of her? Grief for days and family lost? The old feeling of exclusion she'd felt in school? Some of it? All of it? She didn't know. Tears pricked her eyes. She blinked them quickly away and turned her gaze back to the store.

"How did your mom do it?" Tate asked Cassie, glancing at Tia. Cassie could practically hear him thinking, *It could have happened to her*. "She was so young."

"Like everyone else then. Worked two or three crap jobs. Lived with friends. She was lucky. She had Nora. They found a house, got roommates."

"That's why you said you knew about roommates," said Tia.

"Yep," said Cassie, unfolding her legs and stretching them out in front of her. She leaned back on her hands, a smile on her face. "We sure had roommates."

"I hear stories there," said Tate.

Cassie laughed. "Stories I've got."

"Like...?" Tia rotated her hand in a *come-on* motion.

Cassie tipped her head down and to the side, then smiled at Tia. "Like Franco," she said. "He was an actor and comedian. I don't think Franco was his real name, but we didn't care. He could make his face do amazing things. I used to spend hours in front of the mirror trying to mimic him," she said. "He'd act out stories—like Peter Pan—playing all the parts, changing costumes, dialogue, and sometimes getting the characters confused."

Cassie smiled, remembering. "One time he was playing Nana, but he was dressed in Wendy's nightgown—a muumuu Melinda found at a garage sale—with couch pillows stuffed underneath. He hurled himself off one of the chairs, gave this long fading scream like he was falling out a window, and crashed to the floor. Then he lay there singing the Peter Pan song." She put her arms straight out to her sides and flapped them. "I can't fly, I can't fly, I can't fly!"

She was laughing, and so was Tia.

"I'll never hear that song the same way again," said Tia.

When Cassie glanced at Tate, though he was smiling, there a look Cassie couldn't decipher in his gray-green eyes.

"Who was Melinda?" asked Tia.

"A goddess in disguise, I'm sure. She didn't walk, she glided." Cassie made a sliding motion with her hand. "She had rosy chocolate skin—the most amazing color. Very tall—taller than Jim—and slender as a twig, but with this big, deep, boom-box laugh that rattled your chest. She used to hit the garage sales and swap meets, hunting for dolls for me, then making us matching clothes." Cassie was watching a couple of young women who had paused in front of her shop window. "She couldn't have kids of her own, Mom told me later. A bad abortion when she was young." Watching the women walk away, she didn't notice she'd shocked Tia again. "She designs clothes now for some high-end brand up in LA.

"And, of course, there was Jim. I think Nate brought him home." She glanced at Tia and Tate. "Free spirit on a motor-cycle. He was only going to stay for a few weeks." She smiled. "But he fell in love with Nora and convinced her she felt the same." She tipped her head sideways. "I don't think Nora really took much convincing. Anyway, he never left." Her smile slipped a bit, and she swallowed hard.

She was silent for a long time. She almost forgot the two sitting next to her until Tate said quietly, "Sounds like Nora wasn't the only one who fell in love with him."

Cassie looked at him. The understanding and compassion on his face almost undid her. For a moment, she thought she wouldn't mind looking at that face for the rest of her life.

"No, she wasn't," she finally managed to say. She tore her gaze away from Tate and spoke to Tia. "I was just five when Jim moved in. I followed him everywhere. He did these magic things—turned rocks into beautiful gemstones, lit metal on fire. I used to run to the shop after school and vacuum, clean cases, polish jewelry. I loved watching him work. He was my protector." She grinned. "Especially when I was in trouble with my mom."

"It sounds wild," said Tia, sighing.

Cassie felt like she'd been slapped. For a few moments she'd forgotten what a privileged life these two had had.

"Yeah. Well, we were hippies," she said stiffly, sitting up and starting to put their trash into the bags.

Tia looked confused.

"Cassie," said Tate gently, putting his hand out, touching her arm. "You misunderstand."

Cassie turned a shuttered face to him, trying to ignore the sensation of his fingers on her skin.

"Your life—to us—sounds heavenly. You had so much more love, so much more fun, than we had," he said. "At least, after our mom died."

Cassie searched his face and his tone for the condescension she'd so often heard, but found nothing but honesty.

"That's the truth, Cassie," said Tia. "Our dad is all rules and orders." She made a face. "He's okay, I guess, as long as you're doing what he wants. Or, at least, not doing what he doesn't want you to do. I didn't mean anything bad."

Cassie took a deep breath and let it out. "Sorry," she said. "Sometimes I get defensive. I've taken a lot of crap about my family over the years. Especially at school." She reached for a couple napkins. If she didn't break contact with Tate's touch, she was going to reach for his hand.

"Sounds like Tate," said Tia.

"Oh?" Cassie reordered her face and worked to get control of her voice.

Tate leaned back and rolled his eyes. "Fine. Tell all my secrets."

"Long hair. Ponytail. Scruffy jeans. Big bike."

"The issue was the noise, not the size," said Tate.

"The issue was the *bike*." Tia leaned toward him, deepened her voice and shook her finger at her brother. "You are a *disgrace* to the family name," she said.

"You do that well," Tate told her, grinning. He reached up to grasp and shake the finger she was holding in his face.

Cassie was embarrassed. Maybe she was judging these two the way she thought everyone else judged her.

It was an uncomfortable thought.

Tia sighed. "I tried to disgrace the family name. I just wasn't strong enough."

"Eventually you were," said Tate.

"Only because you helped me."

Tia saw the puzzled look on Cassie's face.

"Like I said, my dad pitched fit when I wanted to go to art school. Biology was my second choice. The only reason he agreed to pay for a biology degree was because he thought I'd be a doctor." Tia uncrossed her legs, and folded them to the side, leaning on one hand. "Actually, he thought med school would give me a great opportunity to find and marry one. Particularly a specialist. A rich specialist."

"Good thing he didn't know you were in love with Phillipe Cousteau," Tate teased her.

Tia laughed and sighed. "Yeah. Me and Phillipe. A lost opportunity."

Cassie laughed. "The marine biology?"

"Yeah. But when I wanted to change to landscape architecture, he refused to pay for it. So Tate did." The look she gave Tate was filled with love and gratitude.

"I didn't do that much," he protested.

"You couldn't go to cooking school. I'd say that's a lot."

Tate waved a hand. "I wasn't that sure I wanted to go anyway. No big."

"Was Dad ever nicer?" she asked Tate, changing the subject. "Before me?"

Tate snorted. "No. It was worse. There was Mrs. Garner. You're lucky she died before you were born."

"Mrs. Garner?" Cassie asked, confused.

Tate made a bitter face. "Our grandmother. I always had to call her Mrs. Garner. 'Grandma' was undignified. Even mom had to call her Mrs. Garner. Not 'mom,' not 'Ida.'" He sat up, rolled his shoulders back and stretched before settling his elbows back on his knees.

Cassie felt her breath catch. She felt the same tidal pull, the one she'd felt on the cliff top a few mornings ago, tug her toward Tate.

"She hated our mom," Tate continued. "The only time Martin rebelled against her was when he met mom in Paris and married her." He shook his head. "Mom was beautiful. Smart. Talented. But it didn't matter. Her family didn't have money. The old witch was furious when she found out. She made sure it was the last time Martin rebelled. She tightened up on the purse strings. Threatened to disinherit him. He caved and groveled." He turned an angry gaze out to the ocean, now glinting in the sunlight. "She made mom pay for it every day. And me."

"She lived with you?" asked Cassie.

"Oh, no." Tate threw up his hands in mock horror. "We lived with *her*. It was *her* house. *Her* money." He sighed. "Every day I wished Mom would leave him. Take me with her. But she stayed. Even though *Mrs. Garner*," he placed sarcastic emphasis on the name, "killed her work."

He shook his head. "The smell of the oils gave her a headache. The pastels were too dusty. Watercolors stained the carpet. Clay was dirty." He took a deep breath. "Then fortunately old Ida died. But Martin had become just like her. Bitching every time Mom went into the studio." He looked at Cassie. "Her last resort was cooking, though he even tried to stop that. She taught me. Our joint rebellion," he said with a sad smile.

Tia leaned over and put her hand on Tate's knee. He laid his hand over hers and smiled at her. Cassie felt suddenly outside again.

"Maybe you're right," she said. "I *was* lucky. In more ways than one. I didn't know my grandparents."

"Not at all?" asked Tia. "Not even when you were older?"

Cassie shook her head.

"The only thing I know is that my grandmother insisted Mom get rid of me when she found out Mom was pregnant. She didn't much care how. Or whether it killed my mom."

Both Tia and Tate looked horrified.

Well, it is pretty horrible, thought Cassie.

She looked up to the sky. "And that my grandfather loved the stars."

"Stars?" asked Tia after a moment.

Cassie nodded, smiling wistfully. "Mom used to bring me down here to the beach at night, and we'd spread out a blanket. Sometimes the sand was still warm. We'd lie here and look up, watch stars fall, satellites pass overhead. She'd tell me the names of the constellations and their stories." She paused. "Been a long time since I've done that."

She'd always dreamed that, some night, she and her mom might bring her own daughter down here to watch the stars. The three of them together. She gave a small sigh. Assuming Cassie ever had a daughter of her own.

She looked back at the siblings, eyes shining. Then she sat up straight. The same couple had been standing in front of her window for a few minutes now. They were deep in conversation, the woman pointing to her hand. Cassie knew the signs.

"I have to go," she said, gesturing to her shop. "Potential customers."

She got to her feet quickly. "Sorry," she said, reaching for the blanket.

"I'll bring it back," said Tia. "Go."

Cassie smiled her thanks and went.

CHAPTER 15

THE MORNING MIST OF THE PAST FEW DAYS had disappeared and Eden Beach sparkled in the mild fall day. Tate was in the driveway, head down, polishing the Harley. He'd taken it on a long ride the evening before, and the two of them had come back looking the worse for wear. He had a quiche in the oven, the timer sitting on the front step so he could hear it.

He paid little attention to the footsteps coming up the sidewalk. His quiet neighborhood was always full of walkers and joggers getting in the miles before heading off to work. But then, "Tate?" someone said.

He looked up to see Cassie, paused at the end of the driveway. A bright turquoise tank was tucked into faded jeans, and she wore an old chambray work shirt over it, much too big for her. Her hair was down, loose, tendrils floating around her face in the light breeze. Large silver earrings glinted in her ears, emphasizing the gray streak in her hair.

Tate's heart rolled over in his chest. He was conscious of the stained jeans and shirt. He always seemed to look like a mess when he met her.

"Hey!" he said, rising from his crouch next to the bike. He grinned and reached for a clean rag to wipe his hands. "A thinking walk?"

"Just a walk. I spend too much time sitting at the bench." She looked past him and gestured to the bike. "I never saw you as a Harley kind of guy."

He grinned. "Ah, yes. Sober, hard-working business owner has a dark side."

"Looks like an older one." Cassie stepped closer to the Harley.

Tate was surprised. "You know bikes?"

She shook her head slightly. "Not really. A bit about Harleys." A half smile. "You couldn't live with Jim and not know about Harleys. I'm pretty sure he was born on one."

"What did he have?"

"Panhead. From the late '60s, I think. I only know he had it when he first came to live with us." She ran her hand over the seat of the big bike. "Jim used to take me for rides on the pillion. As his co-pilot, he said." She grinned at him. "You don't really tell a nine-year-old she's 'riding bitch,' at least not around my mom and Nora, if you want to live."

Tate laughed out loud. "No, I can imagine not."

Cassie smiled, her eyes on the bike. "I used to close my eyes, feel like I was flying." Her smile had turned sad. "That's when I knew Jim was really gone. When they found his bike, burned, in the desert. Nothing less than death would have separated him from it."

"I'm sorry for your loss," he said quietly.

She took a deep breath. "Yeah, thanks. Me, too."

A blue jay flew by squawking into the silence between them.

Another deep breath and Cassie looked up at him. "Somehow I wouldn't have thought of you living up here.

Very...yuppie. Not a Harley kind of neighborhood. Must thrill your neighbors when you fire it up."

Tate raised his eyebrows and grinned. "Yeah, well, a few have mentioned it."

Cassie glanced toward the house. "Looks like you're doing a lot of work."

Tate followed her glance. The house was about forty years old and had been a rental for a long time. Some of the screens were torn and the paint was peeling. The oleanders had completely swallowed the fence, which had partially collapsed, and the shrubs against the house, those that weren't dead, were half-strangled with grass. Though he'd mowed what passed for lawn, it was obviously a field of weeds.

"The ultimate fixer upper," he said. "I wanted to be close to the restaurant, but," he rubbed his thumb against the first two fingers of his right hand. "Everything I had went into the business." He waved a hand at the house. "This was a foreclosure. It's been pretty trashed inside and out. Old TVs, busted furniture and appliances inside and in the yard. The carport was falling down. Domingo and I tore that out." He pointed to the left of the house. "Ripped out carpets, blinds, drapes."

"Domingo lives with you?"

"Did," said Tate, "when he first came out. We spent a couple months at night ripping out the worst of it, fixing walls, replacing door frames." He grinned. "Arguing."

"That explains the dumpster."

"That's actually the fourth dumpster."

"Fourth?" Cassie asked, surprised.

"It was bad." Tate gestured to the metal container in the yard. "This one is for the yard crew coming this week to cut things back. That should go some way to reassuring my neighbors that I'm an improvement on the last occupants."

The timer on the porch went off.

"Time for you to leave for work?" she asked.

"Time to pull the quiche from the oven."

She laughed. "Real men *do* eat quiche, then?"

"No," he said seriously, then grinned. "Real men *cook* them."

"I'll leave you to your breakfast." She turned to leave.

"Cassie." Tate put his hand out toward her. "Why don't you join me? I have coffee, corn muffins, quiche. Ambience is lacking, but food's good. At least, I hope it's good." He quirked a smile at her. "I'm hoping to be a chef."

Cassie hesitated. *She's going to say no*, he thought, disappointment already rising.

"Actually," she said, "that sounds great. I'm starving."

He smiled broadly, feeling ridiculously light inside.

"Come on in, then!" He waved her toward the house, snagging the timer from the stoop as he opened the door.

He paused just inside, waving a hand to the right toward a hallway. "A couple bedrooms down there," gestured forward, "living room straight ahead. Of course, you'll have to use your imagination." Right now the only thing there was a garage sale dinette set and two chairs.

The floors were bare wood, sanded but not yet finished. Large areas of white plaster showed where holes had been patched and sanded. "As I said," Tate told her, "a work in progress." He pointed up. When I first bought it, it had that horrible popcorn ceiling—with sparkles."

Cassie winced. "That must have been ugly to get down."

"Oh, I had that done," he said. "There is a limit to my insanity."

"You and Domingo did it all?"

"Most of it, though I had someone in to sand the floors, too." He shrugged. "Have to balance expenditures of time and money."

"You have more talents than just cooking," she said, and

Tate thought he heard surprise as well as approval in her voice.

He lifted a shoulder. "I've done a little of a lot of things. A lot of times I worked in small start-ups. We had to decorate on a small budget. Helped fix up one kitchen after a fire." Another small shrug. "I picked up just enough to get me into trouble. Sometimes, when I couldn't find a cooking job, I could find one swinging a hammer."

Cassie pointed to the sliding glass door in the living room that led to a broken patio, dead shrubs. "Not into yard stuff, though?"

"I can do the maintenance," he said, "As long as it's not fancy. But I don't know what to save and what's weeds." He nodded toward the yard. "But that's not half as bad as when I moved in."

"Wow."

"Yeah," he said. "Kitchen's in here." Tate pointed to the left through an arched doorway.

"Holy cow!" she said, as she stepped into the room. "Guess I can tell what's important to you."

There was slate tile on the floor, new stainless steel appliances—two ovens, a cooktop with five gas burners, double door fridge, dishwasher. The cabinets were of some polished warm wood. Racks of herbs and spices were visible through the glass in one cupboard. The walls were white, the counter, gray marble. The one spot of color: a red KitchenAid mixer.

"You really don't rest, do you?" she said.

"Since my mom taught me, I've never really stopped," he said, as he pulled the quiche out of the oven and put it onto a rack on the counter. He put a small pan on the stove, poured in a bit of milk, and turned the heat on low.

"Plates?" asked Cassie. Tate pointed.

He watched her as she opened the cupboard door and pulled the stoneware plates down. Something warm filled his chest to see her moving in his kitchen, like she'd always been there.

She found him staring when she turned back.

"What?"

"Nothing," he said. "Silverware in the drawer over here. No napkins. Paper towels?"

"The epitome of elegance," she said, laughing, and tore off a couple sheets. Tate cut the quiche and put the slices onto the plates. He turned off the heat under the milk.

"Is this a new recipe?"

He shook his head. "No. Tried and true. Comfort food." He put the plates on a tray, then pulled the corn muffins out of a warming drawer, tumbled them into a basket and tucked them in with a napkin.

"A tray," she said. "And a blankie for the muffins. Now I've seen everything."

He grinned as he poured coffee into a couple mismatched mugs. "Cream?" he asked, then lifted the pan off the range. "Or join me in a *café au lait*?"

"Black, please," she said. "But lots of sugar."

He poured milk into his coffee, pulled the sugar bowl out and handed it to her. "Save a little for me," he said, smiling.

"Did you learn that in France?" she asked, pointing to his coffee.

"What?"

"Heating the milk?"

"Afraid I did. If you'll grab the mugs," he said, as she doctored her coffee, "I'll take the tray. "Let's eat outside. Inside reminds me of too much work to do. Of course, the yard's not much better."

They settled on the front stoop and ate companionably for a while Cassie asking him questions about the quiche, complimenting the muffins.

"So, have you always had Harleys?" she asked, nodding toward the bike before she took the last bite of quiche.

"Almost," he said. "Had a Honda 250 first, but not for long. A friend's father collected bikes. He had an old Sportster. Said I could have it if I could fix it, but I had to buy my own parts. Man, I must have lived at junk yards. Finally got it going." He shook his head and grinned. "It wasn't a 'hot' bike, but I loved it. It took me all over the states. Sold it before I went to Europe." He nodded at the one in the drive. "I didn't think I'd be able to get another. They're not cheap. But a friend in New York knew a woman whose husband had died. She'd always hated his bike. Just wanted to get rid of it. I got it for a song."

Cassie nodded, picking up another corn muffin. "That was lucky. Tia said you had some tough times in France."

Tate looked at her for a long moment.

"What did Tia tell you?" he asked finally.

Cassie stopped chewing at the tone in his voice. "Nothing," she said. "Just that. I'm not fishing," she said hurriedly. "If you don't want to talk about it..."

"No, it's okay," said Tate. He looked out at the street, the Harley sparkling in the sun. What could he, should he, say about Avril?

All of it, his subconscious prompted.

"I was married," he said, not looking at her, but he felt her go still. "Her name was Avril. French. I was twenty-two. She was twenty-seven. I had gotten on in the kitchen of an important restaurant in Paris. I was full of myself and flattered that a beautiful, sophisticated, older woman would take an interest in me." He glanced at her, gave her a small crooked smile. "You'll remember I said I wasn't smart." Cassie didn't smile back.

"We got married quickly, and within a year, she'd lost that

interest. She found out I didn't want to be a high-profile chef. I wasn't interested in being world renowned. Instead, I planned to come back here and open a small restaurant of my own." He shook his head. "She flipped," he said bitterly. "Couldn't see living out her life in a small beach town. She wanted a bigger stage."

He set his plate and empty mug on the tray behind them. "She got even by cheating on me with a friend of her father's. He has lots of money. The kind Avril wanted. The divorce was ugly. And costly." The vicious words Avril had shouted at him still echoed in Tate's mind.

"Were you married long?"

"Three years. Though we only lived together about twenty months of that."

"Not long."

"Seemed like forever. Especially after it went south."

"But even after that, you paid for Tia's schooling," Cassie said quietly.

Tate ducked his head. He wished Tia hadn't said anything about that. "Yeah, well. Tia made it sound like more than it was. She worked while she was going to school. She had roommates. She paid for most of it. I just helped fill in the gaps."

"Still. She said you weren't able to go to the cooking school, like you'd planned."

Tate shrugged. "She deserved a chance to do what she wanted. And maybe schooling would have given me some polish. It certainly would have been more systematic. But I've worked with some of the best." He gave her the crooked grin again. "So might as well dive in the deep end, right?"

He got a faint smile in return.

"Tia seems a bit...unsettled...right now," said Cassie. "Does that bother you? After you helped pay for school?"

"You mean because first it was art, then biology, then landscape architecture, and now working in a nursery?"

"Yeah. Pretty much," said Cassie wrinkling her nose.

Tate sat up and stretched. How on earth did this woman get him to talk about this stuff?

"Yeah, a bit. At first. If I'm honest. But she gave it a couple years. And people get bitter if they're forced to stay in a career they hate, don't you think?"

Cassie laughed, stacked her dishes on the tray with Tate's. "I'm hardly one to ask," she said. "My whole life has been spent around people who do pretty much what they want and damn the consequences." She smiled at him, then leaned forward, hands on the edge of the stoop on either side of her, and put her face up to the sun.

"I think you and I were both pretty lucky. Finding what we wanted to do with our lives when we were young," she said.

"Not being nosy," said Tate, though he was. "Have you been married?"

Cassie shook her head. "Some loser boyfriends. But no loser husband."

They sat there quietly for a moment. "You talked about your 'non-traditional' family the other day, but you haven't mentioned your sister," Tate finally said. "Is she an artist, too?"

Cassie stiffened and went still.

"I'm sorry," Tate fumbled. "Tia mentioned her. I shouldn't have said anything. Forget I asked."

"Sissy," she said quietly. She leaned back and put her hands in her lap. "She wasn't my sister," she said after a long pause. "She was one of our roommates." Cassie was looking across the yard in the direction of his bike, but Tate knew she was seeing a past that was painful.

"I'm sorry," he said again, but Cassie didn't seem to hear him.

"She lived with us for...maybe a year?" Cassie frowned slightly. "I was something like seven? Eight?" A small shrug. "Sissy...always seemed to be listening for voices from somewhere else. She was like an abused kitten. Frightened, but somehow hopeful. Willing to believe. Wanting desperately to be loved. Never finding enough of it." Cassie closed her eyes, almost in a wince, then dropped her gaze to her lap. "Something horrible had happened to her. I don't know what. No one ever told me. Certainly not when I was so young. When I got older...well, I didn't want to know." She stopped a moment as a lone sea gull flew overhead, crying.

"She was small. Not much bigger than I was then. Blondy-brown hair that was always in her eyes. They were literally sky blue. She had beautiful hands." Cassie leaned to the side of the stoop, plucked a long blade of grass, and twirled it. "She used to brush my hair until I was almost hypnotized." Cassie smiled sadly at the whirling grass stem. "Mom said it was the only time I'd sit still."

A long moment passed in silence.

"What happened?" Tate finally asked.

Cassie shrugged. "One day she just went out and never came back. She never said good-bye." Cassie tore the grass stem in half. "Mom and Nora couldn't find her, though I know they looked. Later, when I was older and asked, Mom said someone had probably offered her drugs or love or both, and off she went." Cassie brushed the ends of the broken stem together. "She was the first person I ever lost. The others moved out, moved on. Had other lives. Said good-bye. Sissy." She shook her head. "Sissy just disappeared."

Like Jim, he thought.

"I'm sorry, Cassie." Tate ached to pull her to him and comfort her. He even lifted a hand toward her. But this pain was hers. Hers and her family's. Instinctively, he knew touching her would be a mistake. "You've had a lot of loss," he said simply, dropping his hand.

Cassie took a breath and tossed the grass stem pieces aside.

"My mom used to say loving means losing. If you don't love, you can't lose. But if you don't love, you've already lost."

She sighed.

"Sometimes, though, I wonder how often you can lose before you can't love anymore." She looked at him, sadness in the lines around her dark eyes. "Too much scar tissue."

Too much fear of the loss? he wondered.

"Have you gotten there?" he asked quietly.

"Sometimes it feels like it. You?"

"Sometimes," he said. He leaned forward, forearms on knees. "Then I meet you, and I wonder."

Tate's heart thumped hard. He had not planned to say that. He wasn't even sure he admitted it to himself. *But I'm not taking it back*, he decided. He turned his head sideways to look at her.

She was watching him. She nodded once, straightened and stood. "I'd better get to the shop," she said, bending to reach for the tray of dishes.

Tate put his hand on her arm and smiled. "I'll get them. I've had a lot of experience busing dishes," he said.

She straightened up again, smiling. "Thanks for breakfast." She nodded at the house. "Good luck with the work in progress."

"Thanks."

"...and the neighbors."

He laughed. "Thanks again."

Cassie smiled at him once more, then turned and walked across the lawn. As she reached the Harley, she put a hand out to stroke the handlebars.

Tate called out, "Cassie?"

She turned.

"Would you go riding with me some day? Co-pilot?"

She hesitated, then nodded. "I'd like that," she said. She waved, turned, and headed down the street.

Tate grinned for the rest of the day.

<h1 style="text-align:center">CHAPTER 16</h1>

CASSIE SLIPPED A HEAVY, SILVER CUFF bracelet—intricately carved and pierced—onto her left wrist, enjoying the weight against her skin. What good was being a jeweler if she didn't make herself a piece now and then? A ring set with a carved turquoise went onto her middle finger. She added two rings on her right hand—a plain carved band on her thumb and, on her ring finger, the rhodolite garnet ring she'd finished recently. The bold—and expensive—decision she'd made to add a gold bezel around the stone and a gold inlay down one side had paid off. She was very pleased with the way it had come out and hoped someone would buy it soon.

The turquoise ring echoed the brilliant blue of her slip dress. That and the reddish purple of the rhodolite picked up the colors in the thigh-length woven jacket that Nora had made for her the year before. She gave her hair a last brushing —tonight she was leaving it to fall in waves down to the middle of her back—and stepped into deep purple, open-toed pumps.

Grabbing a handbag, woven to match the jacket and

trimmed with leather by a craftsman she knew from the Pepper Tree, she stepped back to check out her appearance in the mirror. She smiled. No basic black for her.

Her heart beat nervously. She hadn't seen Tate for almost a week, except when he occasionally passed her front window and waved. They hadn't talked since that morning at his house. She wondered what Tate would think of her tonight.

Dangerous thinking, girl, she thought and smiled at her reflection again.

She and Nora moved into the hall at the same time.

"Wow," said Nora. "I'd forgotten you clean up so nicely."

"I think that's a compliment," said Cassie.

Nora smiled. "The turquoise earring is new, isn't it?"

"It is. Finished it this afternoon." The clear turquoise stud, surrounded by a beaded pattern, was connected with a chain to the ear cuff above it on her right ear. Three small, reddish purple garnets, in graded tones, were in her left. She assumed Tia would be at the opening tonight. She was determined to prove to Tate's sister that garnets were something very special, not old-fashioned and boring.

At the thought of Tate, Cassie's stomach fluttered. She wasn't sure she'd eat anything tonight. And she wasn't sure this new feeling about Tate wasn't going to get her into trouble she did not want.

The last few nights, though, she'd found herself thinking that a little romance might not be a bad thing.

"I suppose it's too late to claim a stomachache," said Cassie, citing her favorite get-out-of-school-free excuse.

Nora narrowed her eyes. "If you were going to use that excuse, you should have done it before you got dressed up. Remember, if nothing else, we're promoting both our businesses." Nora tapped her on the arm. "This can be a two-way street, you know."

Cassie looked thoughtful. "Hmm, you're right. Free food

and a chance to promote our businesses. Tate should do this more often."

Nora looked at her. "Actually," she said, "that could be half of a good plan."

Surprised, Cassie said, "I was joking. But you're not?"

"No," said Nora, "though I don't know yet what I mean."

"Oh, well," said Cassic. "So glad you clarified that."

Nora laughed and slapped her on the arm. "Lead on, girl. I'm hungry."

Outside they climbed into the Rabbit and headed downhill. Cassie's stomach was definitely fluttering now and her hands felt damp on the steering wheel.

She dropped Nora off at the door, helping her out of the car and getting her settled on her crutches. She was surprised to see great windows folded back on either side, leaving the center like an entry arch. There were already a lot of people there, some Cassie recognized, though many others were strangers. *Think promotion*, she told herself. *Be a walking ad for my jewelry and Nora's textiles. Don't think about Tate.*

Easier said than done. She'd done little *but* think about Tate lately. It frightened her a bit. She'd made so many bad choices in the past.

She found a place to park at a lot on Canyon and walked back to the restaurant through the alley. As she got to the Ocean Avenue end, she realized that the restaurant opened on this side of the building as well. A half wall separated the alley from a patio just outside the bar. Live music flowed from inside—something Caribbean, she thought—complemented by the chuckling sound of water in a fountain on the patio. Tall space heaters took the chill off the air, and a few people were already sitting at tables.

There was no access this way—probably to control customers. So she walked through a new arbor at the sidewalk, then around to the front.

Nora was waiting for her just inside the door where a *maître d'* was taking invitations. Cassie glanced around and saw the bar in the back left corner near the outside patio. Anna and another two bartenders were hard at work. As Anna served a customer, she happened to glance up and saw Cassie and Nora. She smiled widely. Cassie lifted a hand and smiled back. Then Anna was back to her work.

"Ah, Cassita, I should have run away with you when I had the chance," said a voice at her elbow. "You became beautiful."

She turned to see Fernando, her favorite of Anna's brothers, and his wife Magdalena, hugely pregnant with their third child. Lena rolled her eyes.

"Nandito!" Cassie laughed and hugged him. "I can see your father letting that happen. It was bad enough when he caught us kissing." Fernando, the Casanova of Eden Beach High had surprised everyone by growing up, straightening out, and becoming an immigration lawyer.

Fernando laughed. "Yeah. I spent three months in the barn, shoveling shit, for that. I still don't know why he didn't hand you a shovel, too."

"He loves me," said Cassie. "And besides, I cried."

They laughed, and Cassie hugged Lena around their soon-to-be-third, while Fernando hugged Nora. "Nora," he asked her, "Do you need to sit?"

"Not for a while yet," said Nora. She turned to Lena. "I want to hear about the kids."

"The four-year-old who's discovered the power of credit cards, or the two-year-old I'm giving away?" Lena asked shaking her head.

"Credit cards?"

"Yes. When I tell her no, she can't have something, it's 'Mama, just put it on plastic.'"

Nora laughed. "Where did she learn that?"

Lena tipped her head toward Fernando, who grimaced and produced a mock embarrassed shrug. The women laughed again and started to talk about the kids.

"Your parents are here?" Cassie asked Fernando.

"Of course," said Fernando. "Dad still thinks he has to keep an eye on Anna even though I saw Dale a little while ago. I think half of Eden Beach is here." He leaned close to her ear. "Including the piranha."

Anna had apparently told him Cassie's name for Carla Towne.

"I should have guessed that," she said quietly, "she's his realtor. And she knows all the 'best,'" her hands made air quotes, "people in Eden Beach. And Newport. He'd be foolish not to ask her and all her pals. But if she's smart, she'll stay away from me, especially if there are knives on the tables."

Fernando shook his head sadly. "Ah, Cassie, Cassie. You don't say things like that to an attorney."

She smiled at him, then glanced around. "It's a beautiful place," she said.

The restaurant was huge, with excellent lighting—bright but not blinding. The greenish-gray-blue slate floor rose up the walls about waist high. Above that was whitewashed wood. The tables and chairs were covered in blue and white. Beautiful plant groupings softened the corners and edged a fountain against the wall to Cassie's right. The walls on either side of the fountain were bare except for set-in alcoves. In each was a selection of pottery.

Cassie suddenly clapped a hand over her mouth, and tears sprang to her eyes.

"Cassie? What is it?" asked Fernando. She didn't appear to hear him.

She reached out for Nora's arm. "Nora," she said, "Oh my god, Nora, look." She pointed. Nora turned. Lena and

Fernando followed their gaze. In some of the wall niches around the room were Beth Franklin's pots, plates, and bowls, unmistakable in their porcelain and delicate glazing.

"Yeah, shocked me, too, at first," said Anna who'd escaped from the bar momentarily and come to her side. "Tate's mom was a collector, I guess. He has a ton of it. Not just Beth's, but some people who are really big names now." She slipped her arm into Cassie's. "I like it," she went on. "It'll be like seeing your mom every day. God, I miss that woman."

Cassie couldn't speak. She just nodded. Finally, she said, "You should have warned me."

"No time. He and Tia just put them up today." She said something in rapid Spanish to Fernando.

He turned to Nora who seemed rooted to the spot.

"Nora?"

"It's still some of the most beautiful work in Eden Beach, isn't it?" she said quietly to Cassie.

"Yes, it is." Cassie agreed.

"Fernando," said Nora, "I will take that seat now." Fernando nodded, winked at Cassie, and he and Lena guided Nora to a table.

"I'll bring you a drink, Nora," called Anna.

"Thanks, Anna. I need it," said Nora over her shoulder.

Suddenly, Cassie was standing alone. She looked around, knowing she was looking for Tate and cursing herself for wanting to see him. Instead, she saw Lou Pallis standing at the bar at the same time he saw her. He lifted his glass to her, pointed at it, and raised an eyebrow. She smiled, nodded, and began to work her way through the crowd.

As she did, she caught a glimpse of a group of blond heads. Tia and Tate were laughing at something. Laughing politely with them was Carla Towne, close to Tate's side. Cassie's steps faltered as she realized Carla had her hand tucked proprietarily in the bend of Tate's elbow. Tate said something to the people with them, then patted Carla's hand where it rested on his arm.

Cassie's smile suddenly felt twisted. She was sure her heart stopped for a moment, then her ears buzzed as all the blood in her body raced to her face, burning her with embarrassment.

Carla looked up at Tate, said something, and gave him a soft shoulder butt.

Again, thought Cassie. *I fell for it again.*

Tate had acted as if his world would disintegrate if Cassie did not come to the opening. She'd opened her heart and her past to him. The morning he gave her breakfast, she'd asked him if he felt he'd closed his heart to love. "Sometimes," he'd said, and added, "then I meet you, and I wonder."

How he had taken her in.

He'd acted so angry about his wife cheating on him. Now he was asking Cassie out when he obviously had something going with Carla.

He had from the beginning. She remembered Delia relaying Margot's gossip about the two of them.

Anger surged through her, replacing her embarrassment. Once again, she'd fallen for a liar.

Her heart twisted in her chest.

Fine, she thought. *At least now I know what he is.*

She turned away and continued to the bar, determined not to let anyone see what she was feeling. Especially Lou, Mr. Gossip. *Think promotion*, she reminded herself. *Be a walking ad for my jewelry and Nora's textiles. Focus on that.*

"Lou," she said, walking up to him and giving him her biggest smile. "Good to see a familiar face."

"Can I buy you a drink?"

"I thought Tate was buying."

"He is. That's why I'm offering." Lou smiled at her.

"Ah, Lou, you sweet talker. How can I turn down an offer

like that?" She turned to ask one of the bartenders for something non-alcoholic and found Anna standing there.

"You have a choice," said her friend.

"Oh?" asked Cassie.

"You can have that pre-sweetened stuff you always drink. I told Tate he had to have it here for you, just in case." She put a glass in front of Cassie. "Or, you can have this."

"And this is...?"

"Try it."

Cassie picked it up and sipped. Her eyes got wide.

"This is fantastic! Is that lavender I taste?"

"Yep. House specialty."

"I could get used to this," she said to Anna. "Thanks."

Anna winked and turned away to help someone else.

"So, what's this I hear about you making a stab at the Masters?" said Lou.

"How did you hear that?" asked Cassie, surprised.

"It's Eden Beach," said Lou matter-of-factly. "There are no secrets."

"I'm sorry that got out," said Cassie ruefully. "Now everyone will know, too, when I don't get in."

"Now, now," said Lou, shaking his finger at her playfully. "That's not the right attitude."

"Temporary insanity was the attitude that got me into this," she said.

"You'll get in," he said.

She shook her head. "I don't think so, Lou. Not with my current work. I'm trying to break into something new but everything I try crashes and burns. Some of the ideas I have, they have potential, but I just don't have the skills to carry them off. And I have no way of getting the skills in the next few weeks before Sean's due to shoot them. I started too late, I'm afraid...under duress," she added, as Anna came up to refill her glass.

"Don't look at me," said Anna. "I've got my own duress," and she moved away.

Lou looked puzzled.

"Ah, I see the smoke signals didn't mention that," she said to him. "Anna's applying, too."

"Fantastic!" said Lou his eyes going wide. He caught Anna's eye and raised his glass in a salute. Anna threw her hands up in a what-was-I-thinking gesture. Lou laughed. "She's the best painter in Eden Beach. Don't tell her I said that."

"I agree," said Cassie, and grinned.

"And you're a fine jeweler," said Lou. "I can't say 'the best,' because you're talking to him."

Cassie laughed out loud. "And modest, too."

Lou shrugged. "I simply speak the truth."

"Ah, well, then. I'll take your praise as high praise."

"Do," said Lou, becoming serious. He leaned close to her and put his hand on her arm. "Cassie, Jim gave you great skills. But in the design department, you've far surpassed him. Don't sell yourself short. Keep going. Do whatever it takes to get into the Masters. If you need help learning anything to make a vision come out, just ask. I'll be happy to teach you anything you need to know." He paused. "Because, of course, we all know that I know everything."

Cassie felt tears in her eyes. She had not expected that. "I...thank you," she said. "That means a lot." Then she asked him, "Lou, why did you give up the Masters?"

He grinned and stepped back. "You know me. I'm not much of a team player. I kept pissing off too many people." He shrugged. "Like anything else of that kind, there's a lot of bullshit I didn't want to put up with, and I couldn't keep my mouth shut."

He took a drink, then smiled at her look of dismay.

"That's what I tell people," he said. "Really? I just didn't like the long hours. Working the show, working the shop, paying for someone to sit my booth when they didn't give a damn about my work. It's hard when you're a one-person shop. You'll find that out. But," he said when he saw her face, "it built my name, brought me a good client base and, after a few years, I was able to bail out and become the jeweler godfather I was meant to be."

Cassie laughed.

"Cassie?" said a voice next to her. She turned to find Tia.

Cassie smiled with genuine pleasure. Even though Tate was a duplicitous snake, she really liked his sister. "Tia! It's good to see you." She introduced Tia to Lou.

"Pleasure," he said. "But if you ladies will excuse me, I see a client of mine who has not dropped a lot of money with me lately, and I think schmoozing is in order." He slipped into the crowd.

"I'm glad you came," said Tia. "I don't know anyone except Anna and Domingo, and they're both working like mad. Tate has to work the crowd, and I feel a little lost." She nodded toward her brother on the other side of the room. Cassie followed her glance and noticed that Carla was still glued to Tate.

It was on the tip of her tongue to ask Tia about Tate and Carla, but as she turned to the younger woman, Tia said, "Cassie I wanted to ask you..." She hesitated.

"Yes?"

"Well, I really enjoyed working with you the other day. Carving that wax. It made me remember how much I enjoyed my sculpture classes. I wondered..." Another hesitation. "I wondered if I could come back, sometime, and maybe you could show me more? Only if it's convenient," she hurried to add.

Cassie's heart plunged. Tia couldn't have picked a worse time. If it wasn't bad enough she was trying to create new work and keep the business going, Cassie didn't want to give Tate any reason to come to the shop.

The refusal was forming, but the hope on Tia's face made her pause. She'd told Tate they'd been lucky to find their life's work early. But Tia was obviously floundering.

It will probably only be a couple times, anyway, she thought.

"Sure," replied Cassie. "That would be fun." And it *would* be fun to have company, to teach someone else the way Jim taught her. It would be sad, though, when Tia found out how hard the work was, *or when she finds out how despicable I think her brother is*, and decided not to come back.

Tia beamed. "Good!" she said. "I have Tuesdays off. Would that work?"

"That would be perfect," said Cassie. "Tuesdays are usually quiet."

"Great," said Tia, her smile blazing. "So have you tried any of the food?"

Cassie shook her head. "Only what your brother brought for lunch the other day."

Tia grinned. "Then you have an experience in front of you! Come on." She took Cassie by the arm, and they wove their way through the crowd. Cassie glanced over and saw Tate was now sitting with Nora. He'd apparently brought a spread of food to her. Cassie's heart seized painfully. Then she flushed with anger to see him manipulating Nora. Nora was usually very good at reading people, but Tate had apparently fooled her, getting her to think Cassie was important to him.

"Tia!" A middle-aged couple stopped her. "I'm so delighted to see you here," said the woman.

"Mrs. French."

"I was so surprised to hear Tate was back in town. And with his own restaurant! Your father must be so proud. Is he here?" The woman craned her neck, looking around the room.

"No," Tia told her, shooting a panicked look at Cassie that clearly said, *I hope not*.

"Come join us," Mrs. French said, taking Tia's other arm. "I want to hear about all your adventures. Craig's with us. He just finished at Stanford Law. You remember Craig. You two used to have such good times."

"Mrs. French, I was just taking my friend to the buffet..."

The woman gave Cassie the barest glance. "Oh, I'm sure she won't mind. Old friends catching up and all."

Tia looked helplessly at Cassie. "I'll find you later," she said. "See you Tuesday?"

Cassie nodded firmly. "See you then."

Tia let herself be dragged away, and Cassie went across to the buffet table.

Tate had outdone himself. It not only smelled wonderful, it looked fantastic. Hundreds of small samples of entrées, hors d'oeuvres, breads, desserts, all labeled. No wonder she hadn't seen him. He must have been here twenty-four hours a day for the last week.

She didn't want to see him, she reminded herself. She reached determinedly for a plate.

Cassie was looking over the selection when two women stepped up behind her. She didn't pay much attention to their conversation until one of them said, "Looks like Can't-Keep-'Em-Carla has finally found one."

The other woman snorted. "About time. Her 'best-by' date is long past." They snickered.

"She sure went through them in school," said the first voice.

"No kidding. She took a couple of mine."

"You, too? Hard to believe she's snuggling up to that one, though. A chef. Must be getting desperate."

"Getting smart."

"Oh?"

"Yeah. Dave said she's looking for a money man. Things apparently aren't going smoothly with Daddy."

"Really."

"Yeah. She wants to go out on her own, start investing in large properties. She tried to get Dave to back her. I put the 'no' on that. She also tried Phil Trainer, I hear."

Cassie felt herself stiffen as she looked at the desserts.

One of them laughed. "Wonder if Jana knows that."

"Probably not. Heard she's buying her new house from Carla."

"Someone should really mention it to her, don't you think?"

"Oh, she might come to hear of it. Jana and I have the same stylist." They both snickered again.

"So, you think this restaurant guy has enough money?"

"He's Martin Garner's son."

"Oooooh." The single syllable was drawn out, up and down the scale, heavy with significance. "And he's not hard to look at."

"Not a bad cook, either. Have you tried that little wrap thing? With the bacon? Every calorie worth it."

"Not for me, then. We've got that cruise next week. I don't want to be wearing it at the pool."

Cassie finished filling her plate and turned to find Nora.

She was dismayed to see that Tate was still sitting at the table. It looked like he was talking comfortably to Fernando and Lena.

Cassie put a bland smile on her face, making sure her emotions were carefully tucked away.

Tate stood, as she walked up, and smiled. "I'm so glad you came," he said.

"Quite the event," she said, sitting in the chair he pulled out. "Looks like a success."

Tate made a face. "We won't know until they start coming back."

"The food is remarkable, Tate," said Lena. "I'm sure people will come back."

"It's beautiful, too," said Cassie. "I agree with Lena. You'll soon have it packed."

Tate seemed to hear the polite ambivalence in her mild response. He looked at her curiously. Nora glanced between them. Cassie had the feeling Nora was waiting for an explosion and was trying to figure out how to prevent it.

"Thanks," said Tate. "Cassie." He leaned closer, putting his hand on her arm. Cassie flushed despite her determination not to let him move her. She carefully controlled her breathing and resisted the urge to lean into him. Instead, feeling Nora's eyes on her, she tipped her head attentively.

"Nora was telling me we have some of your mom's pottery on display."

"You do," she said. "Mom would be flattered."

He gave her another puzzled look and a small frown.

"That big pot there?" He pointed. "I had to lug that all the way through Eden Beach to the car when she bought it. She kept telling me to be careful the whole way."

"It's really nice to see it on display."

Tate's smile slipped a bit. "Is something wrong?"

Now Fernando and Lena were watching. They'd known her too long.

"Not at all," she said.

I just wanted to believe, she thought. She'd wanted to talk to him late into the night, to ride that big bike with her arms tight around his waist, hear his heart beating.

She'd wanted to kiss him, and have him kiss her back.

She was mortified to think how close she'd come to making the same mistake.

She was such a damn fool.

Cassie reached for the last of her iced tea, gently disengaging Tate's hand.

Nora, bless her, stepped into the breach.

"You have the pottery," she said, "but you need a few paintings."

"Yes!" Tate turned back to Cassie. "Like those in your shop. Those are some of the most amazing paintings I've ever seen. Who painted them?"

Cassie glanced at Nora, and Nora grinned. Tate looked confused.

"Simply the best painter in Eden Beach," said Cassie.

Tate looked at Nora. "You?" he asked.

"No," said Nora and pointed across the room. "Your bartender. Anna."

Tate looked startled. "Anna?" he said. "Our Anna?"

"That's her," said Cassie.

"Unplumbed depths," he said.

Cassie smiled. Her heart was beating erratically. Whether from anger or desire she didn't know, but she decided anger was safer.

"But I asked her if she knew a painter she could recommend. She said she'd have to think about it."

"That's because I told her you'd consider her 'artsy.'"

Tate made a face at her. "You're not going to let me live that down are you."

"No," said Cassie simply. "But if you're going to buy some of her paintings—large ones—for your walls, then I think it's okay to tell you." *At least maybe Anna can come out of this a winner*, she thought.

Tate grinned at her and put his hand on hers. "You do look out for your friends, don't you?"

She nodded. "I do." *And I'm starting with me*, she thought.

"Tate! Tate, come here!"

Carla slipped between them, forcing Tate to move back,

withdrawing his hand. Her back to Cassie, Carla put her hand on Tate's shoulder, pointedly ignoring everyone else at the table. "There are some people you *have* to meet. I think they can do a lot to help publicize the restaurant."

Tate glanced up and stood. "Please excuse me," he said to Cassie and Nora. He nodded at Fernando and Lena.

Carla gave Cassie a smug look before she turned to tuck her hand into Tate's elbow.

Nora glanced at Cassie who looked back at her blandly. Cassie knew her look as much as said, *I told you so*, and she knew Nora heard her loud and clear.

Nora put up a hand. "Don't say it."

"Okay, so I'll ask," said Cassie. "How did your people reader go so astray?"

Nora shook her head. "He had me fooled."

Fernando looked between the two of them. "There's something your nosy attorney friend should know, isn't there?"

"No," said Cassie. "Not important."

"I'll pry it out of Anna."

Cassie gave him a look that said, *Try*.

"How are you?" Nora asked.

"I'm fine," said Cassie innocently. "How should I be?"

Nora raised an eyebrow and gave her the "mom" look.

Melody dropped into a chair next to them. "This is a great party!" she said. "The food! And the drinks are excellent!"

"Yes," said Fernando, "Nora, can I get you another one?"

"I'll go. I'm going to get more of this special iced tea." Cassie was already standing. "Nandito? Lena?"

Fernando shook his head. "I'm driving." Lena held up a glass half full of soda.

"Nothing for me," said Nora, so Cassie left them all talking fibers, weaving, and babies.

"I know what you'll have," said Anna, when Cassie had finally worked her way through the growing crowd.

"Yes, you do," said Cassie. "And I'll expect my commission," she added, as Anna reached under the bar into the fridge and pulled out a pitcher of tea.

"Why's that?" said Anna, pouring.

"I just sold a bunch of large paintings for you."

Anna's hand jerked as she looked up, startled. Tea splashed on her hand.

"Damn it!" she said.

"Tsk tsk. Where's Consuelo?" said Cassie as she mimed looking around the restaurant.

Anna was mopping up the tea with a bar towel. She grabbed another glass to pour Cassie a fresh one.

"Who'd you sell my paintings to?" asked Anna, handing Cassie the fresh glass.

"Tate. For the restaurant. Make the price high," she added, feeling a bit vindictive. "And make sure he agrees to put your name on the wall on a label."

"Are you my manager now?" asked Anna with a raised eyebrow.

"Payback," said Cassie. "For all those earrings you've sold for me." She held her hand up, palm out. Anna gave her a grin and a high five.

"Cassie, I'm surprised you're not having one of Anna's fine drinks," said Carla's voice at her elbow. Cassie saw Anna's face go blank as she turned to the realtor. Cassie knew she was thinking of poisoning the next drink she gave Carla.

"I don't drink," said Cassie pleasantly, seeing Tate at Carla's side.

"Oh," said Carla. "Of course not. Well, I can understand that, after what happened to your mother. I guess you *would* want to be extra careful. They say alcoholism can run in families."

Cassie saw the surprised look on Tate's face.

You think what you want, she thought with fury.

Cassie pointedly turned her back on Carla, and saw not poison, but knives in Anna's eyes. Her friend's lips were parted, but Cassie reached across the bar and laid her hand on Anna's, which was still around the iced tea glass. *Later*, she mouthed.

Anna narrowed her eyes, then raised an eyebrow, but nodded imperceptibly.

"Anna, I'll have…" Carla started to order, but Anna had deliberately turned her back to put the tea in the fridge. She walked down the bar to help another customer as Carla's request trailed off.

"Cassie," said Tate, as she turned to move away from the bar. She was saved from acknowledging him when she ran directly into Lou Pallis behind her. Lou was holding someone's arm.

"Cassie," said Lou, "I've got someone who wants to meet you. Millie Carter, Cassie Franklin.

Cassie held out her hand, giving Lou a puzzled look.

"Millie wanted me to make a ring like the one you're wearing," he said, gesturing to the rhodolite. "I told her to talk to the woman who made it."

"Oh, hon," gushed Millie, taking her hand. "Can you really make me one just like that?" she asked.

"Actually," said Cassie, slipping the ring off her finger and handing it to Millie, "you can buy this one. I just finished it yesterday."

"Oh," said Millie reverently, sliding it on to her finger.

"I told you she was one of the best jewelers in Eden Beach," said Lou to Millie.

From the corner of her eye, she saw Carla's tight face. The realtor turned away angrily, pulling Tate's arm.

"Do you show your work in the Masters?" asked Millie.

Cassie saw the hitch in Carla's step as the piranha half turned back.

Before Cassie could respond, Lou spoke up. "She will next summer," he told Millie.

"I'll be sure to come by your booth," Millie told her.

As Cassie and Millie began to talk sizing and price, Carla pulled Tate away.

When Cassie finally rejoined Nora, she was laughing with Fernando and Lena.

"Nandito," she said, as they stopped to catch their breaths, "Would you defend me if I killed someone?"

Nora looked at her.

"Who do you have in mind?" asked Nora, but Cassie suspected she knew.

"Carla Towne."

"Cassita," said Fernando, shaking his head. "I didn't hear that. But," he added, "If you need it, I'll give you the family discount."

The three women laughed out loud.

CHAPTER 17

"I'M LOOKING FOR Ms MONET."

Dale Quinn smiled, opened the door wide, and waved Cassie in. "She's in the studio. I think she's swearing, but that Spanish," he shook his head and grinned again, "I don't want to know. I'm staying as far away as possible."

Cassie eyed the paintbrush in his hand. "It looks like she's drafted you."

Dale laughed. "As if. I've got living room detail." He pointed to his right. The walls were about half finished in a dusty rose.

Cassie headed out through the kitchen. The brick patio was a small oasis of potted plants and bird feeders. The hillside behind the house was blackened, dotted with the fast growing shrubs and ground covers Dale and Anna had planted to hold the soil back in the winter rains. Cassie had been part of the "work crew"—Anna's family and friends of Dale's from the fire department—that had done the planting. She noticed that, since her last visit, new construction had started on the lots above.

Her friends had snagged the house the year before, after it had been damaged by the wildfire that threatened to sweep through Eden Beach to the sea. The previous owners had taken the insurance money, done a few cosmetic repairs, then bought elsewhere. Through the firefighter's grapevine, Dale and Anna had heard about the house before the developers and managed to buy it before it went on the open market. They were slowly repairing the fire damage, though, true artists, the first thing they did was put up two studios across the patio: one for him, one for her. Dale's was full of sawdust and wood chips, pieces glued and clamped, massive equipment. It was at least as big as Cassie's home.

Anna's white-walled studio was small, skylit, tidy, with French doors that opened to the patio. An alcove in the right hand wall held a large ceramic plate Cassie's mom had thrown many years before. Cassie had given it to Anna after Beth's death. The painting rack on the left wall was half full. The back wall was Anna's display area, where she hung paintings to think about them. She rarely let outsiders in. Dale, Cassie, Nora, and Consuelo were exceptions. Luis was allowed but rarely visited. Her brothers were banned.

Cassie spotted Anna through the open French doors. Her friend, barefoot, wearing a torn T-shirt over a red tank above ratty, paint-spotted cutoffs, was staring at a painting on the easel. Cassie knocked lightly on the door frame before stepping through the open doors. As Anna turned, Cassie glanced at the display wall and froze.

"Oh, Anna!" she breathed. There, in Anna's signature style, was the burned hillside with a few spring shoots coming back, the sky brilliant above. There was the fire itself—Anna and Dale had gotten far too close to it—brilliant, beautiful, and terrifying. But what caught Cassie's attention was the new work.

Cassie walked closer. Anna usually worked large—more than three or four feet square—and on canvas. The new pieces were all smaller, anywhere from four or five inches across to twenty inches, painted on wood. Some were painted very thinly, looking almost like old Masters with the paint wearing away. On others the paint surface was thick, quickly worked. They were all very intimate and personal. Though not realistic—Anna was prone to sneer at realism—it was clear to Cassie that these were scenes from the patio: the new growth in the burned ground, hummingbirds, the exuberant growth of the oleanders and geraniums. There was, she was sure, even the new construction.

"I take that as approval?" asked Anna.

"Oh, I very much approve," said Cassie. "You've never worked so small before."

Anna shrugged and walked over to stand next to Cassie. "I do when I'm making studies. I usually scrape them off, so you never see them. I like working small. It's quick and it's fun." She smiled. "If it's not fun, why bother? Right?"

Cassie laughed. It had been their guiding principle while growing up.

"Besides," Anna went on, "if it's a flop, I don't have so much time and money in them. So I thought I'd make some small studies, then work them to a finish instead of switching to a larger format."

"And use up some of Dale's scraps in the process."

"Yes, well, there is that, too. He's always stacking bits of cherry, oak, and walnut to the side, saying he'll figure out how to use them. I figured it out for him."

Cassie smiled at the thought of Anna raiding Dale's studio, then went back to studying the new paintings. Anna stood quietly by her side. Cassie kept coming back to two of them—one an intimate look at the fire, and one, she was sure, was a portrait of the Anna's hummingbirds that dominated the patio feeder. She pointed. "I want those two," she said. "Don't sell them to anyone else."

A brilliant smile split Anna's face. "Really? Cassie, you've never bought one of my paintings before."

"No, I never have, have I?" She looked at her friend, puzzled. "I love your work. I love having it in the shop, and I hate when it sells. But these two," she said, turning back to the paintings, "these two remind me of how much I love you. How I almost lost you," she said pointing at the blaze practically burning through the wood it was painted on.

She paused a moment, swallowed a couple times, and blinked back tears. She couldn't look at Anna. She'd been frantic that day, unable to find her friend, knowing she was in the fire zone. Dale had saved her life. And they'd fallen in love.

Cassie cleared her throat and managed to say, lightly, as she pointed to the hummingbird-like one, "And that one because it reminds me you are a force to be reckoned with, never to be denied."

She looked at Anna and saw tears in her eyes. Anna put her arms around Cassie and hugged her. "They're yours," she said huskily.

After a moment, Cassie stepped back, leaving her arm around Anna's shoulders. "So, which ones are you having Sean photograph for your entry?"

"Arrgh!" Anna drove her hands into her already spiky hair. "I don't know! I need you to help me figure it out."

For the next couple hours, Cassie listened to Anna give her the pros and cons of each painting. Eventually Anna picked out two of her large paintings and one of the small, new ones. Cassie, as always, gave them evocative titles. Left up to Anna, they'd have been "Untitled."

"I want the small ones in my shop until the Masters," Cassie said, after they'd raided the kitchen for snacks and drinks and dropped into patio chairs. Although invited to join them, Dale had elected to keep painting the living room. "Give them some display time. I'm pretty sure I can sell a bunch of them."

"Speaking of that," said Anna, dipping into Dale's home-made salsa on the table between them, "I thought you told me not to tell Tate I was a painter. So why did *you* tell him?"

"Did he buy any?"

"Four," said Anna, awestruck. "I've never sold that much at one time." She shook her head. "Not only that, he turned around and sold one of them just yesterday."

"Anna!" exclaimed Cassie, happy for her friend, but feeling a stab of anger at the thought of Tate. "Congratulations! That's double good news!" Anna grinned back at her.

"We've spent half the afternoon talking about my work," said Anna. "How's your work going? Any improvement?"

Cassie's face fell. "None." She sighed. "Anna, to tell you truthfully, I don't think I'm going to make it."

"Oh, no," said Anna. "I'm not listening. I'm not doing this on my own."

Cassie sat up and stared sternly at Anna. "Yes. You are. Those paintings deserve to be in the show." She shook her head and dropped back in her chair. "But my current work isn't enough. I know it. You know it. Even that piece of trash, Carla Towne knows it," she said bitterly.

"I don't know about that," said Anna. "I saw her swallow her tongue when you sold that ring the other night."

Cassie smiled at the memory. "I have to say, that was sweet."

"So, how are you going to break out of this?" asked Anna.

"I truly don't know," said Cassie sadly, smile fading. She watched the Anna's hummingbird chase away imagined threats. "I wish Lou hadn't told everyone I was applying. It'll be bad enough to fail, but to know Carla is smirking," she winced, "it's almost too much."

Anna leaned over and put her hand on Cassie's arm. "You have never failed," said Anna intently. "You won't now. You will figure something out."

"Anna, my photo shoot is scheduled in less than three weeks. It's the last possible date Sean could give me and still get the images done by the application date. Coming up with new, 'spectacular' work," she put her hands up as if framing the word for a camera, "not to mention making three pieces for the shoot, is, if I'm honest about it," she paused for a moment, not wanting to say the word, "impossible," she finished softly.

She looked through the French doors into Anna's studio, where she could see the paintings, abstract and evocative, filling the display wall. Despite Anna's words of support, she was filled with a crushing sense of defeat.

"Sometimes I wish we hadn't grown up," she said. "I wish I still had my chip on my shoulder and didn't feel this need to prove myself all the time."

Anna grabbed her hand. "You keep that chip right there on your shoulder," she said. "Those chips and the need to prove ourselves have gotten us this far, *mi amiga*. And don't you forget it."

Cassie gripped Anna's hand, pledging solidarity as they always had. "Just wish we didn't have to keep risking failure so publicly."

"*Hijole!*" said Anna, laughing, and sat back. "You've got that right."

They munched quietly for a minute, before Anna asked her, "So, what's this I hear about you training a new jeweler?"

"What do you mean?" Cassie was puzzled.

"Tia. She was almost on fire the other night, talking about you teaching her how to make jewelry."

Cassie smiled. "Yeah. She's really interested. I like her. She's nice."

"And her brother? He's nice, too?" Anna grinned at her.

Cassie broke a chip in half, nibbled it, and spent some time looking at the patio, watching Anna's namesake hovering, sucking up sugar water.

"I thought so, but not now," she said. Anger and embarrassment brought a flush to her cheeks.

"What are you talking about? I thought things were getting interesting. Little breakfast at his house..."

"Yeah. Well. That kind of ended when I saw him plastered to Carla the other night."

"I think you got it wrong, who was plastered to who."

"Whom." Cassie gave her friend a small smile.

Anna slapped Cassie on the arm with the back of her hand. "Oh, stop, Ms Dawson." Cassie chuckled.

"Anyway, you go riding with him. You'll find out just who he's interested in."

"Not happening."

"Yes, it will," Anna said with confidence.

"No. He asked me to go with him tomorrow. I said no. And not very nicely."

"What?" Anna's voice went up a notch.

So Cassie told her.

It had been a beautiful Saturday so the streets of Eden Beach were busy. Cassie had had a steady stream of customers and had sold a number of earrings and a pendant. She even had a new commission. She was daring to hope business might be turning the corner.

Tate showed up about 4 p.m. during a lull. Cassie was at the bench, pulling a tourmaline out of a pendant that needed the bail repaired.

"Quiet day," he said, when she looked up as the door pinged. His tilted smile lit his face.

Before she could get control of it, her heart started dancing with gladness to see him. That bright, crooked smile was going to be tough to get over. But as quickly as her heart started doing a little two-step, it plunged down to her toes. Anger replaced it.

"It's just slowed down," she said, keeping her voice noncommittal. She got up, tossed her magnifier back onto her chair, and went reluctantly to the security gate to meet him. She almost reached up to pull the pin from her hair as she usually did whenever she took a break. But that would send a message she didn't want to send. She stayed her hands, brushed imaginary dirt from her cheeks instead, then rested her hands on the gate. "The party the other night looked successful."

Tate smiled widely. "It was," he said. "We were packed for lunch yesterday and today. Last evening we were half full, but everyone seemed to enjoy the menu. We had a lot of compliments. And today, there was a review in the *Union-Tribune*. Turns out my mom's old friend, Sheila, brought someone who does restaurant reviews for them."

Cassie smiled. She couldn't help it. His enthusiasm was so transparent, it broke her heart. "I'm glad it went well," she said, and was surprised to realize she meant it.

"I don't want to keep you if you've been busy," said Tate, suddenly awkward. "But I wanted to ask you if you wanted to do that ride. I noticed from your sign," he turned to gesture at the front door, "that you're closed now on Mondays."

During the season, Cassie ran long hours, staying open six days a week, and until 8 p.m. on Fridays and Saturdays. She could usually catch some of the dinner trade, and it was often lucrative after people had had a few drinks. But starting in October, she shortened her hours, closing Mondays as well as Sundays until May. The extra day allowed her to make work to stock up for the Pepper Tree show and the summer trade, or simply to take a break.

When she hesitated, he said, "The weather is supposed to be good. I thought we could explore some of the canyons. Take a picnic." He smiled. "My quiche is good, even cold."

Reminding her of that morning, reminding her how much she'd wanted to fall for him—had fallen for him, if she were honest with herself, which she did not want to be—brought her anger to the surface.

"No, Tate, I don't think so," she said, tamping down the unwanted disappointment she felt.

"Would another day be better?" he asked.

"No, Tate. No day would be better. I don't need that kind of trouble."

"What do you mean, trouble?" he asked frowning.

"I mean Carla," she said.

"Carla?" he said, looking genuinely puzzled. "What's Carla got to do with this?"

Really? He's going to play it like this? she thought.

All disappointment evaporated, leaving only the anger.

"I'm talking about your involvement," she said. If he didn't hear the edge in her voice, he was deaf, she thought.

"There's nothing between me and Carla."

"I was there, Tate. At the open house," she said tersely. "It didn't look like nothing to me."

Tate waved his hand in negation. "Carla's just been helping publicize the restaurant. The open house was her idea. There is nothing there."

"Yes, I've heard that before," said Cassie. "I'm not getting involved in that again."

"What do you mean?" he asked. "Getting involved in what?"

"It's not important."

"It is to me, if it means you won't go out with me."

"It's not to me," she said. She was not going to talk about Phil. Not to Tate.

"Carla is an excellent choice for you." *If you want to have your head ripped off after sex*, she thought. "You two have a lot more in common than you and I could ever have. And she'll be able to help your business."

"Cassie, you're not listening to me."

"I don't have to," she said. "I have eyes. I can see." She could see him again, patting Carla's hand, jumping up to follow her around, willing to let himself be dragged off. Surprise and—judgement?—when Carla made the remark about alcoholism.

"But it's not what you think you see," said Tate, running a hand through his hair. The gesture ripped at her heart, fueling the fury.

How stupid do you think I am? She wanted to shout in his face. Instead, she took a deep breath, waiting until she knew she could sound rational.

"I'm not a fool, Tate. I will not be lied to and humiliated again," she finally said in her Margaret Hallstrom voice.

Her throat closed up, and she clamped her mouth shut. She was damned if she was going to cry. Not over another liar.

The door pinged, and her client with the great hair cut came in with her daughter.

"I have to go," said Cassie to Tate. She unlocked the gate and moved into the showroom.

"Peggy! Good to see you," said Cassie to the woman. "Is this Jenny?"

She didn't turn when Tate went out the door.

When she'd finished her story, Anna sighed. "Cassie, Cassie, Cassie," she said, shaking her head. "Tate isn't Phil. He's not married."

"So he says."

"Stop it, Cassie," Anna said gently. "You really have it bad, don't you?"

"I do not have it bad. Especially for someone attached to the woman who's trying to drive me out of my shop."

Anna shook her head. "You've got it wrong. You saw what Carla wanted you to see."

"He sure wasn't pushing her away. That's what I saw."

"What *I* saw," said Anna, "was how he watched you the whole time you were talking to Nandito and to Lou. Especially Lou. His ears were almost growing so he could hear what you were saying. He was itching to get away and come over to you. I also saw how Carla looked at you when you were talking to Tate. I'm here to tell you, girl, if looks could have killed, I'd be standing at your grave right now."

"That probably had more to do with her coveting my shop," said Cassie closing her eyes and leaning back in her chair, face to the sun. "Carla Towne has the money to buy anyone. Right now, she wants Tate, that's clear." She shrugged. "He looks happy to be sold."

Anna sighed. "Cassie Franklin, you can be incredibly exasperating."

"That's why you love me."

"I'm beginning to rethink that," said Anna, and Cassie smiled into the sunshine. "Anyway. You know what I mean. I think you should give Tate a chance."

"Anna," said Cassie, tiredly not opening her eyes. "In a perfect world—one without Carla—I would have given Tate more than a chance. But getting involved with someone who's in bed with her, figuratively, if not literally," the thought made her skin crawl, "is asking too much of me. I don't want that bitch in my shop screaming at me in front of customers. Like Jana Trainer. Though, maybe with luck, Carla will have Jana in her face, too."

"Oh?"

Cassie told her what she'd overheard at the open house.

Anna's eyes lit up. "So Carla is trolling for Phil Trainer? And looking to stab Alden in the back?"

"Sounded like it."

"It would be a public service to let people know, don't you think?"

Cassie could almost hear Anna's innuendo-laden conversations with customers at Lydia's.

"Don't. You'll get fired."

"Have I told you you're no fun anymore?"

"Repeatedly."

"So you see," Cassie went on, "it's more than Tate. Carla needs a pipeline to his father's money. The hunt for money is a blood sport to the Townes." She sighed. "I don't want to get caught up in that."

"Tate's dad has money?"

"His dad is Martin Garner." Anna shook her head, puzzled. "He's a big-shot financial guy. Loans money for monster business developments. Phil talked about him like the guy was almost a god."

Anna gave her a faint smile. "Your point?"

"He financed the Towne Center."

Anna stopped smiling. "Wow. That's what they call serious money."

"Yeah," said Cassie. "So if Carla's hoping to poke a stick in her father's eye, what better way to do it than getting backing from the same guy who financed him?"

Anna frowned. "Maybe. But I got the feeling Tate would just as soon run his dad down with a truck than ask him any favors. Why would Carla think he could give her access?"

"Oh, Anna. I don't know." Cassie waved a hand dismissively. She really didn't want to talk about this. "I just know it's something I don't want to get in the middle of."

"But Cassie..."

Cassie shook her head. "No. I have enough to worry about with the business. Not to mention everyone in town gossiping about my failure to get into the Masters."

Anna made a disgusted noise. "Cassie, no one gives a mouse fart for us or what we do or don't do."

Cassie shrugged again. "Maybe not. But maybe it's worked out for the best. I'm worried about Nora."

"What? What's wrong with Nora?" said Anna, concerned.

"She seems to be in more pain than usual lately. I can't get her to go to the doctor. You know she won't take the pain meds unless she's practically screaming. They make her fuzzy headed." She turned to Anna. "Nora needs me, Anna. I'm certainly not going to turn my back on her for a relationship that can go nowhere." *And that will only break my heart*, she thought.

Anna stared back at her. "I don't suppose you've asked Nora how she feels about this."

Cassie laughed derisively. "Nora is too independent to say she needs help, even if she does. She would tell me she could dance if she thought I was getting involved with someone. She's almost worse than you." She pointed at her friend.

Anna reached out and took Cassie's extended finger.

"Cassie," she said seriously. "Listen to me. Or I swear I'll sic my mama on you. You have to open your heart again. The last few years, you've been beat up." Anna held up the fingers on her other hand. "You lost your mom." She folded one finger. "Nora was hurt." She folded another. "And for some bizarre reason, you feel guilty because your mom was driving."

"I don't feel guilty," lied Cassie.

"Oh?" said Anna. "You stopped drinking because Beth had a couple drinks before the accident." She shook Cassie's finger. "That won't bring back the dead or give Nora back her legs," she said gently.

Cassie closed her eyes and turned away, but tears seeped from the corners of her eyes.

"Three," said Anna relentlessly, "you lost Jim," another finger, "and that...despicable...Phil turned out to be very much married and very un-separated." Anna pulled a rag from her back pocket and pressed it into the hand she was holding.

Cassie took it and opened her eyes. She laughed through her tears. "What is this?" she asked. "Am I going to look like Picasso's Blue Period if I use this?"

Anna waved a hand dismissively. "There's a clean corner there somewhere," she said.

Cassie wiped her eyes and nose.

"It *has* been a crappy few years, hasn't it," she finally said.

"Yes, it has," said Anna, "but you have to let people back in."

"I have let people in," she said. "There's Tia. I like her." Though that budding friendship would probably not last long once Tia learned how Cassie felt about her brother.

"Let Tate in," said Anna, then gave a half shrug and lifted her hand. "At least open the door. Talk to him. You'll find out you're wrong." She gave Cassie an evil grin. "I'll take care of Carla."

"Thanks. No. Sorry, Anna. I'm not going to be that big a fool. Not again."

CHAPTER 18

C ASSIE CAME WIDE AWAKE IN THE DARK.

The black clouds that had moved in from the ocean the day before had turned into the first major storm of the season. Rain was drumming steadily on the roof and the gutters were rushing. Tatters of a dream hung in Cassie's mind, snapshots of Eden Beach shifting, sliding, solidifying into stone and metal. The images lit her mind with an idea that ran like fire into her hands. She wasn't sure she had all the skills to make it work, but she knew this was *it*. This was her new work. But heaven help her, she only had a couple weeks to bring it off.

The house was quiet. No sound of the loom. Nora was asleep. It was such a rare event, that Cassie didn't want to risk waking her by making coffee. The silence also worried her. It meant Nora had been hurting so much she had taken her pain meds.

Cassie flipped on her bedside light and reached for her sketchbook.

It wasn't there.

For a moment she panicked, then her heart sank. She'd

left it in Nora's room. She had been showing Nora her failed jewelry designs the previous evening. She'd forgotten to take the book with her when she'd left. Nora was such a light sleeper, Cassie didn't dare creep in to get it.

But her mind was churning. She couldn't lie there waiting for Nora to get up. She had another sketchbook at the shop. She could make coffee there.

Moving very softly, Cassie pulled on her jeans, a shirt, a warm sweater, and bulky socks. She ran a quick brush through her hair and pulled it into a loose braid. As quietly as possible, she dug a couple heavy shoe boxes from the back of the shelf in her closet. They clunked softly as she tipped them into her backpack. With the heavy pack in one hand, her boots in the other, quietly she slipped down the hall and awkwardly lifted her rain slicker from the hook by the front door. She stepped out onto the front porch, inhaling the scent of rain-soaked soil. Gently she closed and locked the door behind her, shrugged on her jacket, and sat down to put on her boots. Pulling the heavy backpack onto her shoulders, Cassie stepped onto the sodden front path and dragged her hood up.

The rain was pouring straight down. The curbside gutters were gurgling as water rushed toward the beach. In places, the streets were flooded almost all the way across. Cassie's jeans were soaked before she'd gone two blocks, but there was no point in driving down to the shop. Cassie wouldn't pay the monthly fees for the lot several blocks away. The closest—free—on-street parking was probably right in front of her house.

She hurried through the dark, splashing through the flooded streets, darting in and out of the circles of light cast by the street lights. She didn't know what time it was, but there were few lights on in the houses she passed. She zigzagged through gray alleys and cut through parking lots.

There wasn't a soul on the streets when she turned down Ocean toward the beach.

Her head down, rain pattering like pebbles on her hood, her mind roiling with ideas, she was shocked when she suddenly slammed into what felt like a soft wall. She staggered and started to fall. Instinctively, she reached out with her free hand and grabbed, her fingers curling into the roughness of a denim jacket. At the same moment, strong hands grabbed her.

Cassie gasped, suddenly frightened. She looked up, eyes wide.

And saw Tate's face.

She froze, all thoughts of new work forgotten. She heard the surf in the distance and the splash of a car passing on Coast Highway. She was aware of the shop signs and night lights reflecting on the watery pavement, her heart jerking in her chest. The rain pattered steadily on her hood, her face. It dripped down Tate's hair into his eyes. Those strange eyes. They were hazel. No, maybe green. Gray?

Her fingers curled convulsively in his jacket.

His hands tightened on her arms. "What's wrong?" he asked urgently. "Are you all right? What are you doing out here at four in the morning?" His face was tight with concern. "Is it Nora?"

"My sketchbook," she said, and the world snapped back as she realized that was a strange reason to be running through a pre-dawn downpour. "My sketchbook's at the shop…Crap! No!" she said. "They're both at home!" Too late she realized the one she'd been showing Nora was her shop sketchbook. The one she kept at home was still in the living room where she'd left it days ago.

"I have to go," she muttered incoherently to him. "I've got to get these ideas down." She started to pull away, but he held her.

"You're soaked," he said. "Come inside. I have paper, pencils, and hot coffee—or I can have hot coffee quickly," said Tate. "It's dry. And warm. Come in." He tugged on her arm, pulling her toward the door of the restaurant. Only as he worked the locks did Cassie realize she was outside Lydia's.

Desperate to get her ideas down, she didn't argue. It didn't occur to her to think it strange that he seemed to understand her garbled reason for being out in the pouring rain. Focused on the images in her brain, she didn't think to ask him if his day always started at 4 a.m.

Tate opened the door, flipped off the alarm and, his hand on her arm, guided her through the restaurant, lit only by a dim light over the bar, into the kitchen. Cassie's stomach growled as her nose encountered the smell of something spicy from the night before. Tate pointed her to the kitchen table where she slipped the pack off her shoulders and dropped it heavily onto a chair. She yanked off the streaming slicker, dumped it on another chair, and pulled the shoeboxes out of the pack.

Tate rummaged in a drawer and brought her a sketchpad and pencils. He flipped through pages covered with sketches —of the restaurant floor plan, Cassie thought. Finding a blank page, he put the pad in front of her.

"I'll get coffee," he said.

"Thanks," said Cassie, but her mind was already elsewhere. She sank into a chair, wiped her wet hands on the still-dry thighs of her jeans, pulled the lids off the boxes, and spilled a cascade of plastic baggies onto the table.

Inside each bag was a stone. Not the kind people usually saw in a jewelry store. These were the kinds that came from a rock shop. Lapidary work—stone cutting—had led Jim into jewelry. In fact, the name of his business, before he had opened in the current location, had been Jim's Gem Jungle.

But Jim had never liked cutting plain round or oval cabochons out of agates or turquoise. He chose stones of any kind, precious or not, for their patterns and textures. When he cut, he followed the patterns in the rock, the flow of the surfaces. Some of these stones were almost carved. Jim had never set any of them into jewelry. He'd always said no one would buy them. Cassie hoped he was wrong.

She began sorting through them. Quickly, she put some back into one box without taking them out of the baggie, but she stopped at one, the one she'd dreamed of, and pulled it out. She rubbed her fingers over the surface, turned it in her hand. Front, back, sideways, the other way. Then she stopped and started to draw.

She smelled the coffee as Tate set it down. He put a bowl with sugar packets next to the mug. She pulled out three, tore them in one movement, dumped them in the mug, and kept drawing. She didn't see Tate smiling at her before he walked away.

When she ran out of sketches for that stone, she put it in the second empty box. She sorted through the pile on the table until she found another one that spoke to her. And she drew.

Empty mugs kept disappearing, and full ones reappeared. Tate refilled the sugar bowl once. He never said a word as Cassie filled page after page with drawings and notes.

At some point she was aware that he was unlocking the back door. She heard loud voices. Tate spoke sharply and the voices got softer. Two men walked into the kitchen. Cassie felt their curious glances, but she didn't look up.

Tate came over to her. "My cooks are in. I've asked them not to bother you. Take your time." He looked at the brilliant blue stone in her hand. "What's that?" he asked. "Is that turquoise?"

"Botryoidal chrysocolla," she said, pausing to pick up the mug and drink.

"Say that three times fast," he said.

Cassie smiled up at him. "Chrysocolla is a mineral," she said. "It's colored by copper, just like turquoise. That's why the colors are similar."

"Looks like bubble wrap."

"Botryoidal is Greek for grape-like. I guess ancient Greeks didn't have bubble wrap," she said.

"How on earth did they send anything through UPS?" Tate asked.

She smiled at him.

"Draw," he said, and walked away.

Cassie did. Another cook arrived. She vaguely noticed the sound of chopping. Later, she smelled bread and something else divine and realized she was starving. She stopped. She had gone through all of Jim's stones and filled Tate's drawing pad.

She looked up. Tate and his cooks were moving smoothly, chopping, mixing, baking. Two of the men were talking softly in Spanish.

"Whatever it is, I hope you have enough for two," she said to Tate.

"Actually, we're all stopping for breakfast," said Tate. "I hope you're not a vegetarian."

"If I were, I'd convert right now," said Cassie.

"Good. We're almost done."

A small dark young guy brought flatware and napkins to the table. "Man, I don't know who you are, but I hope you start coming in every morning," he said to her. "Improves the working environment. Usually all we have to look at is ugly guys." He shook his head. "*Hungry* ugly guys. Armed with knives."

Cassie laughed. He held out his hand and smiled. "Domingo Rivera," he said.

"Cassie Franklin." She smiled. Anna had told her about

Domingo.

"Mingo, stop flirting," called Tate.

Domingo waved his hand at Tate dismissively at the same time he started moving away from the table. "Such a cranky guy," he said to Cassie. "He gets worried because he knows the prettiest ladies like me better than him."

Domingo turned and passed Tate who was on his way to the table with two plates. "*Mucho mejor*," he murmured to Tate. Cassie was pretty sure she wasn't supposed to hear him. *Much better than what?* she wondered.

Tate brought over not only two omelets, but toast, jam, honey, bacon, and orange juice on a tray. "Thought you might have had your fill of coffee by now," he said.

"Definitely," she said. "I think that was a month's worth for me."

He sat down with her, and Domingo and the other two cooks quickly joined them. Things got suddenly quiet except for the sounds of forks and knives against plates.

When her omelet was half gone, Cassie finally looked up. "Thanks. I was about two seconds from starving to death in your kitchen."

Tate's eyes opened wide. "That would have been good advertising for my business," he said wryly.

Cassie suddenly noticed some pieces of slate stacked in the center of the table.

"Why the tile? Planning to put it on the menu?"

Tate smiled and shrugged. "Leftover pieces from the floor out front. I wanted to have some spares that matched in case any of the flooring got damaged. But it's been so hectic that they keep getting moved from place to place without me finding a permanent home for them." He gestured to the pile. "I guess that was their last stop."

"Our house is like that," Cassie smiled. "So tiny everything moves around until it finally drifts into a place where it fits."

The conversation paused, and Cassie found herself just looking at him. *He looks tired*, she thought. She noticed the laugh lines around his eyes and saw the tan he'd had a couple weeks ago was fading. He had the faintest of crooked smiles on his face. Then she noticed the white lettering on his worn and frayed blue sweatshirt.

"Cordon *Who?*" she read out loud. She looked at him quizzically.

He looked down. "Found it at a tourist market in Paris," he said, looking back at her. "Reminds me not to be cocky."

Domingo, who with the others, had just gotten up to go back to work, glanced at Cassie. "You can see how well *that's* working," he said.

Tate closed his eyes, shook his head, looked long-suffering, then shot a stream of very improper Spanish toward Domingo. Cassie laughed, and Domingo grinned.

Tate looked at her sheepishly. "You speak Spanish?"

"I've been around Anna's brothers all my life," she said. "And the horse trainers Luis works with. Oh, yeah," she nodded and grinned back. "*That* Spanish I understand."

"*Hijole*," said Domingo. "We're all in for it now."

Cassie glanced back to the pile of slate tiles. She reached out and lifted one from the stack. She ran her fingers over the uneven, sandpapery surface. She liked the shades of gray and green with a hint of blue. She sat up straighter. "Can I buy one from you?" she asked.

"Take what you need," said Tate.

Cassie slid into the chair closest to the tiles and sorted through them. Tate reached for the sketchbook, then stayed his hand. "May I?" he asked. "I'm curious what drove you out into the rain and the dark."

"You fed and sheltered me and gave me coffee," said

Cassie, gesturing to the book. "And it's your book. I think you almost have a proprietary right to look at them."

Cassie pulled two tiles from the stack, slipped them into her pack, and took her dishes over to Domingo, who smiled and nodded. "You decide not to do jewelry anymore," he said, "I'll make him hire you."

Cassie went back and sat next to Tate. "You draw spectacularly well," he said. "But what is all this? They look more like abstract paintings than jewelry."

Cassie explained about Nora asking her what she loved, and how she wanted to capture Eden Beach in jewelry. She talked about Anna's paintings. She told him the hints that had been coming together in her mind, and how she'd woken in the dark that morning crazy to get the ideas down. Tate simply nodded and smiled, like he'd been there.

"These are the pieces you're going to show at the Festival of the Masters, then," said Tate.

"I really have no idea," she said. She waved her hand at the designs. "I've never done anything like this before. I'm not even sure I *can* do anything like it. Some of the stones will have to be trimmed. Jim taught me the basics, but I was a teenager the last time I cut. I don't even know if his equipment is fit to use after all these years." She studied the drawings. "How I'm going to set these and then add the other details..." She shook her head.

"I'm sure you can do it," said Tate.

"I don't know," said Cassie. "But I do know I haven't been so excited about my work in a long time." She flipped a couple pages. "This time I'm going to do something big. At least if I go down, like Anna says, I'll go down in flames."

Tate shook his head. "I don't think you're going down. I don't know anything about jewelry, but I think that, if you don't get the judges' attention with these, they don't deserve to have you."

Cassie looked at him, into those remarkable eyes—green, she thought, no, gray. "Thank you," she said, feeling a blush spread down her neck. Everything in her seemed to loosen and warm. She realized her anger had drained away. And she didn't want it back.

Afraid her feelings would show on her face, she looked down and flipped through her drawings. She felt excitement rise. They were good. Even if not this year, next year for sure. She nodded to herself. "Yes," she muttered. "This will work, this one." She flipped a page, paused, and tapped her finger on the page. "Maybe this one if I can figure out how to do it. And find the right accent stones."

She was lost again. Tate put his hand gently over hers, and she looked up startled.

He glanced at the clock on the wall. "You might want to head to your shop where it's quiet," he said. "It's about to get busy here."

"Oh, my God! It's nine-thirty!" Cassie leaped to her feet, closed the boxes, and tucked them back into the backpack.

"The pages, your sketchbook..." but Tate was already handing the book to her. "It's still pouring. Keep them dry," he said. She slipped the pad into the backpack, pulled on her slicker, and headed toward the front door. Tate walked along with her.

He switched off the night lights as they passed into the dining room, leaving it dim in the watery light coming through the front windows as they wove their way to the front.

Tate unlocked the doors and held one open for her.

"Tate," said Cassie, as he turned toward her. She stopped, looking up at him haloed by the morning light. "Tate. Thank you." She gestured to the pack in her hand. "For under-standing about all this...this craziness. And for a truly amazing breakfast. Not many people would have gathered in a crazy woman at 4 a.m. out of a pouring rain." She smiled softly at him. "I'm very grateful." She extended her right hand.

Tate let the door fall closed, stepped back toward Cassie, and took her right hand in his left. "You're welcome any time," he said quietly, and softly pulled her toward him.

Suddenly, Cassie couldn't think. She didn't want to think. Not about the Masters. Not about anything. All she wanted was to hold onto his hand, strong and warm. And never let go.

She stepped closer to him. His right hand slid under her slicker and around her waist as he gently pulled her in. Some distant part of her mind heard a thump as she dropped her pack on the floor. Her hand slid up his muscled forearm, bare where the sweatshirt was pushed up, hairs as fine as a kitten's. She vaguely noticed the softness of the old sweatshirt as Tate bent toward her, and her hand traveled up, almost on its own, to touch his face, the angles of his jaw covered with morning stubble.

His remarkable eyes were just inches from hers, and still she couldn't decide what color they were. Ocean gray, this morning, she thought, with just a hint of blue from the sweatshirt. Tiny white lines rayed from the corners of his eyelids, where squinting into the sun had left them untanned.

His eyes seemed to ask a question.

Cassie's hand slipped to the back of his neck, answering. She saw a hint of crooked smile before Tate's lips touched hers softly. After that, Cassie wasn't aware of anything but the feel of him against her, his hair curling under her fingers, her right hand—when had she let go of his?—against his back, drawing him closer.

His lips, tasting of coffee and jam. And him. She wanted more of this, more of him. She felt his hand slip under her thick braid, his thumb stroking her neck. She opened her mouth slightly, felt the softness of his bottom lip. She heard a small throaty sound, part groan, part sigh, part sob, and realized it was her. Tate tightened his grip on the back of her neck and drew her closer. His kiss deepened. Cassie felt her legs get weak as desire rolled through her. She opened her mouth wider.

A cold gust of damp air blew in as the door opened. Cassie stepped back feeling lost and confused in the sudden light. Tate dropped his right arm and partly turned toward the door, his warm left hand still cradling the back of Cassie's neck.

Carla Towne was standing stock still in the open door.

CHAPTER 19

OR A MOMENT, THE THREE WERE FROZEN: Carla in the door, Tate and Cassie trapped in the spill of rain-drenched light from outside, staring at her.

Then Carla spoke. "Well. Good *morning*."

Cassie moved first, bending swiftly to grab her pack. Tate swayed as if a vital prop had suddenly collapsed.

"Cassie," he said, hearing the deep note of desire in his own voice.

"Thanks for breakfast, Tate," she said, and was out the door so fast he wondered if she'd been a mirage. The air around him was suddenly cold.

Tate, making an effort to control his face and assure himself his rubbery legs would hold him, missed the look of calculation and venom that Carla shot at Cassie as the jeweler slipped by her without acknowledgement.

Carla turned back toward Tate.

"I see I'm too late," she said, switching on her smile and focusing on Tate. "I was hoping to get breakfast myself." She stepped in and let the door close behind her. She set a dripping umbrella against the wall next to her where it quickly formed a puddle on the slate flooring.

Tate's body still echoed with the weight of Cassie against him, the heat of wanting her. He could still feel her hands in his hair. Her scent was in his shirt.

He felt a wave of unreasoning anger rise in him. Did Carla have to come in now? *Now?*

"We're not open for breakfast," he said shortly.

Carla turned off the smile and gave him a hurt look, but Tate was in no mood to soothe her feelings.

"Sorry to be rude, Carla," he said brusquely. "We're getting ready for the day. I don't have time to talk."

Carla gave him a measuring look. "Maybe after what I just saw, you should make time," she said.

"Excuse me?" said Tate, his voice dropping dangerously.

Carla jerked her head toward the door. "Cassie Franklin," she said.

"That is none of your business…" Tate started to say, hotly.

"Maybe not," Carla interrupted. "But you're new in Eden Beach and probably don't know about her. Well, you obviously *don't* know about her. So maybe you should hear what I have to say."

Two halves of his mind warred against each other. One wanted to toss Carla into the rain and go after Cassie. In the other, a small bell was ringing, urging him to listen.

Irritated by his own indecision, Tate snapped, "What are you talking about?"

"She's using you," said Carla. As Tate began to retort, she went on, overriding him. "I saw the way she was looking at you the other night, at the open house. It was obvious she was sizing you up. I was afraid something like this would happen."

"Carla, you've said enough," he said, holding up a hand.

Carla ignored him. "It was also pretty clear you were falling for her. Oh, I can understand," she said hurrying on before Tate could interrupt again. "A lot of men in town find her attractive. A *lot* of men," she repeated. "Especially Lou Pallis."

The words bit deep. The image flashed in Tate's mind of Cassie and Lou, their heads close together at the bar at the open house. Jealousy flared.

"I think Lou's wasting his time, though," said Carla into his pause. "He's not her type. Cassie prefers men with money."

"Oh?" said Tate, trying to get a grip on this conversation. "And you know this because she told you? That's surprising. I didn't get the feeling you and Cassie were particularly good friends."

"She didn't have to tell me. I talk to a lot of people. Eden Beach is a small town. I know Phil Trainer."

"Who's he?" asked Tate, the question escaping against his will. *I shouldn't be listening to this,* he thought. "The town gossip columnist?"

"Phil's a financial analyst down in Cabrillo Point," said Carla. "He and his wife are clients of mine." She didn't say that technically only Jana Trainer was her client. Jana was divorcing Phil after he'd had one too many affairs. "Cassie sucked him right into an affair that almost destroyed his marriage. But she didn't care. All she wanted was to find someone to pay the rent on her shop."

Married, thought Tate. *That's what she was talking about. That's why she said she didn't want to go out with me because she thought I was involved with Carla.*

His heart rose.

Then fell.

Why was she involved with a married guy? he thought.

"Phil dropped her as soon as he discovered that," Carla

went on. "After that, I thought she'd be looking for someone else with money. At the open house it was pretty obvious she'd chosen you."

Tate managed to snort. "That's ridiculous. I just opened a restaurant. I don't have any money," he said.

"She probably doesn't know that," said Carla. "All she has to know is that you're from Newport. I'm sure she knows your family has money. Everyone has heard of Martin Garner."

Pain stabbed Tate's heart. *No,* he thought, *not everyone does know about Martin Garner.* Martin liked to work in the shadows. His firm had a nondescript name. Martin's name never showed up on the documents of the projects he funded. But that morning on the bluff, Cassie had known the name. She had immediately connected Tate to Martin Garner.

She'd know about Alden Towne and Towne Center. Even Tate hadn't known that.

Was that when she had developed an interest in him? She hadn't seemed to like him much before that. He remembered the attraction he had felt for her that morning. Cassie had seemed to feel it, too. Had she been playing him?

Tate went cold. Suspicions, primed by memories of Avril, rose in his mind. *Is that why she came to the open house? And why she seemed so willing this morning?*

Had her stop by his house that morning really been accidental?

Carla sighed. "She has to find *someone* before she loses the shop."

"What? What do you mean, loses her shop?" said Tate sharply.

"You shouldn't be surprised," said Carla. "She's in probably the best commercial space in Eden Beach. You have no idea how many people would pay a fortune for that spot. Surely Cassie can't pay for it much longer. I'm sure she's barely hanging on. It probably won't be long before her landlord evicts her."

Tate felt despair for Cassie. He'd watched her this morning. She had been on fire with her design ideas. He recognized that singular focus. He had it himself. It would kill her to lose her shop.

But was Carla right? Did Cassie think he had a pipeline to Martin's wealth? *Was* she using him?

He could almost taste her kiss, feel her hair, soft as silk. Had she been faking?

He didn't notice Carla turn away to hide a small, satisfied smile.

She picked up her umbrella.

"I'm sure you'd have seen it yourself, soon enough," she said. "But I would have hated to see you taken in."

"Well," she said, hitching her shoulder bag higher. "If I'm not going to get breakfast, I'll get on to the office."

She opened the door and went out into the rain.

Tate barely heard her go. When he finally turned around, across the dining room he saw Domingo standing in the kitchen doorway. There was enough light to show the sadness and disappointment on his friend's face. Domingo shook his head and turned back to the kitchen, leaving Tate alone in the semi-darkness.

CHAPTER 20

FOR THE REST OF THE WEEK, CASSIE WAS like a poltergeist, Nora joked to Melody. "I see signs of her, but never see her." Cassie was in the shop before 7 a.m. and often not home until after midnight. Twice she made the long trek to the jewelry mart in downtown LA, driving for more than two hours, through bumper to bumper, morning rush-hour traffic. The first time was for pearls. The second was for unusual colored stones. Both times, she took the freeways to Grieger's, a well-known lapidary shop in Pasadena, for supplies and priceless advice on cutting, trimming, finishing, sealing, and drilling the stones she had. She also found more agates and jaspers that burned in her imagination, but the prize was a slice of finished meteorite.

She spent the weekend in the shed behind the house, cleaning up Jim's old equipment, practicing on the stones she didn't plan to use in her work. She broke stones, dulled blades, crawled into the shower late at night, filthy and exhausted, but exhilarated.

Passion for her work drove her. Even if she didn't get into the Masters, everything about her new work felt right.

Focusing on the challenges in front of her also kept thoughts of Tate at bay.

Cassie would have starved if Nora hadn't made sure there were lunches in the fridge or called Susie to deliver *pad thai*. Cassie laughed the day Dale showed up, "under orders," he said, lugging in a case of bottled iced tea.

A couple times, Anna brought food to her from the restaurant, but Cassie finally asked her not to. She didn't want to take anything from Tate. She was too embarrassed about the kiss, angry at Tate, angry at her own weakness and stupidity.

Of course, she had to tell Anna why.

"Whoa! You've been holding out on me!" Anna grinned. "I *knew* there was chemistry there. And you tried to tell me there wasn't." Cassie didn't respond. "What? He's not a good kisser?"

Cassie glared.

"I'm not getting this, Cass. You like him, he likes you..."

"No. He doesn't."

Her vehemence stopped Anna. She made a face. "He kissed you because he *doesn't* like you?"

"He kissed me because I was *there*," said Cassie.

Anna was shaking her head. "Cass, I keep telling you. You're reading this wrong."

"Am I? What was she doing there at 9:30 in the morning?"

"She probably saw the lights."

"The lights weren't on. She walked in like she was expected, and I realized he was hustling me out because he was expecting her, not because I would be late opening." She shoved her hands into her hair and yanked the pin out. "I was there. I was stupid. I was suffering amnesia. I forgot about Carla." *I wanted to forget about Carla*, she thought. *How stupid could I have been?* "That's why he kissed me. What did he have to lose, right? He'd tried once, and I'd backed him off. Why not try again?"

"Cassie, so what if she was expected? She's his realtor."

"Yeah? So what's she selling him? He has a house. He has the restaurant. What? Is she going to reduce the rent?" Cassie's voice was bitter, just on the edge of tears. "Why was she risking her perfect hair, her perfect pumps to come out in the pouring rain on the off chance the front door of a darkened restaurant would be unlocked?" Cassie threw her hands out to the sides. "What could she possibly need to say that couldn't be said on the phone—if it was business?"

Anna looked at her silently for a while. Cassie finally took a deep, shaky breath and looked away.

"Maybe you should ask him," said Anna quietly.

Cassie gave a bitter laugh. "No. I'm not asking him anything. I'm not going to look like more of a fool than I already do."

She glanced at Anna's worried frown and waved a hand. "I'm okay. I'm just feeling incredibly gullible. And incredibly stupid. It will pass."

At least she hoped it would pass, although it wouldn't be soon. She hadn't felt like Tate had made her feel that morning for a long time. She wasn't sure she'd ever felt like that. No man she'd ever been involved with had cared about her work. None of them had ever appreciated it like Tate.

Or at least pretended to appreciate it. Cassie didn't want to, but she had to force herself to acknowledge that it had probably all been pretense. She'd been a fool. Again.

For those few moments, though, she sometimes thought —late at night or early in the morning when she'd finally gotten home and dropped into bed—for those few moments, she'd believed it was real. So real, she could still feel the strength of his arms around her, feel his hand gently stroking her neck.

Now, there was just a cold, empty spot where her heart used to be.

She buried herself in the work, struggling with the new materials, new techniques. When she worked, everything else disappeared. There was only the stones, the metal, and her hands.

After she broke two of her selected stones, though, she realized she needed help. She put in a call to Lou.

"What can I do for you, Cass?"

"You remember your offer to teach me the skills I needed…"

"You're closed on Mondays, aren't you?"

"Yes," she told him.

"So am I. I'll meet you here first thing—nine or so?"

"But I haven't told you what I want," protested Cassie.

"Doesn't matter," said Lou. "See you then. Got someone here. Gotta go."

Cassie was waiting at Lou's shop when he arrived that morning.

"This is a helluva concept," said Lou, when she'd explained what she was doing with the stones and shown him the drawings. "No one around here is doing anything like this. You are going to get the jump on everyone. Next year, they'll all be trying to copy you."

"But will the jurors like it?" Cassie asked him, as he paged through her designs, turned the stones over in his hands. Before he could answer, she added, "Have you ever been a show juror?"

"Nah," said Lou. "Like I said, I don't play well with others."

"I didn't think Art did, either, but he's in the show every year," she said.

"Don't let him fool you," said Lou. "If Art wanted out, he'd have left years ago."

He flipped another page and shook his head. "After Art sees this work," he said, "he'll really be unbearable. He can't stand not being the one out in front."

Lou pointed to the six stones she had laid on his bench. "So, where do you want to start? Tell me what you want to do and let's see if we can figure out how to do it."

Cassie was there all morning and into the afternoon. With Lou guiding her, she practiced on the throw-away stones. Then, holding her breath and concentrating fiercely, she carefully set four small diamonds in tubing, drilled holes in the botryoidal chrysocolla, and riveted in the tubes. She didn't realize she'd stopped breathing until she turned the stone over, found everything just as she hoped it would be, and blew out a gust of air.

Lou laughed. "Gotta develop nerves of steel," he said.

She smiled weakly. "I think I would have cried if I'd broken that one," she said. "Jim had nothing else like it."

After that, she carefully, but confidently set another piece.

When they finally stopped, Cassie's neck was stiff and her hands were cramped. She looked at the remaining four stones on the bench and shook her head. "Sorry I'm so slow," she said. "I'd hoped to finish all of them."

"Cassie, you're way too hard on yourself," said Lou. "You're really very good. I've worked with jewelers who would never have learned at this pace. They never would have learned, period. If I'm not careful, you'll be taking my place as Eden Beach's jewelry guru. You have nothing to be ashamed of."

He pointed to the other four pieces on the bench. "These are going to be more difficult. Especially since the base stones are unknown or fragile. The basalt has a great surface, but setting into it..." He paused for a while and Cassie let him think. Finally, he asked, "How open are you to altering your concept a bit?"

"Wide open," said Cassie. "I'm looking for a particular feel. Anything that gives me that is fine with me." She explained to him what she was looking for.

By the end, he was nodding. "I think it can be done. Let me sit with it a few days. In the meantime, I think you can finish at least these two." He outlined how she could address the ideas she had with what he'd just taught her.

She pointed at the basalt she was leaving with him. Joking, she said, "I wish I could paint parts of that one with gold. Don't suppose you know how to do that."

"Like gold leaf, maybe?" he said immediately. "Like on icons?"

"Icons?" asked Cassie.

"Religious pictures. Used a lot in the Greek Orthodox church. Lots of them are covered with gold. Here," said Lou, waving her back into his tiny office. On the wall was a small painting of a woman, her golden halo shining softly.

"Wow!" said Cassie. "That's gold leaf?"

Lou nodded.

Cassie frowned. "How would you do that on stone?"

Lou shrugged, hands out, palms up. "No idea," he said.

Cassie huffed and gave him a look of exasperation. "You give me a great idea and no way of doing it?"

Lou shook his finger at her. "I said *I* didn't know how to do it. I didn't say I couldn't tell you where to find out."

Cassie raised an eyebrow at him.

"My great uncle," said Lou. "He's an icon painter. Retired now, but still does a lot of work for St. Paul's up in Irvine." Lou shrugged again. "He may be Orthodox, but his work is not always orthodox. Gotten him into trouble in the past."

"Guess that runs in the family," said Cassie wryly.

"Now, now. Be nice," said Lou, wagging a finger at her. "But if anyone can do it, or teach you how, he can. I'll call him."

"Worth a try," said Cassie.

By time Cassie left, it was just after 3 p.m. Lou walked her out, locked up behind them, and walked her down the steps.

At the bottom of the stairs, Lou turned to her. "Call me any time, if you need help. Or if you just need someone to commiserate. But I think you'll be fine with those two pieces. And I'll let you know what my uncle says."

"Lou, I can't thank you enough. I owe you dinner. A big one."

"You owe me nothing," he said. "Jim was a good friend. He'd be blown away by what you've accomplished. And very proud. And very glad to be an active partner in your work."

Impulsively, Cassie leaned forward and hugged Lou, kissing him on the cheek.

He grinned. "That's pretty good payment there," he said.

She laughed, and he squeezed her on the arm. "See you next Monday," he said. "We'll finish off those last couple pieces."

Cassie shouldered her pack and headed up the street toward home. She turned back once to wave at Lou.

She didn't notice Tate watching her from the shadow of the print shop doorway across the street.

Lou's great uncle Yiannis had known exactly how to apply gold leaf to basalt. He'd been thrilled to be asked for his help. He'd driven down from Irvine the following Monday to her shop.

Yiannis was a small, dark man with a full head of gray hair, still handsome though in his seventies. His easy smile showed a gold bicuspid. He was always ready to joke despite a rather dark history. Yiannis was a legend in the Greek community in southern California, Lou had told her. He'd been a resistance fighter during the war. Afterward, he and his wife, Maria, had fought the communists in Greece. They had been betrayed and forced to flee, barely escaping with their lives. In gratitude to the Virgin, Yiannis had committed his life to painting her icons.

Like his nephew, Yiannis loved to flirt. He'd teased Cassie the whole morning they'd worked together, but he'd been a patient and thorough teacher. "This is good, what you're doing," he told her. "I think I'll steal these ideas."

When Lou came to get him for lunch, Yiannis left her a package of homemade Greek cookies. Powdered sugar sifted out when he set the package down on the table behind her design desk.

"I thought those were for me!" Lou protested.

"No. You are not a beautiful young woman," said Yiannis. He poked Lou in the arm with a gnarled forefinger. "And it gives you a reason to come to dinner some time. Maria loves to feed you."

Cassie grinned at Lou.

"I'm taking him to Tate's for lunch," said Lou. "Why don't you join us?"

Cassie shook her head and hoped she wasn't blushing. She'd been avoiding Lydia's. She even avoided walking down Ocean to Susie's Thai restaurant, choosing to go up Canyon and cut across the bank parking lot to get there. She'd seen Tate from a distance a couple times, running along the boardwalk in the morning. She hadn't tried to get any closer.

"I have some repairs to do," she said. "You two go enjoy." She waved them out and locked the door behind them.

Tate saw Lou come in with an older man and waved. Lou had become a regular at Lydia's. Two or three times a week, he stopped by for lunch, usually sitting at the chef's table in the back and joking with Domingo. Most evenings he had Anna making him a drink before he headed home. Tate usually sat down and talked to him if things were not too busy.

Tate liked Lou, even though it gave him a twinge to think Lou might be interested in Cassie. Or Cassie in Lou. *At least Lou's not married,* he thought with a flash of anger.

Mondays were always a bit quiet, and it was after the lunch rush, so Tate joined Lou and Yiannis after they'd ordered. They had a lot to talk about when Tate discovered Yiannis was from a small village not far from Sparta, where Tate had spent some time hiking the mountains.

"Do you miss it?" he asked Yiannis.

Yiannis shrugged. "Yes and no," he said. "I have very good memories of it," he said, "and I have very bad memories, too. So..." Yiannis shrugged again, hands out. "So, I can't make up my mind, and I don't go back."

Tate thought fleetingly of Paris. "I understand that," he said. "So, how come I haven't seen you before? Do you come to visit Lou often?"

Yiannis made a knowing face. "I'll come back now," he said. "Now that Louis has introduced me to that beautiful girl."

"Who's that?" said Tate grinning. "Maybe I should meet her."

Yiannis wagged a finger. "You are too young. A beautiful—and wise—young woman like that, she prefers someone with experience. Mature." He patted his hand on his chest, winked, and took a sip of ouzo. "Cassiopeia," said Yiannis. "A good Greek name." He gestured to the ceiling. "As beautiful as the stars themselves," he proclaimed dramatically.

Tate smiled. "You'll have to introduce me," he said.

"Cassie," said Lou. "That's her full name. Yiannis came down to help her with one of her projects."

Tate tried not to react, but his smiled dimmed a bit. "Are you a jeweler, too?" he asked Yiannis.

Yiannis shook his head. "I'm a painter of icons. But we both work with gold, so I could help with a small thing," he said. "Like me, she he has magic in her hands."

Lou rolled his eyes. "Unlike you, she's modest."

Yiannis shrugged dramatically. "The truth, it is what it is." Another sip of ouzo. "Someday, perhaps, if she converts, I will teach her to paint icons." Tate smiled, recognizing it as a joke.

Yiannis turned to Lou. "She's very proud," he said seriously. "As you said, she doesn't ask for help easily. But I meant what I told you. I will do anything I can to help her succeed. You make sure she knows this. You tell me what I can do."

He lifted his glass again. "Besides, someone so beautiful. How can I not help her?" He wagged a finger at Lou. "You will not say this to Maria," he said sternly.

Lou snorted and shook his head. "You're incorrigible," he said.

Tate smiled again, but this time, he wasn't sure it was a joke.

CHAPTER 21

CASSIE WAS GENTLY HAND-POLISHING one of her new pieces the Tuesday before the photo shoot, when Tia came in.

"Hi!" she called. "You're just in time to help me decide which three pieces to give Sean tomorrow."

Tia groaned. "My choice would be all of them," she said, reaching over the security gate and letting herself in. "You know I love them all!"

True to her word, Tia had come back to the shop on her day off right after Tate's open house. The same rainy Tuesday morning Cassie had stumbled into Tate's arms, her mind full of her new design ideas. Distracted by the new sketches, the memory of Tate holding her, her humiliation when Carla had walked in, Cassie had almost told Tia she was too busy when she'd come in that day.

But Tia was so obviously excited about learning more, and she'd already driven down from Irvine in the pouring rain. Cassie couldn't turn her away. She'd pushed aside thoughts of Tate, warmly welcomed Tia, given her hot coffee, and set her at the wax bench.

When Tia had walked out the door that day, Cassie had been sure she would not be back, expecting that she would soon hear about Cassie's humiliation that morning. That had made her a bit sad. It had been a very enjoyable day, and Tia had been good company. It had been a pleasure to have someone to talk to, to laugh with, she'd discovered. Cassie had also discovered that she was a pretty good jewelry teacher.

So when Tia *had* come back the following week, Cassie had been surprised—and pleased. Tia had stayed all that day and had started spending her second day off at the shop, too. Cassie had answered countless questions about jewelry making, gemstones, and the custom design process, not really thinking it was anything but idle conversation. She'd been delighted to come out of the bathroom one afternoon, to hear Tia talking confidently—and correctly—to a customer who was looking at earrings.

After that, Tia often talked to customers who were "just looking," giving Cassie time to continue undisturbed with her work. The help had proven invaluable. Tia's unqualified admiration of Cassie's new work, in addition to Lou's enthusiastic support, was good for Cassie's morale, too.

"Actually, I think I *am* going to have him shoot them all," said Cassie, flipping up her head magnifier and smiling. "I just don't know which ones I'm going to put with the application. At least I'll have another ten days or so to procrastinate on the final decision before the images come back from the processor."

Tia leaned over the bench to see the work in Cassie's hand. "Oh!" she said breathlessly.

Cassie was pleased with Tia's reaction. Inspired by Anna's painting of the fire—which hung on the wall next to her—Cassie had chosen a piece of poppy jasper Jim had once carved that looked like an abstract vision of flames. The sense of fire was emphasized by tiny golden and blood red garnets. She'd oxidized the silver frame of the neckpiece until it was almost black. A thin band of bright 18k yellow gold ran through it like flame.

"Definitely put that one into the application," said Tia. "That and the chrysocolla. And maybe the basalt piece with the gilding."

Cassie nodded. "The chrysocolla and the basalt, for sure. But I still have to make a chain for this. It won't be done in time for the photo shoot. I was thinking the meteorite brooch with the gold garnet."

"Yes. I agree," said Tia. "Where are the others?"

In the previous two weeks, Cassie had finished six new pieces. Once she'd finished the Masters entries, she'd started making small brooches and pendants. They would be more appealing to women who liked the work, but were nervous about wearing something so different.

"I put them in the window this morning," said Cassie. "I wanted to see how people react—if they react."

"What if you sell them?" said Tia.

"I'll be thrilled!" said Cassie, laughing. "It would be the best proof I could get that I'm on the right track. But," she said, standing up from the bench, "I'm not sure people will pay the price I have on them."

Lou had talked long and hard, finally convincing her to price the pieces at about double what she had planned. She knew his arguments were right—these were one-of-a-kind pieces that people wouldn't find elsewhere, that her existing work was underpriced for her skills, and that people would value the work more if it was priced higher—but she was nervous about it. They were, after all, still agates and silver, for the most part.

Cassie stretched and glanced toward the street window. Her heart almost stopped. Art Jackson was looking at her work. Cassie had never seen him at her window. She wondered if this was Lou's doing or simply chance.

Tearing her eyes from the front, she turned to Tia. "So. Are you ready to get your hands dirty?" Cassie had promised to show Tia how to clean up the casting of her pendant.

Tia's grin was all she needed to see. As the girl started to sit at the wax bench, Cassie waved her to the second one. "Nope. Today you're at the metals bench."

"Oh!" said Tia. "That's why you have two different benches? One for metal, one for wax?"

Cassie pointed at the metal filings in the catch tray in the metals bench. "You can see how dirty metal working is. You have to keep all the filings and dirt away from the wax. If any of it gets caught up in a carving, it'll mess up the casting."

As Tia sat at the metals bench, she gestured to the light layer of debris in the catch tray. "It never looks like you make that much mess," she said.

Cassie laughed. "I clean it out at the end of every day," she said, "and dump it into the barrel in the back. At the end of the year, I send it all back to the refiner and get a credit against new metal."

"It adds up to that much?" Tia was surprised.

Cassie smiled. "Not a lot, because I work in silver. If I worked in gold, it would be a lot more. In fact, I've heard that long-time jewelers, who move out of their stores or retire, tear up the carpets and even the wood flooring and have it refined."

"You're kidding," said Tia.

Cassie shook her head. "Nope. It can amount to thousands of dollars. Especially the way gold has been climbing in price."

"Holy wow," said Tia. "I can't believe it adds up to so much."

Cassie smiled. "I read a story a while back about a guy in

New York's jewelry district who digs out the dirt in the side-walk cracks and gutters. He finds small stones, like diamonds and sapphires, that walk out of shops on the soles of shoes, along with all the gold. He refines the dirt and resells the stones, and he makes a living doing it."

"No way! That's an urban myth."

"Nope. It's true," said Cassie. She glanced back at the front window, just in time to see Art Jackson walking away. He'd spent a long time with her work. She remembered what Nora said. She wondered what Art had thought about the new pieces. She'd have to ask Lou to find out. Maybe she didn't want to know.

"Where do I start?" asked Tia.

Cassie showed Tia how to use the battered bench pin for support when sawing off the sprues. She explained how to use the Foredom motorized handpiece, gave her a scrap sprue so she could get the feel of the tool, and ran her through the steps involved in grinding and polishing metal.

"Okay, it's all yours," said Cassie, finally. "Just remember, this is not like wax. It's a lot harder to fix if you mess some-thing up. So err on the side of caution. Go slowly. Ask ques-tions if you're not sure."

Cassie picked up the poppy jasper neckpiece and went to the design desk to find a box for it. She took a minute to enjoy the work. It felt so right. She was already getting ideas about how to merge some of her new ideas with her more conservative work, like the pieces now in her cases.

She smiled. She was in love with her work again. It felt great.

She tucked the neckpiece into the box and put it in the safe, then returned to the wax bench to work on a custom piece she was carving.

Cassie kept an eye on Tia. The girl was clumsy and slow at first, but gradually caught on. Cassie gave her pointers when she knew she could help, but mostly left her to discover her own way of working. Making mistakes, as Jim had told her, was the best way to learn. It *was* only Tia's first piece, but Cassie remembered how important that first piece felt. She still had hers at home in her jewelry box.

They worked in silence for a while. With his sister sitting at her side, Cassie couldn't help but think about Tate, even though she tried to keep her mind on the wax she was carving. Suddenly, she found herself asking Tia, "So, how are things going over at the restaurant?" She immediately wished she could kick herself. She kept her eyes on her work.

Tia didn't seem to think the question was odd. She stopped working and flipped the magnifier up. Cassie saw her smile proudly.

"It's going great!" she said. "People seem to really like it! Lunch time it's been full. Most nights, too. And Anna is making the bar a success." Tia laughed. "She is so much fun! She keeps everyone on their toes."

"That's good news," said Cassie, and meant it. Tate was as passionate about his work as she was about hers. She wanted him to succeed.

She sighed sadly to herself.

Tia flipped the magnifier down and returned to her work.

"I'm so happy for him," said Tia. "Tate's waited so long for this."

"I'd guess it takes a lot of money to open a place like that," said Cassie. "With the rent," *especially from the Townes*, she thought, "and all the employees. The loss in food."

"He'd have gotten there sooner if he hadn't been paying for school for me."

"He said you did the heavy lifting on that."

"He always says that," Tia told her over the sound of the burr grinding the metal. "I did work. And I got a couple scholarships when I hit Irvine. But it still set him back quite a bit. Though he won't admit it.

"I feel bad about that," she continued. "There was always money around when I was growing up, you know? I didn't realize how hard Tate was working to help me out. He used to make jokes in his letters about working for food. I thought he was just kidding, being in restaurants all the time. But I think there were times it was true."

They worked quietly together for a while, Cassie thinking about the sacrifices Jim, her mom, and Nora had made for her. She was angry, she discovered, to think that someone as self-centered and greedy as Carla Towne could have as much influence as she did over someone so selfless and good-hearted as Tate. How could he not see through her?

Maybe he was tired of putting off his dream and Carla was the fast track to it. Maybe Tate wasn't the innocent she wanted him to be.

"Tate's an unusual name," Cassie surprised herself by saying. She hurried on. "So's Tia, as a matter of fact."

Tia grinned. "My mom was unusual," she said. "She named him Tate when he was born. She used to joke that she named him for the Tate art museum in England. But I always wondered if it wasn't an old boyfriend." Tia shrugged slightly. "I never thought about it until long after she was gone. I was only eight when she died."

Tia picked up a file and began working a different area of the pendant. Cassie watched. "You're picking this up very quickly," she said. "You have a good feel for the metal. Not everyone has that."

Tia glanced up, surprised. "Really?" she asked. "It doesn't seem that hard."

Cassie laughed. "Girl, you're wasted working with plants!"

Tia smiled and went back to work. She surprised Cassie when she continued her story.

"Anyway, my dad insisted Tate be named Edward Martin. Maybe *he* thought Tate was an old boyfriend, too. The Martin was for him, of course, and the Edward was for *his* father. Mom always called him Tate anyway. Drove Dad nuts. Tate finally changed it, legally. Tate Patrick Garner. Patrick was my mom's maiden name." She filed quietly for a while. "I'm not sure why he didn't change the Garner, too. He really dislikes my dad."

"He probably wanted to keep his connection to you," said Cassie, with a stroke of insight.

Tia looked up startled, peering at Cassie from under the edge of the magnifier. "Of course!" she said. "I should have realized that."

Cassie's heart seemed to twist. How could she help falling for this guy who loved Tia so much he had put off his dream to give her hers, had erased all vestiges of his father's name from his own but kept the hated family name they shared. Who named his restaurant for the mother he'd lost so young. A man who treated Anna so well, loved Beth Franklin's pottery, admired Nora's work, and appreciated Cassie's craftsmanship— even when he'd thought the work was generic.

Who could—and had—apologized multiple times for his boorishness.

Who had kissed her like that. Even though he was involved with Carla Towne.

She had to remember that.

"Your mom was truly an artist," said Cassie, to put a brake on her thoughts. Tia looked at her puzzled.

"To name him after an art museum."

"Oh," laughed Tia. "She was. She was always doing something in her studio. That's where I remember her. Every time I smelled oil paint at school, I'd think of her."

Cassie had a sharp memory of her mom's hands working at the wheel, the earthy smell.

"I know what you mean," she said.

"Tate says Mom was always happiest in Eden Beach."

"Is that why Tate opened Lydia's here, rather than in Newport?" asked Cassie.

Tia nodded her head over her work. "Probably."

Cassie watched Tia work a bit. "Tia, you should probably take a break. Let your hands relax."

Tia straightened, groaned, and flexed her fingers. She flipped the magnifier up, and blinked. "Wow," she said.

Cassie smiled. "Sometimes you forget the world is out there."

Tia got up and stretched, took the magnifier off, rubbed her forehead. She glanced at Cassie's repair box on the desk.

"Do you do a lot of repair work?" she asked.

Cassie nodded as she carved. "If it weren't for repairs," she said, "a lot of jewelers would have to shut down."

Tia watched Cassie work for a while. "I wouldn't have the courage to work on someone else's jewelry."

Cassie shrugged. "Once you learn how to use the tools—especially as well as you're using them—and learn to be careful with them, repair is usually straightforward." Then she glanced up and smiled. "Of course, just when you think that, you find you missed something and a disaster happens."

"Like what?" asked Tia.

"Like almost anything," said Cassie, leaning back in her chair. She pulled off her magnifier, yanked the pin out of her hair, and massaged her scalp. "You discover that the chain that was marked 14 karat, isn't. Or the ring that should be an easy sizing job is made with the solder equivalent of Elmer's Glue and starts to fall apart as soon as you start heating it. You take a turquoise out of a setting so you can repair the mounting and find it's thin as paper and has sawdust or something else packed behind it to make it look thick. Or, because of that, the stone breaks as you take it out and it costs a fortune to have a stone recut for a very angry customer."

"That wouldn't be a lot of fun."

"It's not," said Cassie. "But as long as I've explained the risks that any piece presents, most people understand when things like that happen. I was lucky." She smiled. "Jim had made many of the mistakes, and he warned me against most of them."

Tia nodded. "He's the guy who owned this shop, isn't he? He went missing?"

When Cassie looked at her surprised, Tia explained, "Someone mentioned him at the opening."

Of course, thought Cassie. Eden Beach was a small town, and the jewelry community was even smaller. Get enough residents together, and they were going to talk. Especially with all her mom's pottery on exhibit. She and Nora had not been the only ones to recognize it.

"I think I'd better use the ladies' room," said Tia.

Cassie laughed. "Anna calls it going to Alcatraz," she said, coiling her hair back up and stabbing it with the pin.

"Alcatraz?" said Tia, then laughed. "The Rock!" Still laughing, she headed into the back.

Cassie picked up the wax and a soft brush. Gently she dusted off the debris and began to re-mark the design for her next cuts.

The door pinged. Cassie glanced up. It was Carla Towne.

CHAPTER 22

Today Carla's color was slate gray—pale in the blouse, darker in the suit. Matching pumps. The hoops were white gold.

Cassie stood up, stepped down and through the security gate into the showroom, blocking the realtor's path so Carla could not come farther into the shop.

"Carla, I thought I made it plain you weren't welcome here," she said before Carla could say a word.

Carla smiled. "Cassie, I realize we got off on the wrong foot last time I was here."

"Getting off on the wrong foot? That's what you call threatening to put me out of my shop?"

"That's what I mean," said Carla, still smiling. "A misunderstanding."

You have got to be kidding, thought Cassie. *A misunderstanding?*

Carla waited for a moment, but Cassie simply raised an eyebrow and stared back.

"I should have been more diplomatic," said Carla. "I know things must be hard for you. I mean, with the economy down, people probably aren't buying much jewelry. After all, people aren't even buying important things, like houses." Carla gave a merry little laugh. "So I guess we both were a little edgy."

Edgy, thought Cassie. *And that was before you called my mother a drunk in front of half of Eden Beach.* She continued to stare at Carla.

Who went on, oblivious. "Anyway, I wanted to make amends." More smiles from Carla. Cassie crossed her arms and leaned back on her design desk.

"I know you're applying to the Masters."

I'm going to kill Lou for mentioning that in front of her, thought Cassie. Though she also had to remember he'd brought Millie to her, who'd not only bought the rhodolite ring, she'd commissioned the piece Cassie was carving right now.

"I thought maybe I could help," Carla was saying. "Business owner to business owner. We women have to stick together, right?"

Yep, you're my buddy, thought Cassie. But she simply said, "Oh?"

"Well, the Masters is very competitive you know, only the best get in," Carla said airily.

"Oh, really?" said Cassie. "Imagine. I've lived here all my life and didn't know that."

Carla faltered, and the skin tightened around her eyes. Cassie waited for the explosion. She was surprised when Carla gathered her composure and went on.

She must really want something, thought Cassie. Her eyes narrowed, and she began to listen with more interest.

"I don't want you to take this the wrong way," said Carla.

Too late, thought Cassie.

"But, well, while I think it's smart to try to break into a higher end market"— Cassie could see how it galled Carla to say she was smart—"Jim never really came out of the seventies. And his style"—meaning Cassie's style—"just isn't popular any more. Certainly he was never innovative like Art Jackson."

Where the hell is she going? thought Cassie. *Because she's got about two seconds before I throw her out. Through the window.*

"So I thought maybe I could give you some help getting in," said Carla.

Cassie frowned.

"Carla, the show is juried," said Cassie, as if she were explaining something to a five-year-old. "It's an even playing field."

"Well, maybe not that even," said Carla coyly.

Cassie shook her head. "Every artist who doesn't get in cries conspiracy," she said. "It's just sour grapes."

The predator came out in Carla's smile.

The piranha thinks she has me, thought Cassie. *But for what?*

"Well, I'd want to keep this just between us, you know," said Carla, taking a step closer. "I wouldn't want this to get out." She actually dropped her voice like someone might hear. "You probably don't know. I don't think it's been announced yet, but Art Jackson is going to be one of the jurors this year."

Cassie kept her face neutral, but her heart sank. *Crap. If Art—and that long nose he likes to look down—is part of the judging, I've got about no chance of getting in.*

However, he *had* just spent a lot of time at Cassie's front window looking over the new work.

Then Cassie thought, *I wonder if she's telling the truth?* After all, lying and breathing were synonymous for Carla.

"I'm a really good customer of Art's," Carla was saying. "We go back a long time."

Yes, thought Cassie. *And Art used to have a beer with Jim at our house before he got so full of himself.*

"And I don't want to brag..."

Cassie snorted mentally. *Really*, she thought.

"...but I know he values my opinion. I'd be happy to put a

little word in his ear. You know. Ask him to throw his weight behind your application."

Cassie was irked, but her curiosity was piqued. She knew no one could fix the Masters jury, but she wondered why Carla thought this would work. She also wondered what was behind this sudden offer of help.

Know your enemy, she thought. She decided to lead Carla on by feigning interest.

"Carla, there are seven jurors. Seven. Three of them aren't even from Eden Beach. Even if you could convince Art to assign a high number of points to my work, if the other six panned it, I wouldn't get in."

More piranha teeth.

"I think you underestimate Art's influence," said Carla.

I think you've been paying too much attention to Art's estimation of himself, thought Cassie.

"He has a lot of pull with the other jewelers in this town," Carla was saying.

Cassie just barely kept herself from rolling her eyes. Carla obviously had not talked to many jewelers in Eden Beach.

"And he's been in the Masters for so long, I'm sure his word would carry weight even with the outside jurors."

"You think so," said Cassie, flatly.

More teeth. "I'm sure of it."

"And why would you ask Art to do this for me?"

Carla's smile, if possible, got wider. Cassie could almost imagine feathers sticking out of her teeth. *Do piranhas swallow canaries?* she wondered.

"Well," said Carla, and Cassie couldn't believe the realtor actually started washing her hands together like a villain in an old-time silent movie. "I think we can work together." Carla took a step closer. Cassie only barely refrained from pushing the realtor away from her.

"Look, let's be frank," she said.

Oh, please do, thought Cassie.

"I talked to Rachel about your shop here. I didn't realize she had such an...emotional connection to this place. But I got the distinct feeling she'd like to get more money for these spaces."

You got no such thing, thought Cassie, her hackles beginning to rise.

"Since you remind her of poor Jim, though, she's reluctant to ask you to move out, even if she knows it's really the wrong spot for you and costs her a great deal of money."

Cassie began to straighten up in indignation. She, and Jim before her, paid the same rent as everyone else. Rachel had never given them preference because Jim was her brother.

Carla did not see the signs of the gathering storm.

"However, if you made the choice to move on your own, she wouldn't stop you."

Cassie held onto her temper—just barely.

"And...?" she said, deadly quiet.

"And really, Cassie, if you get into the Masters, wouldn't it be better to be in a quiet place where you can get your work done? Where people aren't always coming in and interrupting you?"

Especially annoying people like you? thought Cassie.

"If you had a shop in a building like the Tropicana, like Lou Pallis, you could work undisturbed."

Cassie just looked at her.

Taking her silence as encouragement, Carla continued. "I just happen to have a great space open on Glen Eden, right across from the library. It's twice the space you have here for just a little more per month. Upstairs, nice and quiet. And," said Carla, like she was handing Cassie an irresistible present, "there are a number of attorneys and financial people in the building. You would have access to any number of potential customers—people who don't usually come down here because of all the tourists."

Cassie knew the building Carla was talking about. It was another of Alden Towne's buildings—or rather Eden Beach Land Management's. Carla was right. The building was full of well-heeled professionals. People who would never look twice at her work. Not only that, Cassie knew very well that, even if she wanted to move into the space, which she didn't, the other tenants would object—loudly—to the smell of burning wax and rubber, and the thought of large gas and acetylene tanks above, below, or next to their offices.

She must have hesitated too long, because Carla was moving in for the kill.

"I know what you're thinking," she said.

No, you don't, thought Cassie.

"Moving would be expensive—the initial rental costs, moving your equipment. But I can help with that, too," said Carla.

"And how would you do that?" Cassie asked her. *My*, she thought, *you are just all kinds of helpful today.*

"Well, just between us, Si Corwin's daughter, Virgie, is starting a little cupcake business."

"Cupcakes?" said Cassie, disbelief on her face. *That will go nowhere*, she thought.

"Yes," said Carla. "Si thinks this would be the perfect place to give her a great start."

"Here. My shop," said Cassie, flatly. Why was she not surprised that Corwin would be part of this.

"Si's willing to pay a, well, a bonus to be able to take over the lease," said Carla.

Be honest, Carla, thought Cassie. *He's offered you a bribe.*

"I'd be happy to give you $10,000 of that as a moving bonus," said Carla.

Cassie was stunned. If this was true, and Carla was really

willing to part with $10,000, the amount Si had offered her must be…beyond her wildest imagination.

She felt her temper rising again. This woman was playing at this like it was Monopoly. It didn't matter that this business was Cassie's dream and Jim's legacy. That didn't even register with Carla. It was simply so much cash to her.

So much power.

"So essentially, you're selling Art's integrity for ten grand," said Cassie, not bothering to hide the contempt in her voice. "Strange that, for someone so close to Art, you don't know he can't be bought."

Carla's smile slipped.

"This is the same way you gave Ron Baxter the old bait and switch," said Cassie, dropping her arms and standing up until she towered over Carla, her fury making her 5'9" seem even taller. "Offer him a great new space, for only a little more money, and promise you'll help him out of his lease so you can re-rent the place to Tate Garner for his restaurant. For a lot more, I'm sure. Only, after Ron broke the lease—and got sued, by your father, I might add—he discovered that, oh, gee, so sorry, the new space was not going to be available—for another year!"

Carla's smile was gone. "Look. I'm just trying to give you a hand here."

"No, you're not," said Cassie, throat tight with anger. She felt herself starting to shake. "You're trying to give *you* a hand here."

Carla went white around the mouth as her lips compressed.

"You have no clue," spat Carla. "This is very valuable real estate. These little artsy tourist shops are a waste of space. There are other, much more suitable businesses that could go in here."

"Like cupcakes?"

Carla seemed disconcerted for a moment, and Cassie realized that the story about Si Corwin's daughter had been a lie. What could Carla want to put in here that would be worth $10,000 to her?

The light that dawned on Cassie was blinding.

"Or, maybe," she said, "a real estate office?"

Carla stepped back as if she'd been hit.

"I should have seen it before," said Cassie. "You want this for yourself. You and Alden will set up here like land barons. Every visitor who comes to town and takes a picture of the landmark theater next door," she waved a hand toward the ticket office she could see out her window, "will have a picture of your real estate office when they decide they want to live here.

"So you want to take my shop, Delia's, Connie's. Take the building from Rachel, maybe? Talk about a waste of space. What'll it be, Carla? Sell the real estate first, sell the air next? Then maybe license the views?"

Carla was rigid, her face twisted with anger. "How dare you!" she snarled. "You think you can sit here and make your tourist trinkets and thumb your nose at everyone. But you can't. This town is changing. The kind of people who are moving in here don't want tacky tourist shops, old hippies, and people who think they're hippies with their little pots and looms and dope.

Cassie stepped toward her. "Take your money and get out, Carla."

"I'm not done," said Carla.

"Oh, yes, you are," said Cassie, astonishing herself with her calm. "Once I let Rachel know you're not only gunning for the merchants, you're gunning for her building, too. Once all the merchants start recommending other real estate agents in Eden Beach when someone asks. Oh, and I'll make sure Art knows you're trying to destroy his reputation, too."

"You think you're untouchable, Cassie Franklin. But before I'm done with you, you'll be happy to find a spot on the beach hammering out spoon rings!" spat Carla.

"Get. Out." Cassie took another step toward Carla.

"And I'll make damn sure you don't get into the Masters!" The realtor spun, threw open the door, and marched out.

"Aiyyi!" yelled Cassie at the closed door, then added. "Bitch!" She pointed at the door. "I will *die* in this shop before I see *you* in it!" She ripped the pin out of her hair and drove her hands into her mane. "And I will *so* get into the Masters and spit in your eye!"

Spinning around, Cassie saw Tia standing in the door to the back room. She was white. Cassie had completely forgotten the girl was there. Carla must not have seen her, either.

The two stared at each other for a minute.

"Sorry," said Cassie, finally, as her adrenalin receded and her heart beat slowed. "I'm sorry you had to hear that. That was ugly. Eden Beach's dark underbelly. Its name is Towne."

She suddenly remembered Carla clinging to Tate's arm at the opening, Carla's look on finding Cassie in Tate's arms.

She closed her eyes. "Tia, I'm sorry, really sorry. I forgot that she and Tate were a thing. I shouldn't have said that."

Tia shook her head slightly and came down the steps. "No worries there," she said, her voice shaking slightly. "I agree with you. She is a bitch. Tate is an idiot." She unlocked the gate and went out to Cassie. "Domingo and I know that, but Tate..." Tia shrugged. "Sometimes he's not particularly smart about women, Domingo says. Though frankly, I think most of it's Carla."

"I'm still sorry," said Cassie. "I honestly forgot you were back there or I would—maybe—not have said the things I did." She managed a half smile. "But then, maybe not. Carla pushes my buttons." She made a face. "Like you couldn't tell."

Tia didn't smile back. "She threatened you."

"Nothing new," said Cassie and sighed. "Carla's a bully. She threatens everyone."

"But she said she'd talked to your landlord. Can she really get you evicted?"

"That's why she was here. She already tried. Rachel will not evict me."

"How can you be so sure?"

"Jim was her brother," said Cassie. "Rachel is kind of like this...eccentric aunt." Cassie shrugged and tried to roll shoulders that were almost immobile they were so tight. "I need something to drink," she said. "You?"

Tia nodded. Cassie let them both into the design area and pulled a tea out of the fridge. "Tea? Water? Soda?" she asked Tia, gesturing to the fridge.

Tia grabbed a Diet Coke and popped the top. "Thanks," she said as they both sat down.

"Are you going to tell Art what she said?" asked Tia, after she'd had a swallow of her soda.

Cassie shook her head. "No. No need to bring Art into this mess."

"Why not?" asked Tia, a bit indignant. "She's telling people she can influence the way he votes as a judge. Couldn't that hurt his reputation?"

Cassie shook her head and took another drink of her tea. She had already finished half the bottle. "No," she said. "The only person she's saying that to is me. And it isn't true. She was making it up. Even if she could influence the voting—which she can't—she had no intention of helping me. She just wanted to get me committed to leaving the shop."

She started to take another drink, then added, "I doubt she's really a customer of Art's. I've never seen her wear a piece of his jewelry. Even at the Masters openings. Women who own his jewelry wear it, believe me. Art's work is a status symbol around here."

They sat in silence for a while. Tia was thoughtful. Cassie's hands had finally stopped shaking.

"What you said," asked Tia, finally, "about her forcing the previous business out of Tate's building, was that true?"

Cassie sighed. "Unfortunately, yes." She shook her head. "She and her father are buying up or trying to control a lot of Eden Beach. They've already forced a bunch of merchants out. Ron was just one more."

"So Carla is really the person who owns Tate's building?"

Cassie nodded. "Well, Alden Towne does, through Eden Beach Land Management." She wondered if Tia knew how her father and the Townes were connected. She doubted it.

"I don't know what Tate will say when I tell him that," said Tia, almost to herself. "He thought she got him such a good deal on the lease."

"Tia," said Cassie, setting the empty bottle on the desk. "Maybe you shouldn't tell him what you heard."

Tia stopped in the process of raising the can of Coke to her mouth. "Why on earth not?" she said, her eyes wide with surprise. "Why would you want to protect Carla?"

"Oh, believe me," said Cassie, leaning back and putting up her hands in denial. "The last thing I would *ever* do is try to protect Carla." She lowered her hands. "But Tate's in, and he's spent a lot of money on remodeling. There's nothing you or he can do about the building's ownership—or about Carla, unfortunately." Cassie looked down remembering Tate's arms around her and the rain pounding outside. She shook her head to clear the images. "His business is going well. And he's... You said he's very happy."

Tia smiled and nodded. "He really is," she said.

"Then don't tell him." Cassie leaned forward and put her

hand on Tia's. "He'll find out soon enough what Carla and Alden Towne are like. Let him just be happy for now."

Tia looked at her quizzically. "You like him, don't you?" she said.

Cassie leaned back. "I appreciate what he's done. I know what it's like to make a dream a reality. He deserves to enjoy that new shine for a while."

Tia shook her head. "I really don't know what he sees in her," she said. "Especially after that woman in Paris, you'd think he'd be smarter."

"I can imagine that was hard."

"Domingo said Tate was really bitter and angry about it," Tia continued. "I didn't know that until Domingo told me." She shook her head again. "That's why I don't get this thing with Carla, why he lets her hang around. Domingo doesn't get it either. He's been pretty blunt with Tate. Told him Carla was trying to haul him in like a big fish. Things are a little stressed between them right now, in fact."

Tia looked straight at Cassie. "I was kind of hoping maybe you and Tate would hit it off," she said. "You seem more his type." She smiled. "Kind of independent. A bit crazy. I think Anna was talking you up to him, too."

I'll throttle her, thought Cassie.

"Yes, well, Anna has tried talking me up for years," she said lightly. "Especially since she got married."

Tia watched Cassie for a minute. Cassie was uncomfortable under her scrutiny. She took a big breath.

"Well," she said. "I think I've had my fill of drama. Back to work for me." She stood. "Do you feel up to it?"

"Absolutely," said Tia.

Cassie smiled, held her hand out and gestured to the bench. She saw the knowing look on Tia's face, though. *I haven't fooled her at all*, she thought.

CHAPTER 23

The noise level at Clancy's was a pleasant background as the waiter set Nora's wine down on the table. Nora lifted it in a toast. "Here's to you! Congratulations!"

Cassie and Anna had gone together the previous day to drop off their applications at the Masters office. For better or worse, it was done.

Cassie picked up her iced tea, smiling, and touched her glass to Nora's. "Thanks, but I think you're a bit premature," she said.

Nora shook her head. "You've taken the biggest step," she said. "You took a risk, came up with some incredible new work, and made your application. I know you'll be disappointed if you don't get in, but," Nora touched the neckpiece she was wearing, which Cassie had just finished, "you already know you did the right thing." While they were waiting to be seated, a group of women had lavishly complimented the jewelry she and Nora were wearing. One of them had bought a small brooch right off Cassie's jacket.

It had been like that much of the previous week. The

small work was selling well. Cassie was scrambling to keep up. Lou was pressing her to raise the prices again.

"In fact," said Nora, taking a sip of her wine, "maybe I'll let *you* buy brunch."

Cassie laughed. "You know, I think I will."

"I was joking!" spluttered Nora.

Cassie smiled and put her hand on Nora's arm. "But I'm not," she said. "Nora, you have been terrific. Feeding me, supporting me. Nagging me. "

Now Nora laughed.

Cassie raised her glass. "Here's to *you*," she said quietly. Nora squeezed her hand gently.

"And since we're celebrating," said Nora, after a moment, "Melody tells me she saw Art Jackson coming out of the shop a couple days ago. What was that about?"

Cassie paused as she was putting her glass down. "I didn't tell you about that, did I?"

Nora shook her head, smiling.

"I guess I keep thinking I dreamed it," said Cassie. "When he walked in the door I was so stunned I almost couldn't speak."

"Hey, Art," was what she'd finally said, taking off her head magnifier and getting up. She'd known Art since she was small, but had never been close to him. He hadn't been in the shop since Jim had disappeared, and had only rarely been in before that. "It's nice to see you." Cassie had walked down to meet him on the showroom floor. "What brings you in?"

Tall and thin to the point of gauntness, long fingers that always seemed to be moving, thinning gray hair, and slightly large dark eyes, Art always reminded Cassie of a praying mantis. Never one to beat around the bushes, he came right to the point. "This new work of yours."

Cassie's heart plunged right to her stomach, and the blood drained from her cheeks. She felt like she was going to be sick. "Oh?" she said, her voice sounding odd and distant in her ears. He was going to tell her it was crap. She knew it. He was going to tell her he was a Masters judge—assuming Carla hadn't been lying—and that she didn't have a prayer of getting in.

But instead, he said, "I'd like to take a closer look at it."

"Be my guest," said Cassie, reaching into her pocket for the case key. Her hands felt like they were shaking, but Cassie was glad to see they were steady when she put the key in the lock.

She pulled out the botryoidal chrysocolla brooch and handed it to him. Art carried it closer to the front window where the light was better. He turned it over in his hands, feeling it all over, looking for rough spots. Then he pulled out a loupe.

Cassie stood next to him, aware of people passing on the street looking in. But her eyes were on Art. He kept nodding.

"Clever catch," he finally said. "Looks a bit like Lou's work."

"Yes, he helped me figure it out," said Cassie. Art's comment made her nervous. She'd never heard you couldn't get help from someone.

"Can I see that neckpiece in the window?" he asked, as if she hadn't spoken.

Without a word, Cassie unlocked the case and pulled the piece out. Her heart had moved back into her chest and was beating normally. *If he'd planned to trash the work*, she thought, *he wouldn't have come in*. She was trying hard not to get excited.

Art set the brooch on the case behind him and took the neckpiece. It was made from a piece of the slate tile Tate had given her that rainy morning she'd walked into his arms. She'd broken the tile on the sidewalk outside and refashioned the most interesting pieces. There were three, of differing sizes, in the neckpiece. Tiny diamonds glittered along the ridges of the slate, bits of gold between them. She had, with memories of Tate, named the piece, "Sun's Morning Kiss."

"Is this gold leaf on the slate?" asked Art, frowning.

Cassie nodded. Moving closer, she pointed out how she'd used it to define the ridges in the slate's texture, explained how she'd had to be careful not to get carried away. She told him about learning from Yiannis.

"Did Jim cut these stones?" Art asked.

"He cut most of them," said Cassie. "I had them in an old shoe box in the closet. But I cut the slate and a couple others."

Art kept turning the piece over and over, his busy fingers touching every surface. Then he went back to the chrysocolla.

"I'm glad to see you using Jim's stone work," he said finally. "I always wondered why he didn't do more. It was his strength, much more than the jewelry work." He looked at her. "You do him proud."

Now Cassie felt the blood rush *up* to her face.

This was Art talking? Art was praising her work? "Thank you," she finally managed to say.

"Is this the work you're entering into the Masters?" he asked.

She nodded once.

"I think you'll do well with it," he said. "Though, I won't lie to you. Some of the judges may have trouble with it."

"Why?"

"Some think jewelry should be all gold and diamonds." He waved a hand at the pieces now sitting on the case. "Your choice of unusual stones could confuse them."

"I'll take my chances," said Cassie.

Art nodded.

"There's only one thing wrong that I can see," he added.

Cassie froze.

"The prices are too low," said Art. He picked up the botryoidal chrysocolla. "This, for example. This stone will be difficult to replace. And the workmanship is excellent. You need to charge what you're worth."

More? she thought. *He thinks I should charge more for it? And the work is excellent?* At Lou's insistence, she'd already doubled the price she'd had on the chrysocolla originally.

"This kind of uniqueness and quality," said Art, "has to come with a price."

Cassie could hardly breathe. "What do you think I should ask for it?" She managed to ask. She was quite proud of herself that she sounded casual.

"Double it," said Art. "Same with that one." His long fingers gestured to the neckpiece in her hand.

"I'm not sure the market will pay that," she said.

"Are they selling quickly?"

Cassie nodded. "Actually, the smaller pieces are."

"Then the prices are probably too low. Raise them. Especially on the stones you can't replace."

"That must have been quite a moment," said Nora, smiling.

"Nora, I thought I was going to fly. I had to go back into the bathroom and scream. I can't believe I didn't tell you this."

"Well, I haven't seen much of you in the last few weeks," said Nora, laughing. "So did you raise the prices?"

"I did," said Cassie, in tones of wonder. "That was one of the new prices that lady just paid for my brooch."

Nora grinned at Cassie. "I told you Art looked at the work of others. Don't be surprised if he uses some of your concepts next year." She raised her glass again to Cassie. "Congratulations."

Cassie put a hand on her heart and gave a mock bow.

"So," said Cassie, as Nora sipped her wine. "Speaking of Melody, what are you two up to? She's been taking you down to her shop an awful lot lately. That usually spells trouble." Nora looked surprised. "Lou told me," said Cassie and smiled. "He loves to gossip, you know that. So what's up?"

Now Nora looked a bit sheepish.

Just then the waiter came up and set their orders on the table. When he'd refreshed Cassie's tea, asked Nora if she wanted more wine, provided more bread, and left, Cassie looked at Nora.

"So?" she said, and took a bite of her meal. She closed her eyes in ecstasy. "This is so good."

"Well, do you remember I said that Tate's opening party was half of a good idea?" asked Nora.

Cassie looked at her blankly, then frowned. "Not really, no."

"You saw how many people were there," Nora went on. "And yes, it was the free food and drink. But I wondered— Melody and I wondered—if something like that wouldn't be nice to do two or three times during the winter months. Except it would include different restaurants and Eden Beach artists."

"Like a Tupperware party but with art?" asked Cassie.

Nora laughed. "Yeah, well, I guess, a little. And without the games!" Cassie smiled, and Nora went on. "We thought it could be held at one of the nicer, more interesting restaurants —like Tate's." Nora paused briefly, but Cassie kept her face non-committal. "Or the Byzantium. Or Cabo's," Nora went on. She took a bite of the Florentine. It was all she ever ordered. "Too bad Clancy's is not in Eden Beach," she said.

"You're not thinking of including The Eden Beach Table?" asked Cassie, with a small smile.

Nora waved away the suggestion. "As if Si Corwin even knows there *are* artists in Eden Beach," she said taking another bite. Then she went on. "At each event, there would be maybe five different artists—a weaver, potter, jeweler, painter, for example," she continued. "It would be invitation only. Each participant would give invitations to their best customers and ask them to invite a guest—hopefully someone who hadn't bought from us before."

Cassie nodded. "It's a good idea. But a big cost for the restaurants."

"Yes," said Nora, and hesitated. "Melody and I are meeting with Tate this week to ask him about that, get his ideas, and to see if he'd want to do another event, maybe before Christmas."

"He might be willing, since he's new in town," said Cassie. She knew Nora was waiting for her to say more. When she didn't, Nora went on.

"You haven't said much about Tate," said Nora, "not since that morning."

Cassie had been so snappish, angry at herself for being a fool, and taking it out on Nora, that Nora had finally confronted her. Reluctantly, Cassie had told her about the morning at the restaurant. Cassie didn't cry easily. She hadn't shed a tear over Phil, although she'd used up a store of profanity that would have shocked Consuelo. But when she had told Nora about Tate's kiss, she'd found herself sobbing on Nora's shoulder. Nora had just held her and let her cry.

Cassie gave a small shrug. "Nothing to say." She concentrated on her meal.

There *wasn't* anything to say about Tate. She hadn't talked to him since that rainy morning. A couple times, she'd seen him pass her store window on his way to Lydia's early in the morning. Each time, her heart had flipped, and blood had rushed to her face as her body remembered the feel of him against her, his hair curling around her fingers. But he hadn't stopped by, not even to apologize. *Carla probably threatened him*, thought Cassie. She didn't know whether she was sad, angry, disappointed, or all of them together. She knew she just felt...empty, when she thought of Tate. So she kept her hands busy, her mind on her work, and pushed all thought of him away.

"Doesn't Tia talk about him?" Nora persisted after a minute.

Cassie shrugged again. "Sure. But not a lot. And it's what you would expect. Big brother stuff." Tia had talked about the postcards, pictures, and letters he'd sent her from all over Europe and the US, and how she'd waited each week to get them. She'd told Cassie how angry she'd been sometimes that Tate had left.

The one thing Tia never mentioned was the morning Cassie had walked into Tate's arms. Cassie assumed that neither Tate nor Carla had mentioned it to her.

"Mostly Tia talks about jewelry," she went on. "Nora, she is learning so fast. I'm thinking of asking her to sit the booth at the Masters during the day, if I get in, or to help with the shop."

"Good for you!" said Nora, letting Cassie change the subject. "I like that you're thinking positively."

Cassie smiled. "She can also help at the Pepper Tree if I *don't* get into the Masters." She and Nora had applied, as usual, for shared booth space at the Pepper Tree Art and Craft Show and been accepted.

"Or if you get into both," said Nora.

"If I need to do both shows and keep the shop open," said Cassie, "Tia better learn faster. She'll have to be making jewelry, too!"

"You'd better talk to her," said Nora. "That just might happen. You remember what happened when Beth applied to those three shows, thinking she'd be lucky to get into one?"

Cassie laughed. "She burned out a wheel trying to make enough for all of them."

Nora smiled sadly. "Sometimes I miss her so much." She got a faraway look in her eyes, and said, "I remember..."

Cassie let her talk. She loved to hear stories about Nora and Beth when they were younger. Their struggles to survive, their friends, their near disasters. So Cassie and Nora reminisced about Beth Franklin while they demolished their meals and finished off the bread. It felt as if Beth were celebrating with them.

When the waiter asked about dessert, they both groaned. He brought the check. Cassie snatched it up before Nora could reach for it.

"I meant what I said," she said.

When she had paid, they got up and moved slowly toward the front of the restaurant, Nora leading. Near the door, Nora hesitated. Cassie, puzzled, followed her glance. In a corner booth Tate and Carla Towne sat close together. Carla happened to glance their way at the same time, catching Cassie's eye. A smug look crossed her face.

Cassie felt a wave of loathing wash over her, but she looked away from Carla as if she couldn't care less. She did not even glance at Tate. She touched Nora's arm. The older woman started moving again toward the exit.

"See?" said Cassie quietly. "Nothing to say."

WONDERING WHAT HAD CAUGHT CARLA'S ATTENTION, Tate turned just in time to see Cassie and Nora leave the restaurant.

His heart twisted in his chest. It did every time he caught sight of her, or when Tia mentioned her work with Cassie. Every time he woke in the middle of the night imagining he could smell the rain in her hair, feel the shape of her body in his hands. He wanted to go back to that morning. He wanted everything he'd believed of her to be true.

What Tate did not want to know is that Cassie had been seeing a married man. After he'd discovered Avril cheating on him, it was the one thing he could not excuse or forgive.

He turned back to find Carla watching him. She nodded as if he'd said something.

"Poor Nora," she said. "It's so sad." When Tate didn't respond, Carla went on. "While Cassie and I don't get along, you do have to admire her. For taking on a burden like that." She nodded her head in the direction of the front door and sighed dramatically. "I expect the guilt is crushing, though."

"I don't think Nora considers herself a burden," said Tate, annoyed, as he usually was when Carla started talking about the merchants in Eden Beach. She had so much contempt for the people running small businesses. He wondered what she said about him when he wasn't around.

Tate was irritated anyway—with Carla and with himself. He had agreed to meet Carla for brunch because she was supposed to introduce him to a radio producer who wanted a cooking show. It would be a good gig—building his name, advertising his restaurant. But when Tate had arrived, Carla was all apologies. The producer had not been able to make it. Instead, she'd spent the last forty-five minutes trying to interest him in a space in Newport. Tate had finally realized that that had been her plan all along. He was waiting until he could decently end the meal.

"I hardly expect Cassie should or would feel guilty because Nora was injured. It isn't *her* fault," he added.

"Oh," said Carla, feigning surprise. "I assumed you knew."

"Knew what?"

Carla hesitated, dropping her eyes, as if perhaps she'd said too much. "Well, it's not a secret. It was in all the papers."

When she looked up, Carla's mask of compassion couldn't quite hide the look of triumph.

I hope you never feel sorry for me, thought Tate, feeling his skin crawl.

"Beth Franklin was drunk," Carla went on. "But then, she usually was. She was an alcoholic. I have no idea why she was driving that night. But she drove off the road and into a canyon." Carla sighed again. "She paid for it, of course. The accident killed her. But poor Nora." More head shaking. "To be crippled like that."

Tate was stunned. Nora had told him about the accident, but not that Beth had been drunk. Now he understood Cassie and Anna's reaction at the open house when Carla had mentioned alcoholism.

"I guess that's why Cassie's trying to get into the Masters," said Carla. "She thinks it will make a lot of money for her. But really. Have you seen the so-called jewelry she's making?"

Tate had. He'd been stunned—and thrilled—to see how the actual pieces had so far exceeded the drawings Cassie had made on that rainy morning.

"Tia says the work is selling well," said Tate, holding in his anger. He wasn't sure he could stand Carla's company for much longer. "She's sure Cassie will get into the Masters."

"Well, of course she's sure. With Lou doing the work for her and Art, well, Art helping her, too," said Carla.

"What are you talking about, Lou doing her work?" asked Tate.

"Oh, please, Tate. Cassie doesn't have the talent to do those kinds of complex things. Everyone's wondering how she learned so suddenly."

That morning, thought Tate, *Cassie said she didn't have the skill*. Then he remembered seeing her coming out of Lou's shop.

"And then, well, maybe I shouldn't say this..."

"You're right," said Tate. "Maybe you shouldn't." *And maybe I shouldn't be listening,* he thought.

It was not what Carla wanted to hear, he saw.

"I don't suppose Tia told you Cassie tried to bribe me."

It wasn't what Tate had expected. "What?" he said.

"She tried to bribe *me!*" Carla let some indignation show. "She offered me $10,000 if I'd put in a word with Art Jackson."

Tate's eyebrows crashed together in disbelief.

Carla nodded. "I don't know how she found out Art's one of the jurors this year. It's no secret that Art is a good friend of mine." She shook her head. "It was sad, really. Made me feel really sorry for her that she was so desperate."

Tate thought Cassie was anything but desperate. He recognized beautiful design when he saw it. He thought the judges would see it, too, though he didn't know what they'd say about someone else doing the work.

"Carla," said Tate, skepticism evident in his voice, "even I know there's more than just one juror. Are you saying Cassie is going to subvert *all* of them?"

"She wouldn't have to," said Carla smugly. "Art has a lot of pull in Eden Beach. He's been in the Masters for more than twenty-five years. Everyone knows him and his work. A word from him would get her in. Or keep her out." Carla picked up her wine glass, swirled the liquid in it. "Of course, I told her no," she said, and sipped the wine.

This is screwy, thought Tate. *Surely the Masters doesn't work that way.*

"That doesn't make any sense," said Tate, shaking his head. "You've told me—repeatedly—that you expect to get Cassie's shop because she can't pay her rent. You've told me that she wanted to get money from me to pay for it, that she'd already asked your friend for money. Yet you're telling me she's offered you $10,000 to bribe one juror with the hope he'll influence the others? Even if what you've said is true, where would Cassie get that kind of money?"

Carla gave a little shrug and a predator's smile, though Tate didn't recognize it for what it was. "She seems to be getting very friendly with Tia."

Tate looked at her like she'd lost her mind. "Tia barely makes minimum wage, Carla."

"But she could borrow it from your father, couldn't she?"

Cold day in hell, thought Tate. Martin had been almost incandescent with rage when Tia had told him she was working at a nursery. He hadn't spoken to Tia since.

The thought gave him pause, though. Cassie couldn't be doing that, could she? Using Tia, hoping to borrow money from Martin? It did make a twisted kind of sense.

No. He could not believe it. He *would* not believe it.

"Of course," said Carla, her eyes on his face, "that uncle of Lou's seems to be very interested in her all of a sudden."

Against his will, Tate remembered Yiannis telling Lou he'd do anything he could to help the beautiful young woman.

"Lou and Art go way back, too."

Tate suddenly remembered. The previous week he'd passed Cassie's shop and seen Cassie and Art, heads bent over her work. He'd thought Art had been admiring it. But maybe something else had been going on. Lou had told him Art never thought anyone's work was any good.

It can't be true, thought Tate. *She doesn't have to do that*. But he realized he was new in Eden Beach. Maybe she *did* have to do that. Maybe that's how things worked. He felt sick.

Then he was angry, angry with himself. He was betraying Cassie just by listening.

"Carla, I have to get back to the restaurant," he said, raising a hand and flagging the waiter.

Carla seemed flustered at his quick change of attitude.

"But we haven't had much time to talk about the location I was telling you about..."

"Carla, I like the place I'm in. I'm not interested in re-opening somewhere else. I'm certainly not interested in opening in Newport."

He stood, took the bill from the waiter, pulled his wallet out, and paid.

As the waiter walked away, he turned to Carla, who was scrambling to collect her purse and jacket. "And just so you know, I really don't appreciate you lying to me about the radio show."

Carla looked up at him.

"That was never really on offer, was it? You just wanted to try to get me into another piece of real estate." He raised an eyebrow. "Maybe *you're* the one who's trying to get money from Martin. Why don't you just call him directly? I understand your dad and he are old pals. He'd probably only charge you a pound of flesh."

Tate turned and walked out of the restaurant, leaving Carla gaping like a fish.

CHAPTER 24

IT WAS JUST GETTING LIGHT, AND THE FOG was heavy, hiding the vastness of the ocean. The waves seemed to come out of the gray unexpectedly to break on the beach.

Tate had already run two miles along the bluff. Now he was pounding along the Main Beach boardwalk. The fog and exertion had soaked through his sweatshirt. His hair dripped into his eyes. With his body working so hard on its own, Tate's mind was free to think and plan.

Their November menu was one of the best they'd developed. There had been several more reviews, one in San Diego and two in local glossy publications. While one had been lukewarm, the others were very good indeed. Lydia's had a full reservation book for most nights and lines at lunch. Sunday brunch was so full, he'd bought a couple more outside heaters so they could use the patio on days like this. Tate had started booking catering events for the holidays and was beginning to bank a bit of money, though he wasn't out of the woods financially, and wouldn't be for a long while yet. But barring disasters, and in spite of redesigning his initial concept, he was off to a good start.

He'd had to replace two of his wait staff, and a couple others had simply moved on. That was normal. By and large, everyone else was working out very well.

Anna had turned out to be his best hire, so much so he'd given her a raise at the first of the month. She kept a close eye on the bar and the liquor. She had recommended he hire—and had trained—her assistant, Jesse, who was just as efficient. She was his first steal from The Eden Beach Table and Si Corwin had been furious. Once or twice a week, Tate had Table staff coming to him looking for work. Anna, who seemed to know everyone, had rejected them all except for Jesse.

Anna's paintings were an unexpected bonus. Tate had bought them because he loved them. But he couldn't keep them on the walls, especially the small ones she'd brought in. They'd sold another one just the past week. Every day he had offers for Beth Franklin's porcelain. He'd become so concerned that they might walk away that he'd had glass cases installed into the alcoves to protect them.

He'd done that as much for Cassie and Nora as for himself. While he would be saddened to lose the porcelains through theft or breakage, he knew it would break their hearts to lose pieces that could never be replaced.

Cassie.

Every morning, just about now as he ran on the beach across from her shop, he thought about her.

Talk about broken hearts, he thought.

He immediately squelched the thought, but it just scurried away to hide. It would come back. It always did. He'd never been like this, unable to shake off the thought of a woman.

But this wasn't any woman. This was Cassie.

Late at night, just as he drifted to sleep, he found himself thinking about the few moments he'd had with her. The morning they'd sat on the bluff, her hair curling around her face, eyes red from crying. Breakfast on his stoop.

That amazing kiss.

The thought of her kiss usually woke Tate up again. Soft. Warm. Her mouth as hungry as his. Her fingers stroking his neck. His arms pulling her close, her body leaning into his, firm breasts and thighs aligning with his.

Once his mind started down that path, Tate would toss and turn for an hour or more. Sometimes, he'd get up to run in the dark streets around his home until he was exhausted.

In the mornings he ran by her shop. Hoping for a glimpse of her. Hoping he wouldn't see her.

You're a mess, Garner, he thought.

He told himself to run somewhere else. But he knew he wouldn't. He wanted to straighten this out, to know—one way or another—if Carla had been telling him the truth.

He could not, however, figure out how to do that.

Both Domingo and Anna despised Carla. Domingo had told him—forcefully and repeatedly—that Carla was using him. Anna refused to serve her. If Carla came in to the restaurant, Anna would be busy somewhere else. Tate had caught the look Anna sent him sometimes, when he was talking to Carla. It was quite clear she questioned his judgement.

That won't be a problem anymore, he thought. He hadn't seen or heard from Carla since their brunch meeting at Clancy's. *Thank goodness.*

He trusted his friends. So why was he listening to Carla? Why believe someone who no one—not even Tate—liked? Who no one trusted?

Simple. Tate hadn't liked Jean-Paul. The *maître d'* of the restaurant where he'd worked in Paris was a liar and a thief, stabbing employees in the back and stealing wines from the cellar. So Tate hadn't believed him when Jean-Paul had told him Avril was sleeping with her father's friend.

When Tate had discovered it was true, he had wondered how many of the other supposed lies Jean-Paul had told were true. Now, while it might well be that Carla had been undermining Cassie for her own ends, it did not necessarily mean she was lying.

What if she is, though? thought Tate.

And what if she's telling the truth?

Tate couldn't ask Lou. He'd be too embarrassed. And he wasn't sure what Lou's relationship was with Cassie. He'd seen them a couple times together, once having brunch at Cabo's. Once on the beach at the foot of the bluffs, heads together, a sketchpad between them.

What if Carla was right about Lou doing the work for Cassie's new pieces?

It was one thing to hire someone to do what you couldn't do in a business. But wasn't the Masters supposed to showcase the artists' own talents? Wasn't it deceitful to pass off Lou's work as her own?

Why would Lou do that?

Tate stepped on that thought.

Then there was the whole bribe thing.

Tate had once talked to Art about the Masters—how long he'd participated, what it took to get in. Art had been derisive about most of the other jewelers.

But he hadn't mentioned Cassie. *Why?* wondered Tate. Did he think Cassie's work was better than the other jewelers he was putting down? Or was it because he'd agreed to get her into the Masters?

He certainly couldn't ask Tia. She thought the world of Cassie. She not only spent as much time working with Cassie as she could, she planned to start taking jewelry-making classes at the Eden Beach Art Institute in the spring.

Although she continued to work at the nursery, and to care for the plants in Lydia's, he could tell that Tia had largely forgotten about landscape gardening.

Tate was sure Cassie wasn't using Tia to get financial support from Martin. That certainly would have soured their relationship.

But what about Tate?

Was it only coincidence that Cassie had warmed to him after she'd learned he was Martin Garner's son?

The ugly thought would not go away.

There had been a girl in high school—Trisha? Trina?— who'd made her interest in Tate very clear. But when he'd gone to pick her up for a date—on the bike and wearing jeans and his leather jacket—she'd been dressed in a thigh-length, sequined dress and spike heels. She'd actually said, "Where's your Mercedes?" After that, she wanted nothing to do with Tate.

And, of course, there'd been Avril. Avaricious Avril.

He'd been sure Cassie was different. He'd needed her to be different.

But if she'd been fishing for money, why hadn't she followed up after that kiss?

That incredible kiss.

Did she think Carla had blown it for her by walking in while she was kissing Tate? Had she found the money she needed somewhere else?

Wasn't that why she was avoiding him?

Tate knew Cassie was dodging through alleys to avoid coming by Lydia's. He'd seen her.

Why was she doing that, if she'd been falling for Tate as hard as he was falling for her?

Wasn't the easiest explanation that Cassie was avoiding him because she'd found someone else more useful to her?

Was Carla right?

Tate had run to the end of Main Beach and was turning to run back along the highway when he saw Cassie, as if he'd conjured her, step from Park and turn north onto the highway toward her shop.

He stopped for a moment, jogging in place behind a group of palms, and watched her.

Now, he thought, *go talk to her.*

And say what?

What could he say that wouldn't sound like an accusation?

Is it true you were sleeping with a married guy?

Are you bribing your way into the Masters?

Were you using me?

Tate watched her for a moment, angry, sad, confused.

Lonely.

He was intensely lonely for her, for the Cassie he thought he knew. The Cassie he wanted to know. The Cassie he wanted her to be.

The Cassie he wanted.

He watched her disappear into the fog, like she'd never existed. Then he jogged up to the highway and turned south, away from Cassie.

Tate returned to his home on the bluff via Glen Eden and Beach, avoiding the run past Cassie's shop. He was annoyed with himself. He knew Cassie was avoiding him. Now he was avoiding her.

So adult, he thought to himself, as he stood in the shower. He felt ridiculous. He hadn't acted like this since high school. *That should tell me something*, he thought.

Still, he found himself walking to the restaurant through back streets rather than going Coast Highway—past Cassie's shop—which would have been faster.

They were just finishing the set up for Sunday brunch, when Tate noticed one of the flood lights in a display case had burned out. He unscrewed it and went into the kitchen. No spares.

Always, he thought.

"Mingo, I'm going to run to Eagle Hardware," he said, holding up the burned out flood. "Anything else you can think of we need?"

"That set of screwdrivers you keep talking about, maybe?" said Domingo, raising an eyebrow and giving Tate a half smile.

Tate snapped his fingers and pointed at Domingo. "That's why I pay you the big bucks," he said. "Thanks!"

"Yeah. About those big bucks..." Domingo started to say.

Tate grinned. "Gotta run! We'll talk later!"

Domingo shook his head and waved his hand in a "get out of here" gesture.

Tate smiled again to himself as he headed out the back door and down the alley to Canyon. It felt like things were getting better between him and Domingo. Maybe now that Carla wouldn't be coming back, he and his old friend would get back onto a solid footing.

The fog was starting to burn off. As he turned down Canyon, Tate saw a shaft of sunlight turn the ocean golden. Glimpses of blue sky showed through holes in the cloud cover. It was going to be a beautiful day.

Tate snatched up a basket, found the bulbs, picked up a replacement and a couple spares. Murphy's law: As soon as he replaced one, another would burn out. Best be ready for it.

He walked quickly down the aisle. He wanted to get the screwdrivers and get back to Lydia's before the doors opened. But his attention was caught by the electrical timers hanging on display. He made a mental note to come back another time to select one for the lamp in his living room.

Eyes on the timers, Tate didn't see Cassie round the corner of the aisle until he crashed into her.

As he had done that rainy morning, he reached out instinctively to catch her as she stumbled backward. Several boxes of Christmas lights dropped from her hands onto the floor.

For a brief moment that felt like eternity, Tate stared at her, his mind a blank, his hands on her arms. All the things he'd wanted to say, questions he wanted to ask, were suddenly gone. He watched a flash of emotions cross her face. Startlement was followed by unabashed happiness and, he almost felt sure, the warmth of fondness. A flash of sadness. Then Cassie took a quick breath, a step back, and a polite smile was all that was left.

"Tate," she said. "Nice to see you."

Nice to see me? he thought. *Is that all?* He looked at her but saw no sign she was being sarcastic.

"Looks like we're both having lighting issues." She gestured at the bulbs in his basket.

Tate didn't quite know what to say. She was acting like they'd never kissed, like she'd never leaned into him as if she wanted to weld herself to him.

When Tate didn't respond, Cassie's smile faltered. She stooped down to pick up the fallen lights at the same time Tate bent to help her, setting his basket on the floor. He found his head next to hers. Her hair brushed his cheek, and he almost reeled as the scent took him back to that rainy morning, and the feel and taste of her.

She glanced up and seemed startled to find his face inches from hers. Tate wanted to fall into those deep brown eyes, edged with faint lines created by grief and laughter. He wanted to lighten that sorrow, share that joy.

Cassie dropped her head, breaking their gaze. "Sorry," she said, as she reached for the boxes around her feet.

A chasm of loss opened around his heart. It would never close, he knew.

Suddenly, he was angry. Angry with Avril, with Carla. Angry with Cassie.

Angry with himself.

He straightened with a couple boxes in his hand. Cassie stood, too, and took the boxes from him.

"Thanks," she said.

"Sure," he said. He didn't trust himself to say more. He wasn't sure what would come out of his mouth.

"Oh. I've been meaning to thank you for the tiles," she said, after a brief pause.

"Tiles?" he said, then remembered the slate he'd given her that morning. Remembered her long fingers running over their surface, touching them gently, following the ridges, the depressions, all her attention focused on the surface of the stones. Remembered the warmth of her touch on his face.

Stop it, he told himself.

"Yes, those pieces of slate flooring," Cassie was saying. "I don't know if Tia told you, but I put them into a neckpiece with diamonds. It came out so well, it's one of the pieces I submitted to the Masters judging."

"You've gotten in, then?"

Cassie laughed lightly. "No, not yet. But I'm feeling hopeful." She held up crossed fingers. "Sean Cleaver—the photographer. He sees a lot of work by different artists—he really liked it. Even Art Jackson was flattering about it!" She laughed again, shaking her head.

Tate felt his face go tight.

It was true then. Lou told him Art never said anything good about other jewelers' work.

"So it's all good with Art then," he said.

Her smile faded, and she looked at him quizzically. "Good with Art?"

"He accepted your offer."

"Offer?" She shook her head slightly. "What offer?"

"The \$10,000 to throw his vote your way."

Cassie became perfectly still. Her face lost all expression.

Tate remembered the look from the first time they'd met. This was Cassie angry. Angry she'd been caught out? Or angry he'd had the nerve to bring it up. Tate didn't know.

"I see you've talked to Carla," she said after the briefest pause.

Tate's heart fell. She didn't deny it.

He nodded curtly, his face tight. "She said you tried her first."

"Tried her first?" Cassie said quietly.

"Offered her the \$10,000 to talk to Art for you."

"I suppose she told you where I got the money to do that, too." Her eyes were almost black, the lines around them tight. She hadn't moved a muscle. Her face was bland. If Tate had not been standing this close, he might not have known how furious she was.

Tate shrugged slightly. "Even if she hadn't, I'd have figured it out. You've been so tight with Lou. And I heard Yiannis himself say he'd do anything to help the 'beautiful lady.'"

Cassie stared at him for a moment. "Well," she said finally, her voice deceptively light, "I guess you know it all, then. Excuse me."

Cassie stepped around him and, without another look, walked to the front of the store.

Tate stood there, motionless, feeling hollow. A moment later, he heard the hardware store door chime as Cassie left.

Tate bent stiffly, picked up his basket and followed, screw-drivers forgotten.

CHAPTER 25

TATE BURIED HIMSELF IN WORK. He was the first to get to Lydia's in the morning, the last to lock up at night. Every Friday morning, he and Domingo came in early to develop the following week's menu. Their holiday catering book was almost full through the new year, and Tate was working extra-long hours to keep tabs on that. He hoped that, come the new year, he could hire someone just for events, but for now he had to shoulder the load.

Tate should have been pleased, and he was. The restaurant was full most days for lunch and often for dinner, despite the rains that had begun to slow tourist traffic down. His crew was excellent: skilled, professional, hardworking. Thanksgiving had just passed, and Tate had been pleased to be able to pay out bonuses so they'd have the cash for the holidays.

But on foggy mornings when he ran—now consciously following routes that would not intersect with Cassie's—he felt the empty spot in his heart that he'd once thought—hoped—Cassie might fill.

When he'd confronted her at the hardware store, he'd

hoped she would fly in his face with righteous indignation, tell him everything Carla had said was lies. But she hadn't.

Which, he figured, meant it was true. Cassie had been using him.

It made it hard for Tate to listen to Tia, bubbling with joy. It was "Cassie says this," and "Cassie showed me that." Every word was a knife in his heart. Every wound made him want to hurt back.

This Tuesday, Tia came in to eat after her work at Cassie's. Lou had stopped by for a drink, as he often did on the way home. Domingo had dragged him into the kitchen to try out a new recipe he and Tate were arguing about.

This was something else that had changed. Knowing that Lou and Yiannis had been involved in Cassie's move to get into the Masters, Tate had cooled toward the jeweler. He disguised it by claiming to be too busy in the kitchen to talk. While they *were* busy, before his confrontation with Cassie, Lou's banter had always been welcome in the kitchen while they were cooking, no matter how busy.

"Now, try my version," Domingo was saying when Tia sailed in the door, grinning widely.

Tate grinned back, as she flew to him and threw her arms around him. Tate raised hands splotched with dough and bent to kiss the top of her head.

"Don't mind me if I don't hug back," he said.

"Guess what?" said Tia, not hearing him. Before he could guess, she went on. "Cassie's application to the Masters was accepted! She's in!"

"Hey! Great news!" said Lou. "I'll have to go congratulate her."

"Not before I get a decision, man," said Domingo, pointing at the plate in front of Lou.

"And," Tia was saying to Tate, "she wants me to help her

next summer. I can work the Pepper Tree show, just like I wanted to when I was a kid!"

"They're both great," Lou said to Domingo.

"That's not a decision that's a cop out," Domingo told him.

They both seemed to notice Tate's stillness at the same time. They stopped arguing.

Tia, however, kept going, oblivious. "In the meantime, she wants to pay me for the two days a week I'm coming down to work with her. She'll pay me *and* teach me! When I start classes, I can work part time on school days."

"What about the nursery?" Tate asked.

"I'll keep working there part time," Tia told him. "Can't give up my day job! Need the money for school."

Tate seemed to notice the dough on the board in front of him. He reached for the rolling pin and began to roll it out.

Lou glanced at Domingo, who frowned and shrugged.

Tate finally spoke, keeping his voice casual. "If you want money for the Art Institute," he said. "I can give you all the hours you need here. You wouldn't have to work two jobs. And I can probably pay more than either Cassie or the nursery."

Tia looked surprised, then frowned. "You mean give up working for Cassie? Why?"

When Tate just banged the dough a couple more times, she said, "What is it? Don't tell me you're going all Martin on me. You're not going to tell me that making jewelry isn't a real profession, are you?" She said it as a joke, but there was an edge to her voice. Chatter in the kitchen began to drop off as the others became aware of the tense conversation.

"No," said Tate, hitting the dough hard with the rolling pin. "But maybe it's time to apprentice with another jeweler. You know. Learn some other techniques. There are plenty here in Eden Beach. Or anywhere, really."

Now there was silence in the kitchen. Tia was staring at him. "What are you talking about? I haven't learned what I need to from Cassie yet. I like her. She's smart. Funny. She makes great jewelry." She opened her hands palms out. "What's the problem all of a sudden? I thought you'd be happy for me. And for her."

Bang. Bang. The rolling pin hit the dough. Domingo opened his mouth, paused, and shut it again. The door to the kitchen burst open as two wait staff came in. They went quiet when they saw everyone staring at Tate. Quickly grabbing their orders, they hurried back out.

"The problem is," said Tate, and paused, attention on the dough in front of him, which was getting tougher and tougher the more he worked it. "What I'm saying, is that maybe you should find someone who is a bit more ethical in their work practices."

"What?" said Tia, staring at him.

"What are you talking about?" said Lou at the same time.

Tate slammed the rolling pin on the counter. He glared at Lou. "You have a lot of nerve asking me that!" he said.

Lou threw his hands out. "Wait. What? How did I get sucked into this?"

"You and Yiannis. You helped her, didn't you?"

"Yeah," said Lou slowly. "So?"

"And Art. Acting like he's above it all. But he's not is he?"

Lou stared at him for a moment. "Before I get really pissed off, Tate," he said, low and quiet, "maybe you should tell me what the fuck you're talking about?"

"What I'm *talking* about, Lou," said Tate, his voice tight, "is the money Yiannis gave her so she could bribe Art to get her into the Masters. What I'm *talking* about is you doing the work for her."

"What?" Lou exploded.

"She told me she didn't have the skill," said Tate. "But hey, all of a sudden, she does."

Lou looked like he was about ready to punch Tate out despite the differences in age and height. Domingo was already taking a step to get between them, when Tia spoke up.

"Carla told you this, didn't she?" she said.

Tate tore his gaze from Lou and turned to Tia.

"Didn't she?" said Tia flatly.

"That bitch," breathed Lou.

"Tia," started Tate.

"And you believed her." She shook her head. "Tate, for a smart guy you are about as stupid as they come."

"I'll drink to that," said Lou, reaching for his glass.

Tate felt sick looking at the disappointment on his sister's face.

"Tia, look I confronted her..."

"Did you?" asked Tia. "And she said it was true?"

"She didn't deny it," he said self-righteously.

"Maybe she thought you should have figured Carla out by now. And that if you weren't smart enough to do that, maybe you didn't deserve an answer."

"She should have..."

"Why? Why should she? Why should she explain herself to someone who'd already made up his mind." Tia stepped closer, seeming to grow with her anger, and looked up at her brother. "Because you had, hadn't you?"

Tate couldn't answer her. *What have I done?* he thought.

"Do you want to know what really happened, Tate? I'll tell you. Because I was there. I heard Carla. I heard every word she said.

"It was Carla. She told Cassie she could get Art to throw the jurors, just because she was such a 'good customer.'" Tia made air quotes. "She said she'd give Cassie $10,000 as a moving bonus, if Cassie would just leave her shop so Carla could move her real estate office in. She'd already tried to get Cassie evicted. But Cassie knew Carla wanted to screw her, like she'd screwed the guy who had this place," she waved her hand around, "before she rented it to you. Carla drove him out of business so she could get more money for this space." She looked at him sadly. "You thought you got such a good deal."

In the silence, Domingo muttered something in Spanish. It was not flattering to Carla. Or to Tate.

Tate looked into his sister's face and knew it was the truth.

"Why didn't you tell me?"

"Because Cassie asked me not to," said Tia. "The restaurant was doing well. She thought you were crazy about Carla, thought you were happy. She asked me not to spoil that happiness." She shook her head. "Cassie could have happily strangled Carla that day, Tate. She should have been ready to tell the world what a miserable human being Carla is. But she asked me not to say anything because she didn't want to spoil your happiness. That's the person you just said had questionable ethics."

Tate turned to Lou, who was looking at him in disgust.

"That's true?" he asked. "About the previous owner?"

"Yep," said Lou. "Offered Ron a bigger place. Got him to break his lease here. Then reneged on the rent agreement on the new place, leaving him with no place to go. Her old man then sued him for breaking the lease on this one."

Tate frowned. "Alden? What…?" But suddenly he knew. He closed his eyes. "He owns this building."

"Yep," said Lou.

That was why Carla had been reluctant to take his lawyer's contract changes to the management company. It was her father's.

Nothing, it appeared, that Carla had told him had been true or honest. Or it had been twisted to suit her purposes. Which meant...

"So Cassie did not date a married man, either, I guess," he said bitterly.

Domingo dropped his head and shook it. "*Híjole*. Dumber than a tomato," he murmured.

"Is that what Carla told you?" asked Tia incredulously.

Tate just looked at her, feeling, if possible, even more gullible.

"Oh, Tate." She threw up her hands, turned, took a couple steps away, turned back to face her brother, and put her hands on her hips. "Cassie dated some financial guy a couple years ago. He told Cassie he was divorced. He wasn't. Cassie only found out when his wife came into the shop and made a huge scene. Anna told me. Cassie doesn't talk about it."

Tate's stupidity overwhelmed him. He closed his eyes. "Shit," he said to himself.

"That about covers it," said Lou, shaking his head. "I'm surprised Carla Towne hasn't cut your balls off and bronzed them for paperweights." He looked at Tate pityingly. "I really thought you had more brains than that."

"So did I," said Tate. He saw Domingo raise an eyebrow. "Don't say it now. I expect you'll be saying it for a long time."

"Damn straight, man," said Domingo, then grinned wickedly. "I'm gonna get a lot of mileage out of this."

Tate glared at him, then looked back at Lou. "I owe you an apology," he said.

"You do," said Lou.

"And Yiannis."

"Oh, I don't think I'd mention this to Yiannis," said Lou, looking Tate in the eye. "He still knows a thing or two about eliminating the enemy from his years in the resistance. He's got a temper. And he adores Cassie."

Tate wasn't sure he was physically at risk from the seventy-something Greek, but he was not in a hurry to face his temper.

"I think I will, however, make sure Art hears that Carla is telling people he takes bribes," Lou continued. "He won't take it lying down. He's pretty blown away by the work Cassie's doing. So am I.

"And for the record," he said, "Cassie might not have had the skills to do the work two months ago, but you better believe she's got them now. I haven't been doing her work, Tate. I've been teaching her.

"There's no doubt she'll get into the Masters. If not this year, next. But she'll do it on her own."

Tate was silent for a moment, as a couple wait staff swung in and out again.

"I guess the biggest apology I owe is to Cassie," he finally said.

Lou picked up his drink and finished it. "You can try," he said.

CHAPTER 26

CASSIE FINISHED SETTING the last chrysoprase in the bracelet she was working on. It was another custom piece in her new style, and it contained three carved chrysoprases set over slate. She would be glad to see it go. It was the last piece of slate from the tiles Tate had given her. Whenever she worked with it, she couldn't help remembering the hopes and dreams she'd held so briefly.

The look on his face in the hardware store.

She pulled the head magnifier off, rubbed the spot where the band had been pressing on her forehead, and looked out into the darkening evening. Winter had arrived in southern California, and as a concession to the chill, she'd worn tall, scuffed black boots and warm socks with her black jeans. Over her long sleeved teal T-shirt, she wore a casual kimono-sleeved jacket Nora had made for Cassie's mother from merino wool in muted pastel colors. Beth had often worn it in the winters while working pots in the unheated shed in the backyard. It had been mended many times. Cassie always felt a connection with her mother when she wore it. Two craftswomen together. Three, if she included Nora's hands in the work, and Cassie did. On a short silver chain around her neck, she wore a simple pendant set with an azurmalachite Jim had cut. She'd smiled at herself in the mirror that morning. *I guess I need to feel my family around me, with the holidays coming,* she'd thought.

While she always had the lights on to show off the work in the cases, they'd made the interior of the shop a bright spot as the fog had rolled in and out all day. It was thickening now, the point of the bluff beginning to disappear into the haze, the sun nowhere to be seen. The small, white Christmas lights she'd hung around the front window and the earring cases cheered her up.

Just the previous Sunday, Dale and Anna had hung one of Anna's new, large paintings on the wide wall near the door. On this dark evening, the bright colors of the hills in spring and the deep blue sky cheered her, too. Anna's new paintings —especially the small ones—were selling as well as Cassie's new work. They were both working hard getting enough pieces ready to sell in the Masters. They were being premature. Their applications had been accepted, but they had to submit actual work for jurying in January. Only then would the decisions be final. But both were feeling confident.

The chill in the air and the fog had kept customers away, and it had been surprisingly quiet for a Friday afternoon two weeks before Christmas. Cassie was grateful for the respite, though. She had four more custom pieces to finish by the twenty-third and needed to get more stock made. Having Tia work for her twice a week had been a godsend. The younger woman was not only terrific with customers, she had started doing the rough clean up on many of the castings. Without Tia, Cassie would not have been able to keep up, even working the long hours she was putting in. Tonight would be another long evening.

She loved the run up to Christmas—people buying special

gifts for themselves or others, the lights in the shops, the fog. But she always looked forward to her ten-day break after Christmas. While other shops closed only for a few days—at max, a week— Cassie always closed until the fifth of January. The fourth was her birthday. She and Nora usually went out for lunch and did something special on that day.

The quiet this evening meant Cassie was able to get into the Zen of doing her work. The last couple weeks had been a rollercoaster, emotionally.

First, Tia had told her about Tate accusing Lou of doing Cassie's work and charging that Yiannis had given her money to bribe Art.

"I swear, Cassie," she had said. "I didn't know my brother could be that dense. Both Domingo and I told him she was a liar." Cassie hadn't said anything. When Tia had tried to get her to give Tate another chance, Cassie had gently said she really didn't want to talk about it. Tia had wisely let the subject drop.

Then Art had come in fuming. Lou had told him about Carla's treachery.

"You should have told me!" he'd said angrily.

"Art, I had no idea she was telling anyone else. I thought it was just her way of getting me out of the shop. If I'd thought she was slandering you, believe me, I would have told you." Cassie had finally calmed him down. When he left, she knew he was off to see Carla. It gave Cassie great satisfaction to think of Art taking Carla apart.

It amused her to think that Carla's invitation to the Masters' opening night would be mislaid this year, but she was beginning to worry about how far Carla's lies were spreading. Much as she didn't like to admit it, Carla did have connections with a lot of Cassie's potential customers in Eden Beach, Newport, Cabrillo Point—all along the South

Coast. Cassie didn't know what the realtor's lies might do to her business, and she didn't know what other stories Carla was cooking up.

Naturally she'd ranted at Nora, who had listened for a while as she worked her loom, then she'd told Cassie to get used to it.

"What? Why?" Cassie had demanded angrily.

"It's part of success," said Nora.

Cassie had frowned, like Nora was speaking another language. "Part of success? People lying about you?"

"Sure," Nora told her. "Envy. Jealousy. Look at what everyone says about Art Jackson. Does he care?"

"Yes," said Cassie. "His hair was practically on fire when he came in to rake me over the coals for not telling him about Carla saying he was taking bribes. You've heard him carrying on about artists he thinks are copying his work."

"Okay. So bad example," said Nora with a small smile. "But Cassie, it will happen. I've heard people claim that Art sends his work to LA. I've heard people also say that he gets to be drinking buddies with the judges so he's sure to get juried in for the next year. It doesn't slow his sales."

"That's sour grapes among jewelers," said Cassie. "Carla's lying to people who might be my customers."

"Is she?" asked Nora. "Sounds to me like the only person she was telling her lies to was Tate." Nora's hands stopped moving, and she looked at Cassie's startled face. "It sounds like this is more personal than professional. Trying to destroy you in his eyes. Building herself up, I'm sure."

"I'm not following," said Cassie frowning.

Nora heaved a large, melodramatic sigh. "Cassie. Think! She started this after she found you kissing Tate."

When Cassie continued to frown, Nora shook her head, reached over to where Cassie was sitting on her bed, and put her hand on Cassie's knee. "Tate is a very handsome, smart, and single man. His restaurant is fast becoming *the* place to eat in Eden Beach. Carla is clearly shopping for someone to wear on her arm at events." Nora sat back and reached for the shuttle. "That was pretty obvious at Tate's open house." She shrugged before she started working the loom again. "It's also obvious she thought you were a threat to her plans."

Cassie remembered the women at the event calling the realtor "Can't-Keep-'Em-Carla." Still, she felt her face harden. "Well, it worked. It's clear Tate bought what she was selling. You saw them up at Clancy's."

"I didn't say he wasn't buying," said Nora gently. "I just said that I doubted she would continue with her campaign against you since she succeeded in driving him away from you." She paused, then grinned wickedly. "And once Art rips her heart out." Nora raised an eyebrow and glanced at Cassie. "Actually, at this point, Art can probably do more damage to Carla than she can to you. Certainly Lou can. That man gets around."

She stopped and looked at Cassie's unforgiving face. "This may end up backfiring on Carla."

"It won't change anything, though, not really," said Cassie. "The Townes will keep buying up Eden Beach."

"True," said Nora matter-of-factly. "There's nothing any of us can do about that. Except make our peace with it."

Cassie sighed. Nora was right. There was nothing she could do about Carla, or about Eden Beach changing. *As for Tate*, she thought, *I can never forgive him*. She ignored the wistful voice in the back of her mind that added, *as much as I want to*.

All she could do was focus on her work, the fact that it was selling well, and that her Christmas season was already better than it had been for the last couple years.

Cassie stood, stretched, and went to the fridge for tea. She looked outside. She loved foggy evenings.

She had just sat down again, when the door opened. Cassie's face brightened when she saw it was Anna, then frowned when she saw Anna was angry. Very angry.

"Wow!" said Cassie with a half-smile. Her tiny friend always seemed eight feet tall when she was upset. "Who set your tail on fire?"

"You did," said Anna, marching to the security gate and letting herself through. She stepped up to the wax bench and dropped into the chair, glaring at Cassie.

What...?" asked Cassie, astonished.

"Why didn't you tell me?" said Anna.

"What?" asked Cassie, trying to think what could have upset Anna so. "Tell you what?"

"That the...idiot...I work for thought you were trying to bribe your way into the Masters."

"Ah," said Cassie. She pulled the magnifier back off and dropped it into the catch tray. "Because I knew you'd react just like this. I was afraid you'd quit."

"Good guess," said Anna. "I just did."

"Anna! No, you didn't!" Cassie shot forward and put her hand on Anna's knee. "Tell me you just threatened to quit."

Anna shook her head. "Nope. Walked out. Told him he was a moron and I wasn't working for a moron no matter how well he paid me. Especially one who was stupid enough to believe the lies Carla Towne spits out."

Cassie sat back and closed her eyes. "Anna, I'm so sorry. You shouldn't have lost your job because of me."

"Cassita, I'm more pissed at you," Anna went on, somewhat calmer. "Why didn't you tell him they were lies? Why did you let him go ahead and believe Carla?"

"What good would that have done?" said Cassie, tiredly,

remembering their confrontation in the hardware store. "It was obvious he'd already made up his mind. If I'd argued, he'd only have been more convinced." She leaned back in her chair.

"You should have heard him. All high and mighty." Cassie felt herself getting angry again at the memory. "He was so sure I was manipulating my way into the Masters." Cassie snorted. "He should have been looking a little closer at the source of his information."

She shrugged. "Carla had convinced him. There was nothing I could say to change that. So why bother? Let him believe what he wants."

They were both quiet for a moment. "But what really hurt, Anna," Cassie finally said, "was that he thought my work was so crappy that I *had* to try to bribe my way in."

Anna shook her head. "I can't believe he's such a jerk," she said, getting up. "I thought he was smarter than that. Better than that. I need a Coke. And chocolate."

Cassie laughed. "Center drawer, where it usually is."

Anna raided the drawer and the fridge, popped the top on a soda, peeled the wrapper off the Snickers, bit off the end viciously, and sat down behind the design desk. Cassie picked up her tea and went to sit with her.

"So now what?" asked Anna, swallowing.

"Now I wish you'd go back and see if you can get your job back," said Cassie.

Anna shook her head. "I'll find something else." Her tone was final. Cassie knew it was useless to try to talk her out of her decision.

"What I mean," she went on, "is what are you going to do now about Carla's lies?"

Cassie shrugged. "Nothing to do but ride it out. See where it goes," she said. She told Anna what Nora had said about it being personal.

Anna snapped another bite off the Snickers. Chewed. "I

should have poisoned her when I had the chance," she said finally.

"Thanks, but I don't think you'd look good in prison stripes," said Cassie, smiling.

They talked a while, Cassie concerned about what this would do to Dale and Anna's finances. They depended on Anna's wages to pay taxes and to remodel.

"So far, the painting sales are helping," said Anna. Cassie didn't point out the obvious—that Tate had sold a number of Anna's large paintings from the restaurant. Anna's quitting would no doubt stop that.

"And Margot Somerset asked me to bring some work to her gallery," Anna added.

"Anna! That's excellent news!" said Cassie.

Anna grinned at her. "Always knew she had good taste."

Cassie laughed. Anna finished the Coke and the Snickers, then got up to leave. "I'd better get home, call Dale and tell him what his wife's done," she said.

"He's on at the fire department tonight, then?"

Anna nodded.

Cassie grimaced. "Is he going to be okay with this?"

Anna nodded. "Actually, he probably will be. He's been trying to get me to focus on painting full time ever since my Masters application was accepted."

"You are very lucky," said Cassie.

"No more than I deserve." Anna winked and grinned, then hugged Cassie and headed out into the growing fog.

Cassie pulled the pin from her hair, massaged her scalp, then folded her dark hair up onto her head, holding it there with her hands as she thought. The gray streak seemed to move like lightning in the dark mass.

What a mess, she thought. All because of Carla Towne.

As she sat there thinking, Cassie realized that Nora was right. Eventually, the whole thing would all blow over. She knew she'd keep the shop now. She was confident that the work would pass the Masters judges' inspection—Art's appreciation of it was proof of that. Even if the judges didn't like it, though, Cassie was happy with it. And no one—not Carla certainly—could take that away.

Anna would no doubt find other galleries, if Margot wanted her work. Maybe she really would be able to paint full time. That would be a dream come true for her friend.

She pinned her hair back into place. If Carla did continue what Nora called her campaign against Cassie, there were no doubt people in town who would gleefully believe her. But Lou and Art knew the truth. And Tia. While Cassie would probably lose a few customers—mostly Carla's contacts—if she was honest with herself, most people would never hear what Carla had to say. Eventually, she would no doubt turn her sights on some other poor merchant.

As for Tate...

For a moment she felt yawning sadness for the loss of something that had never had a chance to live.

She allowed herself to envy Anna for a moment. Dale loved her unquestioningly. He was firmly behind Anna's work and always had been. He'd risked his life to help her save many of her paintings from the fire two years before. Cassie thought Anna was right. Dale wouldn't flinch at the news that Anna had quit. He'd quite willingly make beans for them for a year, if that's what it took for her to succeed.

Tate, on the other hand, had been willing to believe any lies he'd been told.

Cassie sighed and shook her head free of thoughts that could lead nowhere. She got up and went back to her bench. Her night was not getting any shorter.

She was in the back, later, cleaning up the chrysoprase bracelet when the door pinged. Grateful as she was for work, she hoped this was a quick pick up. It was almost five and she was tired. She wanted to close up, go home, have a quiet dinner with Nora, then get back, cast, and finish a setting job.

She set the bracelet on paper towels on the counter and turned to go out front.

Her footsteps faltered when she saw it was Tate.

Even now, when she really didn't *want* to see him, the sight of him made her heart jump, catch, and start beating rapidly. The long sandy blond hair, tousled from him running his hands through it. The long legs in worn jeans. His strong hands and muscled forearms, exposed where the gray Henley and flannel shirt were pushed up. For an irrational moment, she wanted to run down the steps, throw herself into his arms, and start over.

I could, she thought wildly for a moment. *There's nothing to stop me.*

But my pride.

Then Tate gave her a small, sad, half-smile, and just as irrationally, she was furious at herself for reacting like this, furious at Tate for his gullibility, and then at herself again for having expected anything to start with.

Her anger got her moving. She went down to the security gate to meet him.

Tate's smile faded as he saw the look in her eyes. Some part of her mind that wasn't angry noticed that his eyes were gray tonight.

"Tate."

"Cassie." He paused.

Cassie waited while he became uncomfortable.

"I came to apologize," he finally said.

"Thanks for the thought, but I'm not sure you can."

He looked up and over her shoulder, and sighed. "Yeah. I know. That's what Lou said, too." Looking back at her, he added. "You must think I am, as Domingo says, dumber than a tomato."

"You can't joke your way out of this, Tate."

"No. I know I can't," he said sadly. "I know I hurt you."

Cassie felt the edge of her anger blunt at the regret in his voice, but she was determined not to soften.

"It wasn't only me you hurt," said Cassie. "What about Lou? He's your friend. Or Art? He may be a pain in the ass most of the time, but his reputation for craftsmanship and honesty is beyond question."

"Like yours."

"Like mine," she agreed. "So how do you apologize for insulting us all by thinking we'd be such cheats?"

Tate spread his hands out. "Cassie, I didn't know how things work here. For all I knew this was business as usual."

"You could have asked, Tate," she said stonily. "You could have asked any artist in Eden Beach. You could have asked Anna."

"She quit, you know," he said quietly, "when she found out what a mistake I made."

"A mistake?" she asked bitterly. "You even sound like Carla. Trying to tell me her attempt to drive me out of business was a 'misunderstanding.'"

The lines on Tate's face seemed to deepen as her anger flared, but to his credit, she thought grudgingly, he didn't interrupt her.

"But the worst, Tate, the worst were the lies you ate up about my family. That Jim was a drug dealer. That my mother was a drunk who killed herself and crippled her best friend." Tate had asked Melody about Beth and the accident, and word had quickly gotten back to Cassie. "Nora wanted to kill Carla for that one, you know that? Do you have any idea how much pain you've caused? We all trusted you. We thought you were our friend."

She had to stop. There was an edge of tears in her voice, and she wasn't going to cry.

"And you?" Tate asked her quietly.

Cassie waved a hand dismissively.

"I don't matter," she said. "I was just stupid. Putting my trust in the wrong place. It's the hurt this has caused for everyone else."

Tate reached out to put his hand over hers on the gate, but she pulled away. "You do matter, Cassie," he said after a moment. "So much it scared me. I think that's why I listened to Carla. Why I couldn't trust myself, what I was feeling. After Avril..."

"Don't blame this on her," said Cassie. "You think you're the only one who's been used or hurt? You're not. But I was willing to take a chance with you. I thought I could trust you."

As she said it, Cassie realized that was why she was so unwilling to forgive him. She had opened her heart. Risked it. And been betrayed. Again.

Tate looked at her a long time.

"If you'd give me another chance," he said finally, "maybe I can prove to you that you can."

Suddenly, the anger drained away, leaving Cassie sad and exhausted. "I can't," she said. *I won't*, she thought. "I think civil business neighbors will be the best you can hope for.

"Now Tate, I have a long evening ahead of me. I need to close up."

For a moment, he looked so lost, she wanted to take his hand and tell him okay, yes, she would forgive him, she understood. But she couldn't. She just didn't dare.

Finally, he said, "Cassie, I *am* sorry. I'm so very, very sorry." When she didn't respond, he turned and left.

Cassie unlatched the security gate, locked the door behind him, and flipped off the overhead lights. She walked around and turned the case lights out, leaving the Christmas

lights around the front window twinkling against the dark-
ness that had fallen over the fog-shrouded highway.

She had to empty the cases and put all the jewelry away in
the safe. Instead she went up the steps, into the backroom,
and sat down. There in the dark she listened to her heart
break.

CHAPTER 27

NORA FOLDED IN THE FLAPS OF THE LAST box and sat back.

"There," she said. "Done for another year."

Cassie pushed the potted ficus tree, set on a rolling base, back into its corner. It always looked so bare after they took the Christmas decorations off.

The Christmas ficus tradition had started when Cassie was a baby. Beth and Nora had not even had the few dollars necessary for a tree. A sick ficus had been the "rent" paid by one of their previous boarders who had worked in a nursery. Nora had nursed it to health and it had become their Christmas tree. They'd enjoyed the quirkiness of it so much, they'd maintained the tradition. The slender, graceful ficus was just the right size for their tiny living room. The spread of a fir would have had them all sitting outside to celebrate Christmas.

Today, that would have meant sitting in the pouring rain.

Cassie flopped into a chair opposite, yanked her hair down, massaged her scalp, fluffed her hair, and pulled the mass over one shoulder. She stared out at the dark gray sky and watched the palms across the street flail in the wind as sheets of rain battered the dormant plants in their yard. Water poured in the gutters and pounded through the downspout outside. A river of water flowed in the street, lapping at the tops of the curbs.

It had been like this off and on for the last week ruining Cassie's plans for hiking during her winter vacation. While she'd enjoyed the chance to read, to sketch out new designs, to be beaten by Nora at Scrabble, she was getting desperate to get out of the house. She didn't relish driving to Clancy's today, though. There had been reports of mudslides, and the street intersections were sure to be flooded. Her Rabbit was too low and so was Anna's ancient Karmann Ghia. Dale's truck wasn't stopped by flooded streets, but it would not take all four of them.

She sighed. "I think we'd better cancel lunch," she said. "I didn't have the pontoons fitted onto the Rabbit this year."

Nora laughed. "It is probably too much to try to get up to Clancy's, but we could get to Susie's. It's just down the hill. Then we could come back here for cake."

Cassie looked at Nora strangely. "We don't have a cake."

Nora shrugged. "Not yet," she said. "But I could bake one quickly, let it cool while we're at lunch, and frost it when we get back."

Now Cassie laughed. "With Anna in the house? Good luck with that! Remember how you had to fight her for the frosting bowl when we were kids?"

Nora smiled. "You'll have to distract her."

"With the house smelling like chocolate cake?" asked Cassie, grinning back at her. "Not possible. Maybe I should just stick a candle in the *phad thai*."

"So. Susie's?"

Cassie nodded. "I'll call Anna." She pushed herself out of

the chair. "At the worst, if we get stuck in an intersection, we have a friend at the fire department."

"Dale was just saying he was going to get his board out and we could surf to lunch," said Anna, when Cassie reached her.

Cassie laughed. "I can't remember the last time it rained this much. It's too bad I got rid of my water wings."

While Nora whipped up a cake, Cassie pulled down the attic stairs and wrestled the decoration boxes up into the rafters. The rain was deafening in the small space, but a quick glance around showed no leaks.

Downstairs again, Cassie pulled on a warm green wool sweater over her long-sleeved white T-shirt, and her knee-high boots over red socks and jeans. The boots would keep her feet mostly dry wading through the streams along the streets. She pulled her hair into a quick braid, put on Jim's pendant, some of her new earrings, and her silver bracelet.

When she came out of her room, the house was filled with the smell of chocolate, and Nora was waiting in the living room. She, too, was wearing jeans, topped with an old, soft yellow shirt and a woven mohair jacket under her rain slicker. Rubber gardening boots were on her feet. Her flats were in her hand.

"You're kidding," Cassie laughed, seeing the boots. "You're such a fashion leader, Nora."

"Laugh all you want," said Nora. "My feet will be dry." She pulled herself up, fitted her arms into her crutches, and tucked the shoes into the pockets of her bright red slicker, one to each side.

They both flipped up their hoods as they went out the front door and squelched around the gravel path to the carport.

Cassie turned the Rabbit onto Park and headed toward the Coast Highway. As she'd thought, the intersection at the highway was flooded, but not too deeply for the Rabbit to negotiate.

"Seems to be letting up a bit," said Nora, pointing at the rain.

"And the ragtop isn't leaking," Cassie added.

"Can't ask for more than that."

"Not many people on the road."

"Can't blame them," said Nora. "We wouldn't be out here if it weren't your birthday."

Cassie turned right up Ocean away from the coast, passing Lydia's on her left without a glance. Or at least, without much of one. The lights were on and cars were out front. Tate was open for lunch.

A few doors up, she turned left into the bank parking lot across the street from Susie's. Dale's truck was already there, and Cassie pulled in next to it.

"Ready?" she asked. Nora nodded. Cassie quickly jumped out of the car, ran around the other side, and helped Nora get out and up on her crutches.

Her boots made Nora's progress slower than usual as they jay-walked through the three-foot wide puddle at the curb, across Ocean, to Susie's. The few cars on the street stopped at the sight of Nora's canes.

"Wow," said Cassie, as she paced beside Nora. "No one's honking. Must still have Christmas spirit."

Nora snorted. "No, they just know they don't get any points if they run over a middle-aged woman on crutches."

"Such a cynic," said Cassie.

They slogged, ankle-deep, through the pool of water at the opposite curb, and Cassie helped Nora over it. The drumming of rain on their hoods stopped as they stepped under the awning in front of Susie's.

The restaurant was surprisingly full, mostly business people from the surrounding shops and offices. Susie came over quickly, hugged them both, and escorted them to Anna and Dale who were already getting up.

Anna hugged them, too, and pointed at Nora's boots. "A good look, Nora," she said, as she helped the older woman wrestle her jacket off and draped it over the back of her chair.

Nora laughed and sat, bending to pull off the boots, but Dale stooped quickly to help her. Cassie pulled the flats out of the rain jacket pockets and helped Nora put them on.

"Okay, okay!" said Nora, waving them all away. "I'm not the queen. Sit down, for heaven's sake."

Susie brought tea, and soon they were all teasing Cassie about turning thirty. She pointed at Anna. "You should be careful what you say," she told her friend. "You're next."

Over lunch, Anna told them Margot had scheduled her for a solo show in the fall, after the Masters, and that a craft gallery on the Island had accepted several of Dale's small tables on consignment. This called for noisy congratulations and a lot more hugging, with Cassie jumping up and running around the table. Nora reached across and took Anna's and Dale's hands.

"I'm so happy for you both," she said. "This is great news for such a gray day."

They spent the next couple hours eating and talking as Susie's slowly emptied around them. Several times they paused as the pounding of the rain on the roof became so loud they could hardly hear themselves.

Cassie finally looked up and outside. The afternoon was getting darker, and Susie was getting ready to close.

"I don't know about you two, but I'm ready for chocolate cake," she said.

Anna leaped to her feet. "I'm halfway there!" she said. Cassie laughed.

"And," said Anna, waving at Dale, "I'm bringing the fire department to handle all the flames on that cake."

Cassie shook her finger at her friend. "I'll get even," she said. "You know I will." Anna made a face at her.

Nora reached for her purse, but Dale stopped her. "This is our treat," he said. "I'll take care of it."

Cassie helped Nora get her flats stowed, and Dale and Anna helped her into her jacket.

"We'll see you there," said Anna, walking them to the front door while Dale went to pay Susie.

The rain pounding on the awning outside was deafening. While they'd been inside, the street in front of them had flooded all the way across. Water swirled over the curb and washed almost to Susie's door. Cassie glanced quickly up and down. There was no easier place to cross. One car rolled slowly toward the beach on the other side of the street, water almost up to the bottom of the car's doors.

Cassie felt a moment of panic, wondering if her Rabbit would be able to make it through the surging water. It was still high and dry in the parking lot across the street. She thought briefly about asking Dale and Anna to take Nora home. She could walk back to the house, and though she'd be soaked when she got there, she wouldn't get stranded with Nora.

But as she'd hesitated, Nora had stepped off the curb and begun to wade slowly and deliberately, water almost to the tops of her boots. Cassie quickly followed her.

The power of the water rushing down the street caught her by surprise as she stepped off the curb. As she tried to hurry to catch up to Nora, Cassie watched their left to guard against any cars coming up the street.

Nora had just reached the center line, and Cassie, a few steps behind, was reaching for her arm to support her, when there was a roar above the sound of the rain beating on her hood. Cassie quickly turned to the right expecting a car.

Instead, not a hundred yards away, was a wave of filthy,

roiling water. At least knee high, it poured around the corner at Beach, throwing up a rooster tail of spray as it hit the planters there and rounded onto Ocean. It slammed into the bank building on the opposite corner, flipped over on itself, and came at them furiously, growing in height. It tore out part of the fence in front of the historical society and crested over a silver Porche Turbo, setting off its car alarm.

Stunned, Cassie was momentarily rooted in place. Nora, attention focused on her feet and the water in front of her, stepped ahead.

"Nora!" Cassie screamed.

Nora glanced back over her left shoulder as she lifted her right crutch. Cassie fought the weight of the water suddenly swirling around her calves as she tried to get to her friend.

She was reaching out for Nora, when the wave slammed into them. Nora staggered as the water knocked her off balance, swung her around, and swirled a crutch between her feet. She fell and went under.

Her other crutch flew backward, hitting Cassie at the knee. Cassie went down. Her eyes, mouth, and nose filled with stinking water as she was swept and rolled down the street. The sweater under the rain jacket soaked immediately and became dead weight. Her hood pushed forward over her face.

Cassie fought to get to her knees, but the raging water kept forcing her down. Choking and coughing, she finally managed to get her head up above the water. She had barely staggered to her feet, and got the hood shoved back, when a large branch caught in her legs, knocking her back to her knees again. She caught a flash of red in the water, just down the street, before the water washed over her head. Something heavy in the current hit her hard behind the ear.

When she came up again, she was horrified to see a car at the curb begin to float and slide down the street. Cassie thought someone called her name, but she was desperate to get to Nora.

Kicking and pushing against the street, flailing against the current, Cassie tried to keep her head above water and use the power of the flood to get to Nora. She was slammed against a parked car that had wedged itself against the curb. Using the bumper, hidden under the rising and churning water, Cassie clawed her way to her feet.

"Nora!" she yelled, and saw her, legs half wedged under another car, weakly reaching for the car's side mirror, her head barely out of the water. "Hold on! I'm coming!" She didn't know if Nora heard her.

Pulling herself along by the sides of the car, struggling to keep her footing in the now waist-high water, Cassie reached her friend. Bracing herself against the awesome power of the torrent cresting against the side of the car, she grabbed the back of Nora's jacket and pulled. She managed to get Nora's head up above the water level, but the rubber gardening boots, now filled with water, were caught under the car. Cassie couldn't drag her free.

The water pushing hard against her back, breaking over her shoulders, Cassie bent and shoved her arms under Nora's armpits, wrapping them around Nora's chest. Her crutches had pulled away somewhere in the water.

"Nora! Nora! I'm here. I've got you. You'll be all right," said Cassie. "You'll be all right."

Nora coughed, gagged, then vomited into the water in front of her. Cassie felt Nora's hand clutching hers convulsively as she retched. Her head fell weakly back onto Cassie's shoulder. She continued to cough, clutching Cassie's hand each time.

Cassie was freezing. She saw a streak of red flow away from her in the water and knew one of them was bleeding. She had to get Nora out of the water, but she didn't dare loosen her grip. Leaning back against the water, she tried to take a deep breath to call for help, but the air caught in her lungs, and she began coughing violently.

"Help," she managed to call weakly, doubting that even Nora, in her arms, could hear her. "Help," she tried again.

She heard scraping from the front of the car, and her heart almost stopped to think the car was moving. But then someone slid from the hood, dropping into the water in front of her. Cassie looked up into Tate's face, tight with fear and worry. His hair was plastered around his face, his thin shirt glued to his body.

"Cassie," he shouted, leaning into the flood. "Are you hurt?"

She shook her head. "I don't know," she said and began coughing. "Nora," she managed to choke out. "Nora's caught." She coughed again.

"Can you hold her?" he asked Cassie.

"I think so," whispered Cassie. Tate seemed to understand her.

Tate grabbed a breath and went under. It seemed an age. Suddenly, Cassie felt the release as Nora's legs came free. As Nora floated, her weight dragged suddenly at Cassie, and the water threatened to push them both under again.

"Tate!" she shouted, as he popped up, dripping and spitting water. He was already reaching one arm around Nora's waist, his strong bulk holding them both against the push of the flood.

"Cassie! I've got her. Can you stand?" With both of them locking arms around Nora, their faces were inches apart. For the briefest moment, Cassie looked deep into gray eyes, flecked with green.

Cassie nodded, relinquishing her hold on Nora. Tate stood up, pulling Nora out of Cassie's grasp, lifting her, pushing his other arm under her limp legs. Cassie dragged herself upright with the aid of the car's side mirror. She staggered as the flood hit her.

"Hold on," said Tate. "Don't move and don't let go. I'll come back for you."

Cassie just nodded.

"Don't move!" he told Cassie again, then stepped past her, toward the rear of the car, planting each foot firmly against the water.

Cassie hung on, the muddy water swirling around her. Plastic bags, branches, empty cups rushed by. She saw more blood. *It must be me*, she thought.

She pulled against the mirror, reaching for the door handle, hoping to pull herself around the car.

The car shifted. Terror seized her as she lost her balance. The water knocked her feet from under her. She twisted as she fell, wrenching her shoulder. But she did not let go of the door handle. The torrent washed over her head, and her nose filled with water.

She was coughing, gagging, and trying to get her feet under her when, suddenly, Tate was back. He slipped a strong arm around her waist, bracing himself against the flood.

"I've got you," he said.

He held her as she got first one foot, then the other under her. The water shoved against the back of her knees. Cassie clutched desperately at Tate.

"I've got you," he said calmly. "I'm not letting you go."

She tried to speak and started coughing. He held her until the spasm passed.

"Okay?" he asked.

She nodded.

"Lean on me," he said. "We're going around the end of the car and into the restaurant. Can you do that?"

Cassie nodded again. She looked up into his face, into gray eyes tight with concern. Time froze. For a moment, with the rain falling on her face and dripping from Tate's hair, she was back in October, on the rainy morning when she first fell in love with him. Her hand curled tightly into the front of his shirt.

She tried to smile. "We've got to stop meeting like this," she managed to say hoarsely, then started to cough.

"Oh, for Pete's sake," he said, with exasperation. "You almost drown on my doorstep, and now you joke about it?" He shook his head, took a tighter grip on her waist and began to pull her up the street against the flow. "I expect you'll live."

Tate guided her to the restaurant door. It took a couple customers, waiting inside, to push the door open against the weight of the water. Cassie had just a moment to see Tia's white face as Tate pulled her through the narrow opening. Water gushed in after them. The door slammed shut.

The restaurant floor was covered with ankle-deep, muddy water. Domingo bent to stuff soggy cloths back against the door as Tate helped Cassie toward the kitchen. A half dozen or so customers were helping other staff stuff towels and table cloths around the folding doors where water was pouring in waterfalls through the seams.

"Where's Nora?" Cassie croaked.

"She's in back. We have a cot back there for emergencies. We called the paramedics, but I don't know how they'll get to us through this," he said.

The cot was in a small room off the kitchen, and the water there was less. Someone had taken off Nora's wet clothes and pulled a dry sweater on her. Her legs were wrapped with a blanket, and another was thrown over her. Dry white socks peeked from under the blanket. She was either asleep or unconscious.

The sight of Nora so silent and helpless frightened Cassie. She tried to pull away from Tate and stumbled dizzily. He grabbed her.

"Slowly," he said. "You're bleeding." He pulled her jacket off.

"Nora," said Cassie. "Tate, is she... Is she okay?"

"She's alive," said Tate, answering her unspoken question. "But she's half drowned."

One of the cooks splashed across the wet floor, bringing in a chair. He set it next to Nora. Tate helped Cassie sit down. The cook handed Tate a clean towel.

"Tia," he said to his sister, who'd followed them in, "grab that blue sweatshirt from behind the back door. Then bring me the First-Aid kit."

Tate reached for Cassie's left hand and pushed her soggy sweater sleeve up. She looked down and saw her bracelet was missing. In its place was a jagged gash on the outside of her forearm that ran several inches up from her wrist. She was so numb with cold, it didn't hurt, but it was bleeding freely.

Tia came back carrying the First-Aid kit and a heavy UC Irvine hooded sweatshirt. Cassie recognized it as one she'd seen Tate wearing during his runs.

Tate, who was obviously no stranger to cuts, quickly and skillfully cleaned and bandaged the cut on her arm.

Then Tia shooed him and everyone from the room and helped a shaking Cassie peel off her sodden sweater and shirt. Cassie was intensely grateful for the dry warmth of the sweatshirt as Tia zipped her into it. Tia wrapped a folded blanket across her shoulders.

"I'm sorry we don't have any dry pants for you. Or boots," she told Cassie.

"Thanks," said Cassie. "This almost feels like a miracle." She pulled her chair closer to the cot and reached for Nora's hand. She saw Tia frown, and felt her friend push her sodden braid aside.

At a tap on the door, Tia let Tate back in. He was carrying a large mug of hot tea.

"Tate," said Tia, who was standing behind Cassie, "she's bleeding here, too." She gently lifted Cassie's soaked braid to show him where blood oozed down her neck from a cut beneath her hair, staining the sweatshirt.

Tate's fingers were warm on her neck. Cassie realized how very cold she was.

"See if we have any more clean towels. We'll have to let the paramedics take care of that one, but at least we can slow the bleeding," he said. He turned concerned eyes on Cassie. "I think you'll need stitches. It looks like you hit your head."

Cassie nodded and a wave of nausea swept her. "I think I'm going to be sick," she said, suddenly sitting up straighter.

Tate quickly grabbed a waste basket from beside the cot. He got it to Cassie just in time. The horrible taste of flood water filled Cassie's mouth. She retched again and again.

When she finally stopped, Tia was there with a glass of water and a damp cloth.

"Here. Rinse," said Tate, handing the glass to Cassie. She took it with shaking hands. Tate wrapped his warm hand around hers, guiding the water to her mouth. "Now spit," he said indicating the waste basket. She did as he asked.

"Tia," he said, toeing the waste basket, "I hate to ask…"

"Done," she said. She gave Tate the cloth, grabbed the basket, and was out the door.

Tate knelt down in the water and dirt on the floor and put an arm around Cassie as she wiped her mouth. "Do you think you can drink a bit of this?" he asked her, holding the mug of tea to her. "It might help warm you and settle your stomach."

Cassie looked into his eyes, just inches from hers. She saw worry and fear in their gray-green depths. *Gold*, some part of her mind said. *There are flecks of gold there. Why didn't I notice that before?*

She also realized, with a shock, that she was looking straight into his heart, a heart full of love. For her. It was there, too, in the gentle strength of his arm around her waist. No man had ever looked at her, held her, like that before.

"You saved our lives," she said wonderingly, as she heard a commotion of loud voices and heavy boots out in the kitchen.

Tate gave her a small smile. "If I hadn't," he said, "do you think Tia and Anna would ever have let me hear the end of it?"

Cassie tried to smile, but her face refused to cooperate. She dropped the blanket from her shoulders and slid from the chair onto the wet floor and into his arms. Tate quickly set the tea down and wrapped both arms around her as she began to cry.

CHAPTER 28

W HEN THE PARAMEDICS HAD ARRIVEd, Dale had been right behind them, tiny Anna swimming fiercely in his wake. The paramedics had wrapped Nora warmly, covered her to protect her from the rain that was still falling, strapped her securely to a stretcher, then bundled her out the door into the flood waters. Cassie almost panicked watching her go.

Dale got both Anna and Cassie, armed with the waste basket, down the back alley to the parking lot and packed into the big truck. Going up and around the culvert blowout on Beach, and working through back streets, he eventually got Cassie down the coast to the hospital. She'd been sick once more on the way.

Dale left them with the truck and hitched a ride with the paramedics back to town to help with rescue work.

A nurse stitched Cassie's arm and the back of her head, filled her with antibiotics, and tried to get her to stay the night. She refused. Anna assured them that Dale was a trained paramedic and that they would be home with Cassie all night.

Anna leaned over to Cassie who had a tight grip on her hand. "I told her that means half of the fire department will be watching over you," she whispered into Cassie's ear. Cassie smiled. At least, she thought she did.

She insisted on seeing Nora. Although Nora had regained consciousness, she was sleeping when Cassie went into her room. She was on oxygen, and nurses told Cassie they would keep her for a couple days to be sure she did not develop pneumonia. By the time they left the hospital, it was after eight in the evening. The rain had started to taper off. Cassie stirred when Anna turned off onto Talisman, heading into the hills toward their home.

"We're going to your house?"

"Yes," said Anna.

"Anna, I just want to go home."

"No," said Anna in a tone that Cassie knew well. "The streets downtown are still flooded. Even if they weren't, you're hurt. You're in shock. And I promised the nurses I'd watch you all night."

Now Cassie did smile. "You promised the nurses Dale would watch me all night."

Anna shrugged.

"I have to check on the shop," said Cassie, serious again.

"The nurses were saying there's more than two feet of water and mud on Coast Highway and more still rushing down Canyon and Ocean," said Anna, steering the truck around curves as they climbed. "There is nothing you can do tonight. You're going to take a hot bath, get into some warm clothes, have some food, if you can keep it down, take your meds, and go to bed."

Cassie gave her tiny friend another smile. "*You're* going to lend me clothes?"

"Of course not," said Anna. "Dale is."

Cassie didn't try to argue any more.

She had a hard time sleeping though. The vile taste in her mouth would not go away, no matter how many times she brushed her teeth. She continued to feel sick. Every time she started to fall asleep, flashbacks of being in the water would jerk her awake. When she managed to doze, nightmares of Nora being washed into the ocean woke her, heart racing.

Lying awake in the dark, trying not to think of the flood, she'd see Tate's face, his forehead creased with worry, and she'd feel an intense rush of love, warmed by the memory of the love in his eyes, of feeling safe in his arms, of finally belonging.

Then she'd see Nora's face again, white and still, her graying hair filled with grit soaking the pillow, and terror would send Cassie's heart pounding. She'd come so close to losing her second mother and dearest friend.

She might still lose her. The ER doctor had told Cassie that Nora was at risk of developing pneumonia or some horrible infection from all the filthy water she'd swallowed. When Nora was able, they would check for any further injury to her back or legs, which were bruised from her tumble down the street. While Cassie had been able to struggle to her feet, Nora had been at the mercy of the flood. Doctors were afraid it might have exacerbated the injuries from the accident.

In the dark, the weight of responsibility pressed down on her. Cassie could never think of leaving Nora. Nora had helped raise her, had been an unfailing source of encouragement and support. She'd lost her mother and then she'd lost Jim. Even if this disaster had healed the rift between Tate and her, Cassie couldn't desert Nora. No matter the cost to herself.

Sometime in the early morning hours, exhaustion finally carried Cassie into a deep sleep. She did not wake until almost ten. She had just rolled over—momentarily disoriented at finding herself in Anna's spare room—to look out the window at blue sky, when Anna came in.

"Good," she said. "Dale told me to wake you if you weren't awake already."

"He's home?" asked Cassie.

"No," said Anna. "He called. There was so much to do last night, he stayed at the fire station and just went into his regular shift today. Hey, take it slow!" she added, when she saw Cassie was about to get up.

The warning was well timed as Cassie felt a bit sick and dizzy at first.

"How do you feel?" Concern was strong in Anna's voice.

"Icky. Dirty. Like I've been beaten with a stick," said Cassie.

"That was me," said Anna. "I pounded you last night while you slept for scaring the crap out of me."

"So kind," said Cassie, making a face at her friend.

When her head cleared, and Anna was sure she'd be okay, Cassie climbed into a hot shower. She scrubbed repeatedly, thinking she'd never get the sour smell of floodwater washed away. Finally, she got dried off and dressed. Anna had washed her jeans and underclothes and Tate's sweatshirt. She borrowed a flannel shirt from Dale. Anna had hosed out the boots, but they were probably going to be a total loss. Cassie padded around in two pairs of Dale's socks.

"Any idea how things are downtown?" she asked Anna, as she sat down to toast and tea. Suddenly, she was starving. "Can I get some peanut butter to go with this?"

Anna rolled her eyes and put the jar on the table. "It's a mess. Mud everywhere. But the road crews have been working all night clearing the worst of it." She sat down across from Cassie, coffee in front of her.

"Did anyone else get hurt?" asked Cassie.

Anna shook her head. "Dale helped pull a bunch of kids from the preschool, though."

"Poor kids must have been scared to death."

Anna laughed. "Dale said they didn't even notice. The teachers kept them busy and fed. It was their parents who were totally freaked out."

"I can imagine," said Cassie. Images flashed through her head. Ropes of filthy, churning water slamming into the buildings. The car floating. Nora, white-faced on the cot in Tate's restaurant. She shivered. They'd been so lucky.

"I don't suppose Dale was able to check the shop," she said.

Anna made a negative noise around the coffee she was swallowing. "He didn't want to set off the alarm." She made a face. "Cass, it's going to be a mess. Dale said some businesses had a couple feet of water in their shops. Not to mention the mud.

Cassie felt sick.

"That below-ground restaurant on Hillside was really hard hit. They got the water pumped out, but they're cleaning up the mud today."

Cassie winced. She liked that place.

"Susie's?"

"Water damage. Mud. Same story over most of downtown," said Anna.

"Speaking of restaurants," she went on, "Tate called this morning to check on you. I think you scared him to death."

"Sounds like you've forgiven him," said Cassie.

"He saved your lives. I think I can forgive him," said Anna. "What about you?"

"How is Lydia's?" Cassie asked, sidestepping Anna's question.

"Okay, considering," Anna told her. The staff and customers had gotten the chairs up out of the water, she said, but the tables would have to be replaced, or, at the very least, refinished. The water was pumped out and the mud shoveled. They were hosing out the rest of it. "The slate floor will have to be scrubbed down, but not replaced. Tate said he'll probably have to replace the bar, though. Fortunately, the slate ran up the walls. Since it was so new, the restoration contractor thought the grouting would have protected the wall underneath. They won't really know until they get it cleaned out. The kitchen, though." She shook her head. "Tate called the health inspectors to come in and see what he needs to do to get it back up to standard."

It'll probably cost a fortune, thought Cassie. She felt sick for Tate. Tia had said he had just been starting to get ahead from the holidays, and that he'd paid everyone bonuses.

"Oh. And you'd better be prepared for another thing," Anna went on.

Cassie felt her stomach tighten. "For what?" she asked.

"Dale said Main Beach is pretty much gone."

Cassie sat bolt upright. "What do you mean *gone?*"

"The water just poured down Canyon, Hillside, Ocean and there was only one place for it to go. The beach and the boardwalk were in the way."

"The beach is *gone?*"

Anna nodded. "Scoured right down to the bedrock."

Cassie shook her head, thinking. *It really is lucky we're alive*, she thought.

"You'd think we'd be used to this, wouldn't you," said Anna, pouring herself more coffee. "After all the floods we've had. Maybe we should start putting all the buildings on stilts. Run the channel right through the center of town and out to the ocean. Make it a tourist attraction."

Cassie smiled, as she knew Anna hoped she would. "I can see that going through the city council, can't you?"

"You have flood insurance, right?" asked Anna, changing the subject.

Cassie sat back, surprised. "You know, I hadn't thought about it. But I do. After the shop flooded in the 1970s, Jim got flood insurance, even though it cost a fortune. I've never changed the policy. I'd forgotten all about that." A weight seemed to lift from her shoulders. She'd have to call the agent after she'd seen the shop.

Cassie sat quietly for a moment. "You know," she said finally, "for someone everyone considered a laid-back hippie, Jim was a surprisingly thoughtful business owner. I still learn something from him every day."

Cassie thought about her mother's life insurance policy, which had paid off their mortgage when her mother died. Cassie had never thought about her own mortality. But suppose she'd been knocked out yesterday by whatever had hit her in the head. She might have drowned. What would have happened to Nora? Who would take care of her?

Since the accident, Cassie had felt a responsibility to help Nora in any way she could. But she'd never thought about what would happen to Nora if she weren't there. When she talked to her insurance agent, she'd have to look into insurance for more than just the shop.

Cassie sighed. She wasn't sure she was up to all this.

"I need to get down there," she said finally. "I need to get the car, if it didn't float away. Can you take me?"

"Whenever you're ready," said Anna. "And the car is fine. Dale said the parking lot was flooded, but not enough to damage the cars there."

Cassie got up and took her breakfast dishes to the sink. "First, I have to go see Nora, though," she said.

They gathered up brooms, mops, rags, bleach. When Anna grabbed the shovel, Cassie shuddered to think what she'd find at the shop.

They loaded everything into the back of Dale's truck and headed down the coast to the hospital, making a short detour through muddy streets to Cassie's house so she could get some shoes.

"I'm going to get Nora some flowers," said Anna, turning toward the gift shop as they went into the hospital lobby. "You go on up."

Cassie found Nora alone in her room, the bed propped up at a comfortable angle. There were already two small bouquets of flowers set on the bedside stand and a large one on a table across the room.

Nora opened her eyes as Cassie walked in, and a gentle smile lit her face. She held out her hand, and Cassie took it as she stepped up to the bed, tears stinging her eyes. She blinked rapidly and tried to sound upbeat as she said, "You're looking better."

Nora wheezed a short laugh and pulled Cassie's hand indicating she should sit down on the side of the bed. "I'm not sure that's saying much."

Cassie smiled back. "Actually, it is. Last I saw you, you were covered in mud and white as a sheet. At least you're clean now."

"Still white as a sheet?"

Cassie waggled her free hand in a so-so gesture. "Moving toward beige," she said.

"How's the bump on the head?"

Cassie looked at her quizzically. "How did you know about that?"

"Tate was here earlier." Nora lifted her free hand and pointed to the large bouquet on the table across the room.

Cassie's grip on Nora's hand tightened. "I'm glad he found us," she said, and felt tears start again.

Nora squeezed her hand. "None of that," she said hoarsely. "We're both alive."

Cassie made an exasperated noise and brushed at her eyes. "I've been leaking like a faucet," she said. "The doctor said I probably would. Shock and a little bit of concussion."

"Me, I just keep falling asleep in the middle of words," said Nora. Cassie smiled at her, then became serious.

"Nora, I'm so sorry," she said.

"For what?" asked Nora in surprise.

"I let you down," said Cassie. She swallowed hard. "You could have died. I should have seen the flood coming. I mean, the streets were almost flooded across. We shouldn't have been down there."

She stopped. Nora was looking at her oddly.

Cassie took a deep breath. "I want you to know I won't let you down again. I'll always be there to help you."

"Cassiopeia Andromeda," said Nora sternly. "Stop right there."

"No," said Cassie. "I need to tell you..."

Nora squeezed her hand tightly. "Stop."

Cassie stopped.

They looked at each other for a long moment.

"This," said Nora finally, gesturing to her legs, "was not your mother's fault. It is not your fault. It's about time you stopped feeling guilty for it."

Cassie didn't say anything.

"Don't give me that stubborn look," said Nora. Cassie raised an eyebrow.

"The doctors say..." she started.

"Oh, screw what the doctors say," said Nora angrily. Then she went into a coughing bout. She waved at the water glass, and Cassie jumped up to get it.

She helped Nora drink and got her settled again. Nora lay back with her eyes closed.

"Maybe I should come back later," Cassie started to say.

Nora moved surprisingly quickly and grabbed Cassie's hand. Cassie sat back down and waited.

It took a moment for Nora to get her breathing under control. "The doctors haven't been so right before," she finally said. "I think I wasn't supposed to walk again, if I remember rightly."

"My miracle girl," said Cassie, smiling.

Nora snorted. "No miracle. Stubborn." She took a few moments to catch her breath. Cassie let her take her time.

"Cassie, neither of us saw that flood coming," Nora said after a few minutes. "We probably should have, given the amount of rain we've been getting. But whatever. *It was not your fault*," she said emphasizing every word. "There was nothing either of us could have done about getting caught in it. But when it hit, you saved my life. Even though you'd been hurt."

"Tate saved both our lives," said Cassie.

Nora shook her head. "If you wouldn't have gotten to me first, I probably would have drowned before Tate could help."

Cassie didn't know what to say to that.

"I should have said this to you a long time ago," said Nora, "but I kept hoping you'd figure things out on your own. I want you to listen without interruption."

"Say what?" asked Cassie.

Nora lifted the hand she was holding and shook it back and forth vigorously, as if she could shake Cassie. "I am not your responsibility," she said firmly. "I'm not helpless. I'm not witless. But your constant determination to 'do for me' is a burden I don't want to carry any more."

"You're not a burden."

"Then stop making me feel like one," said Nora.

Cassie sat as still as stone, staring at the determination in Nora's eyes. "I never..."

"No, you never meant to," said Nora. "But isn't that why you've built the wall between you and Tate?"

"What? Tate believed..."

"You could have explained that he was wrong. He would have listened to you. Oh, don't look skeptical. We had a long talk this morning. Instead, you chose to let him believe Carla. You *let* him go. In the back of your mind, you were thinking, 'What would poor Nora do if I fell in love and moved out?' Weren't you?"

Cassie felt shot through the heart. She *had* felt that. She'd spent all night feeling that. Worse, now with Nora saying this, Cassie realized that, deep beneath her outrage that Phil had lied to her about being married, she'd suspected. She'd known it was a relationship that would go nowhere. That she could stay and take care of Nora. Stay where her mom would have wanted her to be.

She knew Nora saw the truth written on her face.

"Cassie," said Nora more gently. "You cannot continue to live your life feeling responsible for me. Or Beth. Or Jim. You have to grow up, stop living in the past. Live your *own* life. Otherwise, some day—and sooner than you think—you'll regret it. And you'll hate all of us for it." She lay back and closed her eyes, focusing on her breathing.

Cassie started to speak, but Nora squeezed her hand tightly. Cassie closed her mouth. Apparently Nora wasn't done. She smiled to herself. The woman was a force of nature.

"Live *your* life, Cassie," said Nora again, quietly but fiercely. "Take the risks you need to take to do that. Beth took a huge risk. She left her family to have you. That was probably the greatest lesson you should learn from her. Take the risks love demands of you. Trust your heart." She squeezed Cassie's hand. "Don't waste the life Beth gave you." Nora lay back against the pillows again and closed her eyes. She was breathing hard. "She would have hated that."

Cassie bit her bottom lip. She felt... How did she feel? Hurt? Maybe. After all, she was only trying to do what was best. But Nora said she made her feel like a burden. How was that best?

Guilty, yes. But as she sat there, holding Nora's hand, Cassie realized that some of the guilt was from the fact that she felt released. Free. Free of, she had to admit, the *burden* of trying to do what was right for everyone else. Keeping Jim's legacy alive. Caring for Nora in her mother's place.

Nora, in her love and wisdom, had set her free.

Cassie felt a wave of gratitude.

She looked at her friend, lying quietly on the pillow, and realized that Nora had fallen asleep. *At least,* Cassie thought, smiling, *she finished her sentence.*

She got up carefully, leaned over and kissed Nora softly on the forehead. Nora stirred. "Love you," she said quietly.

"I love you, too," said Cassie. "I'll be back tomorrow."

Nora responded by squeezing her hand.

Cassie turned to go and saw Anna standing in the doorway, flowers in hand, tears in her eyes. Quietly, Cassie took the flowers and set them on the table next to Tate's. Then she linked her arm in Anna's as they walked slowly to the elevator.

CHAPTER 29

WHEN THEY ARRIVED AT THE SHOP, it was almost 2 p.m. Cassie saw a long hose trailing from the movie theater, emptying muddy water at the curb. A couple of employees were shoveling mud out into the plaza, then pushing it to the street where bulldozers were pushing it into huge piles.

"It looks bad," she said to the theater manager, who was push-brooming water and mud to the curb.

"It is," he said. "The whole auditorium is floating."

So Cassie wasn't surprised when she opened The Green Lotus' door and water flowed out. She and Anna quickly grabbed brooms and started shoving water to the curb, too.

Inside, the carpeting was hidden by inches of silt, and the smell of mud and wet wood filled the air. She raised her hands helplessly.

"Where do we even start?" she asked Anna. Her friend simply handed her the shovel.

"I'll call Tate and get the number for that restoration contractor," said Anna, and squelched through the muck to the security gate, then turned to Cassie. "So I guess you'd better start shoveling here, so I can get back to the phone."

"If it's working," said Cassie. Surprisingly, it was.

Fortunately, the contractor was at the restaurant when Anna called. He promised to come by when he was finished at Lydia's.

"Now you'd better call your insurance agent," said Anna, taking the shovel from Cassie.

Not long afterward, Tia and Domingo, who'd been at Lydia's, showed up bringing their own broom and shovel. They helped Cassie and Anna carry the three display cases outside. It made Cassie sick to see the mud and water stains on the beautiful wood work.

Anna saw her face. "Don't worry," she said. "Dale will know how to fix it."

She and Domingo took over shoveling the muck out the door, while Tia and Cassie swept it into the street.

"Man, this is like shoveling out stables," said Domingo, as he tossed another shovelful out the front door.

"No, it's not," Anna told him. "This smells worse. And it's heavier."

The restoration contractor stopped by, gave Cassie a bid, and promised to send over a couple men to rip out and remove the carpeting and set up fans by the evening. "It would have been so much worse," he told her, "if your shop had been all on the same level. As it is, only your showroom was damaged. Though we'll have to see how much water that platform absorbed." He pointed to the raised section where her benches and design desk sat. The insurance agent came in just as they were talking about the work that would have to be done.

The four of them—Cassie, Anna, Tia, and Domingo—took turns shoveling, brushing, hosing. Water continued to drain from the theater next door. Cassie hated to think of the damage inside.

Tate drove up just as they were washing the last of the mud into the street.

"Time for a break," he said. "The oven's hot and the pizzas are about to go in."

The four mud-spattered friends gave a weak cheer. Cassie quickly locked and alarmed the door. She turned around to see Tia and Domingo climbing into the bed of an old truck at the curb. Tate was holding the door for her.

"We need a ride to the restaurant?" she said.

Tate shook his head. "House. Don't want to use the restaurant until it's been inspected."

"What's this?" Cassie asked, gesturing to the truck as Anna slammed the door on her right and Tate climbed in on her left. "Next generation Harley?"

Tate lifted a shoulder as he turned the key. "Sold it," he said. "I was going to make some changes to the patio at Lydia's, but now I guess it will pay for clean up."

"I'm so sorry, Tate," Cassie told him.

Tate shook his head as he pulled into traffic and headed up to the bluff. "Don't be." He grinned. "I'll get a bigger one next time."

Twenty minutes later, soggy, muddy shoes kicked off, the five were demolishing three pizzas in Tate's kitchen.

Cassie had finished several pieces before she finally spoke. "I had no idea I was so hungry," she said, reaching for another slice. "This is absolutely the best pizza I've ever had in my life."

Tate bowed.

"I'm sure," said Anna. "All you've had since you dumped your lunch yesterday is one piece of toast and peanut butter. Dirt would probably taste good to you right now."

"*Excuse* me?" said Tate, raising his eyebrows.

"No," said Cassie. "I had my fill of dirt yesterday. This is much better. It's finally gotten the taste of asphalt out of my mouth."

"Yeah, so what the hell *was* that yesterday?" asked Domingo. "I never saw so much water."

"Unfortunately, it happens," said Cassie. "But it always comes as a surprise."

"Why?" said Domingo. "This is, like, sunny California, right?"

"Not always. Winters when we get a lot of rain, the ground gets saturated, and the canyon funnels the runoff right to the ocean." Anna shrugged. "We're just in the way. This time it was worse because the hills burned two years ago."

"The road work up the canyon probably didn't help, either," said Cassie. Crews had been re-grading and widening a section of the road at the head of the canyon near the freeway. People had been complaining about the mess and the delays since summer.

Anna nodded. "The by-pass channel up on Beach couldn't handle all the water. Dale said that's what blew out."

"You sure you should be working so hard down at your store?" Tate asked Cassie, a slight frown between his eyes.

Cassie nodded. "Yeah," she said. "I'm fine. It's the best thing for me, I think. It's something I can control. Yesterday, nothing was in mycontrol." She pointed to the last bite of pizza in her hand. "And this," she said, "this is like a miracle drug. I could move mountains." She popped the last piece in her mouth and reached for another slice.

"You keep eating like that," said Anna, "and even Dale's clothes aren't going to fit you."

Cassie made a face and waved a hand at her friend, like she was waving away an annoying insect. "As you pointed out," she said, around another bite of pizza, "I lost my lunch yesterday." Suddenly she stopped chewing. "The cake," she said. "We forgot the cake."

"My chocolate cake!" said Anna.

"What cake?" asked Tate.

"My birthday cake," said Cassie. "We were going back to the house for dessert when the flood hit."

"It was your birthday yesterday?" asked Tate.

Cassie nodded. "Some way to celebrate, huh?"

Anna put her hand out. "House key," she said. "I'll go get it."

"No way," said Cassie standing up. "I want to move those benches and everything else up into the back room. The contractor and my insurance agent think it's best to tear out the platform and rebuild it. Make sure there's a good water-proof barrier between the cement and the wood."

She looked at Anna's stricken face. "*Then* we'll have cake."

"That's blackmail," said Anna. Cassie grinned and wiggled her eyebrows at her friend.

When they got back to the shop, there was an apologetic phone message from the contractor saying his men would not be able to get there until the next day.

Cassie sighed, when she told her helpers. "I really wanted to get this mess out of here today," she said.

Tate looked at Domingo who rolled his eyes, then dropped his head against the nearest wall. Tate grinned.

"I'll be right back," he said, heading out the door.

"What?" Cassie asked Domingo.

"We can tear it out," he said. "We did it a couple times in New York when pipes broke in the winter." He made a face.

It was hard, heavy, nasty work. They pried off the base-boards, pulled up the carpet and padding, cutting it into strips with sharp knives, so they could muscle it out the front door. Then they pried up the tack strips, brought in the hose, and washed all the cement free of mud.

It was after 7:30 p.m. by the time they finished, and the bed of Dale's truck was loaded with the filthy carpeting. They carried the showcases back into the shop and locked up.

"*Now* do I get my cake?" asked Anna.

"Absolutely," said Cassie. "Everyone does."

After hurried consultations, Tate headed to the parking lot, promising to bring sandwich fixings from home. "And the rest of that pizza!" Cassie called after them. He turned and grinned. Walking backward, he blew her a kiss. Her heart rolled over.

Domingo and Tia went, too. They both wanted a shower and a change of clothes.

Cassie narrowed her eyes. "I thought Tia was living in Irvine with friends," she said to Anna.

"Umm. *Most* of the time, she is," said Anna, then waggled her eyebrows.

"Ah. I see," said Cassie, grinning. "Does Tate know?"

Anna nodded. "He pretends not to, but he does."

Anna took the truck and its cargo home to switch it for her Karmann Ghia. They'd take the carpet to the dump in the morning. "I'm taking a shower, too, so don't you *dare* touch that cake without me!" she called to Cassie over the top of the truck cab, as she stood on tiptoe on the running board.

"No guarantees if you're not there in forty minutes!" Cassie answered her. With a glare, Anna threw herself into the cab and pulled away from the curb. Cassie double checked the locked door, then walked up Ocean to the lot where she'd left her Rabbit. The wheels were muddy, she saw, when she got there, but the water had not risen enough in the lot to get into the car.

"Thank goodness," she muttered. "I don't think I could clean up any more mud."

Ten minutes later, she was home and in the shower, her muddy clothes—and Dale's shirt—in the washing machine.

Fifteen more and she'd pulled on a big, old, dark red cotton sweater over stretch pants and bulky socks. Her damp hair was twisted up into a knot and skewered on the top of her head. Phone tucked between ear and shoulder, and phone cord stretched across the kitchen, she checked in with Nora as she put a salad together, updating her friend on the condition of the shop and the upcoming finale to the birthday party.

"Glad to hear Tate is keeping you fed," Nora told her, her voice sounding stronger than it had earlier that day. "I've had nightmares of you living on granola bars."

Cassie laughed, gave Nora her love, and hung up, feeling happier than she'd felt for a very long time. She kept smiling to herself as her heart seemed to beat, "Tate, Tate, Tate." She flicked on the radio and her smile got broader, as she heard Bonnie Raitt singing, "That's just love sneaking up on you."

"Sing it, Bonnie!" she said, laughing again. She joined in, singing as loudly as she could and dancing in place as she tore lettuce and grated carrots.

Their duet was interrupted by a knock on the door. It was Tate, heavy windbreaker over a blue plaid flannel shirt that turned his eyes gray. He grinned at her, holding out a bag and a box. She took the box and waved him in. "Down the hall," she said, directing him to the kitchen.

"Compact," he said when he got there, taking in the tiny space as he set the bag on the dining table, slipped off the windbreaker, hung it on the back of a chair, and rolled up the sleeves of the flannel shirt.

"You wouldn't believe how many people you can fit in here during a party," she said putting the box on the counter.

"There are just enough people here right now," he said, as he stepped toward her and took both her hands in his. His grip was warm and strong. Cassie knew she would not let go of him again.

"Cassie," he said, at the same moment she said, "Tate." They laughed then grinned at each other.

"I brought you something," he said, pulling folded papers out of his back pocket. He unfolded them and laid them on the counter, then pointed. "They're in French, of course, but the important word is the same as in English."

Following his finger, Cassie saw Tate's full name, Avril something or other, and the word "divorce."

She looked up.

"Just so you know," he said quietly and smiled. "No lies, no secrets."

"No lies, no secrets," she repeated, putting a hand on each side of his face.

Tate was leaning toward her as the front door opened.

"Thirty-seven minutes," called Anna. "If you've cut that cake, I'll have revenge." She walked into the kitchen just as Tate stepped back from Cassie. "Ah," she said. "Maybe I should have taken another five minutes?" She gave Cassie a knowing look.

"I assume that's beer," said Cassie, pointing to the bag in Anna's hand.

"After today? I deserve it," said Anna, as there was a knock at the door, and Cassie went to let Domingo and Tia in.

"Where's Dale?" she called over her shoulder.

"On shift tonight."

"Again?"

"Covering for someone."

"Man's a saint," Cassie called to her. "You don't deserve him." She heard Anna blow her a raspberry from the kitchen.

It was a riotous evening, one of the best in a long time, thought Cassie, considering the work they'd all put in that day, Nora lying in the hospital, the damage to the shop and to Lydia's. They sat on the living room floor around the coffee table, eating sandwiches, left over pizza, and salad. They polished off half the chocolate cake and half a gallon of Rocky Road. Domingo told them stories about his family and trips to Puerto Rico. Tate told stories on Domingo, who retaliated with stories about Tate, and the two of them insulted each other for a while. When Cassie saw Anna's eyes light up, she warned, "Don't," but it was too late. Anna soon had them laughing so hard their sides hurt.

As the evening passed, Anna curled up in the upholstered rocker that had been Beth's favorite. Domingo and Tia moved to the small loveseat and sat close together, not quite touching, Domingo oddly quiet. Tate, long legs stretched in front of him, stayed on the floor, leaning against the old wing-back chair that was Cassie's usual place in front of the window. Cassie, coming back from fetching another iced tea from the kitchen, hesitated only momentarily before slipping into the wingback behind him. Tate, gesturing with his mug of coffee to make some point, casually slipped sideways to lean against her leg, setting his free hand on her stockinged foot. As Tia answered him, Cassie gently stroked Tate's hair. He leaned softly into her hand, sending a wave of warmth flowing from her feet to her heart.

This is how love should feel, she thought. Safe. Content. Happy.

It was almost midnight when Tia yawned and stood up. "I have to go," she said. "I have to be at the nursery in the morning." She groaned. "I'm not sure I'll be able to move anything heavy, though."

Domingo rose as well. "Yeah, my day starts early, too. This grouchy guy I work for, man, he's a pain."

"I'm sure he can find more mud for you to shovel," said Tate. Domingo waved him away and started to pick up plates, but Tate shook his head. "Leave it. I'll help Cassie clear up," he said.

"I'm off, too," said Anna, and Cassie saw her quick glance between Cassie and Tate. "I'm not saying I'm getting old, but I'm pretty sure some of the muscles I'm feeling haven't been used in fifteen years or more." She nodded at the cake pan, still on the coffee table. "I should probably take some cake home," she said. "For Dale, of course."

Cassie raised an eyebrow almost to her hairline. "Of course," she said. "I'll call him tomorrow to see if he enjoyed it."

Anna sighed. "You're evil, you know that?"

In the end, Cassie sent the rest of the cake home with Anna. After she waved Domingo and Tia away, she found Tate in the kitchen, washing dishes. He was singing softly to himself, in Spanish. Something romantic, she thought. The water was running and he didn't hear her come in.

Cassie stood in the doorway for a moment, just watching him, at home in her kitchen. He'd draped the flannel shirt over a chair by the table, and shoved up the sleeves of his cream-colored Henley. No crazy T-shirt tonight. As he stood, bent slightly at the waist over the low sink, and washed, rinsed, and set the dishes in the drainer, she could see the muscles in his back tense and relax. Her eyes flowed down the line of him, from the broad shoulders, to the narrow waist and hips, very nice butt, and long strong legs. His hands and muscled forearms darted in and out of the water.

Her heart expanded, cracking all the barriers she'd put up around it, driving out any lingering fear and uncertainty. She felt the blood rushing to her skin, as if love were pushing its way through her pores.

Tate flicked off the water, snatched up a towel to dry his hands, and turned, startled to find her behind him. Cassie knew he had to see everything she felt glowing in her eyes. Another time, she would have slammed the gates, made a joke, picked a fight. Not this time. She stood there quietly, just looking at him, watching him look back.

Cassie saw her heart mirrored in his eyes, saw desire ignite in his face. She'd seen it before. That distant morning on the cliff top, on the anniversary of her mother's death. That rainy morning when he first kissed her. Now she let him see her return the look to him.

Tate, his eyes steadily on Cassie's, set the towel on the counter and stepped toward her. Cassie moved forward into his arms, lifting her hands to his waist, briefly resting them on the firm muscles of his stomach before sliding them to his sides. Tate raised a hand to her face, gently cupping her cheek in his palm, and stroked her bottom lip with his thumb. With a small smile, Cassie slowly turned her head and kissed his palm.

At Tate's quick intake of breath, Cassie lifted her face and looked into his eyes, soft with desire. With his free hand, Tate reached up to Cassie's hair and tugged the hair pin free. Her thick dark mane tumbled free. Cassie took the pin from him, set it up on top of the refrigerator next to them, and smiled. Tate was already burying a hand in her hair and pulling her to him.

Her lips parted and she lifted her mouth to his. Tate bent and kissed her softly, then more deeply. Everything left her mind except this moment, Tate's hand in her hair, his breath on her cheek, his mouth moving on hers. His hand dropped from her cheek, and slid down her back, pulling her closer. Cassie moved into him, every part of her going soft, turning to liquid, as she wrapped him ever closer.

Slowly she moved against him. Distantly, she was aware that the music had changed in the other room: Michael Bolton, "I Said I Love You But I Lied."

Tate's hand at her waist moved down, gently stroking her hip before sliding under the hem of her sweater. When she felt the warmth of his hand in the small of her back, she heard herself make a noise deep in her throat. Her hands curled reflexively into the shirt at his back.

Slowly, she disengaged from the kiss, leaning back from Tate, looking up into his eyes, those remarkable eyes, now almost blue around enormous pupils. She crossed her arms in the space between them, gripped the hem of the sweater, yanked it over her head and off. She dropped it on the floor behind Tate. Tate brought a hand up and traced a line with his finger, from the hollow of her throat, down to where her breast bone disappeared behind her bra, then followed the curve of her breast, just under the bra's edge. His large hand cupped her breast and she dropped her head back. Tate bent his head and kissed her throat. He slipped her bra strap off her shoulder, and gently kissed the spot.

Cassie lifted her head and softly kissed the top of his ear. She dragged her hands around from his back, just under the waistband of his jeans. She leaned back, her hips pressing into him. She worked her hands between them and unfastened the button above the zipper.

Tate raised his eyes to her. Slowly she unzipped his jeans, then tugged him toward her as she turned.

"This way," she said. She flipped off the kitchen light and led him, in the semi-darkness, down the hall.

CHAPTER 30

THE SUMMER MORNING SUN was warming the beach, and the first sunbathers were arriving to bake themselves. Tons of sand had been trucked in during the spring, and Main Beach was now back in place. Cassie was setting up the store before going to the Masters to set up her booth for the day. Tia would be in shortly. It was turning out to be a busy summer, but Cassie wouldn't have had it any other way. Her work was getting excellent reviews. It had been mentioned in a *Town & Country* magazine article, and she had a half dozen commissions. It was better than she expected. Better than she could have dreamed.

Best of all, Carla hadn't been able to do the damage Cassie had feared. Lou and Art had made sure the merchants in town knew Carla had been spreading lies, and they were on guard against her now. Most had been supportive of Cassie, who hadn't realized how much she was respected around town.

Carla had not been at the Masters opening. Although Cassie saw the realtor periodically in town, they didn't speak.

She was finishing the front window display and, as she always did, she ran outside to see how it looked.

"Nice store, young lady," said a voice behind her.

Focused on how she might make the display better, she only half paid attention, saying "Thanks!" over her shoulder.

"I hate to say it, though. The name's kind of weird."

A chill ran up her back. She turned and faced a tall man in his early sixties, very thin, leaning on a cane, white hair curling over his collar. His bright blue eyes watched her over a bushy white moustache that flowed into mutton-chop sideburns.

"I'm...sorry?" she said. Suddenly her heart was pounding in her chest. For a moment, she thought she might faint.

"Should be something catchy," the old man said. "Something like Cassie's Gem Jungle." His mouth quirked up in a lopsided half-smile she knew as well as her reflection in the mirror.

Cassie was across the sidewalk in two steps, her arms tight around his waist. "You're alive! You're alive! You're alive!" was all she could say, her voice muffled against his chest. His free arm was around her so tightly she could hardly breathe. She didn't care.

"Did you ever doubt it?" he asked.

She looked up into his face, tears streaming. "All these years missing you, you miserable old...old...coot!

"Easy on the 'old,' darlin'. I'm feeling every year."

"You couldn't write? You couldn't call?" Cassie stepped back far enough to swat him on the chest.

"Hey! That anyway to treat an old man back from the dead?"

"If I wasn't so...so...*damn* glad to see you, I'd be tempted to kill you," she said.

Jim laughed and hugged her to him again.

"I don't suppose you have a bench for a broken down old jeweler, do you?" He asked her, letting her go.

"You idiot, the store is still yours," said Cassie. "After all, the weird name was your choice."

Jim shook his head. "Store's yours, Cassie. It has been since the day you first sat at my bench. When I left here, I knew you were better than I'd ever be and would only get better." He nodded to the window. "I see I was right. That is flat out amazing work."

She looked up at him suspiciously. "Does Rachel know you're alive? Of course she does," said Cassie, answering her own question. "That's why she was always sure you were going to come back. I thought she was just in denial. Why else did she keep me here?"

"I think we have a lot to talk about," said Jim. "You have to finish your window. I don't suppose you have any of that vile bottled tea you're so fond of."

"Just for you," she said.

Cassie took his arm as they walked around to the door.

"What happened?" she asked.

"I don't really know," he said. "One night Dwayne and I were running down the highway in Utah. It was clear and cold. Maybe we were a bit high. Next thing I knew, I woke up in a hospital in Orem with a bunch of nice Mormons asking me if I was LDS. I thought they got the letters confused and were asking about my drug habits. I told them I never touched the stuff. I was strictly a grass man."

He stopped inside the door and took in the white-washed brick wall splashed with Anna's paintings, the pale slate floor, the wood and bronze cases in an Art Deco style. "Wow! Cassie. This is great! When did you do this?"

"Just after the flood last January. If it happens again, it'll be easy to sweep the mud out. Though I shouldn't have to. I had a flood gate installed."

Cassie released the security gate, and Jim stepped up behind the design counter and sat down. Cassie pulled iced teas out of the fridge for them both. He smiled. Jim was the one who had gotten her started on it.

"Go finish your window," he said. "I'm not going anywhere."

"Fine. But you keep talking," she said. She went back to the window and began to rearrange the pieces.

"What happened to Dwayne?" she asked.

"Dwayne disappeared."

"What?" Cassie turned back to him, disbelief on her face. "You're lying in a hospital, and he disappears?"

"Yeah. The police didn't believe me, either. But it's true. Never saw him again."

Which told Cassie that Dwayne had probably been carrying a lot of stuff he shouldn't have in his saddlebags.

"So why didn't you let me know you were all right?"

Jim pulled from the tea. "Cassie, for the first few months I was pretty scrambled. Took me that long to remember Rachel's name. When I finally did, those nice Mormons tracked her down, and she flew out to Utah so fast they thought she was a bullet."

"She never said a word," said Cassie.

"Honey, I don't think she believed I'd ever have my mind back. I think she half expected me to die. She didn't want me to die for you twice."

Cassie fiddled with a neckpiece in the window. She wiped the tears with her shoulder.

"Anyway, Rache stayed with me in Utah until things settled down, I got some of my mind back and was able to travel, even flat on my back. Then she figured out a way to get me home."

"Home was here."

"Cassie, I wasn't walking, wasn't talking much. I wasn't doing much of anything. Rache took me home with her."

"How did she get you from Utah to Connecticut?"

"I have no idea. She only ever said she'd worked miracles. You'll have to ask her if you want more details. Most of that first year is a blank for me."

Cassie closed and locked the front case.

"So why weren't you wearing a helmet?" she asked, as she walked toward him.

"I always wear a helmet, Cassie. Ever since the day I met you. I always wanted to see you grow up. They said without the helmet, I wouldn't have made it. You could say you saved my life."

"Rachel should have told us."

"Darlin', for a couple years I was working with doctors, physical therapists, occupational therapists, speech therapists. I'm not sure, but I think Rachel even brought in a couple psychics."

Cassie smiled.

Jim smiled back.

"Like I said," he continued. "Rache wasn't sure I'd pull through in any kind of condition to come back. When it became clear I was on the mend, well, that was my fault. I wanted to be as whole as I could be before I came back to you." He paused. "And Nora."

"Oh my God," she said, stricken. "Nora."

"I wanted to ask, but was half afraid to."

She gave Jim a stern look. "We cannot spring you on her like this."

"What are you going to do?"

"I'll think of something before I get home. I have to get her for the Pepper Tree." She picked up her purse from under her bench.

"You okay to watch the store?" she asked Jim, smiling.

"Darlin', you just watch me."

She leaned over and kissed him and hugged him. Then she ran out the door. She immediately ran back in.

"The pretty little blond who will be here in a minute?" she said. "She's Tia. My apprentice."

Jim waved her on out the door. "We'll be fine," he said.

Nora was waiting for her at the front gate, face lifted to the sun. She smiled as Cassie pulled to the curb. Cassie had taken to parking downtown. She could afford the monthly parking fees now, and she had to be too many places at once to be walking.

She leaped out of the car and ran around to Nora.

"That excited to get to the Masters?" Nora laughed, stepping out onto the sidewalk.

Cassie put her hand on Nora's arm stopping her.

"Nora, I was just thinking... Don't you wish Jim could see this? If he were still here, he could watch the store or work at the Pepper Tree for me."

Nora's smile faded. "Cassie, stop. You're sounding like Rachel," she said.

"But what would you think if Jim came back?" insisted Cassie.

"First, I'd have to shoot him then, I'd be able to forgive him," said Nora, tears in her voice.

It was so much like what Cassie had told him, she started to laugh. Then she started to cry.

"Nora," she gulped through the tears, "you'd better polish your guns!"

"Cassie, what are you..." Then she saw the tears in Cassie's eyes and the look on her face. She became the stillest stone.

"Where is he?"

"At the shop," said Cassie.

"Take me to him."

A few days later, Cassie was alone in the shop. Alone except for the customer who was buying two pairs of earrings, the one waiting to pick up her repairs, and the one showing off her new custom ring to the repair customer. The noise level was delightfully high.

Jim could not have come back at a better time, she thought. Between the three of them—Cassie, Tia, and Jim—they were just keeping up with the work and covering the booths at the Pepper Tree and the Masters. Jim had moved back into their house with Nora. Cassie had moved in with Tate at the top of the bluff. It had seemed strange at first, to leave the only home she'd ever known. Now, though, she was looking forward to the two of them making the little bungalow their home. Together.

She was just finishing the earring sale when she saw Tate come in. Cassie smiled at him and lifted her chin in acknowledgement. She delivered the finished repairs, rang up the sale, and made an appointment for the woman to come back with her husband to talk about a custom piece.

Finally, she turned to Tate.

"Yes, sir. And what can I help you with today?" she asked him.

"Hmm," he said, making a show of looking around. "I'm not sure. Something artsy, I think."

Cassie smiled at him.

"Did you have anything particular in mind?" she asked.

Tate reached into the watch pocket of his jeans and pulled out a white gemstone paper. He laid it on the case and carefully unfolded it, just as Tia had shown him.

Inside was a tsavorite garnet. Brilliant green. Cushion cut. Just over a carat.

Cassie gasped.

"Lou got it for me," said Tate. "I was hoping you could make an engagement ring."

Cassie looked up at him, heart in her throat.

"It'll have to be very special," Tate went on. "She's very particular. She makes show-stopping jewelry."

Cassie smiled broadly at him. "I know just the thing," she said.

Dear Reader,

Thank you for reading *Trust Not the Heart*, part of my Eden Beach Main Street series. I hope you enjoyed it. I'd love to know what you think of Cassie, Tate, Domingo, Anna—and even the devious Carla Towne. Drop me a line at LizHartleyAuthor@hotmail.com.

If this is the first of my books that you've read, I'm truly grateful you took a chance and gave it a try. I hope you enjoyed visiting Eden Beach so much that you'll come back again.

Whether you're a new reader or a returning reader, I'd like to ask a favor. If you're comfortable with it, I'd love you to review *Trust Not the Heart*. Honest reviews—what you liked, what you didn't—help other readers discover a new book or author. If you have the time, here's a link to my author page at Amazon, where you can find all my books and post your review.

If you freeze at the thought of doing a review, I've posted some guidelines on my website that can help you get started, whether you're reviewing my books or anyone else's. All authors will be grateful you took the time. I know I will be.

To learn more about Eden Beach and the quirky people living there, visit www.LizHartleyAuthor.com. You can follow me on my blog or subscribe to my quarterly newsletter.

If Facebook is where you keep up with friends, family, and favorite authors, you can follow me there, at LizHartleyEden-BeachNovels.

Again, thank you for reading *Trust Not the Heart*. I hope to meet you again in Eden Beach.

Now, please read on for a sample of my book, *Dangerous Visions* from my Eden Beach Crime Novels series.

Gratefully,
Liz Hartley

DANGEROUS VISIONS

Stacie shivered slightly in the foggy February dampness. Flipping up the collar of her navy blue pea coat, she shrugged the jacket closer around her. She watched the koi scrolling through the pond next to the interpretative center of the Lillian Becker Botanical Preserve, where she volunteered, as she waited for her group. Today, a hand-spinning group from Costa Mesa wanted a tour focused on dyeing plants. She'd researched the topic herself and was looking forward to sharing what she'd learned.

The thick fog blurred and softened the colors and shapes of the bougainvillea, yucca, and even the ground-hugging succulents. The path behind her disappeared into gray folds of drifting mist. The stone wall of the interpretive center, twenty feet away on the other side of the pond, was ghostly. Even the sound of trickling water falling into the pond was muffled.

It would have been warmer to wait inside, but Stacie loved the way fog made the familiar strange, mysterious. Anything could happen. Sherlock Holmes could appear.

Stacie smiled at the thought. *That's what I need,* she thought, *a deer stalker cap to keep my ears warm.*

Absently, she pulled the chain at her neck, drawing her pendant from inside her soft, teal-colored turtleneck sweater. The deep violet amethyst crystal, an old, family heirloom, had been broken at one time. It was now wrapped with gold bands and capped on the base where the bail connected to the chain. Her great aunt Amelia had worn it before her, and had given it to Stacie when she had graduated from Orange Coast Community College with her certificate in accounting. She always wore it, its perfect termination lying just next to her heart.

After all, it was said to be magic.

Magic, thought Stacie, as she idly ran the pendant, warm from her body, along the sturdy gold cable chain. Her smile faded. *Some kind of magic.*

Family legend had it that the crystal would announce the wearer's true love. But even though Stacie had been born on Valentine's Day, love had eluded her.

Anything like a normal life had eluded her.

She watched one white koi, curling in and around the other jewel-colored fish. *You can try to blend in*, she thought, *but, sooner or later, they'll see you're not really like them at all.*

Amelia had called it a gift. For Stacie, it had been a curse. No matter how she had tried to suppress it or deny it, somehow it had always come out and left Stacie standing alone, smarting, among the shards of broken relationships, broken friendships.

It wasn't that she didn't have friends. She did. Good ones. But after the disaster with Drew, her otherness was a constant, hard kernel of ache, a stone under her heart she could actually feel.

Even her own mother had called her a freak. Her and Amelia.

Yes, well. Pamela, thought Stacie bitterly. *To know her is to despise her.*

If it hadn't been for her dad...

She shook herself mentally and took a deep breath of damp air. *Enough*, she told herself. *I've got a sweet little home, work I enjoy, and I live in the most beautiful spot on the South Coast. I even have a dog. So. Just. Stop.*

Stacie didn't often feel sorry for herself, but she had just turned twenty-nine. Sometimes—no, all the time—she just wanted to be like everyone else. To talk to people without being afraid of what she might unwittingly say. To fall in love, have a family.

Love, she thought, feeling a familiar flicker of resentment. It had never happened for Amelia. It would never happen for her. Magic crystal or no.

But the hope of love, she'd found, didn't die easily.

Her thoughts spiraled, like the koi, back to the man she'd met at the South Coast Heritage Park the previous Wednesday. Early in the morning, with few other hikers around, she could walk, meditate, clear her mind. Even when it was foggy at the coast, it might be clear at the top of the canyon. Wednesday had been just such a morning, with the sun turning the grasses golden, and mockingbirds mimicking every bird in the area and even a few car alarms. Her pea coat draped over one arm, her daypack slung over the other shoulder, Stacie was headed back to the parking lot after a peaceful walk.

As she rounded the curve at the bottom of a hill, she was surprised to find a photographer waiting patiently for a shot. He knelt at the side of the path, his camera mounted on a shortened tripod. His attention was riveted on something in the grass. Stacie stopped to wait.

She hadn't seen him on the trails before, and she studied him as she waited. Worn, tan boots toed into the dirt and gravel of the trail, his legs in faded blue jeans were folded, his butt settled firmly on his heels. The leather elbows of the battered, camel-colored corduroy jacket were scratched and rough. The collar of a faded royal blue flannel shirt poked out untidily next to his right cheek.

Obviously he was outside a lot. His dark, curly hair had been shaped in what she thought of as a military cut, but he was at least a couple weeks past a haircut, which softened the look. His face in profile was strong, all planes and angles, a bit of stubble over tanned olive skin. *No shave this morning, but not unshaven for days,* she thought. His hand on the cable release was square, nails trimmed.

Precise, neat, not a slob, but not a slave to fashion.

The morning breeze, warming as the sun rose, flipped the shirt collar against his cheek. He might have been a boulder on the hillside for all the notice he took. She smiled. The quiet patience of this man waiting for the perfect shot made her content to simply wait with him, the sun on her face, its warmth penetrating her shirt. The amethyst crystal, hidden just next to her heart, warmed as well.

She was so focused on her study of him, she started slightly when the shutter clicked. The stranger smiled as he rose smoothly and gracefully to his feet. There was a flash of movement in the grass. When he turned, he was startled to find her watching.

Stacie was startled, too, by the intense blue of his eyes. It was as if a piece of evening sky had fallen into them. The blue was brilliant against the warm tones of his skin.

"Looks like you got your shot," she said, surprised to see a mask of neutrality slide over his face. It was as if he were embarrassed to find her watching, seeing him vulnerable, wrapped in the joy of the camera and the subject.

"I did," he said, and in one quick glance, she realized, he

had examined her as thoroughly as she had taken minutes to examine him. "Thanks for giving me the space."

"May I see?" she asked.

Then he smiled fully. "It's not digital," he said. "It's an old single-lens reflex. You'd have to wait until I print it."

"That makes you almost a dinosaur, doesn't it?" She smiled back and stepped down the trail. He was about six feet tall or slightly over, and as she got closer, she found herself looking up. "Black and white?"

He nodded, bending to lift the camera affixed to the tripod. When he looked back up at her, hands automatically adjusting the legs of the tripod, he asked, "Are you a photographer?"

Stacie laughed. "No," she said. "I took a class once. Too... I don't know. Unimaginative. I was no good at it. I'm a book-keeper," she cut the air at a diagonal with her hand, "tax preparer. Numbers I can handle. Anything to do with art, I'm at a loss."

He smiled at her. "Maybe you just never found the right art," he said. "I'm sure you're good at something."

If you only knew, she thought with a pang. For years she'd wished she could meet someone who'd accept her for who she was. But every time, her wretched gift had made itself known, and it had been a disaster.

But not today. Today, she would let the past lie. It was her birthday. The sun was warm, and so was the stranger's voice. Rather than think about what would never be, Stacie was content to simply stand on the hillside and talk.

"Do you sell your work?"

He hesitated, then shrugged, glancing down to remove a filter. "I've participated in a few shows," he said, "and sold a couple."

Before she could ask anything more, he gestured with his head to the path behind her. "What's up ahead?"

"Your first time up here?"

He shook his head. "I've been to the park before, but I usually hike out of the Live Oak Canyon parking lot."

Stacie raised an eyebrow.

"Don't you have to dodge mountain bikers?"

He grinned. "Sometimes. But usually not this early." He pointed up the trail. "Is there really a lake up there?"

"Normally," she told him. "But the drought has been very hard on it. It's not much more than a puddle right now." She pulled her daypack forward, unzipped a pocket and unfolded her tattered map of the park. "For some interesting images, you might try these areas." She pointed out a couple paths, giving him a short synopsis of what he might see on each.

"You must come up here a lot," he said.

"I'm up here most mornings," she agreed, then winced inwardly. *I shouldn't have said that*, she thought, *telling a stranger my habits*.

Stacie was not generally secretive, trusting in the basic goodness of people. But she was alone, and she had seen no one else on the trail that morning.

As she talked about one of the trails, she casually put her pea coat back on and slipped a hand into her pocket to hold the quartz crystal she always kept with her. She'd found it at a gem show in Pasadena when she was just twelve. Clear and colorless as pure water, nestled in a spray of tourmaline crystals, the crystal had called to her so strongly it had practically stuck to her hand. Her great aunt had bought it for her and told her to carry it always. "It will protect you," Aunt Amelia had said.

She'd been right. Like an amplifier, the stone augmented Stacie's natural intuitive gifts. Over the years, she'd learned to read the crystal's signals.

The touch of the stone confirmed her sense that there was nothing in this man to fear. She sensed only calm happiness, though it was underlain by sadness, caution, a touch of bitterness and, oddly, she thought, confusion. There was strength and sureness there. Trustworthiness. Safety.

"Anything in particular you're looking for?" she asked him.

"Not really," he said, lifting the strap on his camera bag over his shoulder. "Anything with a strong pattern. Lots of contrast. Close-ups, usually."

"Ah. Then maybe you would like the lake. All that cracked mud. But I'd also recommend heading up here," said Stacie, moving closer to the stranger's shoulder and pointing to an area of the map. "The bark on the sycamores is always fascinating, and there's a stand of scrub oak that casts some great shadows this time of day." She mentioned a few other plants that might give him what he wanted and told him where to find them.

He was surprised. "You really know your plants for a bookkeeper," he mimicked her slash through the air, "tax preparer."

Stacie laughed. "I love plants, particularly California natives, though they've been outnumbered by imports. Our climate is so good for so many plants."

They talked a while more about the park, the plants, the weather. Gradually, the guarded look fell from his face. She even made him laugh. His voice was warm, baritone. His laugh was a throaty chuckle. When Stacie spoke, there was focused attention in those sharp, blue eyes. She could have talked to him all day.

She had to go, though. She had a shop to open.

They exchanged good-byes, and he headed up the trail, taking Stacie's map with him. It wasn't until she got back to her car that Stacie realized she hadn't asked his name.

But she'd thought about him since then—many, many times.

Now, as she stood in the dense fog, waiting for the hand-spinners, a baritone voice behind her said, "Well, hello!"

Slipping her pendant into her sweater, she turned, her smile already in place. Her memories of the stranger were so strong, she expected to see him there.

The man standing behind her—far too close to her—was not the dark-haired photographer.

He was about her age. His straight, blond hair folded over the collar of his camo jacket and fell across his forehead to light, ice blue eyes under dark blond brows. A straight nose, angular lips. Some would say he was strikingly handsome, but there was something in his eyes. Or rather, something *not* in his eyes. Stacie wondered if she would have noticed if she hadn't been remembering the dark-haired stranger in the Heritage Park.

Stacie's smile slipped as a sudden headache hit her between the eyes, as if she'd eaten ice cream too fast. She had a sudden sense of vertigo. She stepped back instinctively to create more space between them. Her boot heel knocked against the rocks at the side of the koi pond. Her hand went immediately into her jacket pocket to hold the quartz crystal.

Her heart kicked into a racing beat at the touch. The crystal was ice cold, the edges between the faces like razors slicing her hand. She felt blood running over her fingers.

There was no doubt what it meant.

Danger. *Extreme* danger.

Adrenaline surged through her.

She saw him register the change in her face.

"Guess you were expecting someone else," he said, his smile cooling, but still firmly in place.

"Yes," Stacie managed to reply calmly. "My tour group." *Please, please, please,* her mind chanted. *Don't let him be part of it.*

The stranger laughed, a forced sound. "I guess I should have known," he gestured at her jacket.

Stacie flinched. Every instinct made her desperate to step away from his hand, but the pond behind her barred her escape.

"Your name tag. Stacie," he read. He gave her the creeps looking pointedly at her chest. She was devoutly glad her last name was not printed there. Cappella was not a common name. The Internet would lead him right to her. "Do you often lead groups here?"

"No," she lied. "I'm just filling in."

"Lucky for me," he said. He put out his hand. "My name's Troy."

No, it's not, thought Stacie.

She cringed at the thought of touching him, but he had her trapped. She had to pass him to get to the path. She was afraid to take her hand out of her pocket in case she truly was bleeding, afraid to let go of the crystal. As if it could help her.

Cursing the cultural training that indoctrinated women to be "nice," and praying for her garden group to arrive, she reluctantly let go of the stone and put out her hand. It wasn't bleeding.

His grip was hard, warm, and slightly damp. He held her hand too long, pulling her subtly, but strongly toward him. Stacie pulled back, trying to release her hand.

"Careful," he said. "Don't fall in." His smile was triumphant.

The door to the interpretive center burst open, and the air was filled with the sound of fifteen or more chattering women.

Stacie almost sobbed with relief. She tugged her hand free, not caring how rude it was. "My group," she said. "Excuse me." She stepped unwillingly toward him, steeling herself to shove past him if he tried to stop her.

He looked amused and stepped back, clearing her path.

"Perhaps we can take a tour together some day," he said,

as she passed him. "I'm sure there's *lots* you could show me." His slippery, insinuating tone turned her stomach.

Stacie glanced back as she moved away. "I don't think so," she said firmly. She hurried down the path, anxious to get away.

"Then perhaps we can meet for coffee some time," he called to her.

"Good morning!" Stacie walked quickly to her group, pretending not to hear him. The women's voices rose in pleasure as they saw and surrounded her.

As she began to tell them what they would be seeing this morning—or not seeing, given the fog, she joked—she felt Troy watching her. She tucked her hands into her pockets, wiping her right one on the handkerchief there. She clutched the crystal. The feel of razors was still there, but not the sense of bleeding.

She and her group moved away. When she was sure it would not be obvious, Stacie glanced back. Troy was gone.

Gradually, her erratic heartbeat slowed, became more regular. The sharpness of the crystal slowly faded until it was as it always was.

It took a long time, though, for Stacie to stop shaking.

Dangerous Visions is available at Amazon, Kobo, Nook, and Apple Books. To learn more about Liz Hartley and new books, go to www.lizhartleyauthor.com. You can also follow my blog, sign up for my newsletter, or follow me on Facebook at LizHartleyEdenBeachNovels.

ACKNOWLEDGMENTS

No author can do it alone. I was lucky to have the help of a number of people in writing *Trust Not the Heart*.

Custom jeweler John Thompson shared his personal experience of the Laguna Beach flood of 1995. My fictional depiction of what happens in Eden Beach is more dramatic, but I depended on John's basic recollections as well as news reports and online images.

Lori Cole, Harley groupie, helped me choose the bikes that both Jim and Tate ride.

Sonia Allen lent me some of her family names for Domingo Rivera and Anna Rodriguez.

Deb Spencer and Mary Wong, of Trios Studio in Lake Oswego, Oregon, read the first draft and vetted the jewelry process descriptions.

Lynn Kacy and Linda Walsh Lapinski, realtors extraordinaire, assured me that a Carla Towne could indeed exist.

Lauri Nutting Martin read the draft and made valuable suggestions. Linda Tamasiunas, Eileen Hicks, and Darcie Preuitt generously took time to proof the final version. Naturally any faults in the final product are mine, not theirs.

The beautiful cover is by Kim Killion, of Killion Publishing.

Devon Monk, dear friend and amazing author of more than 20 speculative fiction novels and countless short stories, provided her experienced eye, wise counsel, and support during the entire writing and publishing process. I think it's fair to say, I really couldn't have done it without her. Thanks, Devon!

ABOUT THE AUTHOR

Liz Hartley is the author of two series set in the small town of Eden Beach, California: The Eden Beach Main Street Novels, and The Eden Beach Crime Novels.

Liz has worn jewelry and picked up rocks since she was old enough to stand. She was probably fated to spend more than twenty-five years writing about jewelry and gemstones. She has both Graduate Gemologist (GG) and Fellow of the Gemmological Association of Great Britain (FGA) diplomas. So it's no wonder that jewelry and gemstones play a prominent role in her novels.

An enthusiastic traveler, Liz has lived and studied in Japan, traveled with gem and mineral enthusiasts to Brazil, journeyed to southern Africa with members of the Los Angeles Zoo (where she was a docent for five years), and made two "grand tours" in Europe.

She does not own a TV, but loves movies and will read just about anything that doesn't get out of her way.

facebook.com/LizHartleyEdenBeachNovels

ALSO BY LIZ HARTLEY

Dangerous Visions: An Eden Beach Crime Novel